Pyrate Rising

Second Edition

ISBNs: 979-8-9852206-0-5; 979-8-9852206-1-2

Pyrate Publishing

Cover art and images by:

Roger C. Ambrose

RCA Designs

For my grandson, Drake

Always be inspired

Always be yourself

Always be truthful

And always be proudly who you are

Never give up

Never lose faith

Never let others down

And never stray, though travel far

Forever smile

Forever care

Forever empathize

And forever follow your north star

Inspired by True Events

Though based on historical events, this book is not intended to be a precise historical record of Drake's life and adventures. I have chosen to introduce dialogue, insert fictitious characters, create text for letters and messages, and slightly modify aspects of some events. This enables me to be relatively true to Drake's story yet bring some nearness of life to it. I hope I have done no injustice in this.

Also, while we have paintings of Drake in formal attire, and rather fanciful drawings of 'Golden Age' pirates by American Illustrator Howard Pyle, we have little knowledge of how Drake and his men actually dressed while at sea. So you'll have to excuse me for taking some liberties with that.

The life of my fictitious character, Garret Connachan, is inspired by two famous pirates of the early eighteenth century.

Pyrate Rising

Prologue

No one with family should be alone. That was the thought running through my mind. Yet there I was—alone; in a crowd; surrounded by dissonant voices, clamoring to be heard. Horses passed by in four-beat gaits, their hooves clopping on damp cobblestones. A few pulled aging wooden carts that creaked and strained under their loads. Children laughed, chasing each other. Two shabbily dressed men stumbled along, singing a bawdy shanty, off-key. It seemed everything, everyone, was in motion. Except me. I remember watching the droplets of heavy mist settle on my coat, unflowing, just like the tears welled up in my eyes.

I recall an animal-skin ball rolling up to my feet, with pace. I trapped it. It was damp; heavy. Boys nearby yelled for its return. I kicked it back. 'Thank you then', they shouted. For that one brief moment, I had become part of the bustling throng. And then, just as quickly, I was alone again. Memories of playing ball at Ritchfield Academy crossed my mind, bringing a longing to be back there. But that could never be. I had been expelled. My classmates, my only friends, were no longer accessible to me. Having just turned twelve, the life I had known was dissolving away in the drizzle. I was leaving behind those I loved and cherished most—my father and older sister. Images of them coursed through my head, tugging at my heart. Imminent departure threatened to turn my once-bright future into a gloom as dull as the air enveloping me. It took a deep breath to fight back the emotion lurking inside. I sensed it stemmed from weakness. That felt odd; uncommon. I had always prided myself on being strong.

"Out the way, child," a rugged-looking sailor shouted. I stepped aside as he and a handful of others brushed by, carrying provisions for their vessel. My eyes followed them. In the distance, tall-masted ships, their sails mostly furled, swayed with the rhythm of the water in Plymouth Harbor. They drew my attention, sharpening the edge of my uncertainty. Longboats were shuttling back and forth among the ships, accompanied by the persistent hum of hammers and saws deployed by carpenters.

Life on the ocean was something I had never envisioned. Yet there I was, about to join the esteemed Captain Drake and his crew, as a midshipman. There were only three such highly coveted openings available. My father had paid dearly for mine; not for the cramped quarters we mids would share, but rather for Drake's mentoring. His ship, the *Pelican*, was of the latest design— tailored for speed and engineered to withstand a long, treacherous voyage. Though largely dark, its bright, freshly painted trim made it stand out against the blended grayness of harbor, sky and ocean-weary vessels. Almost stationary in the undulating water, it would soon become my new home; yet I knew none of its crew. What possible good could come of this, I wondered. Should I turn and run? But then, where would I go?

The coachman patted my back. "Good luck to you, Master Connachan." He had just unloaded a small seaman's chest, placing it near my feet. It contained the only familiar things I would have in this new world— clothing, books and a few personal items. He turned and mounted the coach that had delivered me to this lonely, crowded harbor. My father's last words came back to me: "Remember Garret, be most careful. You must not let anyone know your truth."

The crack of the coachman's whip interrupted my thoughts. The horses' hooves clopped loudly on the cobblestones as they whisked away the coach. The quickly dissipating sound forced an involuntary sob. They had left me here. Truly alone. Suspended precariously between the past and the rest of my life.

A large, rough hand unexpectedly grasped my shoulder from behind.

I

Eight years earlier…

He was unusually tall and slender, his hair graying, his beard tightly trimmed. The clear, cool water rippled as he slid the small boat calmly into the lake. A child sat in the boat, quietly. The aging man waded into the water and jumped in, effortlessly. The boat rocked and glided forward. He untied the square-rigged sail from the mast, securing it to the spar to catch the modest breeze. The sound of the water lapping softly against the boat brought him peace of mind—solace from the normally hectic pace of his days. The morning sun burned through a light, rising fog, glistening the water and offering a wave of warmth.

"Alright, Garret, now put your foot against the larboard side and push the tiller for me," Daniel Connachan instructed. "And remember. Keep your head low, to avoid the boom." The four-year-old did as told. The sail flapped while the two waited a moment for it to fully grasp the wind. Garret beamed as the boat pulled forward, skating along the water.

"Well done." Daniel nodded, smiling proudly. He was a man of means. Irish-born but English-raised, his parents had left him extensive properties throughout the two countries and up into southern Scotland. A graduate of Magdalen College, Oxford, he'd put his law degree to beneficial use. Over the years, his meticulous work and reputation had earned him the right to counsel many of England's wealthy merchants involved in maritime

4

trade. He'd also been appointed to chair the board of Briscoe Bank and found his days filled with unlimited opportunities to accumulate wealth. His earnings enabled him to acquire even more property, including land bordering this fair-sized lake. It was his favorite place to spend cherished leisure time. The serenity helped clear his mind from the stress of business.

But there was something even more pressing; a constant haunting of his soul, like a dark, stuffy room without a door to exit. It was the troubles brought on by his mentally challenged daughter, Gwendolyn. At the age of fifteen, Gwendolyn had been captivated by the charms of a tall, handsome, uniformed soldier, whose interest was solely prurient. The soldier took full advantage of her fascination for him and her mental incapacity. Daniel believed his daughter's resulting pregnancy would embarrass the family, blemish his reputation and potentially disrupt his business endeavors. Seeking to avoid these outcomes, he had Gwendolyn secluded on one of his estates, where she later delivered the child now seated across from him. In order to cover the tracks and preserve his reputation, Daniel had paid the local priest handsomely to have the church records show, among other things, that the child was his own, and that his wife's then-recent death was a result of the delivery.

"Look, Father," Garret said, pointing to a school of silvery fish wriggling jauntily alongside the boat, reflecting the sun's light. "Might we catch one?"

"Not just yet. We shall stop later and let down the lines. Hopefully, we shall catch something more substantial. Now, let us tack to starboard."

Though disappointed, Garret liked the way Daniel spoke—calmly, confidently, reassuringly. He was in charge but not demanding. They would fish at some point; Garret was certain of that. Daniel never promised anything he didn't deliver. He was a man to emulate.

Garret moved the tiller into position. Daniel smiled, "You shall make a fine sailor one day, son. Mark my words."

II

The smallest of six ships rolled gently in the coral blue water just inside the Caribbean harbor. Viewed from afar, the *Judith* bore an air of tranquility. That was deceiving. It was about to launch an historic beginning for the daring young captain standing on its deck. His long, sandy-blond locks, sun-bleached from months at sea, flowed like a soft wave in the calm breeze. A tight, scruffy beard edged along his sharp jaw, coming to a point a little below his chin. The stern look on his rugged, tanned face communicated he was in charge. Not a particularly tall man, he was chiseled for strength. He wore a dark-brown, leather doublet. It felt calming against his broad chest. His silver breastplate-armor and helmet lay close by, in the event the action became heated. A brown bandolier ran across his right shoulder to his left hip, securing the scabbard that sheathed a freshly sharpened cutlass.

Next to the captain's side was his seasoned master's mate, Charles Prouten. A man of similar size, he too had the broad-shouldered, narrow-waisted, muscular shape reflecting years of strenuous work onboard ocean-going vessels. Specks of gray peppered the curly dark hair on his sideburns and beard surrounding his leathered face. Known for his still-sharp eyes, Prouten offered an observation, "The building is just to the right of the town's center." He pointed that way.

"Thank you, Mr. Prouten," Drake replied. "I see it now."

With his ship double-anchored to minimize its movement, the newly appointed captain focused in on the main square of Rio de la Hacha, Spanish for River of the Axe. His eyes scanned up and down the building, home to the town's Treasurer, Miguel de Castellanos. Two years earlier, Castellanos had led this town in battle, humiliating an English sea captain. Prouten was one of the survivors. Here, now, was the duo's opportunity to exact revenge.

Fleet Commander John Hawkins looked on from his flagship, the *Minion*. He'd chosen Drake to take the lead, judging his small ship would present the hardest target for shore-based cannons to hit. This was the new captain's opportunity to prove himself. To support him, Hawkins had assigned his best gunnery team, led by Master-at-Arms Lee, to the *Judith*.

Drake smiled at Prouten, confident they were ready. He turned to the fleet's interpreter, Robert Langton, to hail the shore in Spanish on his behalf. Langton was a Lincolnshire man, educated at Cambridge. His powerful voice was a must-have for any seafaring interpreter. On Drake's order, he called out, "Hail residents of Rio de la Hacha! We are a merchant fleet, in need of fresh water and provisions. We are anxious to trade and have various goods on board for exchange. We request your approval and blessing."

Drake smiled as Langton shouted the words. It was all a ruse, of course, intended to give Commander Hawkins the ability to claim high ground if things went as anticipated.

Treasurer Castellanos was on shore, watching the English fleet. He heard Langton's request but wasn't buying it. Spain was not on friendly terms with England; the two nations were in a virtual undeclared war. The town's residents considered the English their enemy. They were rightfully nervous about this fleet's appearance. It had drawn a small crowd from the moment it assembled near the edge of the harbor, causing others to gather valuables in preparation to evacuate.

At Castellanos' order, the town answered Langton's call with a thunderous volley from two of the shore-based cannons. Warning shots. They splashed threateningly close to the *Judith*. Drake smiled, welcoming the opportunity to reply. While the cannonballs' wake passed beneath his ship, he conferred with Prouten on the distance and angles they had earlier given the gunners. Prouten nodded agreement. Drake gave the order, "Cannons at the ready, if you please."

"Cannons at the ready," Prouten echoed loudly. Gun ports slammed open. The noses of the *Judith's* black, cast-iron weaponry rolled through.

"Cannons ready," relayed Lee.

"Ready captain," said Prouten.

Drake's eyes locked in on Castellanos' home—a weathered, aqua-colored building with a second-story balcony wrapped in peeling, white fencing. A charming-looking house, it was about to turn ugly.

The rolling out of cannons had shifted the ship's weight, slightly. Drake had Prouten shout to the gunners, modifying his earlier estimate of the angle. He waited a moment for them to adjust. As the *Judith* settled nicely between two mild undulations, he gave the order, calmly, "Fire at will, Mr. Prouten."

"FIRE!" Prouten shouted.

"FIRE!" echoed Lee.

Four six-pounders roared almost simultaneously. The guns flamed and recoiled as iron balls screamed toward their target, leaving a trailing cloud of dark smoke. One shot ripped through the far-right side of the upper balcony, shattering the edge of the wall behind it. Another followed closely, hitting within feet of Castellanos' front door.

"Knock, knock," shouted Drake, drawing his cutlass and thrusting it high in the air. His men laughed and cheered, anxious to disembark for a beachfront assault.

The front-right wall of Castellanos' house had shattered, sending wooden shards spearing through the air in several directions. The balcony began peeling away. On the street below, residents scattered, seeking shelter to avoid fragments of the disintegrating residence. English sailors on the remaining five ships cheered in unison at the boisterous opening volley on this otherwise calm summer day.

The roar of battle heightened as Hawkins' entire fleet joined the assault. Streaking orange flames lit billowing clouds of black and gray cannon smoke. Several of the larger buildings were hit, damaged to varying degrees. The Spanish shore battery returning fire was mounted on a six-foot fortress wall. Eight cannons, each staffed by a handful of gunners. It, too, was targeted by Hawkins' fleet, with the kind of precision he demanded. Still, the Spanish gunners scored damage of their own, hitting two ships—one below the waterline.

Hordes of sailors descended the sides of Hawkins' ships, jumping into longboats they had already lowered into the water. Armed with finely honed swords, pikes and axes, they thirsted to take the village.

The residents of Rio de la Hacha fled, cherished belongings slung over their backs, loaded on donkeys or thrown hastily in wooden carts. Viewed from the approaching longboats, they appeared as a fast-flowing, churning river of humanity. Animals, too, raced helter-skelter—goats, dogs, hogs, chickens—barking and squawking in panic, though not understanding why. The Spaniards controlling the shore battery began fearing for their own lives. Many left to join their families in the frantic run for survival. A few remained bravely in position, reloading and firing their cannons as best they could. But as the wave of longboats neared the shoreline, even the most courageous cannoneers left their positions. They had no desire to engage in hand-to-hand combat with this flotilla of ferocious, well-armed warriors.

As their boats ground onto the beach, the sailors scrambled out, sprinting toward the town like dark, wind-blown sand, undeterred by stray rifle shots—though two men breathed their last. By the time they reached the edge of the now-smoking village, they were shocked to find no opposition. Rio de la Hacha had become a stilled axe.

———

The glowing, pulsating orange in the blackened remains of the wood dying in the fireplace saddened Garret. It meant the day was ending. Daniel finished reading sections of Marcus Aurelius' book: *Meditations*. Reading was something they did every evening. Seated on his lap, Garret liked watching the expressions change on his face as he read, seldom understanding everything he was saying. The softness of his voice was soothing. He often pointed out when he had replaced the actual words with ones summarizing the essence of the text. He said the books all shared a common theme—great men, doing great things; doing what they thought was right, and striving to learn from their experiences. Garret hoped to one day be just like these men he so admired.

Daniel closed the book. "Time for bed."

Garret slid off his lap, grabbing his large hand as he rose from the chair. "Did you know Marcus, Father?"

Daniel laughed. The Emperor-cum-philosopher had lived in the second century. "I *feel* as though I know him. But he died long before I was born."

"Was he an Englishman?"

"He was a Roman. An Emperor."

"What is an Emperor?"

"An Emperor is like our Queen."

"But the Queen is a woman."

"Yes, she is. A great woman at that. One to be admired."

"Did the Queen write a book?"

Daniel laughed again. "Not yet. Her story is still being written." He stopped and knelt down. "Your story, too, is now being written, Garret. By you. You can make your story whatever you want it to be. I have no doubt you shall write a truly remarkable one. That greatness is within you."

"But I am not writing a story."

"You are, Garret. Just not the way you imagine it being written. You are writing it with your actions, your decisions, your observations, your passions. You shall write it with your heart."

"Okay," Garret replied, not fully understanding.

Daniel smiled, picking up and carrying Garret to bed.

———

Over several days, Hawkins' men occupied and pillaged the buildings in Rio de la Hacha, searching for valuables. They even scoured through the dusty rubble of buildings that had borne the brunt of his fleet's hellfire. He'd set up headquarters in the chapel, where his captains came to report the results of their search. Much of the news was disappointing; the residents had removed their most precious belongings.

Near the outskirts of the village, a lone messenger arrived, carrying a white flag. Castellanos had sent him to request terms of settlement. He was met by Hawkins' men and taken to the chapel. They entered while Hawkins was seated at a table, reviewing the latest report. He was an older commander with a receding hairline, a well-cropped goatee, and oddly pale skin. Dressed more like a gentleman in a Bristol tea shop than an ocean sailor, Hawkins was a cerebral man who prided himself on being England's foremost sea captain. He handed the inventory list back to an officer as the messenger approached. The man was younger than Hawkins had anticipated. His facial hair wanted to be a beard but was more a series of light, stray clumps on his rosy cheeks. His clothes were in good order and he had a pleasant demeanor. He showed no obvious signs of nervousness—surprising, given his youth.

"Good day, sir," the messenger said. "I am here on behalf of Señor Castellanos, Treasurer of our village."

"My compliments to the Tesorero. What is it he wishes to tell me?"

"He wishes to discuss the return of the village, in exchange for a gratuity from our residents."

"Please inform the Tesorero that we shall be happy to return the village," he glanced through a window at the nearby devastation, "in its recently modified condition, of course." Hawkins' men smiled and traded glances, enjoying the irony of the devastation being made so light of. The Commander paused to gauge the messenger's reaction. It was a mere nod; a rather reserved acknowledgment, he thought. He continued, "In exchange for our generosity, the Tesorero shall be expected to provide a…gratuity, as you say. Twenty thousand gold pesos." Hawkins knew the amount was exorbitant. He simply wished to set the bar high, to maximize the ultimate settlement. "I welcome the Tesorero's visit, to agree on these terms. Shall we say on the morrow, at the sun's zenith?"

"Of course."

"Excellent. Please have him bring the gratuity with him." Hawkins knew full well that wouldn't happen. He simply wished to set the tone. "We shall meet on the beach, where the view is unobstructed. That will allow both sides to ensure no weapons are raised by or against each other's forces."

"As you wish, sir. I shall share your message with Señor Castellanos." The messenger bowed, turned and left, accompanied by his English handlers.

A stiff breeze swept along the soft beach the following afternoon. Drake sat at a make-shift table, flanked by an English flag, flapping noisily in the wind blowing from behind. He wore his dark blue naval colors, a sword at his hip. Hawkins' other captains flanked him. The Commander had asked Drake to lead negotiations with Castellanos. It was a time-tested strategy— without Hawkins' physical presence, Castellanos would be unable to gain immediate closure on whatever he might request. Hawkins believed that, of all his captains, Drake was the most articulate, and therefore likely to be the most able negotiator.

A dozen fully armed sailors were stationed behind Drake, swords sheathed. A decanter of wine and two tankards had been placed on the table, to facilitate the discussion. The men patiently awaited Castellanos' arrival, grains of sand dusting their heads and necks.

In time, the Treasurer approached in the distance, accompanied by a handful of militiamen. Drake thought them an untidy group. Not exactly the King's soldiers. Their cutlasses swayed on their hips as they walked the beach with some difficulty, trenching through the soft sand in their boots, against the sometimes-stiff breeze. Their heads were mostly down, to shelter their eyes from blowing sand. Hands held their hats. One Spaniard carried a flapping white flag, a sign of truce. When they reached Drake's table, Castellanos doffed his feathered hat and bowed in greeting. He was formally dressed, befitting his status. The absence of his hat betrayed a balding head, though he had a full, and tight, gray beard. His eyebrows, on the other hand, were anything but tight; more like the trailing streaks of geese flying off in a multitude of directions. The Tesorero's face was a pale white, almost as though he'd powdered it. Not being a man of labor, he bore a pear-shaped physique. He took a seat at the table, opposite Drake, who had risen in recognition of the man's role.

"Good day, Señor Castellanos. I am Captain Drake." He sat. "Please be assured, we have no desire to further damage your lovely village, nor to harm your people. Yet I must tell you, we are deeply troubled by your unfriendly response to our request for water and provisions."

"I understand, Captain. I regret that decision. You must know, the history of our relations with the English has not been…" Castellanos searched for the right word, "pleasant. We based our action on that history, expecting your intentions were less than honorable."

"You misjudged us." Drake poured wine into the tankards. He slid one across the table.

Castellanos was convinced the surprisingly young captain was lying, to mask his real intentions. But there was nothing to gain by arguing the matter. "Again, I regret our decision."

"It was a costly one; both for your village and for our men. A generous gratuity is therefore in order, to cover damages we have suffered and to provide for the families of our fallen sailors. Of course, there must be an added payment for your unfortunate insult of the English flag."

"My good sir, may I humbly submit that your Commander's request is well beyond the modest means of the town's residents."

"That may be so, Señor. But surely you can imagine the depth of their loss if we are forced to burn your village to the ground, for lack of good faith on your part." Drake let that sink in, using the opportunity to sip his wine. "Nor would we stop there. We would scour the woods for villagers and valuables. It would not end well for them." He leaned back, letting the images simmer in Castellanos' mind. The request for twenty thousand pesos needed to be accompanied by a certain degree of fear. Drake peered deeply into the man's eyes, measuring him. He would wait for the Spaniard's response. Castellanos also waited, well aware that in any negotiation one must be willing to sit patiently, hoping for the other to speak first, offering a concession.

Drake eventually broke the silence, conceding nothing. "We have already secured everything of value from our search of the buildings. It appears the most precious valuables had already been removed."

Castellanos nodded. "In truth, there was little of value to remove. And surely you would agree that such action was prudent, under the circumstances. The residents took what little they had." Drake chose not to respond, waiting instead for a response to his initial request. It finally came. "Might I humbly suggest a gratuity of one thousand pesos." Castellanos raised his cup slowly, finally taking a sip of what he recognized was wine from his village's own storeroom.

Drake laughed. Some of his men joined in. The laughter was brief. He rose from his chair, placing his hands on the table and leaning in toward the

Treasurer, for emphasis. "I appreciate, sir, that the resources of the village may not be sufficient to meet our request. But do not test our patience with a trifling offer." He paused, returning slowly to a seated position. "I am a generous man. Given your circumstances, I am prepared to settle for something less. Let us agree on ten thousand. In exchange for this lesser amount, we shall not inflict further harm on your village or your people, though we reserve the right to search the woods for hidden valuables."

Castellanos hesitated, wondering how far he could go without devasting the economic well-being of his villagers or putting their lives at further risk. "We appreciate your most generous offer, Captain. Unfortunately, we have nowhere near that amount of gold among all our residents combined. Might I suggest two thousand, which still represents a trying hardship to my people? We are a simple village, sustained only by meager crops and modest trading with occasional visiting ships."

Darke parried, "You may be aware that we have taken up residence in your church. There is much in the way of gold plate and religious artifacts there. They are no doubt cherished by your people. We shall be obliged to take these with us, to make up for the shortfall in your most unreasonable offer."

Castellanos knew that was not an outcome his people would accept. The religious artifacts had value to them well beyond their worth in gold. After further discussion, and Hawkins' later approval, the two sides reached a settlement. Castellanos would deliver four thousand pesos and needed provisions, in exchange for the return of his village, with no further damage. The religious artifacts would remain in the church.

Revenge had been served.

<h1 style="text-align:center">III</h1>

The artfully carved wooden sword was heavy. It took both hands to swing it at a similar cutlass held by Daniel. Garret raised it high in the air and then slashed it down diagonally. Its speed surprised Daniel, jarring his weapon enough that he almost lost his grip. He laughed aloud. "You shall make a fine swordsman."

Garret lunged at him with a big smile and swung hard again, making solid contact with Daniel's sword. He offered more resistance this time. Then he countered with a rapid but slow-ending swing against Garret's trailing edge, dislodging the child's sword. It glanced off the ground, bouncing away.

"Do you see how vulnerable to attack you are after you have swung your sword?" Daniel asked.

Garret stepped back with a frown, retrieving the sword, determined that wouldn't happen again. Tightly gripped, the sword swung back hard toward Daniel's, now hanging near his side. It flew out of Daniel's hand, landing on the grass. "Do you see how vulnerable you are when you think you have won?" Garret smiled, pointing the wooden weapon toward his stomach. "I have beaten you."

"Indeed you have," Daniel chuckled. "Perhaps I shall get the better of you next time."

"No, you will not." Garret pressed the dulled end of the wooden sword into his gut, to emphasize the point.

Daniel smiled proudly at the child's tenacity. He reached down and picked Garret up. "I love you, my little warrior. One day you shall rule the world."

"I shall slay my enemies. Just like Ulysses."

"You may slay them, or you may win them over," Daniel countered, putting his index finger to Garret's temple, "but you must always use your head to determine the better course."

"But why, father?"

"Because if you spare a man's life, you may make him a friend forever."

Garret thought about that for a moment. "Can we eat now?" The hunger was no longer for battle but for food.

———

Within days of collecting their ransom from Castellanos, Hawkins and his men had replenished their provisions and completed preparations to leave Rio de la Hacha. Before the ships hauled anchor, the captains joined their commander for supper onboard the *Minion*.

"Welcome to you all," Hawkins began, as they stood at the table ahead of the meal. The wine in the tankards now held in their hands swayed gently with the sea. "This evening we celebrate our rich success." He raised his tankard, "To victory!"

The captains echoed his call, "To victory!" They sipped briefly.

Hawkins continued holding his tankard aloft. "I also wish to toast our newest captain, young Drake, for taking the lead. And for his excellent marksmanship in personalizing our opening statement to Señor Castellanos!"

The men laughed heartily and cheered "To Drake!" They drank to the making of the bright young captain—and continued drinking that evening, for many other reasons.

"Welcome back, sir," said Prouten, greeting Drake at the entry-port of the *Judith*. "I trust supper was enjoyable."

"Indeed it was, Mr. Prouten. 'Tis an honor to serve with Commander Hawkins. He is the finest of seafarers and a confident leader. I have learned much from the man. And will continue to."

The two men proceeded in silence to the stairwell leading to his cabin, their hard-heeled boots clattering on the dry, hardwood deck. They were oblivious to the creak of the rope lines, the flapping of the English flag, and the sound of the water lapping against the hull—the constant background noise of a ship, with which they were so familiar. Nearing the stairwell, Drake slowed his pace, then stopped and turned. "I am honored to have you at my side, Mr. Prouten. I believe we shall do great things together."

"Thank you, sir. I believe we shall."

"But for now, I must rest. Suppers can be quite tiring. Especially when the wine flows like a river. Let us confer over breakfast."

———

Torrential rain and sixty-knot winds whipped the sea into a writhing, angry kraken. Towering walls of water slammed Hawkins' fleet, at times attacking from a variety of angles. Sailors slipped and scrambled as they struggled to secure the decks and tightly furl the sails, frequently finding themselves covered and pummeled hard by surging water. With lines secured around their waists, they still struggled to hold onto whatever they could, to avoid being swept over the rail or slammed against the side. Ships' masts, strained beyond their design, cracked under the relentless pressure. Some ultimately broke apart, crashing dangerously down on the deck, wrenching ropes and torn sails with them. Two of the ships were so harshly battered that they lost steering ability. With no way to avoid a broadside hit from soaring waves, both simply tumbled sideways into cratering troughs, smashed by crushing waterfalls. The shattered ships and forlorn souls onboard made their way to the bottom of an angry sea, together.

By morning, the storm had subsided. Now well beyond the west coast of Hispaniola, Hawkins' four remaining but badly beaten ships, including the *Judith*, hobbled to the safety of the nearby port at San Juan d'Ulua. It was a smaller seaside village than Rio de la Hacha—a few handfuls of wood-built residences surrounding a central church constructed of stone. A small fortress stood about sixty paces from the shoreline. Its mud-brick walls, measuring eight feet in height, bore two cannons mounted on top, aimed at the harbor. But the fortress offered no resistance to Hawkins' pathetic-looking fleet as it arrived, without English flags flying.

"Haul anchor," shouted Hawkins, intending to take shelter, rest his weary crews and make needed repairs. Armed crewmen loaded the longboats and rowed ashore, taking unopposed control of the town. They didn't bother looting, it being such a sorry outpost. The only treasures here were the calm and the much-needed rest.

Two weeks passed slowly as the crews completed repairs at a leisurely pace. In retrospect, they'd taken too long. Dusk was soon to fall when one of Hawkins' lookouts spotted a fleet of thirteen multi-masted ships off the coast. Approaching slowly due to a lack of wind, the vessels emerged over the horizon in full sails, like a creeping layer of air-borne confetti, flickering in the silvery light of the setting sun glancing off the water. Among those on board was the newly appointed Spanish Viceroy, Don Enrique Martinez. When word of the ships reached Hawkins, he realized there was little time before they would reach the harbor. With only four ships on his account, still not fully repaired, he faced overwhelming odds. He ordered his captains to make ready for battle and man the Spanish cannons on the fortress wall. At the same time, he sent Langton in a longboat to intercept the oncoming flagship.

Langton's face showed his youth. Tall, thin, better-dressed, and more polished than the typical sailor, he'd been well-educated in languages, speaking impeccable Spanish, French and Latin, among others. Now at the furthest end of the harbor, he called out to the Spanish flagship as his longboat, bearing a white flag, came within hailing distance. "Permiso para abordar," he shouted, requesting permission to board.

Unarmed, he was assisted aboard the ship. Only one of the six sailors who had rowed him over accompanied him. The rest waited patiently in the longboat. Langton was taken to the Viceroy. Martinez was a robust, white-bearded man who clearly enjoyed his drink—a bit too much given his bulbous, veiny nose.

"I thank you for your willingness to meet with me, Your Excellency." Langton bowed slightly from the waist. "My name is Langton. I come at the request of Commander Hawkins, noble servant of Her Majesty, Queen Elizabeth of England. I extend the Commander's warmest personal greetings."

"My compliments to your Commander, Señor Langton. May I ask what your intentions are?"

"Our small merchant fleet has sought refuge in the harbor. We are guests of the village, repairing our ships which were battered by the recent storm. We are conducting modest trading with the villagers for needed supplies. We seek a few more days to complete our repairs and provision our ships before returning peacefully to England."

Martinez had learned of the English attack on Rio de la Hacha but didn't wish to make this emissary aware of that. He responded with a level of disdain. "Your ships, Señor, have more the appearance of warships than trading vessels."

"We carry only defensive weapons, Viceroy. We mean you no harm. Nor do we have any intentions to harm the villagers."

Martinez considered this for a moment. Was Langton's comment about not harming the villagers a veiled threat? He wasn't about to be played the fool. "Thank you, Señor. You shall have two days to complete your mission. Please give my regards to Commander Hawkins."

Langton looked searchingly at the Viceroy. It was clear this short visitation had ended. He wondered whether Martinez was being truthful. His face was difficult to read. He thanked the Viceroy, bowed and took his leave.

After Langton disembarked, Martinez instructed the commander of the Spanish fleet, "We shall not be denied access to our own port by English pirates. Let us prepare immediately for an assault in the dark of this night. We must take control, both of their ships at anchor and the battery of cannons onshore."

———

"What word from the Spanish?" Hawkins asked Langton.

"The Viceroy sends his compliments, sir. He stipulates that our departure must occur within two days."

"Is that all?"

"The meeting ended abruptly."

"I see. Thank you."

As Langton turned to leave, it occurred to Hawkins that he should probe more deeply, "One moment, please." Langton stopped, turning back toward him. "You are a most gracious diplomat. Yet I worry that your diplomacy may mask the reality of the situation at hand. I would like to know what your instincts tell you, even if you fear it may be something I would prefer not to hear."

Langton thought for a moment, choosing his words carefully. "I have no wish to give any undue concern, sir."

"But?"

"There can be no guarantee that the Viceroy shall choose to withhold his forces for the next two days."

Hawkins wasn't a man who managed his ventures by simply hoping for the best. For his fleet's safety, he knew he must prepare for the worst possible turn of events. He had quickly summoned his captains, who were now assembled before him in his cabin. He rose from his creaky wooden chair, a shard of pain emanating from his right knee. "Mercy!" he exclaimed as the pain coursed through his entire leg. "Thank you for coming, gentlemen. Mr. Langton has informed me that the Viceroy has given us two days to complete repairs and be on our way. I suspect, however, that the Spaniard may have different designs." The men's faces showed concern.

"I cannot risk the safety of our fleet. We have no time to spare. Captain Drake, since the *Judith* is in the best condition of our ships, you shall take the front, nearest the Viceroy's fleet. With all haste, please."

"Aye Commander."

"The rest of you, prepare your ships to sail, ready or not. And stay alert for any signals from the *Judith*."

"Aye, sir."

"And you, Captain Drake, be sharply vigilant. We shall follow your lead." He sat back down in his chair, cringing with discomfort. "God be with you, gentlemen."

IV

The blood-curdling scream coming from the residence shattered his quiet morning like disintegrating glass. Taking a break from preparations for his upcoming arguments at court, Daniel was strolling the grounds, alarmed by the shriek. Another frightening scream followed closely, pressing him to rush to the house with whatever speed his stiff, old legs could muster. He opened the door just as Garret raced down the staircase and ran straight to his arms. He knelt and embraced the child, looking up the stairs as Gwendolyn's maid descended

"What is it, Garret?" Daniel asked, with concern.

"She hit me," Garret sobbed.

"Who hit you?"

The maid, now by his side, whispered in Daniel's ear so that Garret couldn't hear. "Your daughter, sir. She struck Garret hard. On the face."

Daniel pushed Garret back gently, looking at the small face, tears streaming down its cheeks. One cheek was still red from the back of Gwendolyn's hand.

"Oh my. Why?" He directed the question to the maid.

"If you please, sir, there was a disagreement. Gwendolyn was unhappy about Garret's choice of clothing. The pants, in particular."

Daniel recognized his own accountability in the matter. He'd set in motion a difficult dynamic between his daughter and her child ever since paying the priest to falsify church records. Listing the mother as his own deceased wife had pained Gwendolyn. She resented his demand that she be constantly presented as Garret's older sister, rather than mother. It was a source of increasing conflict between the two of them. Daniel could see that the stress of the situation with Garret had only deepened Gwendolyn's debilitating depression and anxiety. She had even exhibited signs she might harm herself.

Things were becoming far more complex than Daniel had ever anticipated. He knew he needed to resolve things soon, both for the sake of Garret's relationship with Gwendolyn and for his daughter's own mental well-being. "I shall talk to her," he said to the maid. He rose to head upstairs, Garret clinging tightly to his leg.

"Please, Garret, let me go. I must speak with Gwendolyn."

"No," Garret insisted, tightening the grip. "I hate her."

Daniel kneeled once again, bringing their faces together. "Your sister is not herself. She loves you but she has troubles that confuse her, and sometimes cause her to behave badly. It is not her true intent." As he said this, he thought about the two things he'd recently been considering. One was to institutionalize Gwendolyn at Bridewell, a hospital for the indigent and mentally challenged; assuming they would have her. The other was to send Garret off to a private boarding school. He'd been leaning toward the latter. Among his clients were a handful of wealthy merchants who were funding a private academy—Ritchfield. It offered training in arithmetic, natural philosophy, cosmography, navigation, military sciences, languages, history, politics and civil law. Having Garret benefit from the academy's offerings seemed far preferable to institutionalizing Gwendolyn. Though the thought of losing close contact with Garret tore at his heart, he decided in that moment to message his friend, Robert Doughty, who oversaw Ritchfield Academy. Still, he recognized it might be a few years before Garret would be eligible to attend.

———

"Mr. Prouten," Drake called as he boarded the *Judith*. "Join me in my cabin, if you please."

Prouten followed Drake down the stairwell and into his quarters. The two men stood. Drake wasted no time explaining the situation. When he was done, he gave his orders, "Accordingly, Mr. Prouten, we shall move slowly into position, as to be unnoticed. Have young John (Drake's younger brother) scale to the crow's nest and keep a sharp eye on the movement of the Spanish fleet. He must maintain a count of their ships at all times. Put the gun crews on notice. They must be prepared at any moment to rain fire. Have the anchormen at the ready, to weigh in haste. All sails to be fully unfurled, on my order."

"Aye Captain, on your orders." Prouten nodded and left.

Drake was excited for action. There would be no Spanish surprise. Not on his watch.

A hard knock on the door awoke Drake in the middle of the night. He'd dozed off at his desk, while reading, his head now laying atop the book. He bolted up reactively, shaking his head in the process. There was no need to dress; he'd kept his clothes on in readiness. "Enter," he said, rising from his chair. It was Prouten, a worried look on his face. "What is it, Mr. Prouten?"

"Young John sends his compliments, sir. He reports that three Spanish ships have disappeared from view, heading beyond the harbor."

Drake thought for a moment. "It suggests they are preparing a land-based assault. Alert the fleet."

Prouten left hastily for the main deck. He ordered signal flags to the rest of Hawkins' fleet and sent messengers in longboats to the men on shore, ordering them to abandon their posts immediately.

It was a mere two hours later when the Spanish ground forces charged the village shore battery, in the dissipating dark preceding dawn. They were shocked to find the cannons deserted. No matter, they would ready them to fire on Hawkins' fleet. More surprise, however—the gunpowder and fuses were missing. Still, the English were in a perilous position. The Spanish fleet's cannons began showering them with heavy fire, inflicting severe damage on one of Hawkins' ships.

Following Prouten's alert from the *Judith*, Hawkins had prepared well. Crewmen on every ship had been positioned on the masts to unfurl the sails on short notice. Others awaited orders to weigh anchor on command. When the inevitable attack came, his gun crews responded with cannon fire of their own. But they were hugely outnumbered and outgunned. There was really no choice but to take immediate evasive action. Hawkins shouted to his master's mate amid the ferocious exchange of cannon-fire, "Full sails, if you please, Mr. Allan!"

"Aye sir," Allan replied. "Set full sails," he shouted to the men. "Lively now."

Except for the one severely damaged ship, the English fleet came alive with men rushing to unfurl and set the mainsails, mizzens and topsails. The canvas quickly fluttered down, came taut, and filled with the wind. The *Minion* slowly began moving toward the wide mouth of the harbor while returning fire.

The Spanish continued their heavy barrage, setting the midsection of the one crippled ship completely ablaze as its gunpowder stores ignited. Sailors were thrown onto the deck and against the rails by the force of the blast. Bright orange flames stretched high into the darkened sky, their light dancing off the choppy waters. Charcoal-colored smoke billowed into the darkness.

Hawkins maneuvered the *Minion* into position behind the burning ship, to avoid taking direct fire from the Spaniards. He signaled Drake to come around in the *Judith*, to offload precious cargo from the failing ship before it could sink.

Amid the flames, smoke and general chaos, Drake's men scurried to help the sailors on the doomed ship unload as much cargo as they dared. Hawkins, meanwhile, spotted a favorable opening. On his orders, the helmsman made the turn. The ship, now with good speed and a favorable wind, slipped between the right wing of the Spanish blockade and the shoreline, though not without damage from opposing guns. Cannon shots peppered through the mainsail. The foremast was splintered. Sections of taffrail were destroyed. Several sailors were injured, others killed, by rifle shot, flying wooden shards, and cannonballs streaming across and through the decks.

The burning ship in the harbor began tilting into enveloping black water. Drake ordered a hasty evacuation. The men scrambled off the flaming remains, heading for the *Judith*. Some couldn't wait their turn to board the longboats, of which there were too few. Instead, they jumped into the water, hoping to grab onto a boat or swim for the rescue ship. Many wouldn't survive, dying in the flames or drowning under the cratering remains of the floundering ship.

The battle raged on, cannons flaming like the fiery breath of competing dragons. The *Judith* gathered up the retreating sailors as best it could. Drake's ship was small, fast and highly maneuverable. It pressed its way through a large gap in the blockade created by the two Spanish ships that had left to hunt the *Minion*, with limited damage and no return of fire.

The early morning unfolded darkly, under a heavily overcast sky. Though the crush of battle was now well behind them, danger of a different nature bore down on Hawkins' ships. The intense winds that had enabled the more streamlined English vessels to flee their oppressors, now gusted violently, completely separating the *Minion* and the *Judith* from each other's sight. In the turmoil, Hawkins and Drake had failed to establish a place where they might later meet. Instead, their ships were forced to sail separate, chaotic courses, twisting and turning like foxes evading Spanish dogs.

By late morning, Drake realized he was on his own, having to navigate back to England with limited fresh water and food supplies. These he would have to parse out among not only his own men but also those he'd rescued from the burning vessel that now lay at the bottom of the harbor at San Jun d'Ulua. Lightly bruised in battle, the *Judith* would require constant pumping and a myriad of carpentry repairs to maintain its seaworthiness, especially in the cold, heavy, winter waters of the North Atlantic as they approached England. The ship was now far slower than its full capability given the weakening structure, the water it was taking on, the addition of survivors, and the weight of cargo taken from the burned ship. The journey home would be challenging, with some men sick, all of them hungry and, after a time, having only the rainwater they could catch in unused canvas to quench their unrelenting thirst.

———

It was one of the colder gray days in January when Drake and his hobbled crew heard young John's excited shout from the crow's nest on the mainmast. "Land ahoy! We are home!" Though the sight of English hillsides was still beyond those on the deck below, their hearts lifted them to a height where their minds could envision them.

"Well, Mr. Prouten," a somewhat emaciated Drake said to his weary master's mate, "God has seen fit to bless us. Let us cherish his blessing and use that gift to further our efforts on his behalf."

"Most certainly, Captain. Though England is home, the oceans will always beckon us. Let us one day take ownership of them from Spain."

"We must," Drake nodded, "and we shall."

The *Judith* soon limped into Plymouth Harbor amid the rousing cheers of the crew and ceremonial cannon fire. They had arrived home safely, their hold filled with precious cargo. To a man, they hailed Drake's skill in guiding them back against challenging odds.

It wasn't long after setting foot on English soil that Drake learned Commander Hawkins and his men hadn't yet returned. No one knew what had become of them.

V

Four candles waved their light across the walls and ceiling of the tiny room at Ritchfield Academy. Garret sat wrapped in a warm shawl, reading an English translation of *The Art of War*. It was attributed to Sun Tzu, a Chinese General who supposedly lived in the centuries preceding Christ. It was required reading for the class on military history. Unlike the books Daniel had read to Garret, there was no hero. This was purely a treatise outlining the man's thoughts on military strategy—as though he were playing a game and defining how it should be won, under various conditions. The book had totally absorbed the last two evenings. But this night, Garret's mind tended to wander elsewhere. To home. To family. The time apart had never been so long. Years had passed since living at home. Though summers brought visits back, Daniel was often away on business. Gwendolyn, on the other hand, was always at home. At least physically. For the poor woman, there was no such thing as an emotional home—at least not as Garret had come to think of it. Home was a place of love, comfort, peace. Gwendolyn had none of those. Her mind wouldn't let her. She was tormented for reasons Garret couldn't understand. The woman had one time even threatened to cut herself with a knife. The incident was disturbing. It had happened only a week before Daniel brought Garret to Ritchfield. On the way, he had explained how the academy was a vessel for shaping the future. Though that was clearly true, Garret sensed something more lay behind Daniel's decision—possibly Gwendolyn's unpredictable and potentially dangerous moods. Nonetheless, Garret was determined to excel at the academy and make the family proud. There seemed

36

little doubt that finishing at the top of the class was possible. Nothing would get in the way of that, whether in academic or athletic endeavors. Emulating the heroes from Daniel's books was the objective. It may well have been *his* wish but it was now Garret's own vision. The road forward meant learning as much and as quickly as possible. It was like running a race with others who might not realize they were even in it. In fact, it seemed few chose to do little more than walk it.

Unable to concentrate on the reading, Garret closed the book, set it on the small table, blew out the candles, and crawled into bed, throwing a shawl over the woolen blanket to provide sheltering warmth. Thoughts drifted to the conversation with Daniel over dinner, just days before originally leaving for Ritchfield. The server had presented a plated flank of roast pig, bordered by boiled carrots and sprinkled with sprigs of mint. He'd placed it gently on the table where the two were seated, and then withdrawn. Daniel had said a brief grace before taking up silver tools to carve the meat. Garret's mouth puckered at the memory of the pink-colored juice oozing onto the serving plate. Reflecting on it now, it was clear Daniel had carefully prepared for the discussion, wishing to counsel a seven-year-old headed for life at the Academy. He had opened indirectly.

"We shall leave for Ritchfield the day after the morrow. An early start is in order." He laid thin slices of pork on the plates. "Our days at home together have been a blessing to me, Garret. I shall miss you dearly, though I know in my heart this is best for you."

"I look forward to it, Father, though I worry I may not be as happy as I am here."

"You shall make your own happiness. I know this to be true. It is in your nature."

"I shall take your word, then."

Daniel added carrots to the plates. "There is something you should be aware of while you are at Ritchfield."

"What?"

"Each of us lives a life that becomes filled with truths and falsehoods. Some have more of one than the other." Garret looked confused. Daniel smiled. "It is most important that we be thoughtful about both. Some truths, and some falsehoods, should always remain private. Others may be shared." He sat.

"I do not understand."

"At this point you may not, though in time you shall." Daniel cut his pork and took a bite. Garret and Gwendolyn followed his lead. When Daniel finished chewing, he sipped wine from his cup before continuing. "Your truth is who you really are—mentally, emotionally, spiritually. Even physically. Including the many things you believe. All of these you must thoughtfully defend, sharing carefully. Sharing only with those you most love and trust."

"Of course."

"Some of these things, in particular, are the most sensitive and personal. Your body, for example. That can be shared with no one except the person you love—the one you choose to marry. And not until you marry. You must never disrobe before others. Ever. In fact, a person must avert their eyes if another is disrobed, or disrobing. It is a required courtesy. Nor must you discuss bodily functions since that may lead to awkward conversations." Daniel looked Garret in the eyes. "Do you understand this?"

"I do, Father."

"Excellent. We shall discuss more about truths and falsehoods during our trip to the academy."

Thinking back on it now, some two years later, Garret appreciated Daniel's counsel, though there was no point at which disrobing in front of others was done at the academy. In fact, it was prohibited by policy, according to the headmaster. Thoughts of Daniel's counsel, and feeling blessed to have him as a father, carried Garret off to sleep.

———

Ever since returning to England, Drake had spent countless hours reviewing the successes and failures of his voyage under Hawkins. Committed to becoming the best commander on the high seas, he carefully retraced the fleet's maneuvers, battle tactics, coordination and other strategies, intending to reinforce things that had worked well and identify weaknesses. One thing stood out—the treachery of Viceroy Don Enrique Martinez at San Juan d'Ulua. The man had no honor, in his mind. His deception put Hawkins' fleet at great peril, serving to heighten Drake's hatred and mistrust of Spaniards. He pledged to avenge his fallen sailors, devoting the remainder of his life to striking King Philip's empire at every opportunity.

Taverns all across England were commonly abuzz with discussion of Drake's exploits. His crew had spread word of the young captain's seafaring skills, unaccompanied by the arrogance found in most commanders of the day. They said he had an uncanny ability to turn visions into reality, attributing it to his intense passion and focus. He'd demonstrated a quickness in adapting to unanticipated developments in battle. What's more, he was viewed as masterful at aligning and motivating his men to achieve the mission at hand. His reputation as a daring and powerful leader was being richly etched. People who came into contact with the man remarked on his cheerfulness, sense of humor, and fondness for engaging with others. They drew close to hear his fascinating stories of adventures and battles with the Spanish. Many wished they, or their sons, might accompany him on his next voyage. Some had already approached him, offering handsome payments to take their sons aboard as midshipmen, believing he would be the best possible mentor for boys of a seafaring nation.

————

The forest was still damp from a short, overnight rain. Several horsemen assembled at its edge, their foxhounds noisily jostling alongside. Daniel Connachan had organized the hunt on one of his properties, serving as Master of the Hounds for the sport that was quickly gaining popularity among England's elite.

Garret, at Daniel's side on a white pony, was already experienced. This was not the first hunt. That first, now more than a year ago, was still a vivid memory. At its end, Garret had been welcomed into the hunting fraternity with a ritual ceremony. As Daniel drew blood from the dismembered fox, Garret, on bended knee, was circled by the other hunters. They watched as Daniel streaked blood across his child's forehead and down both cheeks. "Garret Connachan," he proclaimed, "you are hereby made a member of the Fraternity of the Foxes. May you fare well and long in your pursuit of prey." The men had laughed and cheered the addition to their ranks. It made Garret feel part of something special—a brotherhood, etched in blood. Being a full member had brought a sense of power to every hunt since then.

The excitement and anticipation this morning were in stark contrast to Garret's typical placid mornings at Ritchfield Academy. The hounds paced anxiously, sensing the imminent start. The men's robust conversations came to a halt. They looked to Daniel, who had raised the bugle high. He drew it to his mouth, waited a moment, smiled, and then blew the charge. The hounds yelped, racing headlong into the woods, in search of their quarry. Two of the many horses reared up as the rest took the bleating of the horn in stride. At their riders' commands, the horses trotted ahead, following the hounds.

Garret relished the familiar sounds—the distant howling of dogs, the crunch of shrubbery under the horses' hooves, the swish of tree branches brushing by, and the banter of the men. Their conversations were assisted by a dram of whiskey prior to the start. Breathing in the blended scent of damp forest, morning mist and white pony, Garret thought forward to the finish— the exhilaration of the capture, followed by the bloody sacrifice of the fox. Exciting, yet appalling. It felt wrong to take the animal's life for mere sport;

especially since it had done no harm. The killing seemed a sheer display of man's dominance—masters of the world. Still, it was accompanied by an expression of reverence for the animal—the prayer for its soul; the use of its blood in marking Garret's passage into the fraternity; the auctioning of its parts as trophies. The surprising amount of money raised from the auction would be contributed to Ritchfield Academy. The fox's life would therefore extend beyond the moment—trophies and memories for the men, and funding for the education of their sons.

In time, the initial excitement of the chase dissipated. The dogs ceased barking, focusing more on sniffing plants in search of the scent they craved. The horses' gaits slowed. Even the men's conversations withered. It was surprisingly quiet for a time as the search continued in earnest.

Several of those who'd joined Daniel for the hunt were his clients. One was Robert Doughty, lead investor in Ritchfield Academy. In his late sixties and completely bald, Doughty had long ago taken to wearing a white powdered wig. But not this day. He felt it might interfere with the proceedings. Daniel leaned over to speak with him, out of earshot of Garret. "Tell me, Sir Robert, what have you heard from the headmaster regarding Garret's progress at the academy?"

The question wasn't unexpected. Daniel had asked Doughty to make the inquiry at the time he invited him to the hunt. "If I may speak candidly, Daniel, young Garret is not the best-mannered student. The most intelligent, perhaps but, shall we say, disruptive. Not as obedient as one might like."

Daniel laughed. "I shall take the blame for that. It is actually a point of personal pride. I have always taught that one must challenge the thinking of others, albeit in a respectful way. After all, if one does not push the boundaries, no progress can be made."

"Indeed," replied Doughty. "Boundaries are being pushed," he smiled. "I am told Garret is a fierce competitor in the field as well. One might think the child's size a disadvantage in physical competition with older boys, yet that is offset by an apparent understanding of how the games are smartly played."

"I am pleased to hear that. Garret chooses not to share with me the success of competitions, for fear of undermining others at the academy. I respect that." Daniel paused before redirecting the discussion, "I find Garret has developed a deep love for courses on naval and military strategy."

Doughty nodded, "The headmaster concurs—definitely points of excellence"

"Good. Good. I thank you for following up on my inquiry."

"You are most welcome."

"Now tell me, how is your son faring in your many businesses?"

"Thomas is doing fine, thank you. He, too, is an intelligent man, as you know. It serves him well. I worry, though, that he has an air of self-importance. I find it uncomfortable. He has little empathy for those of lesser intellect. At times, it causes ill-will with our customers."

"Perhaps you are too harsh, Sir Robert. That is not an uncommon trait among children of wealthy intellectuals."

Sudden barking of the hounds interrupted the conversation. They'd picked up a scent. The chase was now fully on. The horses trotted again, brushing against the trees in their haste, giving off a light spray of fallen rain from the whip of the branches. Garret smiled, holding the pony's reins high and firm, enjoying its rhythm.

The chase didn't last long. The fox had gone to ground, taking cover in a den beneath the surface, surrounded by the hounds. Daniel dismounted, ushering the dogs back with a long, firm stick. He raised his pistolet in the air and fired, as did others. The noise of the shots was intended to flush the fox. It didn't have the desired effect.

"Bring up the terrier," Daniel ordered. One of the attendants had brought a terrier in a cage on the back of his steed. He dismounted, untied the cage, and placed it on the ground, setting the little dog loose. It jumped and barked fiercely. The man walked to the hole, motioning his arm swiftly toward the den's entrance and snapping his fingers. The terrier wasted no time, rushing in with a growl. The frightened fox fled its den quickly, rushing straight into a mesh that had been thrown over the opening. It became entangled as the attendant pulled the strings to tighten the enclosure. The hounds yelped in delight.

Garret watched in sorrow as the mid-sized, red fox, defenseless but for its bite, shivered in fear. It would soon be beheaded. The tail and feet would be removed. Six parts available for auction—the head being the most prized. Garret's heart bled for the defenseless animal. Its death had a way of haunting the soul. At least for some.

VI

Two ships sailed beyond Plymouth's outer harbor, under a warming spring sun—Drake's flagship, the *Pascha*, and its consort, the *Swan*. His return from San Juan d'Ulua years prior was now a distant memory. It had taken far longer than he'd anticipated to arrange funding for this voyage to the Southern Seas. His pitch to investors was the promise of generous returns based on capturing what he termed the 'treasure house of the world'— Nombre de Dios. It was where the Spanish warehoused gold and silver, mined in places as far away as Peru, awaiting arrival of the treasure galleons and warships that would transport it to Spain twice a year. Preparing ships and amassing a crew had gone quickly once the funding was secured. Hundreds of men had begged to sail with Drake, many drawn by the adventure of hunting treasure in the mythical Southern Seas. Others sought to free themselves from a dismal life in England. Only seventy men were chosen.

Captaining the *Swan* was Drake's younger brother, John. Though inexperienced as a captain, John had grown up on the sea alongside his famous sibling. He carried himself just as confidently, with an athletic swagger and a frequent smile. His light-colored hair and tanned face closely mirrored his older brother's. The crew had long ago taken to calling him 'Little Drake' because, at the time, he was shorter than his brother. But now that he was taller, they'd turned to calling him "Captain John."

Drake stood at the *Pascha's* stern, looking back at the *Swan*. He saw John at the bow and waved, proud to see him taking on his first command. He turned and walked the deck, his thoughts immediately rotating to the task at hand. Given Spain's extensive fortifications around Nombre de Dios, he knew that a seaborne attack with only two ships was unlikely to be successful. Instead, he'd settled on a land-based assault. But it would likely take more men than he had at his disposal. He believed there was a good chance he could garner the help of the black slaves he'd heard about who, over the years, had managed to escape their Spanish captors and now lived freely in the forest, beyond the village. These 'Cimarrones' had turned outlaw, stealing what they could from their former overlords. Their experience could prove beneficial. He was confident that having a common enemy would encourage them to partner with him.

"Full sails," Mr. Prouten. "Time is our most precious currency."

———

The headmaster was displeased. "We have never accepted a girl into Ritchfield, Mr. Doughty. You must understand, she would be surrounded by boys, some of whom are almost young men at this point. It could present a most awkward situation for her."

The elegantly dressed Thomas Doughty, son of Sir Robert, sat beside his daughter Rose. "I appreciate your concern. But, as you are well aware Mr. Frankum, my father's funding of the Academy is unmatched. Should you choose to keep his granddaughter from being admitted, you may soon find yourself in search of other employment."

"I do not appreciate your insinuation, sir. Your father is a gentleman. He would not stoop to such bullying."

"My father's health is failing him. No doubt I shall soon take over management of his affairs—including oversight of Ritchfield."

Frankum leaned back in his chair. He was aware that Sir Robert's health was deteriorating, though not to the point of having to hand over his responsibilities at Ritchfield. The headmaster valued his role here. It gave him high standing, in the best social circles. He had no interest in surrendering that. "Very well," he said. "We shall admit your daughter. But I cannot be held responsible for any untoward actions that may result."

Doughty glared at him, his eyes filled with the ferocity he felt. "You, sir, will do well to watch over her at every turn. Are you quite clear on that?"

Frankum shuffled uncomfortably, feeling the sweat from his armpits soil his blouse. He nodded, begrudgingly. He would need to find a way to ensure the girl's safety and prevent her from being bullied. Or worse. Perhaps he could assign one of the older boys to take Rose under his wing—one he could trust.

Though she was assigned a protector, a fourteen-year-old named Christian, it hadn't taken Rose long to find a friend on her own. She was particularly fond of Garret, who struck her as smart, fearless and a natural leader, even among boys who were two and three years older. Garret was actually a year younger than Rose—only nine. But to her, he seemed older, tall for that age, a superb athlete, and a gifted swordsman. With a rather sweet face. The two of them had grown close through their participation on the same football team. Rose hadn't seen the sport played before. Garret had taken the time to teach her the rules of the game and the many ways in which the ball could be maneuvered with the feet—making it look easier than it really was. Garret was always patient with her.

The two shared a love of history, though Garret's preference was for military and naval history whereas her own interests were in the political vein. Admittedly, the two were tightly intertwined. After all, military might was the ultimate tool of political leaders and rulers.

Though Christian was always nearby, Rose and Garret often completed their homework together at a table in the study hall. On one particularly gloomy afternoon, they were preparing for an examination on naval history. Sitting near a window, they listened to the rain pinging hard against it. Rose was not a fan of inclement weather. "Can you imagine," she whispered, "what it must be like to be a sailor in Her Majesty's Navy, in a driving rain such as this? Constantly wet. And cold." She shook, as though shivering.

"I don't mind the rain," replied Garret. "I find it refreshing at times. The cold, however, is another matter. I prefer to be warm. I imagine if one were sailing the Southern Seas, it might not be so bad."

"I suppose. Still, I have no interest in being on a ship at sea."

"Would you not wish to visit other worlds? Perhaps Africa or the Indies?"

"Not really," replied Rose. "I have everything I want here, at home."

"Well, for myself, I should like to see other countries at some point. Greece and Italy, for example. They have such rich history. And the islands in the Southern Seas. They offer a myriad of new opportunities."

"Would you not miss your family and friends?"

"I would make new friends."

"Would we still be friends?" Rose asked.

"Of that, I am certain," Garret assured her.

Rose sensed her fondness for Garret was growing beyond mere friendship, though it seemed clear Garret was not picking up on that. Not in the least.

———

Leaving their ship behind, they moved quietly in a pinnace and longboats under a dark, overcast sky. Drake and his raiders approached shore on the outskirts of the now-sleepy treasure town of Nombre de Dios. Though unable to connect with the Cimarrones by this point, he'd felt a deep need to proceed with the assault anyway. His men were impatient to capture a prize. Best not to disappoint them. He felt the first spittle of rain as they skidded onto the sand. By the time they pulled their boats toward the nearby foliage, the rain was pelting them. They waited anxiously, it being too dark and too wet to proceed through thick jungle.

In the early hours of the morning, the moon finally broke through the cloud cover, spreading whiteness on its underbelly—sufficient light for

Drake's forces to get underway. He ordered Prouten to remain behind with a handful of men. They would guard the boats until the raiders returned, hopefully with treasure in hand.

The going proved exceedingly slow, the men having to hack through thick plants to forge a usable path. It was almost dawn by the time they reached the outskirts of the village. Dark, heavy clouds once again covered the sky. Drake turned to his brother, John. "I shall lead my men down the main street, toward the market square. You and your men shall approach from the flank—he pointed right. Once the town is secured, we shall take the storehouse."

"Understood," said John, extending his hand. "I wish you joy of success."

"And you, John." Drake grasped his hand, thinking how his brother had developed into a fine young man, a good friend, and a confidant. Suddenly worried about John's safety, he ordered some of his most capable men to accompany him. Despite John's youth, there was little question among the men about his capabilities to lead them. After all, he'd come from the same stock as Drake himself. His height, strength, intelligence and self-assuredness also gave them confidence. He issued orders with a degree of certainty that belied his level of experience.

Rain once again fell steadily, making a plinking sound as it pitted against the men's swords and pikes, like tiny pebbles. The two groups followed different paths, proceeding to the very edges of Nombre de Dios, doing their best to maintain silence. As the town square came into view, Drake held his hand high in the air, signaling a halt. He scanned the buildings, looking for anything in motion. Nothing moved. He searched for a sign that John's men had reached their flanking position. Again, nothing.

The loud chiming of church bells suddenly pierced the silence. Someone was signaling the residents—perhaps a sentry who'd heard or spotted the invaders. Within moments, a rhythmic beating of drums added to the noise, rousing the military. The town was better prepared than Drake had imagined. Still, he was confident that immediate action provided him the upper hand against an unassembled opposition.

"Forward," Drake shouted, "with haste!" The raiders charged, armed with swords, pikes, crossbows, pistolets and axes. Storming like a black wave, they startled the few militiamen who were readying their arquebuses. Battle yells filled the air—coyote howls, screeching hawks, laughing hyenas. The chilling cacophony unnerved awakening villagers.

First among Drake's raiders was Musa, a giant, dark-skinned, heavily muscled sailor. His tattered shirt and dirty pants clung to him in the rain. A bright red bandana covered his head, its primary responsibility being to hold back the sweat his enormous frame constantly generated in the daytime tropical heat. Unquestionably the strongest warrior, he served as Drake's personal bodyguard. Both feared and admired by the crew, many called him Black Musa. It wasn't merely for the color of his skin—it was the blackness he'd brought to a myriad of Spaniards and others who'd foolishly sought to challenge him. His preferred weapon, which he handled with blinding speed and surgical precision, was an executioner's axe, its head curved on both ends and freshly sharpened. The long handle was made of rock-hard, black ebony. A line of near-parallel scratches ran along its edge, each one marking a man he'd disposed of. Running at Drake's side, Musa's face bore a menacing grin, welcoming imminent battle.

The make-shift Spanish militia grew haphazardly. Hastily set arquebuses took aim at the surging raiders. Smoke mingled with rain as the militia fired shot after shot. One of the leading raiders took an iron ball to the head. Blood oozed from the entry wound as he crumpled into the damp mud. Drake took a hot, stinging blow to his thigh, causing him to stumble and fall as his leg gave out. Musa reached down, pulling him off the ground. The two pressed forward, Drake's pumping adrenaline masking his pain.

Hard rain hammered the raiders as they fired back with pistolets and crossbows. Others clashed head-on with the militiamen who were ill-prepared for such vicious hand-to-hand combat. The pikes and cutlasses wielded ruthlessly by Drake's men tasted Spanish flesh. Musa wielded his axe with ferocious force, crashing it down on unprotected shoulders and slashing at necks. The Spaniards took their own toll on the raiders. Blood seemed to flow more than the heavy rainwater in the muddy street, as warriors on both sides collapsed heavily into the muck.

And then they came—John's men flooded the town's militia from the flank. Overwhelmed Spaniards reacted to the horror of looming annihilation. They fled in terror, casting their weapons aside. The town's residents were streaming out of their homes, seeking cover in the jungle. Women screamed and children cried as they raced away, soaked and barefoot, carrying nothing, most covered only by sleepwear.

The vicious battle ceased within minutes of the first shot. Drake, John and their raiders now stood unopposed in the drenching, ceaseless rain, in complete control of a town emptied of residents. The men gathered round their two captains, while a few stood watch. A handful of Spaniards had been taken prisoner. Drake ordered them brought forward. He addressed them directly, having Langton translate. "My good gentlemen," he opened, "you have defended your town bravely. But you have lost this battle. Your life is now in our hands. We promise you no harm and ask in return that you direct us to the Governor's house." Drake suspected the Governor would be storing gold and other treasures in his residence—easy to access and carry away.

"Please sir," one of the prisoners stuttered in Spanish, "spare us. We have families." He pointed down the street. "The Governor's house is that way. The large, white house."

"Thank the man, Mr. Langton. Tell him he can go now, to be with his family."

The prisoner, surprised he was being set free, paused for a moment, glancing at his fellow militiamen. Seeing Drake nod his head in the direction many of the villagers had fled, he quickly came to his senses and dashed off in that direction. The rest of the prisoners remained held by Drake's men, for possible further interrogation.

John led most of the raiders to the storehouse. Drake, with Musa's help, led eight raiders down the mucky street to the Governor's residence. There was no response to their pounding on the door. Drake nodded to Musa, who smiled back, stood to the side of the door, and swung his mighty axe at it sideways, shattering a gaping hole in the middle. The others stood back, worried a pistolet shot might come through. When nothing happened, Musa took a heavy run at the door, crashing through as though it were merely false wood. He stood inside the entry, slivers of the shattered door still hanging on his broad shoulders, wood-dust sticking to his wet clothing. Drake limped in, cutlass raised, followed closely by the rest. He placed his arm on the wall to steady himself, now forced to worry about the blood seeping through his pant leg.

"Search the house," he directed. "Lively now!"

The men scoured the residence, grabbing some of the more easily transportable gold and jewels found in casks, in the closets. They emptied a large clothing chest from the bedroom, to load the treasure in. Drake ordered two of them to take the chest back to the boats. One of the raiders hailed him to the rear of the house. He hobbled to an enormous hallway, running the entire length of the residence, some seventy feet long. He stood quietly for a moment, using his cutlass as a crutch, astonished by what he saw. The hall was filled end-to-end with foot-long bars of silver piled twelve feet high and ten deep, like a shining, regal wall inside a palace vault. An incalculable fortune. But it was more than his raiders could carry and load onto the boats. Nor was this the more prized and valuable gold they sought. He thought for a moment, exhausted and a little dizzy from the loss of blood. "Take as many bars as we can carry. Leave the rest. We must head to the storehouse." Before exiting, he ordered a few men to search for carts that could transport any treasure.

Musa helped Drake struggle forward through the slick, squishy mud now layering the street. The entire group of raiders soon stood outside the storehouse, pummeled by rain coming at them almost sideways in a torrent. The streets were a virtual river of sludge, sucking at their boots. They sought shelter under the porticoes of the buildings, waiting impatiently for the intense rain to subside. Drake, increasingly woozy, worried that the passage of precious time would give the Spaniards time to reassemble, possibly with reinforcements. He sought to proceed the moment the rain eased up. After a few minutes, it obliged. Even the wind softened.

"Now!" Drake yelled, his voice cracking. A sharp pain surged through his leg. It was bleeding profusely. He bent over, his face in agony, barely able to get the words out, "Break down the doors." Stepping forward, he stumbled and fell into the muck. Musa and John picked him up, the right side of his face fully covered in mud. One of the men wiped and bound his leg tightly with a scarf, to stem the bleeding. Drake lost consciousness, unable to command further.

John realized he was suddenly in charge. He ordered Musa to attack the door. A mighty swing of his axe hit the heavily reinforced door, with minimal effect. It was clear much more time and effort would be needed to break into the storehouse. John was concerned. Even if they could get in, the river-like streets and thick forest would make transportation of heavy treasure impossibly slow. He also worried that his hobbled, unconscious brother, and other wounded raiders, would be sluggish in returning to the boats. He addressed the men. "This is not our time. The obstacles and risk outweigh any potential gain here. We must take our leave and wait for a better time."

Although they shared disappointment, the men sensed John was right. And they valued Drake more than the treasure itself. They knew his leadership would bring other opportunities to secure treasure. This wouldn't be the end of it. Disheartened, drenched, and concerned for their leader's health, the raiders trudged their way back to the boats. A large Scotsman, with a broad back and heavy red beard that dripped constantly in the rain, handed his pike to one of the men. With a little help, he hoisted Drake onto his back. Tough-as-nails, the man was called 'Caber' by his mates, owing to his reputation for winning caber-toss competitions in his homeland. The nickname was easier to pronounce than his real name—Farquhar. He was reputed to have singlehandedly hauled a seaman's chest filled with gold and jewels, and often carried full barrels of water without help. He now plodded along, carrying the wounded Drake through the damp forest, without the slightest grimace.

The raiders eventually returned to their boats. The treasure taken from the Governor's residence had already been loaded. The men were soon on the water, in retreat, in the morning light. Drake, covered in mud, lay in one of the boats, blanketed, his eyes closed. He was gasping haltingly for air more than breathing it. Together, the men prayed for his life, fearing he might not see the coming of the night.

VII

He'd never experienced it before—his body shaking nervously, beyond his control. He felt it most in his hands. Standing before his furious headmaster, Christian was nervous, apprehensive about what might follow.

"Have you lost your mind?" Frankum yelled at the top of his vocal range. "Was I not perfectly clear that you were to keep the girl from harm?"

"Yes, sir," Christian replied sheepishly, head down, eyes staring at his too-large feet.

"Then please, tell me how this could possibly have happened."

"I am afraid, sir, that she was off to attend to personal matters. One of the older boys followed her. He had a knife and threatened to slice her if she did not do as he wished."

"And where were you?"

"I had gone for water, sir. We had just finished our game. I was most thirsty. I told Rose I would meet her back at the square."

"And?"

"I waited but she did not return. I went looking and found her crumpled on the ground, sobbing. There were bruises on her face and arms. She pleaded with me not to tell anyone what happened."

"Do you know who did this?"

"She would not say. He threatened her if she were to reveal his name."

"We shall find this bastard and deal with him accordingly," insisted Frankum. A moment of silence followed—an uneasy moment for Christian.

Realizing the precariousness of his own situation if word of this were to reach the girl's father, Thomas Doughty, Frankum cautioned the young man, "Keep this entire matter to yourself. Do not speak of it to anyone. Am I clear?"

"Yes, sir."

Still livid and disgusted, Frankum yelled once more, "You are dismissed. I am enormously disappointed in you."

Christian walked out, head still down, wishing he'd never been pressed into taking the girl under his wing in the first place.

Following the assault, Rose had come to find Garret. She needed comfort and there was no one else to confide in. Or trust. Garret was her best friend. Potentially more at some point, she hoped. Though Garret hadn't picked up on her one very subtle advance, she was confident he would protect her from her assailant.

Garret was shocked by the sight of Rose—her clothing ripped, her face bruised. "What happened?"

The girl sobbed, barely able to speak, "I was attacked." She fell into Garret's arms, both of them speechless in the moment. The two held each other until the shaking stopped and the tears slowed.

"Who did this?"

Rose shook her head. Saying his name would only bring back an image and a memory she sought to suppress. She held on, comforted in Garret's arms.

This cannot stand, Garret thought, wanting desperately to crush Rose's assailant. That emotion oddly brought back a memory of the bloody dismemberment of a fox, after the hunt. The only difference here was the anger, fueling a rage within her. Garret realized that doing nothing might subject poor Rose to even more abuse. Reciprocal action had to be taken—to send a message that the girl was untouchable. There had to be a way. In the morning, when Rose might be feeling less traumatized, Garret would press further, for the attacker's name.

———

Drake's men had returned from Nombre de Dios to their encampment at nearby Isla de Piños. They carried their commander to a small tent, pleased to see that he was still breathing. It wasn't until the following morning that Drake finally regained consciousness. It may have been the pressing ache in his leg that brought him to. Fighting a mental grogginess, he tried retracing his last events but could only remember the beginning of the assault on

Nombre de Dios. The rest was a blur. Had their attack been successful? John interrupted, poking his head through the tent's opening.

"Come, John," said Drake.

John entered and sat on the ground, hands on his folded knees. "I am pleased to see you are awake. The men are concerned. How are you feeling?"

"The pain tests my mood." Drake shifted his weight a little. He rose slowly, a grimace wrinkling his face. "How are the men?" It was his first concern, even before his own health.

"I am afraid we lost four fine crewmen. Several are wounded. All but one should recover. Including you," John smiled.

"I am sorry to hear that. Their loss is more painful than my physical ailment." A moment of silence passed, during which Drake closed his eyes. John sensed his brother was saying a prayer.

Drake opened his eyes, "Were we successful?"

"We returned with a modest treasure, from the Governor's house. Do you not recall?"

"My mind is blanketed by fog."

"We were not able to break into the storehouse. Conditions were difficult. The main door was heavily reinforced."

"I see."

The two brothers paused, both thinking about what came next. John spoke first. "We shall not be able to repeat this assault."

"Indeed," Drake replied.

John offered thoughts on what he'd observed during the assault: the village militia's lack of preparedness for hand-to-hand combat; the positioning of sentries; and the presence of small ships in the harbor, only one of which might be considered a warship. "Rather than a direct attack on the town, perhaps we might raid one of the mines."

Drake contemplated the thought. "That might indeed yield a better outcome. Still, I worry about the distance over which we would need to transport heavy treasure; all while having to avoid opposition. The Spanish would have time to mount a formidable attack." He paused to consider other possibilities. "Perhaps we might intercept the gold while the Spanish transport it from their mines to Nombre de Dios."

"Finding that trail might prove difficult. Through a most unpleasant forest, I might add."

"Do we have prisoners?" Drake asked.

"A few militiamen and some slaves. Africans."

"Perhaps one of the Africans might have knowledge of the route and be willing to cooperate. Ask Mr. Lee to bring me the one who appears to speak for the rest. Have Mr. Langton join us as well. We may need his help."

John left, returning soon with Lee, Langton and a large, balding, well-groomed black man. His skin was more caramel than black, as though he were of mixed race. He wore an unusually frilled blouse and relatively clean, white-cotton pants that ended mid-calf. They were held up by a belt of white rope, bearing a sheath that at one time had contained a dagger. The dagger had been taken from him.

"Captain Drake," said Lee, "may I present Diego. He speaks reasonable Spanish, having been their slave for many years. I believe he might be of service in helping us understand their operations."

"Buenos dias, Diego. Como estas?" It was some of the little Spanish Drake knew.

Through their conversation, with Langton's assistance, Drake found he liked this man. He seemed honest, of decent intellect, and had a sense of humor, accompanied by a pleasing smile, full of large teeth. After years in captivity, Diego had become a trusted advisor to the governor himself and supervisor of the slaves serving in his household. He'd hidden in the town during the assault. After the battle ended, he'd walked directly up to some of Drake's men, holding a white cloth in upraised hands, signaling surrender. Diego had much to share. Drake sensed he would be helpful in establishing contact and relations with the Cimarrones, the former slaves now living and hiding in the jungle outside Nombre de Dios—men he could use to supplement his own.

———

Garret waited until after breakfast in the assembly hall. Together with Rose, they returned to their dormitory. Now seemed a suitable time to open discussion about the attacker.

"Rose, you know you can trust me. I have slept on this matter and I must insist that you share the name of the boy who did this to you. If we say nothing, and do nothing, he will only be encouraged to take further advantage of you—perhaps even encouraging his friends to do so as well."

Rose thought about that. In her gut, she suspected Garret was right. She teared up and shook her head. "I am so afraid."

Garret wrapped an arm around the girl. "You are precious to me, Rose. A truly bright blossom. Let me be the thorn that protects you."

Rose wiped away a tear. "Thank you, Garret."

"Now tell me, who is this villain?"

"You promise you will not tell anyone?"

"You have my word." Garret stopped walking, placing both hands on Rose's shoulders and looking her in the eye, awaiting the answer.

"Henry." The name was almost inaudible. Rose hung her head as she uttered it.

Garret knew him well—one of the bigger, older boys. He was always aggressive on the football field, making tackles with no concern for the safety of those he challenged. He sought to intimidate others as a way of weakening their game, making their moves hesitant. His general demeanor was one of arrogance and superiority. The boy was no pushover. Avenging his assault on Rose wouldn't be easy. But Garret was determined to find a way. There was really no choice. As they walked on in silence, the upcoming wrestling competition came to mind. A match against Henry might be possible, though he would be in a higher age grouping. It would require the coach's approval to wrestle at that level. No, not *require approval*, Garret thought—demand the right.

———

Over a period of several days, John, Diego and a few others traveled the coast, far from Nombre de Dios, seeking to contact the Cimarrones. In time, they came across a handful of them near a river that spilled into the sea. Discussions followed. John was disheartened when he learned that the Spanish didn't transport their treasure from the mines frequently. It would be at least five months before the next mule train would traverse the well-worn trail. If that were to be their objective, the raiders would simply have to wait. The good news was that the Cimarrones were willing to partner with them, happy to attack their former overlords.

Upon hearing the news from his brother, Drake thought it best to build up their current encampment and wait for word of the next mule train. The men spent several weeks completing construction. When they were done, Drake named it Fort Diego, honoring the slave who'd proven so valuable.

The wet sand and cool water felt good on their feet as Drake and John walked the shoreline. The morning was calm, the sun low in the sky, gleaming down on the white-sand beach. They discussed strategy for their next assault and reminisced of their childhood. As they often did, they teased each other about past mistakes and shortcomings. It was John's turn to tease his older brother, "It continues to amaze me that, for such a small man, you have such an oversized reputation."

Drake laughed. "You have much to learn, John. It is not the size of the man that matters but rather the strength of his passion and the size of his heart."

John laughed, "If you say so, *little* brother."

As they walked on, Drake mentioned he had decided to sail to Cartageña, to gather supplies and seek further information on the pattern of movement of the Spanish gold. Perhaps an assault at sea might be possible during the transport from Nombre de Dios to Cartageña. In the meantime, John would stay behind, taking charge of Fort Diego. The two strolled on, laughing and sharing a friendship that doesn't always come simply from being brothers, unaware that this would be one of the last conversations they would ever share.

———

Another of Drake's younger brothers, Joseph, sat in the warm sun on a hillside overlooking Fort Diego and the blue Caribbean Sea. His eyes wandered from ocean to land and place to place, amid the boredom of the watch. A flash of white on the deep-blue water suddenly caught his eye. He looked closely for the flag but couldn't make it out clearly. Judging from the breadth of the sails, it was a wide-bodied ship. Possibly a Spanish merchant, he thought, though he couldn't rule out its being a warship. He watched it closely for a few minutes, trying to discern its direction. It appeared to be moving at an angle, rather than directly toward the island. Minutes passed. Finally, he could make out the Spanish Burgundy flying on the stern. No time to waste, he thought. He sprinted off to his signaling point and waved his flags vigorously, heralding his sighting to those in the fort below, ecstatic that his time on the hill hadn't been wasted.

With Drake already in Cartageña, John was attending to various tasks as the fort's leader. When word came of the presence of a Spanish ship, he worried the fort might have been spotted. If so, the Spanish might assemble ships and forces for an assault against it. He thought it best to capture the vessel, to prevent that from happening. He quickly ordered his crew to ready their ship. With John leading, the *Swan* soon set sail to hunt their prey.

It wasn't until the following morning, under a clear blue sky, that sharp-eyed, young Joseph in the crow's nest caught the white sheeting of a ship. "Sail ho," he called to the deck below.

The *Swan* was already at full sail, taking maximum advantage of the stiff breeze. "Where away?" John shouted.

"Two points, sou' sou'east, if you please."

John hurried to the bow and stood at the gunwale, to the left of the bowsprit. Squinting his eyes, he scanned the water in the direction noted. And there it was, a ship flying the Cross of Burgundy. It was still unclear whether this was a merchant or a ship of the line—a Spanish warship. Both were known to use the same flag. In either case, it appeared headed in a more southerly direction than the *Swan*. Wishing to head him off, John shouted instructions to the helmsman.

"Hard to larboard, eight points. Lively now!"

The pilot gripped and spun the tiller, carefully guiding the ship in the direction John had ordered. The *Swan* glided through the water, narrowing the gap with its prey. Since it was closing quickly, John assumed this was a merchant, not a warship. By late afternoon he was within cannon range. But from this vantage point, he could see it was in fact a ship of the line. It must have spotted them and feigned being a merchant by traveling at a much slower speed than it was capable of.

The Spanish captain had expected the ship now fast approaching him was either English or French and had no good intentions in coming at him this quickly. He smirked at his deception, which had clearly fooled this would-be predator. He welcomed the opportunity to mete out punishment.

John ordered the *Swan* into a broadside position, readying its cannons to fire. He noticed then that his prey had beaten him in turning broadside, its gunports springing open. He could see the noses of the cannons roll through the ports; at least eight of them pointed his way. As the Spanish gunners secured their deadly weapons, John realized his ship was in peril. Unable to turn fully broadside fast enough to return fire, the *Swan* was both defenseless and a larger target than if it were approaching head-on.

Spanish cannons flamed and roared. A few of the shots tore through the *Swan's* sails and crashed onto the main deck, sending shattered wood spearing through the air. One of the incoming cannonballs struck John in full flight, separating his body into two pieces, killing him instantly. Prouten looked on in horror. He turned his head away, hand over mouth to hold back the vomit he felt rising. Bits of it spattered out of his mouth, between his fingers. He needed to regain his composure immediately, though he wondered if that were even possible. He was now, shockingly, in command of the ship. Spitting out the last of the bile, he yelled out in full voice, "Hard about! Lively now." The crew scrambled to reset the sails amid the continuing volley of cannon fire. The small, agile ship turned quickly, allowing Prouten to avoid most of the incoming fire and make his run back toward Fort Diego. The heavier warship followed but was unable to keep pace, eventually losing the *Swan* in the darkness of the encroaching night.

<h1 style="text-align:center">VIII</h1>

Following receipt of Headmaster Frankum's carefully worded report on the incident involving his daughter, Thomas Doughty hastened to visit Ritchfield Academy. It had been weeks since the event. He was appalled it had taken this long for word to reach him. He came not only to check on his daughter but also to chastise Frankum and release him from his position. While racing to Rose's dormitory, he found her on the grounds, in the company of a friend.

"Father!" Rose exclaimed, running to him. Garret watched as Doughty dropped to his knees, embracing his daughter. Tears flowed down Rose's cheeks.

"My dear Rosie. I am so sorry for what has happened." Rose sobbed, unable to say anything. Doughty glanced up at her friend, who was approaching. "Who is your friend?"

Rose turned. "This is Garret," she sniffed. My best friend."

Doughty stood up, one arm around Rose's shoulder. He extended his hand. "It is a pleasure to meet you, Garret."

"And you, sir." Garret shook his hand.

"Would you mind giving us a moment? I should like to talk to Rose in private. Perhaps you and I can talk later."

"Certainly, sir." Garret walked off, thinking how cold and impersonal the man seemed, despite his obvious feelings for his daughter.

Within the hour, Thomas Doughty returned to see Garret. He was a rather small man, impeccably dressed, wearing a powdered white wig. His eyes seemed unfriendly. Perhaps that was simply a result of the unfortunate circumstances that had befallen his daughter. Garret doubted Rose had shared with him the full details of her encounter with Henry. Doing so would not only be uncomfortable but also force her to relive an exceedingly painful experience. Now face-to-face with Doughty, Garret pondered an answer to the question he'd just raised. How much to share without violating Rose's trust?

"I am afraid I know little of what happened, sir. I was not there."

"I understand. But did Rose share any details with you?'

"Only that she had been taken from behind, and that the boy had a knife," Garret responded, choosing not to be completely open with him. It was up to Rose to share the details with her father—if she chose to.

Doughty looked at Garret intensely. "I sense you know more than you are telling me."

"No, sir."

"What about the name of the boy who attacked her?"

It was clear Rose hadn't disclosed Henry's name to her father. Not my place then, thought Garret. "Rose has not shared that with me."

Despite the denial, Doughty judged from Garret's manner that something was being withheld. "I sense you are not being truthful with me.

Let me assure you, young man—if I find you are attempting to deceive me, I shall have you expelled from the Academy."

"I am sorry, sir; I cannot help you."

Doughty turned and left, walking in the direction of the headmaster's office. Garret watched him go, first impressions confirmed—the man was unlikable, despite being Rose's father. There was a distinct iciness about him, and a distasteful aura of arrogance. Perhaps he would learn Henry's identity through some other means and have him expelled. In the meantime, Garret felt it best to wait for the upcoming wrestling competition, to deal with Henry.

———

Drake returned to Fort Diego, unaware of the tragedy that had occurred while he was gone. Prouten met him at the shore. Drake looked questioningly at his master's mate, wondering why his own brother had chosen not to greet him. "Where is John?"

"My apologies, sir. I am unsure how to say this." He looked down at the sand. "John is no longer with us. He met his end in a confrontation at sea."

Drake's knees unexpectedly buckled at the news. He reached out to Prouten, stabilizing himself. His shock buried any would-be tears. "How can this be?" he replied.

"A Spanish warship. John died a valiant death." Prouten chose not to disclose the gruesome details. Drake sensed from Prouten's brevity that it had been a bitter experience, best not shared.

The two men walked toward the fort in silence. When they reached it, Drake immediately recognized the sorrow in his men's faces. He nodded to them but didn't speak. Instead, he retreated to his quarters, where he could privately release the tears compelled by such a devastating loss. Never again would he be able to enjoy his brother's company and good humor. He recommitted himself to fighting the Spanish to the end of his days.

John's death wasn't the only unwelcome news for Drake. Many of his men had become violently ill, including his younger brother, Joseph, who had joined as a midshipman, not yet a teenager. There was much speculation about the nature and cause of the dreaded illness. But there was little that could be done for those who contracted it; most simply died. Eventually, the sickness claimed the lives of more than twenty men, young Joseph among them. It was another demoralizing blow, causing Drake to withdraw for a time, barely able to interact with his men.

Each day that one of the fallen crew was to be buried, a brief service was held on the dead man's behalf. Preacher Fletcher would read a passage from the Bible. Drake would say a few words, commenting on the deceased man's contributions to the expedition. Others were invited to add their own memories. When the time came to bury Joseph, Drake was simply unable to comment. He did his best to summon the courage to speak, but the dual loss of his brothers was more than he could bear without weeping openly—something he felt he couldn't do in front of the men and still maintain their respect. Prouten spoke on his behalf.

Having lost two brothers and several crewmembers, Drake needed time to work through his sadness and reengage his passion for an attack on the treasure caravan bound for Nombre de Dios. He spent his days walking the shoreline or alone in his tent, reading, reviewing maps, and rethinking the many aspects of his assault plan. He would avenge John's death by seizing Spanish gold on the Panama trail and leaving behind a cross of gold in John's honor.

In Prouten's mind, Drake had mourned and self-isolated for too long. He came to his leader's tent one morning, following breakfast. "Good morning, Captain. Will you join me for a walk up the hill?" There was no specific matter Prouten wanted to discuss. He simply wished to get Drake out of his tent for a little fresh air. Hopefully, it would return the Captain to a degree of normalcy and help him get on with the rest of his life. After all, the men were beginning to question Drake's enthusiasm for the mission. And even his readiness for battle.

"Certainly, Mr. Prouten." Drake stepped away from the map he was reviewing. "The air shall do me good."

The slight, cool breeze coming off the sea was pleasant, midst the growing heat and humidity of the late morning. As the two men wound along the path up the hill, they barely spoke. Not wanting to talk unless his captain was so inclined, Prouten waited for him to make the first comment. But Drake was busy absorbing the beauty of this far-off place. The deep blue sky was sparsely spotted with puffy white clouds of varying shapes, drifting like ships in the heavens. The lighter blue and turquoise waters nearest the shore lapped softly against the white sand. Palm tree fronds rustled in the breeze, their sound mixing with the morning songs of several varieties of colorful birds. Two larger birds hung almost motionless in the stronger winds aloft. This was a paradise, Drake thought. And for a time, it cleansed his mind of the crushing sadness he'd been wrestling with over the loss of his brothers…and too many other good men.

Nearing the top of the hill, Drake slowed to watch a reddish-brown squirrel cross by. The little rodent scaled a rock, stopped for a moment, and stood on its hind feet, looking directly at the two men. Its bushy tail stood tall, directly behind. The squirrel remained motionless, as did they. Drake felt an odd connection with it—as though it had a soul of its own. It moved slightly toward him and then once again stood on its hind feet, as if it wished to share something with him. After several seconds of searching each other's eyes, Drake sensed the squirrel was a sign—a sign that his brothers had passed on safely to the other side and were now one with God. It brought him peace. And warmth. A few more moments passed before he turned to Prouten. "A capital idea, my good man. This walk has renewed my spirits. I feel a happiness I have not felt in some time." He looked back. The squirrel was gone.

"Rightly so," replied Prouten. "We have all felt the sorrow of loss on this island. Absent that, this place would be a paradise."

"Indeed. Unfortunately, it has become our Slaughter Island." The name would stick.

IX

The great lawn served primarily as the exercise and football field. It stretched across the front of the administrative and classroom building at one end, down to and across the dormitory at the other. The air above it was filled with laughter and excitement as the schoolboys assembled for the wrestling competition. Some were participants, others merely observers. The latter pushed and shoved each other, jockeying for favored positions while waiting for the key match of the day. As far as anyone knew, this had never happened before. Garret's insistence on wrestling up two age groups had been approved. The wrestling coach was initially leery. But, being pressed, he believed Garret had the necessary combination of speed, physical talent and knowledge to compete at this level. Garret was also tall enough, though underweight. Eventually, he was persuaded. The new headmaster had signed off as well. After all, the match would be supervised, to ensure no severe harm would befall either wrestler.

Garret's competitor was Henry, the boy who had assaulted Rose. Stalky, strong, and known for his roughness on the football field, most thought Henry an outright bully. He smiled wryly, anticipating his take-down of the smaller Garret. He disliked the fact that Garret was a more skilled baller, and well-liked by others. Both combatants were viewed by their classmates as leaders—Garret by way of influence and intelligence, Henry by way of sheer intimidation. Henry was surprised that Garret had already defeated two opponents in this age category, in order to challenge him. He had no idea that his competitor's motivation was the opportunity to deliver payback on behalf of Rose—in a legitimized way.

The sound of the coach's whistle pierced the air, silencing the crowd and gathering their attention. The competitors began circling the space between them, each seeking an opening. Their classmates cheered them on. Henry made the first move—a clumsy, unexpected dive at the ankles, attempting a quick take-down. Stepping aside to avoid the attack, Garret tripped on his right arm as it whipped by, falling backward. Henry was on top in an instant. He reached for Garret's head, placing it in an arm lock and forcing it into the dirt. Garret pushed up hard on his elbow, creating enough of an opening to pull the head through and out. Popping up and backing away to create space, Garret felt blood drip from a wide forehead scratch. A split lip bled as well.

"Are you okay to proceed?" asked the coach. Garret waved him off. Henry had scrambled to his feet. Seeing the red smear on his opponent's face, he grinned, meanly. Again, he lunged, this time going directly for the head. Garret instinctively reacted to Daniel's words—*after the thrust, you are most vulnerable*. Ducking and stepping to the side provided the opportunity to turn and launch at Henry's back as the force of his offensive carried him by. Garret grabbed his right arm, bending it upward, behind him. Henry swore in frustration while being forced slowly down to his knees. His head pressed into the dirt, he spit some of it from his mouth. Garret increased the upward thrust against his bent arm until it neared the breaking point. Though Henry tried not to evince any pain, the excruciating agony forced a scream.

"Time," yelled the coach. The new headmaster appeared concerned.

Garret was slow to release, wanting to inflict as much pain-filled retribution as possible. "Time!" the coach reiterated loudly over the continuing sound of Henry's screams, stepping forward.

The headmaster, furious with Garret, shouted, "Let him go." The coach grabbed Garret, forcing the two apart. Yanked to the feet, Garret wrenched free from the coach's grasp, glaring down at Henry and breathing heavily, as though ready to pounce again. Henry lay on the ground, writhing in discomfort, dirt lingering on the side of his face. The coach stepped between them, placing his hands on Garret's shoulders. There was a deafening silence among the shocked classmates. They hadn't expected such a violent attack—especially from Garret, who had always seemed so mild-mannered and thoughtful of others. Dusting off dirt and wiping a bloody cheek, Garret glanced and winked at Rose. She winked back.

The headmaster swore at Garret and waved his arms, instructing everyone to return to their rooms. Henry rose to his feet slowly, his sore arm hanging limp, his dignity as tarnished as a rusted iron wheel on abandoned farmland. Watching Garret walk away, he vowed this would not be the end of it. He would take his revenge on the bastard. And soon.

Garret strode away confidently, head high, heart racing, finally having tasted blood in action. The adrenaline rush was something new. Something euphoric. Intoxicating. It seemed a battle was not something to fear but rather to relish. Turning to look back at the now-dissolving crowd, a smile drew across Garret's face. Rose came running, wearing a matching smile.

———

It finally came—word from the Cimarrones that a phalanx of Spanish guards had been observed journeying from Nombre de Dios to their hub on the west coast of Panama. It marked the start of preparations to move their precious metals through the forest; the beginning of the journey that would carry the precious cargo to the eastern shore. Drake was relieved; his long wait had ended. Convinced that the Spanish had strengthened their defenses in and around the town itself, and that warships would be gathering in the harbor to accompany the treasure galleons, he was fully committed to an assault on the less-protected caravan hauling treasure along the Panama trail. His two ships would take up position well off the coast, miles from the town, where they would go unobserved. The raiders would then take longboats in the dark of night, to the landing site suggested by the Cimarrones, who would meet them there and guide them to the trail. Knowing his success depended on catching the Spaniards by surprise, Drake had been careful to ensure the plan's secrecy, sharing it only with Mr. Prouten and Diego, his link to the Cimarrones.

From the shore, the Cimarrones spotted Drake's two ships sitting at anchor in the calm sea, backlit by a crescent moon. It wouldn't be long, they thought. Onboard the ship, Drake stood at the taffrail, observing the flickering light from two small fires set by the Cimarrones. It danced on the surrounding foliage, marking the landing site.

"It is time, Mr. Prouten. Prepare to disembark."

"Aye, sir," Prouten replied. He turned and barked the orders, "Prepare the longboats. Man the oars. Lively now."

Drake's men poured over the sides, filled the longboats, and rowed toward shore. The water was calm; the only sound being the lapping of oars entering and drawing it. With the aid of the mild surf beginning to push them forward, the boats quickly skated to shallow water. Their hulls slid onto the beach, grinding softly through damp sand. The raiders jumped out of the boats, some dragging them into the jungle. Others covered the tracks left on the beach by running tree branches over them.

The men rested a few hours, awaiting the morning light. After a quick breakfast of hardtack, they followed Diego and a handful of Cimarrones along a narrow, winding path through the jungle. They were soon enveloped by the jungle's thick humidity and the sun's oppressive heat. Sweat poured down their faces and necks as they wound along the lightly but incessantly inclined trail. They found themselves inordinately bothered by unrelenting mosquitos and various other flying insects. Slithering snakes added to their misery. But for the lack of fire, this was literally Hell's

jungle.

In time, the raiders met up with a larger group of Cimarrones. They continued forward another hour, to the base of a demoralizingly high hill. Already fatigued, Drake's men were uninclined to ascend the challenging slope, despite Diego's insistence. Drake suggested they break, for food and water. Diego conceded, though he was surprised at how these well-muscled men were so easily exhausted. He didn't understand that a sailor's life, filled with hard labor, tested and built muscle but did little for building stamina.

Following the break, a handful of Drake's men joined him and the Cimarrones in slowly ascending the hill. The remainder proceeded to a point further along, at the base of the hill, where they would later meet. The sun frequently peered through thinning shade, searingly. Sweat flowed from the tops of the men's heads, like rivulets down a mountain face. When they finally reached the summit, Diego pointed to a grand old macondo tree rising high above the surrounding vegetation. It had been bent severely by wind over many decades, leaving its main trunk sweeping low to the ground, before angling gently toward the sky. The Cimarrones had long ago notched rudimentary steps into the tree's trunk and along the main branch, enabling them to use it as a lookout point, to scan the vast territory below.

At Diego's insistence, Drake ascended the tree. Carefully. Climbing until he felt he could go no further without too much risk, he settled into a comfortable position and then scanned the panoramic view. On one side he could see the familiar and inviting blue Caribbean Sea. In the other direction, he looked down along the tropical rain forest to a white sand beach highlighting the shallow, light-blue water glistening in bright sunlight. Beyond the beach was the vast Pacific Ocean he'd heard about in his teenage years. Now here he was, seeing it for the first time, amazed and intrigued. He sat motionless, breathing it in, promising himself he would explore this Ocean one day. It was something no English sailor had ever done. But for now, he had a specific task to attend to. He noticed the small village alongside the beach—an assembly point for caravans from the mines. Hundreds of slaves hauled gold and silver, loading the precious metals into wheeled carts and leather pouches that would later straddle the mules. Roughly two hundred mules were feeding and resting in a large enclosure. Elsewhere, Drake could see a line of wooden carts loaded with chests of gold and silver bars. Numerous guards supervised the activities, talking among themselves. Their cutlasses gleamed in the sunlight. Drake could see arquebuses positioned around the encampment, though none appeared manned. He descended the tree and turned to Prouten.

"The mules have not yet been loaded, though it appears they will be soon. The carts are already loaded. We must move into position, with haste." The men quickly exited the summit, leaving two Cimarrones behind as spotters, to keep watch for the caravan's departure. They descended the hill along a different path, this one heading east. Following the Cimarrones' lead, they reached the point where they met up with the rest of the raiders. They stopped at dusk, to set camp.

Morning found Drake and his men scouting the well-worn Panama trail, where the mule train would carry freshly mined treasures through the dense jungle. They surveyed a few sections, looking for a suitable place to set their ambush. Drake chose a long, straight stretch anchored by sharp curves at each end, making a hurried escape difficult. This location would give his men the best opportunity for success. It was here that he would take some small measure of revenge on the Spanish for killing his brother.

X

If there was a moon this night, it was unable to make itself known. Thick clouds and distant thunder threatened heavy rain. Garret hurried across the square, hoping to avoid getting wet. A short walk after completing studies had become a daily routine before turning in. The evening air floated a scent of coming rain. Nearing the corner of an old stone building, a shadowy figure emerged. Garret recognized it. Henry stopped in the path and stood there, saying nothing.

"What do you want?"

"Payback, you bastard."

They were not alone. Movement at the corner of the building caught Garret's eye. Two other boys were watching. Henry's back-up. Bracing for danger, Garret's adrenaline and thirst for a fight kicked in. Fleeing wasn't even a consideration. This bout with Henry, unlike their last, would be unsupervised. This time his arm could be broken, if that opportunity presented itself. Garret's mind searched for the best order of combat, alert to the likelihood his accomplices would join in. The blade of a knife Henry was trying to conceal in his right hand was illuminated briefly by lightning-lit clouds. Smaller than a dagger, the blade's point was barely visible behind his sleeve. From that position, Henry would need to raise his arm high in order to thrust the blade downward. Garret avoided looking at it, needing Henry to believe it wasn't visible and therefore not in need of a change in position. The rain began falling, with more force than expected, causing Garret's eyes to blink.

Intending to keep Henry stationary until the gap was sufficiently narrowed, Garret approached him slowly. Henry waited, gripping his knife tighter while the rain grew in intensity. Within moments, he raised his arm quickly, as expected. Garret lunged at it, grasping his tricep with the left hand before he could begin the downward plunge. Henry stumbled backward. Bringing his clenched left fist around, he landed a feeble punch to the right side of Garret's head, forcing it left. Garret's right elbow deflected another blow from his left fist while the grip on his tricep slid quickly to his forearm. Planting a leg alongside and jerking the shoulders sharply left, Garret forced a toppling of both to the wet ground. Henry landed punches on the upper right arm with his weaker left hand. Garret scrambled to the knees, seeking to gain stronger leverage on his right arm. Knowing the flailing of his free left hand would distract his focus from the knife, Garret concentrated on dislodging it, absorbing multiple hits to the right arm and cheekbone, though they lacked full force.

With Henry still on his back, Garret shoved a knee hard into his groin. He screamed in agony, losing complete focus on the knife. Slamming his hand hard to the ground, Garret knocked the knife free and scrambled to grab it. Henry brought his right arm crashing down. It caught on the upturned blade, slicing through the skin on the underside of his arm, just above the wrist. Garret tried getting up on the now slippery ground, only to be tackled from behind by one of Henry's friends, knocking the knife to the ground. The third boy joined in. Henry's two accomplices pinned Garret in the slippery muck.

Henry scrambled to his knees, blood racing down his wrist and seeping through the fingers of his left hand. He struggled to stand, remaining bent over as he did, wrestling with the pain in his groin.

"What do we do with Garret?" one of the boys yelled. Garret squirmed beneath them.

"Knife the bastard!" Henry shouted. One of his accomplices spotted the knife on the ground and quickly grabbed it, rising to his feet. Garret tried to wriggle free from the other attacker.

"I need help," Henry cried out, in panic, startled by the blood now streaming freely onto his feet. "I need to stop the bleeding." He dashed off toward the infirmary. The boy with the knife kicked Garret hard in the rib cage before hurrying after Henry. The other accomplice, having freed himself from Garret, took his own kick at the right shoulder before running to catch up with his friends.

Laying exhausted in the muck, in pain, drenched by showering rain, thoughts raced through Garret's head—unprepared, yes; overwhelmed, yes; beaten, no. Now, more than ever, came a thirst for blood. Henry's blood. He was not some defenseless fox.

———

A chorus of insects serenaded Drake's raiders in the night's stillness. The men sat at their makeshift camp along the trail, near their intended point of ambush. They ate a meager meal of fruits and roasted rodents they'd caught and skewered. Drake rose. "Gentlemen," he said. "I expect the mule train will pass by on the morrow. Our success requires that you follow our plan. Those of you with Mr. Prouten shall be positioned at the rear of this section of the trail." He pointed in that direction. "You must wait in complete silence for the mules to pass. My group shall be near the far end, awaiting the caravan's approach. We shall attack first, at Diego's signal—a bird call." He nodded to Diego, who formed his mouth and mimicked the call of a seagull. Some of the men nodded.

"We shall attack the guards, not the slaves. Swords, pikes and axes only. No pistolets. We must keep the sound of our attack from reaching Nombre de Dios. The Cimarrones carry bamboo pikes for use by the slaves. We believe they shall be happy to join us." He looked around to ensure they were all paying attention, before continuing. "Once our attack is in progress, the guards will be in disarray. The mules are likely to scatter. The Cimarrones will be responsible for capturing them and securing the treasure. With the chaos at the front, the guards at the rear can be expected to rush forward to assist their mates. Mr. Prouten's group shall attack at that point. Once the guards have been overcome, we shall regroup here and then transport the treasure back to the boats." He paused to scan the men's faces. "Does everyone understand?"

"Aye sir," the men replied.

"Any questions, then?" There were none. "Thank you, gentlemen. Now, let us bed for the night and proceed to our designated positions at sunrise."

———

Dawn brought the jungle to life, offering up the songs of birds, the screeching of monkeys, and the wind rustling through the leaves high above. The sun soon filtered through the trees, brightening the colorful birds flying deftly through the forest. Drake was intrigued by the large multi-colored parrots in particular, making a mental note to draw them upon his return to the ship.

It wasn't long before he and his raiders took up position along the trail. They waited impatiently, fighting bothersome mosquitoes and flies that bit relentlessly. The men smeared mud on their bodies to defend themselves but enough insects pierced their skin to bring frustrating discomfort. After an agonizingly long wait in overbearing heat and humidity, the raiders finally heard distant bells, worn by mules. But another sound came as well—galloping hooves of a single horse, approaching from the opposite direction. The lone rider, dressed in sun-glinted armor, galloped past them on a sleek, brown steed, throwing up clumps of earth behind. He was a messenger, sent by the authorities in Nobre de Dios. A rogue Cimarrone had leaked word of the ambush, for which he'd been handsomely rewarded.

Upon reaching the caravan, the soldier dismounted. He spoke with the lead guard, ordering a return to the mine until reinforcements could be mustered. The guard instructed his men to make an immediate turn. But he smartly decided to let six pack-mules continue on, with a handful of brave guards. It would distract potential raiders, enabling the rest of the caravan to retreat safely. The six mules carried mostly supplies and a small amount of silver—intended to confuse any raiders into thinking this might be all the treasure being transported.

The mules, six slaves and three guards inched along the trail, giving the rest of the caravan more time to retreat. As they finally neared the end of the straight section, Diego whistled his bird call. Drake's group stormed from their hiding places. The guards' horses reared up, whinnying loudly. Cimarrones emerged, quickly distributing bamboo spears to the slaves accompanying the mule-train. Others secured the mules. The Spanish guards threw their hands high in surrender, releasing their weapons, as instructed.

Drake walked onto the trail, assessing the situation. He was disheartened, though not surprised, at the small size of the caravan. It seemed clear the Spanish had been forewarned. The treasure and revenge he sought had eluded him. He would once again have to find a way to tap into the multitude of Spanish treasure. But for now, with the raiders' presence in the jungle known to the Spaniards, he expected soldiers would soon come looking for them. He ordered his men to tie the prisoners to trail-side trees, so that they might be easily found and rescued. He had no desire to treat them poorly. They were merely pawns who had immediately surrendered. The raiders then coaxed and pulled the mules with their meager supplies through the thick jungle, beginning the long trek back to their boats.

Within minutes of leaving the trail, the raiders heard more galloping hooves. At least a dozen armed soldiers approached from Nombre de Dios. They spotted the prisoners tied to the trees. Dismounting rapidly, some soldiers freed the guards. Others set their arquebuses to fire into the jungle. Shots soon began clipping trees and brush. Drake's men took cover, waiting for the first barrage of shots to finish. While the Spanish reloaded, the raiders made a screaming charge, led by Drake and Musa. A shot from a pistolet grazed Drake's scalp, stinging him and dropping him to the ground, bleeding. A raider running near him was also wounded. Another was impaled through the chest by a long, thrown pike. He fell backward, bleeding heavily and gasping his final breaths. Musa took a pistolet ball in his enormous bicep but continued the charge, running fiercely and wielding his lethal axe. He uttered a blood-curdling yell as he bore down on the soldiers. Caber was close behind, pike in one hand and cutlass in the other. The soldiers were unnerved by the frightening image of the two enormous men and a rushing horde following them. The ferocity of the charge spurred the soldiers to turn and run, dispersing fragmentedly into the jungle on the far side of the trail. The raiders gathered up the arquebuses left behind before resuming their hike back to the boats, now with heightened initiative. Drake hurried along, holding an oilcloth to his head to stem the bleeding. The danger of pursuit was over. At least for now.

Shortly after dusk, the raiders arrived at a small fishing village. They took charge without opposition and spent the night there, resting, nursing wounds and contemplating their exit. They slept only briefly, for fear Spanish forces might now be trailing them.

Drake was up before dawn, his head pounding. The bleeding had stopped. He rousted the men, insisting they leave immediately. They proceeded along the water's edge, mules and silver bars in tow, returning to the boats. As they rowed away, Drake looked back at the shrinking landmass they left behind. He knew he needed to lay low for an extended period—long enough for the Spaniards to believe he'd given up on stealing their treasure—assuming they ever would.

XI

It was late in the morning when Christian arrived, instructing Garret to accompany him to the new headmaster's office. When they arrived, both noticed a rugged knife lying on a white cloth on the otherwise clean desk. Henry's knife.

"Stand right where you are." The headmaster rose from his seat and walked around the desk, a harsh look on his face. "How far this star has fallen," he said, shaking his head. "I am most disappointed in you, Garret. I came here and found you to be a bright student with much promise, though rather undisciplined at times." He said this, recalling vividly how Garret had failed to end the wrestling match with Henry in a timely way. "Now I find you have ambushed master Henry. In the dark of night. With a knife in hand, no less!" He pointed to the weapon on the desk, a residue of dried blood discoloring the blade. "Would you care to explain yourself?"

"You have the facts wrong, sir," Garret responded, calmly.

"Pardon me?" There was indignance in the headmaster's voice.

"I was not the attacker."

"Surely you do not expect me to believe that?"

"It is the truth, sir."

"Two witnesses say otherwise."

90

Garret was momentarily speechless, backed into a verbal corner, contemplating whether to continue the protest, in likely futility, or offer an apology and hope for reasonable punishment. The headmaster surmised Garret was trying to piece together a story.

"If you cannot accept my word, sir, then I have nothing more to offer."

"You realize, of course, that you must be expelled from the academy." It was a statement, not a question.

The shock of the headmaster's words hit hard. The severity of the punishment hadn't been anticipated. Nor wanted. Garret loved the studies here, and the friendships. The headmaster continued, "I shall send my recommendation to Mr. Doughty. It may take a few days for his response. In the meantime, you shall be confined to your room and precluded from engaging with others." He returned to his seat. "Now leave this office and let me not set eyes on you again."

"Yes, sir." Turning and walking to the door, Garret took one last shot. "Things are not as you say they are…"

"Enough! Off with you," the headmaster yelled, with a flurried wave of his hand.

———

Returning from Panama, Drake and his men spotted a French-flagged ship, captained by Guillaume Le Testu. The Frenchmen were seeking Spanish prey. Drake hailed the vessel, later boarding it peacefully to meet with Le Testu. The two captains exchanged pleasantries and sat in Le Testu's cabin, discussing their recent experiences over cups of port. Le Testu said he'd learned that a Spanish galleon was headed to Nombre de Dios. It served to heighten Drake's desire to separate King Philip from his gold. While the two captains conversed, Drake revisited his thoughts about a second attack on the treasure-laden mule train. He'd originally thought it best to wait a while. But with the approach of the Spanish galleon, he felt a need to try again soon. Perhaps the Spanish might think him foolhardy to attempt another ambush so soon, thereby leaving their guard down. When the right moment presented itself, Drake broached the topic, "We share a common enemy, Captain. Perhaps it would serve our interests to combine forces."

Le Testu didn't hesitate, "Most certainly. Our combined fleet would allow us to impose our will on all but the finest of Spanish warships. Perhaps even challenge a galleon," he grinned.

Drake liked this energetic man immensely; he had a sense of humility yet no shortage of confidence. "Excellent. But I must tell you, I have something in mind which is not a seaborne venture." He told Le Testu of his recent assault along the Panama Trail. "I believe it would serve us better to attack at a location closer to Nombre de Dios. The guards are likely to be exhausted from their journey through that miserable jungle. And, close to home, they are certain to be less alert." Le Testu liked the idea. He particularly liked the chance to secure Spanish gold. "Let me be clear," Drake closed, "the plan must remain unknown to your men. I have no tolerance for any leak that might once again jeopardize such a mission."

A mere two weeks later, Drake and Le Testu's men had positioned themselves along the Panama Trail, this time closer to Nombre de Dios. Drake had once again selected a suitable location for the assault. Two of his Cimarrones traveled west along the path, toward the Spanish assembly point on the west coast. They returned the following day to report that three mule trains were being readied—some two hundred mules and forty to fifty guards. This was indeed the treasure caravan Drake sought. The assault wouldn't be easy, given the number of Spanish soldiers, but with the addition of Le Testu's men and the element of surprise, Drake was confident they could succeed.

The raiders spent two nights in the biting jungle before word came that the mule train had left for Nombre de Dios and would reach them soon. They took up positions along the trail, expecting to attack in a fashion similar to their prior ambush. Waiting impatiently, they once again cursed the mosquitos and flies that brought so much agony.

This time there was no leak. No advance warning for the Spanish guards. Approaching the perceived safety of Nombre de Dios, they were happy and boisterous, their senses numbed from cups of beer they'd enjoyed during an earlier break. They looked forward to a well-deserved siesta in town.

Drake's raiders heard the far-off sounds of the approaching caravan. The tinkle multitude of bells, braying of mules, creak of wooden carts, rumble of hooves, clank of armor, and humming voices of the guards proclaimed a large procession. The breeze carried the pungent smell of mules and horses taking turns dropping their waste. The Frenchmen at the near end of the trail remained silent as the caravan made its noisy way past. They could see just how heavily loaded the mules were. No wonder they were constantly defecating. Le Testu judged there were at least fifty. Numerous carts carried chests and metal bars. The guards, fully dressed in shining, metal armor, carried long pikes in hand. They were only about twenty in number, this being merely the first of three separate caravans, each spaced a couple of hours apart.

As the front of the caravan approached Drake's group further up the trail, his raiders burst onto the path, attacking with speed. They pulled many of the surprised Spanish guards down from their horses before they even had an opportunity to throw their pikes or reach for other weapons. One guard nearer the middle of the caravan had sufficient time to draw his cutlass. He slashed an oncoming Cimarrone across the neck, killing him instantly. Other Cimarrones quickly overwhelmed him, taking brutal revenge. Another guard near the rear of the procession pulled out a pistolet. He took aim, shooting Captain Le Testu in the stomach. The Frenchman dropped to his knees, falling sideways. Severely wounded, his face tasted the damp soil. Blood oozed through his fingers as he pressed his hand against the wound. After taking the shot, the guard was pulled from his horse and slayed savagely by Le Testu's men. They left parts of his body strewn along the path.

The Spanish were quickly overwhelmed. A few managed to flee into the woods. Most were hunted down by Cimarrones and slaves, who showed no mercy. Other Cimarrones up and down the length of the caravan hastily secured mules that were scattering in the chaos.

Within a handful of minutes, Drake's raiders took complete control. It was immediately obvious, however, that the carts were so wide and heavily laden that they would never make it through the narrow path the Cimarrone's had created in this dense part of the jungle. And there was too much heavy treasure to carry on the mules, or by hand. Drake instructed the men to forget the silver, take only as much gold as they could, and bury the rest of the treasure. He hoped to one day return and retrieve it. Of necessity, they buried it nearer the trail than they would have liked.

While the men were digging, Drake took an oilcloth from inside his doublet. With a piece of charcoal, he sketched out a rough map, noting the position of the distant mountain top between the two largest trees along the trail. When he finished, he stuffed the map in his blouse and turned to check in on Le Testu. The Frenchman had been dragged off the trail by his men and propped up against a tree. He was bleeding profusely from his stomach wound, in no position to move. He struggled to speak as Drake came by and kneeled to face him.

"Congratulations, Captain. We have won," whispered Le Testu. He eked out a pained smile before continuing in a stilted voice, his breathing intermittent. "I am afraid I must remain here. Two of my men shall stay with me. Our fate shall be in Spanish hands. There is no choice."

Drake nodded his understanding. "I admire your courage, my friend." He paused a moment, realizing this might be the last he would see of the Frenchman. He extended his hand. "It has been an honor to partner with you. I assure you, the treasure shall be split evenly among our men, with special allowance for your own family." He touched Le Testu on his shoulder and smiled. "With any luck, I shall return to find you imprisoned by the Spanish, and set you free."

"Thank you." Le Testu forced a smile. "As others say, you are a man who is larger than life."

"Larger-than-life simply means smaller-in-reality," Drake smiled.

Le Testu had trouble responding, his words separated by pauses, "Perhaps so. But for a man lacking in size, you lead with outsized courage."

Drake echoed the comment he'd shared with his brother John months before. "A man's courage must trump his size." With that, he embraced Le Testu gently before rising. He parted, fully expecting Le Testu faced impending death. Even if he were to live long enough for the Spaniards to find him, they were not known for their forgiveness.

———

It was just another of several seemingly endless days. Garret sat in the room, longing for someone to speak to—someone with a sympathetic ear. But Rose and the other classmates were all attending lessons. For the first time, Garret felt crushingly alone. Deserted. Change was forthcoming. Daniel had been informed. He would be disappointed but surely would accept a truthful explanation. He might even appeal to the Academy, for reinstatement. Garret wondered whether that was best. All the learning at the school brought a sense of growth. But the mindless discipline that pervaded Ritchfield was tiring. The use of the birch stick to address even minor misbehavior was revolting. The new headmaster believed it was the best means of bringing the students into compliance. Garret felt it had the opposite effect—driving defiance. As someone who disliked being constrained by questionable boundaries, pushing the envelope was a road often taken. A game really; a welcomed opportunity to challenge the system while avoiding punishment. Of the several times crossing the line, only one had led to being caught. And that was only because Rose had given them away. They had sneaked out of their rooms after curfew. Garret wanted to hunt for and capture a small animal spotted in the yard from the window above. Its eyes had shone in the moonlight, drawing attention. It looked as though it might be a pine martin, though how it had ever made its way to this part of England was inexplicable. The two went out through Garret's window, laughing as they scaled down from the second story of the building by tying their bedsheets together. They headed out onto the grounds with a clothing bag, hoping to find the critter. For Garret, it was reminiscent of the foxhunts with Daniel. For Rose, it was a little frightening. Garret had spotted the animal and flushed it out of the shrubs, laughing as it ran toward Rose. The poor girl screamed frantically, drawing the attention of one of the attendants. That was when they were caught. Both had felt the sting of the birch stick the following morning. One thing Garret was now sure of— punishment would never prevent being adventurous in the future. It only strengthened the desire to push boundaries. And make the stakes more interesting.

Garret smiled at the memory but regretted the likelihood of not seeing Rose before leaving the Academy. More than any other classmate, the girl shared common interests and similar feelings. There was an inexplicable bond between them. Garret couldn't put it in words. The girl had become the closest of friends—someone to share even the most personal of feelings with. Knowing Rose would go on living a separate life brought a wave of sadness. Perhaps one day they would be fortunate enough to meet again. Would they be much older? How would they look? Would they even recognize each other? More importantly, would they be able to immediately reengage as close friends? Or might it somehow be awkward? Garret chose not to give it further thought. It was too difficult a thing to deal with in the moment. And there was a far greater concern to think on.

———

Within hours of Drake's raiders leaving Le Testu alone with his guards, a group of Spanish soldiers came across the Frenchmen. Realizing the hopelessness of his situation, and the likelihood of being executed there in the forest, Le Testu pleaded with the soldiers to spare the lives of his men. The Spaniards chose not to respond. One drew his cutlass, an evil smile emerging on his rugged face. He waved the gleaming weapon crosswise in the air by his head. Walking slowly toward Le Testu, he glared at him, speaking in a hushed, angry voice. Le Testu knew what was coming. He looked the soldier in the eye, refusing to flinch. The Spaniard stopped within range. The cutlass seared through the air with the speed and artistry only an elite swordsman could generate, severing Le Testu's head cleanly. It balanced on the stub of his neck for a split moment before toppling to the ground, as though in slow motion. The soldier stooped down to pick up the head by the hair. He lifted it high in the air, spitting at it. He would carry it back to Nombre de Dios, to display in the village square.

Le Testu's guards were summarily tortured by the Spanish for fifteen minutes before one of them finally disclosed the direction Drake's raiders were traveling, and the approximate distance from the harbor where they'd left their boats. The man's cooperation didn't benefit him or his crewmate. They were slain on the spot and carted back to Nombre de Dios, to hang in the square alongside Le Testu's head.

By order of the governor, Spanish soldiers launched a small ship, to intercept Drake and his raiders at the harbor Le Testu's men had spoken of.

———

Heavy rain pounded on the thick jungle with a drumming sound, drenching the raiders as they guided heavily burdened mules along the narrow path. For two days, they had trudged along the rain-slicked, muddied forest floor. Burdened by weather, wounded men, and the heavy weight of chests bearing gold bars, navigating the path in reverse seemed an endless task. Drake worried about their slow pace. He sent a small party ahead, to alert those guarding the boats that they would soon arrive with treasure in hand. The following day, the advance party came within a quarter mile of the harbor, hearing distant voices. As they moved closer, they became alarmed. The words were Spanish. Peering cautiously through the foliage, they could see a group of armed soldiers milling about, their longboats pulled well up onto the beach. A small ship was anchored in the harbor. The appearance of a lightly smoldering fire and scraps of food littering the ground suggested the soldiers had been there overnight. Maybe longer.

A messenger hurried back to alert Drake that the raiders' boats and men were nowhere to be found and that Spanish soldiers were now encamped there. Upon hearing the news, Drake imagined they might be surrounded—by those at the harbor and by soldiers pursuing from behind. There was no choice but to wait out the enemy at the harbor, hoping they would give up and leave before any pursuers in the forest might reach them. He ordered his men to hunker down quietly in the damp foliage and rest. Three men were sent to the rear, to relieve others who were keeping an eye out for approaching Spaniards.

Drake's thoughts turned to the fact that there was no sign of his men who'd stayed behind with the longboats. It meant there would be no way to escape the mainland, even if the Spaniards were to leave the harbor. He contemplated an ambush, to slay the soldiers and take their longboats. But his men were exhausted from their journey. An ambush might be difficult to pull off. And there might still be more soldiers on the ship anchored nearby.

Soaked and weary Spanish soldiers pursuing from behind found it difficult traversing the thick jungle in search of the raiders. The Cimarrones had created alternate paths to confuse the pursuers. It caused them to decide to return to Nombre de Dios and leave the soldiers at the harbor to deal with the brigands. But those at the harbor had also lost hope. Two days had passed with no sign of the thieves. Wet and tired themselves, they suspected Le Testu's tortured guard had lied to them about the location, simply to end his pain. With their food supplies gone, the Spanish captain ordered a return to Nombre de Dios. His men shoved their longboats into the water, jumped in, and headed back to their ship.

Word of the soldiers' departure from the harbor came to Drake from his advance party. Encouraged, he gathered the men to continue their slog through the forest, mud-caked and insufficiently rested. He hoped his men who'd stayed behind with the boats might be found hiding somewhere near the harbor. Instead, when they reached the site, there was no sign of them; no way to return to their ship with their treasures. The men felt deserted, tired, helpless, and concerned for their lives.

Drake wasn't about to abandon hope. He organized a handful of men to build a raft, using whatever materials they could find. When the storm finally passed, the work began in earnest. The raiders cut down small trees and branches. They stripped the green skin off tall saplings to tie logs together. They used the men's shirts to create a rudimentary sail. Within a day, they'd crafted a useable vessel with a tightly secured mast, a workable sail, a rudder and a set of oars. It was large enough to carry four men but unlikely to survive challenging waters for any length of time. Drake was not dissuaded. Having spent most of his life at sea, he was confident the raft would enable him to find his ship.

With the weather finally calm and promising, Drake left at dawn. He and three others waded into the water and scrambled onto the makeshift raft, leaving Prouten in charge of those onshore. Musa stayed behind as well, instructed by Drake to protect Prouten. Besides, he was too big a man to be supported by the crude raft. Those on the beach looked on, fearing for their commander's survival, let alone his ever returning for them. Drake called out. "Rest assured, God smiles on us. I shall return within days and together we shall celebrate our capture of the treasure."

The fair weather failed to hold. Drake's raft was battered by another storm and turbulent seas. Though it held together, it was becoming water-logged, challenged to support the full weight of the four men. They took turns getting off and swimming alongside as they held on, to keep from overburdening the small craft. When the rain finally ceased, the blazing Caribbean sun burned down on their weakened skin, drying it to the point where it split open as easily as a freshly sliced fish. Saltwater stung their raw flesh as it washed over them. With no more water to drink, the four men became despondent, fearing the worst and praying to God in soft, parched voices, either for his intervention or to bring a quick end to their misery.

The men who had stealthily fled the harbor ahead of the approaching Spanish were now returning in longboats, hoping that by the time they arrived, they would find the Spanish gone. They spotted Drake's failing raft with its tattered sail, bobbing in open water. Altering course, they rowed hard to reach it. The rescuers told Drake they would return immediately to the ship, to get treatment for him and the others. He was having none of it. "God has blessed us," he said in a faltering voice. "We are saved. But the rest are counting on our return. We must free them first."

As the longboats finally made their way into the harbor, the stranded raiders onshore heartily cheered Drake's return. He'd kept his promise, beyond their wildest expectations.

XII

The horse-drawn coach was new. Imported from Hungary. Its deep-red, velvet interior seemed to glow in the prism of the crystal drinking glasses strapped inside. Garret's hand stroked the smooth fabric. It felt comforting. Daniel was outside, instructing the coachman. The footman soon opened the door. Daniel climbed in.

"Well, Garret, we are off to Dashwood's."

"Dashwood's?"

"A bookseller, here in Kent. The headmaster has provided a list of books the Academy uses for its instruction. You may be denied attendance, but you shall not be denied the knowledge. I have arranged for someone to instruct you daily, at home." Though grateful, Garret was saddened by his comments, having hoped for a different outcome—an appeal that might extend the cherished camaraderie of classmates, the sporting activities, and the military exercises at Ritchfield. All of that was suddenly beyond reach. "My good friend, Colonel Tyndale, has agreed to provide your further instruction in the military arts." Daniel patted Garret's leg in reassurance. "He has recently retired. His teachings shall be far superior to anything you might have received at the Academy."

The coach bounced roughly along the cobblestones. Moments later, it passed by Rose, dressed for football, waving farewell. Garret expected this might be their last sighting of each other. Waving back brought a separate wave—one of sadness. Daniel noticed. "Things may seem dark to you at the moment. But believe me, there is light ahead. Things will get better. Much better. You shall once again find joy in life. Happiness is not an event—it is a choice.

Garret didn't react right away. Life seemed unfair; sometimes cruel. Henceforth, taking charge of events would be crucial. Anyone who might choose to stand in the way would be the worse for it. Any challenge that might present itself would be thrust aside. 'Happiness is a choice,' Daniel had said. I shall manage my own happiness, Garret thought.

————

Drake's crew and Le Testu's men assembled at Fort Diego, where they rested for several days in the warm Caribbean sun, soft white sand and comforting breezes. They amused themselves with games of bowls, dice and cards, the stakes of which came from their share of captured treasure. They hunted wildlife and enjoyed fine meals of roast boar and rabbit, accompanied by ample cups of grog.

Following a late meal one evening, Drake asked Prouten and Lee to join him in his tight quarters, careful not to hit their heads on the hanging brass lantern bearing the light of a candle. They gathered around a small table on which lay his crude, hand-drawn map of the location where his men had buried treasure along the Panama trail.

"Gentlemen," said Drake, placing his finger on the small charcoal X he'd drawn, "I believe enough time has passed that we can return to the forest, to recover the treasure buried here. And perhaps the Cimarrones shall inform us of Captain Le Testu's fate. If he is being held prisoner, I should like to free him."

"I am all for recapturing the treasure," replied Prouten. "My only concern is transporting it. Experience tells us just how difficult that is. As for Le Testu, I cannot imagine he is still among the living."

"Let us hope for a different outcome, Mr. Prouten. I gave the man my word that I would return." Drake paused briefly, thoughts of Le Testu bleeding by the tree passing through his mind. "What think you, Mr. Lee?"

"I concur, sir. We should recover the silver. But I am inclined to agree with Mr. Prouten, that Le Testu is no more."

"Alright then, gentlemen, let us proceed. Make all preparations for our departure. We shall leave within the week. Following that, we shall make our return to England."

They landed quietly in the middle of the night, meeting up with the Cimarrones. Over the next two days, they once again fought the stultifying combination of heat, humidity and insect hordes as they wound through the dense Panamanian foliage. The Cimarrones had informed Drake that Le Testu was beheaded by the Spanish. Those thoughts weighed heavily on him during the miserable trek through damp jungle. He'd lost a friend. He seethed inside, enraged by the story of the man's brutal demise. It was just one more reason to continue seeking revenge on this heartless enemy.

The raiders finally reached the trail. Memories of the noise and clash of battle filled their minds. But for the sounds of wildlife, the men found the place eerily quiet. Drake pulled his oilcloth map from inside his doublet and guided the search for the spot where the two tallest trees aligned with the distant peak of the mountain, just as he'd drawn it. As they approached the position, they saw mounds of dark, moist soil piled up. Dead, yellowing foliage was spread all around, though new green growth had pushed through and smothered much of it. The Spanish had found and removed most of the buried silver. Finding only a few dozen silver bars scattered in the vicinity, the men returned to their longboats at the harbor with diminished joy.

On the evening of their return to Fort Diego, Drake arranged for the men to celebrate the conclusion of their combined efforts at Nombre de Dios. They enjoyed a sizeable feast and altogether too much grog. With the celebration well under way, Drake had to work hard to gain their attention.

"My good men," he called out several times. When the voices quieted, he continued, "God has blessed us all. Upon return to our homes, we shall be rich beyond our dreams." The men cheered and drank to their good fortune. Drake smiled and watched in joy. He waited for the right moment and then raised his hand for silence. When it came, he continued, "Yes, we have gained much. Yet we have also lost many brave men—men such as Captain Le Testu, who served with the intelligence of a fox and the courage of a lion." With that, he raised his cup in his right hand. "To the fallen. May God be with them."

"Hear, hear," shouted the men.

After another pause, Drake turned to the task at hand. "The time has come to finish our journey. Come the morrow, let us begin careening and provisioning our ships for the return voyage." The men cheered more wildly than before, suddenly anxious to be back among family and friends, to share their stories and spend their newfound wealth.

Within the week, the raiders bid Fort Diego and Slaughter Island farewell, having experienced both the joy of captured treasure and the tragic loss of friends to sickness and death. Their journey home would be one of mixed remembrance.

Outside the remains of Fort Diego, a golden cross nestled neatly between two rocks. Drake had placed it there, in memory of brothers lost.

XIII

"You have performed exceptionally well in the use of weaponry, Garret. But there may come a time when you find yourself without weapons," noted retired Col. Tyndale. They were in the yard, taking a break from cutlass practice.

"You must never assume you are in a fair fight. Never. Be alert for surprises…unforeseen circumstances. Perhaps a hidden, secondary weapon—possibly a small dagger taken from the back of your opponent's belt. Or a sharpened stick he may have picked up. If you always expect the worst, you shall be better prepared for any surprise." He let that sink in before continuing. "The worst situation is where you have no weapon and no access to anything you might use as one, against an armed assailant. In such a case, you must take the defensive, avoiding any blows. You must spot an opening to attack. There are three areas of significant vulnerability that may present themselves. The first is the groin. No man can withstand a well-placed attack on his testicles, whether by foot, fist or any hardened part of your body."

"The testicles, sir?"

"Yes," Tyndale replied, wondering how Garret could not know at this point what the testicles were. "The two balls in the scrotum, behind and below your penis."

"Yes, of course," Garret nodded, masking shocked surprise. What was the old man talking about? Penis? Testicles? Garret made a mental note to bring it up later, with Daniel.

"This is the greatest of the three vulnerabilities," the Colonel continued, "because the pain can be both excruciating and debilitating. Your opponent's lower body is often less well-defended since most of his focus is on his upper body. A swift, well-placed kick can win the day." Tyndale demonstrated a kick against the air.

"Perhaps I might practice against a target."

"In fact, you will. I shall bring a straw man to our next session, to practice on." He paused before proceeding, "The second point of vulnerability is the throat, most specifically the larynx—the bulge in the neck." He pointed to his own larynx. Though the testicles are the first choice, an effective blow to the larynx can be just as devastating. It is ideally delivered while ducking low, striking hard and fast with your right-hand knuckles. Like so." He ducked and jabbed at Garret's throat in a lightning move that brought his knuckles within inches of Garret's larynx. It was shocking. Impressive.

"Finally," Tyndale continued, "you shall find the eyes to be an exceptional, though more challenging, target. If you can obtain a position that enables you to thrust your fingers directly into the eye socket, you can immediately incapacitate your opponent."

"I see," Garret said, repelled by the thought of such a ghastly measure. "I hope I shall never find myself in such a situation."

"I too. But one must be prepared."

That same evening, seated at table and waiting for Daniel to finish filling the plates, Garret sensed the time was right. "Tell me, father, where might I find my penis and testicles?"

Daniel stopped. He looked at Garret. Slowly, he placed the utensils on the plate, uncertain how to respond. He hadn't yet prepared for this discussion. How had the question even been prompted, he wondered. He wanted to stall, to give himself more time. "Pardon?"

"Colonel Tyndale instructed that I might hit a man in his testicles, behind his penis. He indicated they were in the area of the groin. I do not understand."

Daniel nodded without saying anything, realizing there was no choice—this was the time for the discussion he had imagined would come at an older age. He leaned back in his chair, opting for an indirect, Socratic-oriented approach. "Tell me Garret, is it your wish to be a person of substance? Someone who might influence and lead others? Perhaps even change the world?"

Garret was puzzled. He hadn't answered the question. Why would he now ask a different question—one that had an obvious answer? Nonetheless, a response was in order, "I would, yes. I hope to be a man of consequence one day. Someone whose story shall be remembered by others. Just like the men in your books."

"Do you imagine that becoming the kind of person you envision would be easier for a man, or for a woman?"

Garret glanced at the frail, confused, Gwendolyn—the woman with whom she was most familiar. The only adult females she really knew were household maids. The answer, once again, was obvious, "A man, of course."

"Without question?"

"Yes."

"So, if a person could somehow have a *choice* to be either a man or a woman, would it not make sense to choose the former?"

"Assuming that were even possible, then yes—if that person wished to be someone of consequence."

"I believe in my heart, Garret, that you shall be a person of great consequence." Garret smiled, sensing Daniel's pride. He continued, "Which is why I made a choice for you."

"What choice?"

He leaned in, grasping Garret's hand, uttering his next words softly, warmly, "That you should be raised as my son rather than as my daughter."

"Your daughter? I do not understand." Garret had responded before Daniel's full implication had even sunk in. "What are you saying?"

Daniel's face was filled with love and caring. He knew the answer would come to Garret. There was no need to utter the actual words.

Garret's heart raced, causing an unexpected rise in body temperature. "No!" Garret rose from her chair, pulling away and shaking her head, "No. No. No."

Gwendolyn rose from the table. She ran from the room in tears, her mind in turmoil. She recalled how, after Garret was born, Daniel had told her he needed to take steps to keep the girl from suffering the very violation she herself had suffered. So he'd paid the priest to certify Garret as male, as his own son. And he'd raised her that way, so she wouldn't even realize she was a girl. In time, he'd assured Gwendolyn, he would share this secret with Garret, though he'd expressed no specific date or age. He would simply tell her when he deemed the time was right. And now it was finally here. The recollection and pain of the many years that had passed—the lost opportunities—were overwhelming.

Daniel stood, glancing briefly at Gwendolyn's departure. He stepped toward Garret, reaching out and once again grasping her hand. "Garret, dearest, you are who you are—an amazing individual. Male or female is of no matter. You shall one day be a remarkable person. Indeed, you already are. I have simply chosen to give you an advantage you would not otherwise have."

Garret breathed heavily, fighting back tears, needing to be strong. She now kept her eyes firmly locked on the floor, unable to look Daniel in the face. "What shall become of me? I am not even the person I thought I was."

Daniel moved in close, hugging her warmly. "You are the person you have always been, Garret. You are simply in disguise. For *now*," he assured her. "There shall come a time when that disguise is no longer required." Garret sobbed, nodding acknowledgement of his words though not fully believing them. "But you must first earn the right to shed that disguise." He touched a finger to her forehead. "Earn it with your intelligence. With your actions. Your words." He pressed the finger lightly against her chest. "Earn it with your heart." Garret breathed in deeply, nodding once again. "You must work harder and smarter than any man around you. The more you dedicate yourself to that, the sooner you may share your truth."

Daniel held her, lovingly. Neither spoke for a few moments. Garret sobbed. She felt uneasy, though Daniel's warmth, his hug, comforted her. "I shall do my best, Father."

"You are already doing that, Garret. And you must continue to do so, for as long as necessary. But trust me, you shall know when you have earned the right to speak your truth. So find and take every opportunity to earn it. Push hard for it. Until that time comes, and even after then, you shall have my complete, unconditional support. And my love. Always."

Garret wanted the awkward conversation to end. It was time to move on. "The meat is getting cold." She forced a nervous laugh and gathered herself. "Might I have a cup of wine with my meal?"

"You most certainly can," Daniel smiled.

In the weeks that passed, Garret wrestled constantly with her new reality. She often relived experiences from her past, wondering how her actions might have differed if she'd known her truth at the time. In each instance, she could recall nothing that suggested they would have. That was reinforced repeatedly. In light of that, Daniel's words seemed right—she was who she was—the same person she had always been. There was no reason to think less of herself; to think she was not every bit the equal of any boy her age. Yet how would things be, going forward? And why couldn't she simply be herself from now on?

In the end, Daniel's words kept coming back to her—"I have given you an advantage you would not otherwise have." They'd come from a place of love. Deep love. They'd come from a place of knowledge. Of experience. From a man she admired. One she trusted. A man she loved dearly. He knew better than she did. He wanted only the best for her. He'd demonstrated that always. She had to agree that there were advantages to presenting as a man. The people she knew or read about as leaders were all men. Except for the Queen, of course. Yet hadn't the Queen herself had an advantage? Hadn't she been born into the role? So, if wanting to be someone of consequence, someone to be admired, meant taking advantage of something you'd been given—like what her father had given her—then wouldn't it make sense to do that? It appeared to make sense. And given that it did, she would need to continue hiding her truth; to protect herself from being discovered; to enable her to fully benefit from that advantage. It would mean being a constant learner—highly observant of situations, of people. Being cognizant of her own actions; of her appearance. Everything would need to be carefully thought out; planned even. Orchestrated.

Daniel's other words seemed important as well—"for *now*…There shall come a time when that disguise is no longer required." That had to be her goal. The sooner she could reach it, the sooner she could truly be free, to be herself in every way. "But you must first earn the right to shed that disguise," Daniel had said. *Earn* the right. Earn it. "By your actions. Your words," he'd said. If her actions and words could convince people to accept her as a leader, as someone of circumstance, without knowing she was a girl, or a woman, then wouldn't they still accept her as a leader once they learned her truth? That made sense to her.

The goal was clear. It was now simply a matter of timing. How long might it take to earn the right? That was the question. There was no clear answer. But she would proceed down that path. She would seek opportunities to prove herself. At every turn. To earn the right to come clean—as a girl. Or a woman.

In time, Garret came to appreciate the difficulty Daniel must have had in making the decision about how to raise her in the first place. And then having to share the shocking news with her. Despite her own misgivings, it made her appreciate Daniel even more. She felt lucky to have him in her life.

———

Following his return to England, Drake wasted no time seeking investors for his next endeavor—navigating the Pacific Ocean, along the west coast of the Americas. The thought of it had pulled at him continually since he'd spotted it from high up on the macondo tree in Panama. One potential investor was Thomas Doughty, an English nobleman. Son of the highly regarded, though now deceased, Sir Robert Doughty. The two men met one afternoon at Drake's favorite tavern in Devon—The Blue Anchor.

Doughty was a small man who carried himself pretentiously—head high, shoulders back. His brown hair was balding severely, as his father's had, so he covered it with a powdered white wig whenever he was in public. His eyes were those of a cat, suggesting the mind behind them was constantly scheming. He was clean-shaven and well-dressed in silk finery, with a ruff collar at his neck. He carried a holstered sword, a carryover from his brief stint in the military, though he'd never seen action in battle. He'd simply purchased the rank of a captain and taken much pride in it. A lawyer by schooling, he'd inherited, and now managed, his father's business interests.

"Good of you to come," said Drake, standing as Doughty entered the tavern and approached his table in the back. He'd met the man before but only in passing.

"It is my pleasure and honor, sir. The Queen holds you in high regard." Doughty casually referenced the Queen as a way of suggesting he had some level of closeness to her—to raise his standing in Drake's mind. The truth was, he had no relationship with the Queen. She knew him only as the son of his much-respected father.

"Please, have a seat." Drake motioned to the chair across from him.

"Thank you." Doughty sat. He went immediately to the business at hand. No preliminary social banter. "So, you are seeking investors for your next voyage."

"I am indeed. I was told you might have an interest in financing a search for Spanish treasure." Drake smiled, knowing how much English investors liked the sound of the word.

"I would not be quite so blunt, Commander. I have an interest in financing a *trading* voyage. If there is treasure to be had along the way, that would simply be an added blessing for my family's interests."

Drake's smile dissolved, though he saw through the remark. It served Doughty's dual interests—suggesting he thought at a higher level than Drake and enabling him to distance his reputation from that of a pure treasure hunter. It would give him an air of righteous standing, befitting a gentleman of his background. Drake was fine with that; he simply wanted Doughty's money. Unlike this arrogant man, he himself had come from little, carving his own standing and reputation. He knew many wealthy men of England resented his inclusion in their exclusive community. Some even considered him an outright pirate. It didn't bother him; they mattered little, except when he required their funding. "Of course, Mr. Doughty. Our primary purpose is that of exploration and trade. We shall sail the Southern Seas and cross to the Pacific Ocean, in search of all nature of," he paused, "tradeable goods."

A server interrupted, his comment directed at Doughty, "Your wish, sir?"

"Your finest port, if you please." He gave the server a coin, then turned back to Drake, "I shall be pleased to invest in your enterprise, Commander. I have but one stipulation."

"Which is?"

"I wish to join you on this voyage. And bring a few of my closest friends."

Drake hadn't imagined this man was an adventurer. He had neither the appearance nor the demeanor. Perhaps it was simply for the glory of the voyage, much like the glory of his benign military experience. "I presume your friends are all men. We cannot have any women onboard our ships."

"Of course, of course. Men only."

"How many?"

"Five or six, including my brother, John."

Drake saw no harm in it, though he believed firmly that any men traveling with him should be prepared to fulfill the same duties as those of his crew; just as he himself did. He was not in the passenger business. "That shall be fine. I presume I may call on them, and you, to serve as would any members of my crew."

"I assure you, Commander, you may indeed." Doughty said it knowing full well it was a hollow promise. "I, of course, would be honored to captain one of your ships."

There it was, thought Drake. Doughty's money for a Captaincy. He hesitated. It wasn't common to grant such a vital role to someone who'd never proven themselves on the seas. Still, he wanted Doughty's funding. Where was the harm, he thought. Should anything not go well, he could always remove the man from the position. It was his right as Commander. "That can be arranged," he replied.

The two men spent the balance of the afternoon working out the details and terms of Doughty's investment in the voyage.

Some three years had passed before Drake was ready to embark upon his ambitious voyage. Drawing on his own wealth and that of investors like Doughty, he'd spent much of his time designing and building a custom warship—the *Pelican*. His passion for the project had consumed him, as he fussed and worried over every minute detail of the vessel. It was a sleek, three-masted, hundred-foot-long ship—twenty-two iron and brass canons, three-hundred-ton displacement, and over four hundred fifty square yards of sail. A state-of-the-art warship. It had crow's nests on both the main and mizzen masts. His personal cabin featured a wide-framed stern view, with a built-in bed, a sitting bench with velvet cushions, and a large table mounted firmly to the floor, serving variously as a dining table, his desk and a map table or drawing board. The hold was capable of storing not only ship's supplies but also tons of cargo. The overall design contemplated navigating the treacherous voyage through the hellacious winds and turbulent seas off the southern tip of South America. That path, or the almost-as-difficult Strait of Magellan, would lead him to the glorious Pacific Ocean. Perhaps beyond.

————

Charles Prouten spotted the auburn-haired boy standing alone on the cobblestones, looking out over the harbor, a small seaman's chest at his feet. Colonel Tyndale had arranged for him to meet the boy there. Prouten was aware that Tyndale's patron, Daniel Connachan, had provided handsome funding for Captain Drake to take the boy aboard as a slightly under-age midshipman. Such positions were much in demand. Wealthy Londoners sought to have their sons sail with the highly regarded Drake as a way of schooling them in the emerging arts of navigation, global trade, management of an ocean-going vessel, and naval warfare. There were other midshipmen joining the voyage as well, though Connachan would be the youngest. Maybe too young, Prouten thought. He grasped the boy by his shoulder.

"Garret Connachan?"

Garret turned, "Yes, sir."

"My name is Prouten. Master's Mate to Captain Drake. I am here to accompany you. My longboat awaits." He pointed to a boat along the shoreline. "Let us grab your chest and get aboard."

"Yes, sir." Garret reached down for a handle on the wooden chest that looked as lonely sitting on the ground as she felt in her heart.

"Have you sailed before?" Prouten asked as they began walking, the chest held between them.

"I have indeed, sir. On my father's lake."

Prouten rolled his eyes. Another landlubber, he thought. So much to learn yet believing otherwise. "I suspect you shall find the ocean a little less friendly than your lake."

"My father has instructed me on sailing in stormy weather, sir," Garret said confidently. She thought it important to assure him she wasn't a mere landsman—someone completely unfamiliar with sailing open water.

"Tell me, how high are the waves on your pond?" Prouten smirked.

"A lake, sir, not a pond," she corrected him, adding proudly, "I have experienced waves of almost two yards, trough to peak."

Prouten was a little surprised. It was more than he'd anticipated. Still, the scale of the ocean's waves was not to be downplayed. "You shall see waves more than ten times that size."

Garret stopped in her tracks. The chest yanked at her arm since Prouten hadn't stopped right away. She remembered just how challenging a two-meter wave could be—especially in the high winds that it took to churn the water to that degree. The risk of capsizing the boat was always present under such conditions, though she'd never lacked faith in Daniel's ability to keep them afloat. She understood well the need to manage the sail and the heading of the bow. But a wave of twenty yards would most assuredly sink any vessel, she thought. It gave her pause.

Prouten had stopped walking by this point. He understood the boy's hesitancy. It was time for a little motivation, he thought. "I assure you, Master Connachan, we have challenged waves of that size in ships smaller than the *Pelican*. Captain Drake is one of the finest seafarers England has known. You shall see wondrous things and learn more than you might ever imagine."

Garret took a deep breath, now looking intently at the *Pelican*. It appeared so small against the backdrop of this enormous harbor. A strange combination of fear and excitement embraced her. Though worried about the ocean's overwhelming power, she was intrigued by Prouten's words. Men like Drake had overcome any fear they may have felt and found a way to master whatever the seas and weather had tested them with—just like the heroes in the books her father had read to her. And she remembered how, during her days at Ritchfield, she had embraced the thought of traveling to far-off places. That opportunity was now here. The door had opened. No more looking backward, she thought. Only forward.

As she and Prouten resumed their walk to the longboat, Garret realized her sadness had dissipated, replaced by the knowledge that she was now stepping into the next phase of her life—one promising a degree of adventure she suddenly craved.

Daniel's words once again echoed in her mind, "Be very careful. You must not let anyone know your truth." She felt confident she could do that. Presenting herself as male wasn't just second nature—it *was* her nature.

XIV

"All secured and ready, sir." Prouten had come to Drake's cabin in a hurry, anxious to share the news and get underway. All preparations had been completed and the provisions stored, including the animals. The crew were now at their stations.

Drake was pouring over his recently acquired navigational materials for what he was certain would be an era-defining voyage. "Thank you, Mr. Prouten." He drew back from the table and followed him out to the main deck. They continued toward the bow of the ship, Drake breathing in the salt air deeply as the wind wafted it briskly across his face. This was precisely what he was born to do, he thought—sail the world's limitless, challenging oceans, scribing his signature on them. He grabbed hold of the rigging and looked back toward Plymouth, something he always did when leaving the harbor. His familiar sense of uncertainty about how long the journey might take, or whether he would ever return, washed over him. It passed quickly, propelled by the rush of adventure that always preceded a voyage. "Let us get underway, Mr. Prouten."

The frigid wind gusted harshly, accompanied by darkening skies threatening to dispense harsh rains. Still, the *Pelican* departed Plymouth Sound leading a fleet of five ships, including the *Elizabeth*, the *Marigold*, the *Swan*, and the *Benedict*. One hundred sixty sailors in total, including Drake's younger brother Thomas, and Diego, the former slave from Nombre de Dios who was now Drake's personal assistant. Also joining him were his teenage cousin, John; Thomas Doughty and his entourage; a preacher—Francis

Fletcher; and a nephew of his former Commander, John Hawkins. Besides Prouten, his officers once again included Mr. Lee, his master-at-arms, and Mr. Langton, his interpreter. And to his great delight, Musa and Caber had signed on without hesitation.

The fleet's crews hustled noisily, weighing anchors and setting sails. Many sang as they worked. On the *Pelican*, the men were assisted by a handful of midshipmen. The crew understood that these 'mids' were well-to-do boys whose fathers had paid Drake generously to be their mentor. But the Captain had made clear to them that the mids were to be treated no differently any other crewmates. He wanted them to learn the many aspects of a ship's operations and its ocean-going culture, just as he himself had—without special privileges.

One midshipman in particular had caught Drake's attention. He understood the boy's father, Daniel Connachan, was arguably the foremost lawyer in London's merchant circles. But the rumor was that the boy had been expelled from a private academy for knifing a classmate. Drake hoped that wasn't predictive of his behavior during the coming voyage. He required his men to treat each other with respect. As equals. It was something he'd learned under Commander Hawkins—a fine naval captain though not necessarily the most thoughtful leader of men. Drake observed during his time with Hawkins that men were less likely to give their best effort if the captain failed to treat them fairly and equitably. Treating them well had therefore become a cornerstone of his own leadership style. Without their trust, he knew his ship would underperform. Yet that approach still demanded an elevated level of discipline. It was in everyone's best interests. Those who violated the rules could well put the lives of their fellow sailors at risk. That was unacceptable.

Consequently, he had informed his officers to keep a close eye on young Connachan. If he were to pull his knife on a member of the crew, Drake would send him to the brig and abandon him on the nearest point of land— inhabited or not. But he had no idea exactly what deception was about to unfold onboard his ship.

Garret herself had already heard murmurs among the men regarding the knifing at the Academy. She was uninclined to set the record straight. For one thing, it gave her a sense of strength and standing among these older men. For another, it aligned more with the actions of a boy than a girl. And finally, the rumor had no bearing on her current situation. Yes, she might test the limits. That was her nature. But she was determined not to be a disciplinary problem for Drake. She was there to learn, excited by the thought of just how rich that learning experience might be. She'd already proven to be an exceptional student under the daily instruction of her scholastic tutor. And she'd excelled in her intense, one-on-one military training under Colonel Tyndale. She now welcomed continuing her learning under Commander Drake. When Daniel had disclosed that this was her best next step, she was conflictingly hesitant and intrigued. Hesitant because it would mean leaving behind everything she knew; intrigued because it promised adventure. Daniel had shared this decision well after their discussion about the truth of her gender. More recently, he'd shared other thoughts with her. Though she knew she was tall for her years, he'd told her that she hadn't yet 'come of age'— that in a short time her voice, and most especially her womanly attributes, might begin to disclose her truth. She understood well that her path to advancement and opportunity lay in effectively presenting herself as a male. At least until she could prove herself. And she was fine with that. She knew she could ride a horse with the best of them, artistically wield a cutlass, and hunt skillfully with both crossbow and pistolet. She felt confident that she was in no way second to boys when it came to physical endeavors. And she was deeply committed to treading carefully in this place, surrounded only by men. Everything she did needed to be thought through carefully. Precisely. There could be no slipping up. If her truth were to be discovered, she suspected she would be confined or imprisoned. Or worse yet, left behind in some foreign land, unable to return to England. Never seeing her family again. There was simply no margin for error. She was a keen observer and would use that skill to mimic the nature and mannerisms of her fellow sailors, to deceive them convincingly.

One thing Garret didn't know was that Daniel had ulterior motives for sending her off to sail with Drake. Besides enabling him to continue maintaining the family secret, it would preserve his good reputation at a time when that challenge would be heightened by her coming of age.

———

"Mind your angle there, Master Tovery," Drake instructed. The midshipmen were assembled on the main deck, holding their astrolabes and trying to determine the ship's current latitude. It was their first use of the richly engraved, circular metal disc. Drake had told them it was originally designed by followers of Mohammad, as a representation of their universe—

they believed they were at the very center of it. He was now checking to make certain the mids had the correct plate inserted, given their current position north of the equator. The line between two raised points on either side of the disc represented the horizon. They were to hold that line at eye level and align the slider on the back in the direction of the sun.

"Note the readings in your log gentlemen. I shall be grading you based on how close they are to our actual latitude." Garret was first to make her notations. Drake accepted her logbook, checking her observation while waiting for the others. Tovery was quick to follow, as was Drake's young brother, Thomas. Yates and young cousin John were taking a little longer.

"How are we doing Master Yates?"

"One moment, sir."

Drake waited patiently until Yates recorded his reading and handed him the logbook. The Commander nodded, pleased to see that all of his mids had been close to the *Pelican's* true position. He smiled, "Well done lads. We shall use our astrolabes later this evening, to find selected stars, weather permitting. Now, be about your chores."

Garret and Yates headed to the edge of the foredeck. It was their turn to clean the wooden slats, through which the men often did their business. The mids agreed this was the most menial of their many tasks. Yates, holding his nose and smiling broadly, turned to Garret. "I hope no one has visited the foredeck recently."

Garret held her own nose. "Why sir, I believe you have a strong preference for older excretions. I myself prefer more refreshing arrivals. They are far easier to clean."

Yates laughed. "Have you ever seen the Captain clean the slats?"

"I believe it is his privilege to avoid this particular task."

"Then let me be a captain."

"You shall have to ask him about that," replied Garret. "In due time, of course. For now, you and I are captains-of-the-schitte."

Having finished her assignment with Yates, Garret moved to her next station—at the crow's nest, high in the mainmast. Warmed by a bright sun, she stood several yards above the deck, looking in the direction of the fast-approaching Southern Seas. She'd been told that crossing the equator was a cause for celebration. No one had mentioned it was also a point of initiation for those who'd never made the cross before.

Garret always enjoyed her time as the lookout. It afforded an opportunity to observe the many operational activities on the deck below. The *Pelican* was a constantly busy ship. Drake saw to that. He believed it was best to keep the men heavily occupied with chores. It served two purposes. One was to keep them out of trouble. The other, the more important of the two, was to ensure that the *Pelican*—the foremost privateering vessel of its generation—would perform at her best, at all times. On this day, the gun crews were firing their cannons at distant targets. Garret particularly loved this activity. The view from the crow's nest was far superior to that from the deck below. It surprised her just how accurate the gunners had become over the past several weeks. Watching the cannonballs fight the crosswind on the way to their target, she felt the short tail of her auburn-colored hair flow in the breeze beneath her white bandana. The hair was braided in the manner that many sailors preferred, to keep it from getting in the way of various chores. She thought about how well she was now blending in with the crew. Her oversized, brown calico shirt, flowing with the wind, would most assuredly hide evidence of her womanhood, whenever that might come. A shark's tooth she'd purchased from one of the men hung at the end of a leather strap around her neck, just like those of others who'd taken to wearing shark's teeth, beads or even small bones. Her slightly torn and soiled beige, cotton pants were no different than those worn by most of the men. She even walked with a typical sailor's swagger. But one thing she had to constantly work on was her voice—keeping it in a lower register than normal. And she forced herself to become comfortable wielding the same vulgar vocabulary these seamen favored. All things considered, she felt confident no one suspected her truth. At least not yet.

Scanning the sparkling blue water, she reminisced fondly of her childhood days on the lake with her father. The thunder of the *Pelican's* cannons, however, contrasted sharply with the serenity of the lake that she and Daniel deeply cherished. She was aware Daniel had inherited much from his parents' estate, though not the property on the lake. That was his own doing. Having studied the law at Magdalen College, Oxford, he'd put himself on a firm path toward financial success. He'd accomplished much in his life, enabling him to grow his combined land holdings to more than ten thousand acres, much of it dedicated to farming.

The property surrounding the lake was where Garret had been primarily, and discreetly, raised. It was a place of joy. She remembered fondly the horses she'd ridden and taken care of, the many foxhunts she'd participated in, and the countless hours of sailing—occasionally fishing and frequently swimming. The lake was also a place where she'd trained daily in the use of weaponry, under Colonel Tyndale. It wasn't simply the nuanced handling skills the Colonel imparted regarding any weapon she was learning; it was also the insight he shared on reading the circumstances of any given encounter with an enemy. He'd taught her to anticipate her opponent's potential countermeasures, and to practice the less common, least expected, and therefore most effective, maneuvers. Through the old Colonel's efforts, she'd found joy in placing a well-hit blow on any target. She recalled Daniel's insistence that she become sufficiently skilled to compete with the best of the young men in the military. In that way, he thought, she would always be well prepared and extremely comfortable defending herself. As these reminiscences passed through Garret's mind, a distant speck of light suddenly captured her eye. "Sail Ho!" she called down to the deck.

Drake had been reviewing the navigational charts in his cabin at the *Pelican's* stern when the call was echoed down to him. He placed a weight on the papers, left the cabin, and headed to the main deck. Prouten met him there, pointing in the direction of the sails. "About two points off the bow, sir."

"Thank you, Mr. Prouten."

"It bears a Spanish flag."

The ship was the *Santa Maria*, loaded with precious goods from the Caribbean, principally molasses and sugar cane. Drake followed its movement closely over the next hour, as the *Pelican* closed on it. "We are in good fortune, Mr. Prouten. This appears to be a trading vessel; not particularly well-armed. Let us prepare to send a warm greeting," he smiled. "A single warning shot across her bow, if you please."

"Aye sir." Prouten left quickly to find Mr. Lee. He was already in the low-ceilinged gun deck, in anticipation of firing.

"The Captain sends his compliments, Mr. Lee, and requests a warning shot, forward of the vessel, on his signal."

"Aye, Mr. Prouten. On the Captain's signal." Lee understood this meant using the chaser on the bow, rather than the broadside guns. He raced to the foredeck.

Drake awaited Prouten's return.

"All is ready, sir."

"Excellent," Drake replied.

"Ready at the bow," called Lee.

"Patience…patience…," Drake mumbled softly to himself, seeking just the right moment. Prouten watched as they drew within range of the *Santa Maria*. It began making a starboard turn—an apparent attempt to outrun Drake's fleet.

Drake welcomed the expected maneuver. "Fire at will, Mr. Prouten."

"FIRE!" Prouten shouted.

A single bow-chaser roared, firing a two-pound shot. Rather than following a direct firing line, it flew high in the air, landing thirty yards in front and twenty yards aside the *Santa Maria*. It dropped almost vertically, spewing water high into the air. The hunted ship's captain immediately interpreted Drake's message. He also recognized the futility in trying to escape confrontation. He ordered the lowering of the flag as a show of surrender, before more threatening cannon shots could be fired. Unfortunately for him, one of his crew had taken the liberty of firing a random shot at the *Pelican* with his arquebus. It was an amazingly lucky shot, though not so lucky for Yates, the midshipman. He'd been standing at the taffrail, his eyes following the trail of the cannonball. The shot from the arquebus pierced his skull, killing him instantly.

Drake was appalled. Seeing Yates fall, he ran and knelt beside him, placing his hand behind the boy's neck. The body shook briefly, then went limp, the color draining from its skin. The tragic loss of one of his youthful charges brought a wave of sadness and regret. He'd always enjoyed his daily lessons with the midshipmen, instructing them on navigation, the ship's operations, management of provisions, military strategy, maintaining a healthy culture among the crew, and basic leadership skills. By this time he knew each of them personally. They were the closest thing to children of his own that he'd ever known. This loss was personal. It triggered a recollection of his young brother Joseph, who had similarly died in his arms years ago, on Slaughter Island. He called for his men to tend to the body. As he walked away, a tear welled up in his eye.

Having seen Yates fall, Garret had raced down from the crow's nest. She saw the sadness in Drake's eyes as he walked toward her. She shared his sense of loss; Yates had been one of the better friendships she'd developed thus far. She felt a pressing need to say something to her commander. "Sorry to bother you, Captain. Yates was a good friend. I know how much he appreciated your lessons and admired your leadership. I shall miss him." She wanted to say 'miss him *dearly*' but worried that might be an uncommon thing for another boy to say.

Drake acknowledged Garret's comments. Something about them struck him—more in their delivery than their substance. A certain softness. A sense of caring. They'd come straight from the heart. For the first time, he noticed something different about Garret that he couldn't quite put his finger on. He saw it in the youngster's eyes too. "Thank you, Master Connachan. I, too, shall miss him."

Garret turned to leave, not wishing to risk close scrutiny of her person. Drake raised his voice, "Tell me, Connachan, do you have siblings?"

"Aye, sir. An older sister. Much older."

"And are you close to her?"

"Indeed I am sir, though she is not of right mind."

"I see," Drake nodded. "Cherish her, Connachan. Family is everything." He said this while once again recalling the painful loss of his brothers, John and Joseph.

"I will, sir. Thank you."

As they parted ways, thoughts about Garret raced through Drake's mind—a fine boy, mature beyond his years. With a very personable demeanor. And self-confident. Officer material, perhaps. In time.

———

The lead navigator aboard the captured *Santa Maria* was Nuno da Silva, a native of Portugal. He was deeply experienced in sailing in and around the Americas, having spent most of his life in the Southern Seas. Drake felt he could be valuable in navigating to the Pacific Ocean; particularly in making the cross from the Atlantic. He arranged for da Silva and the *Santa Maria*'s captain to room as his guests onboard the *Pelican*. Da Silva was soon asked to take charge of the fleet's navigational responsibilities. Aware that Connachan had studied navigation at Ritchfield Academy, Drake insisted da Silva take the midshipman under his wing, to learn the finer points of ocean navigation.

As for the *Santa Maria* itself, Drake chose to rename it the *Mary*. Reflecting on his promise to Thomas Doughty, he appointed him captain of the ship—an appointment that would soon haunt him. Doughty's arrogance, and that of his friends, didn't sit well with Drake's crew. Nor with Drake himself. The man had originally promised that he and his friends would serve as equal members of the crew, yet they were clearly unwilling to lower themselves to that level.

Garret was among those who disliked Doughty. Upon learning of his presence on Drake's fleet, she immediately recalled her unpleasant encounter with him following the brutal assault on his daughter Rose, at Ritchfield. Though she cherished her friendship with Rose, she'd found her friend's father both disagreeable and pompous.

Doughty had never been at sea before. Nor was he used to the daily drudgery of sea-going life. His position as captain was unearned and the crew knew it. Over time, their displeasure with his appointment boiled and festered. In frustration, he'd treated his crew harshly, further stirring their resentment. They accused him of stealing some of the goods taken from the *Santa Maria*; goods that would ordinarily have been shared among the crew. There was some truth in their accusations, though their claims were exaggerated. Eventually, Drake had no choice but to address the problem. He knew Doughty would be unable to effectively command the ship without the confidence and support of his sailors. He decided to reassign him. But since Doughty was an investor, Drake felt it was important for him to save face among the other officers. He gave Doughty command of the *Pelican*, and took personal command of the *Mary*, to mollify its crew. That decision brought more unfortunate consequences. Doughty wasted little time sewing unhappiness among the *Pelican's* crew.

Garret and the other mids joined Drake on the *Mary*, to continue their daily instructions. All were aware they'd be crossing the equator within a week because they'd shortly need to switch out the metal disk in their astrolabes. The night before the actual crossing, the crew was preparing for the usual celebration that accompanied it. Garret noticed sailors filling a large wooden tub with saltwater. She had no idea why. The whole thing seemed to her nothing more than an excuse to drink and make merry. That evening, the mids, and others who hadn't ever made the equatorial crossing, were escorted to the crew's quarters and informed that they must remain below deck until after the cross was made, sometime during the middle of the night. In the morning, they were awakened early, blindfolded, and led up to the deck, each accompanied and held by a crew member. Drake smiled as eight boys and men were lined up. The entire crew had assembled to watch.

"Gentlemen," Drake said loudly, "we gather this morning to please the ghosts of seafarers' past, each of whom has enjoyed the grand crossing of north to south. In their honor, let the initiation of these new crossers begin."

Garret felt two men grab and pull her forward. They carefully tilted her back onto a plank and had her lie on it. She lay still as they strapped her to it tightly with ropes. Through the dark blindfold, she sensed even greater darkness was to come. One man began applying tar to the left side of her face. She shuddered at the touch but said nothing. When the man finished smearing tar over the rest of her face, he rose and looked to Drake. Three large blocks supported the plank on which Garret lay—concerned for her welfare but confident Drake wouldn't let any actual harm befall her. At his signal, the two blocks on the ends of the plank were removed, causing it to tilt on the remaining block that was attached to a large dowel. Garret felt her feet angle downward, unaware that the plank was next to the large tub of water she'd seen men filling the night before.

"Let the christening begin," Drake yelled. Two sailors pushed down hard on the plank near Garret's head, plunging it into the water in the tub below. She heard the muffled sounds of the men cheering and laughing as her head went under. It remained there as she held her breath, until she felt her lungs screaming for air. Suddenly, the plank was reversed, bringing her dripping head back above the water, her soaking body now once again angled with her feet toward the deck.

"May God bless the soul of this seafarer and keep it safe from the grasp of the ocean's ghosts." Midst the laughing and snickering of the crew, Garret gasped for air, recognizing Drake's voice but not fully making out his words.

"Have you anything to ask of these ghosts, Master Connachan?" Garret breathed heavily, not ready to speak. "I say again, have you anything to ask of these ghosts?

Finally able to respond, she spit out the words, "Pray sir, let them keep their foul hands to themselves."

The sailors roared and cheered young Connachan's initiation. "To Master Connachan! Huzzah! Huzzah! Huzzah!"

XV

The mids' daily training sessions with Drake continued as normal, though without the presence of Yates. His death had served to bond the young midshipmen more tightly. William Tovery was one of them. He stood next to Garret. Dark-haired, with friendly brown eyes and an engaging smile, William was destined to become a much-desired object among the young women he would meet. He waited until the end of the day's lesson to raise a question the mids had been discussing the night before, "Tell us, Captain, before leading the charge against the treasure caravan outside Nombre de Dios, were you at all in fear?"

Drake smiled at the boy, observing that he was both intelligent and unafraid to ask tough questions. His father, Robert, was a personal friend—a Portsea merchant interested in the possibilities of trade with the Southern Islands. Robert believed Drake's taking William aboard would better prepare the boy to become a global trader.

"A fine question, William. Good of you to ask." The compliment was his way of encouraging the mids' questions, ensuring a more robust learning experience. "What man could claim to be unafraid when facing the possibility of death?" He scanned the mids' faces. "Yet men of courage must overcome such fear. The lives of their mates may well depend on it." The mids' eyes were all lit and focused. Drake raised his index finger, "Remember this, whenever you face battle—'tis better to die a hero than to live a coward."

139

The mids were dumbfounded. Speechless. That thought had never crossed their minds. Seeing a path to make a related point, Drake continued, "Even when there is no battle at hand, but perhaps simply a question of whether to tell the truth, a man must find the courage to speak truthfully. To do otherwise would cause regret that he will carry for the remainder of his life. And the more regrets a man accumulates through the years, the more haunted his soul shall become."

The mids nodded. Whether it was in agreement, or merely their understanding of what he'd just said, Drake couldn't be certain. He only hoped to continue reinforcing this line of thinking, so that these boys would grow into honorable men and courageous leaders. "Now, see to your assignments," Drake closed.

As the boys left, Garret lingered. Inspired by Drake's words, she gathered her own courage. "A moment, sir?"

"Most certainly, Master Connachan. What is it?"

"Might I ask—do you have a son? Or perhaps a daughter?"

"Neither, I am afraid. With God's blessing I shall have one in the future," he smiled.

"Do you have a preference?"

"A preference?"

"Boy or girl."

"I think perhaps I would be a better father for a boy. Men have struggled for eternity to understand women, whether young or old," he smiled again. "Why do you ask?"

"I am curious, since there are no women among the crew, if you *had* a daughter, would you welcome her as a midshipman?"

"I have never thought of such a thing. It is not a question to be quickly answered."

"Indeed. But would you have confidence in your daughter's ability to be a valued member of your crew? Perhaps just as valuable as a son?"

Drake squinted his eyes, wondering why Garret had even asked. The majority of work on a ship was physical in nature, for which men were better suited, due to their size and strength. Yet some women he'd come to know were both physically and mentally strong. In fact, their mental strength often seemed more grounded and seasoned than that of similarly aged men. There was no doubt women could just as easily handle certain tasks, such as navigation or managing provisions. But they would need a certain strength of character if they were to influence and lead others; as would any man for that matter. Most of the women he knew were too demure, unwilling to speak their minds or challenge the thinking of a man. Not that they weren't capable of doing that, but more likely to avoid conflict. He wished all his crewmen would have the courage to speak their minds, to challenge his own thinking without worrying that he might disagree with them. He'd often found that those who challenged his thinking, simply by doing so, helped him arrive at a better decision than he might otherwise have made. And there was no reason a woman couldn't do that as easily as any man, if she were so inclined.

Garret waited patiently, hoping there might be an opening she could navigate through, at the right time—whether that time was now or not.

"I suppose a case might be made for a woman to be a valued member of the crew." Garret's heart jumped with hidden hope. "But this would be a difficult proposition," he continued. "A ship is a place where men can be themselves and speak freely concerning things that might trouble a woman. And since men have certain needs, any woman would be challenged to avoid their pursuits. There could also be animosity among crew members who might have similar designs on the same woman. That would make it difficult to ensure harmony among the men. Besides, men are superstitious about having women onboard, even as passengers. They believe it to be a bad omen. The only woman they are comfortable with onboard ship is the one they sometimes carve in wood on the bowsprit."

Garret wrestled with how to respond. She'd opened the door and found an apparent openness to the possibility of a woman's presence among his crew. But Drake's concern about harmony onboard ship, something she'd been taught was crucial to the success of any voyage, was worrisome. If she were to disclose her secret, would he be inclined to lock her up, or put her ashore at the first chance, in order to avoid disharmony? Yet hadn't he just commented on the need for courage when facing a difficult situation? And hadn't he just told the mids that a man must always do the right thing? She felt she could draw on his own words for support, knowing he cared for his mids as though they were his own children. Maybe that was because his own younger brother, Thomas, was among them. Drake had taken them all under his wing, committed to protecting them and developing their skills. There was no reason to believe that would change if he were to learn that one of them was in fact a girl. Her decision was quickly made; she might never have a better moment than this. Summoning her courage to keep her voice from trembling, she responded, "I agree, sir; a woman might serve the crew well in some ways. Yet I understand she might also be a distraction for the men. But if the crew were not aware that she was a woman, then I believe she would be able to serve her captain well."

"Perhaps," Drake replied, thinking it didn't matter at this point anyway.

"Captain, with all my courage, I must disclose that my family and I have maintained a particular secret for my entire life."

Drake studied his mid's face carefully, curious where Garret was heading. She looked back at him defiantly, chin up, head back. It suddenly hit him—the look, the line of questioning, his prior feeling that Connachan was somehow different from the other mids, and now Garret's raising questions about a woman's place. There was only one conclusion to draw. He felt his temperature rise. Realizing what Garret was about to say, he shook his head and held up his hand, causing her to pause.

"Enough!" he shouted in frustration, louder than he intended; loud enough for others on deck to overhear. He grabbed Garret's arm, pulling her toward the door to his cabin. She followed him through it, choosing not to speak. He closed the door.

"Do you have any sense of the difficult position you have placed me in?" Drake asked. He proceeded to his table and sat.

So, he knows, thought Garret, still not responding.

"My men are borne of the sea. They fear its wrath. And almost to a man, they are convinced a woman's presence onboard does not bode well. Even my own feelings lean in that direction. A ship is no place for women. Of any age. Certainly not one as young as you."

Silence followed. Garret let it float, sensing the need to let him exhaust his emotions. She stood there, unabashedly proud of who she was.

Drake rose. He walked to a small olive jar containing wine. His left hand grabbed a cup; his right poured. There was no pour for Garret. Walking to the stern and gazing out the tall windows, he slowly raised the cup to his lips, taking a longer than normal draw. Garret remained quiet, observant. Drake turned to face her. "You must *never* speak of this. To *any* crewmember." He approached, unhurriedly. "Nor must you ever give them any reason to suspect your true nature. If you do, I shall set you ashore the moment we land, regardless of the place. You shall have to fend for yourself. Do you understand me?" His voice was overly loud.

"Yes sir," Garret nodded. Though feeling her entire body begin to shake, she stood stoically, unwilling to exhibit any emotion. Be strong, she thought.

Drake took another sip. He placed his cup on the table. Breathing in deeply, he continued. "What a fine muddle, Connachan. Your, and your father's, mess now becomes mine as well." He sat once again. "The trust and support of my men is the one thing I need above all else. You have placed that at great risk. Unfathomable risk." He shook his head. "Any other captain would confine you to the hold and lock you in chains, to be done with the matter."

Garret held back. Courage, she thought—demonstrate your strength, your resilience. She wanted his support, not his sympathy.

Drake blew his breath heavily through his teeth. He looked directly into her eyes. They were dry, not moist. "Tell me, Connachan. Why? Why would you and father do this?"

"My father raised me as his son, so that I might have all the advantages that come with that."

Drake nodded gently. Her very presence here was proof of that advantage. He softened. "I must say, Connachan, I find you to be an excellent student. A quick learner. Though you greatly disappoint me with this news, I understand the position you find yourself in. Replacing your deceit with the truth is something I respect." He leaned back. "Though we are now partners in this ruse, you realize of course that I must find a way to extricate myself from that situation."

It was an opening. Garret took it. "I shall not let you down, sir."

"You most certainly shall not. Indeed, you must do more than that. You must prove to the men that you are every bit as worthy as they, to be a member of my crew. Perhaps more so."

"And I shall. You may count on that."

Drake rose and approached her, placing his hand on her shoulder. "You make a fine midshipman. I admire your mastery of the knowledge I have shared. But you must now accelerate your learning as never before. In return for your commitment to that, I shall maintain your secret. For now. But do not disappoint me. Ever. Do you understand?"

Garret nodded. Despite the roughness of his voice, she felt the warmth of Drake's soul through his grip on her shoulder. Tears of gratitude threatened to well up in her eyes. She breathed deeply, blinking them away. "Thank you, sir. I shall not disappoint you." She turned to leave.

"One more thing," Drake offered. Garret paused. "If there is anything I can do to assist you, please come to me in private for such support." He didn't know how else to phrase it. He worried that if one of the crew members were to somehow stumble across her secret, he might take a fancy to her and make an unwanted advance. He hoped she would understand his offer in that context, not as some form of oblique sexual overture.

"Thank you, sir. I shall."

As she left, a hundred thoughts raced through Drake's mind. He knew he must be extremely careful in maintaining this secret. It meant showing her no favor, and placing her in the same potential danger as he might any other midshipman. It was simply one more challenge he now had to face. And not an insignificant one.

Closing the door behind her, Garret's heart still raced. Smile or cry? She felt a need to do both. A deep breath of ocean air calmed her. The moment had come and she'd met it head-on. And survived. Captain Drake was now, in fact, her accomplice. It meant he would be as motivated as she was, to find every opportunity to prove herself. She could barely wait. A smile emerged, alongside tears.

XVI

The sand of the small Brazilian harbor was soft and white. Warm, too, against her bare feet. Garret sat next to William, near the lapping water, sharing a short break. The anchored fleet swayed lightly in the harbor. It was peaceful, save for the noise emanating from the one ship being careened. Men aggressively scraped barnacles off the wooden hull. There was a brief lull in their conversation about their upcoming crossing to the Pacific. Garret gazed far beyond the ships at the dark blue water, framed by a differently blue horizon. William interrupted her thoughts, "If there are to be any assaults on land, I hope to take part in them."

"I, too, would welcome that," replied Garret.

"My preferred weapons are the pistolet and dagger. I have spent much time practicing with both."

"I myself prefer the cutlass. It does not require reloading and can be lethal in multiple ways."

"I wonder how we might fare," William looked to the sky, as though the answer might be hiding among the wispy clouds. He threw a stone into the air. "I so wish to make my father proud."

"But your father is not a soldier. I suspect he would find greater pride in your returning with knowledge of the trading world, rather than experience in battle."

"Perhaps. Still, I hope to prove myself in combat, to earn the respect of the men, and the Commander."

"Hopefully, we shall both have that opportunity. And soon," Garret smiled. She had already tasted blood in hand-to-hand combat—Henry's blood. At Ritchfield. Though she couldn't explain why, she'd found it…exhilarating. She had no desire to share that with William at this point; he might think her bloodthirsty. The truth was that her bloody confrontation with Henry had given her a sense of power; of freedom from domination; of revenge, accomplished. Having such feelings didn't cause her to think herself abnormal or somehow less human than others. But despite her deep friendship and growing trust with William, she doubted she could explain it to him. Perhaps one day, after they'd participated together in battle, they might discuss their experiences and feelings. Maybe then he would understand.

At her core, Garret felt she was not a bad person. She was simply unafraid to defend herself or mete out punishment—even if doing so meant bloodletting. Rather than fearing such an engagement, she almost welcomed it. With that in mind, through her time at sea, she had frequently measured herself against the men she worked alongside. They had more years building their muscular frames. But brute strength didn't always translate into effectiveness in combat. To her, fighting was an intricate combination of strength, skills and intelligence. And her skills were already finely honed. In fact, she noted with some satisfaction that her daily exercises on deck with her cutlass had drawn both observers and admiration. The only men she truly felt might have some advantage over her in that regard were Musa and Caber. Both men were enormous in stature. Musa's reach, extended even further by his lethal axe, would be difficult for anyone to overcome. If ever she were to face an opponent like him, she would need to rely on her positioning, speed and agility for advantage. Perhaps best to simply sling a dagger to a vulnerable area, rather than to his massive chest. Thank goodness these two men were on her side—better mates than menace, she thought.

Though Garret was comfortable with herself in these terms, she still wrestled with being female, rather than the boy she'd believed herself to be for virtually her entire life. It was difficult to think of herself in that way. The vast majority of her interactions with others had been with boys and men. Daniel had seen to that. Their mannerisms were common to her. Comfortable. She fit in that world. There was no doubt in her mind that her experiences with them had shaped the way she walked, talked, carried herself, dressed, and even thought. So she wasn't even certain what being female truly meant. Surely she would find that out, in time.

"Have I lost you, Garret?" William asked. "Your eyes suggest your mind is elsewhere."

Garret shook her head, unshackling her mind from its thoughts. "My apologies. I was thinking of days at home. Of just how much my world has changed. Our world. And it changes still. We shall have to adapt well." She thought of that adaptation primarily with respect to her gender—something William wouldn't even understand.

———

About two weeks into their stay at the harbor, Drake became concerned that several of the men were finding too much comfort among the local women. He worried it was hurting relations with native leaders and weakening his crew's discipline. It hastened his decision to leave, as pleasant as this place was. When it came time to depart, he was therefore pleased to still be on good terms with the locals. More than anything, he appreciated what they had shared regarding their philosophy and understanding of how their world worked. And how best to live in concert with it. Their spirituality amazed him. Though it was unlike his own—they believed in the constant presence of the spirits of the dead— it strangely comforted him. He contemplated their further belief that every creature had a soul, from the giant spotted cats that roamed in the wild, to the snakes that slithered through the jungle, and even down to the smallest of insects that inhabited virtually every millimeter of land. It reminded him of the squirrel he'd encountered on Slaughter Island, following the death of his brothers, John and Joseph. As a religious man, he believed God had created the heavens and the earth, and all living things. So why wouldn't he have imbued them with a soul? Besides, who was he to say that these natives were wrong? Theirs was a simple life but a rich one. He felt a renewed sense of purpose and a fervent desire to be more in touch with the world around him.

It was a cool, cloud-filled morning when the fleet left the harbor, heading south. Based on navigator da Silva's recommendation, they would use the Strait of Magellan as their crossing point to the Pacific, rather than attempt the more threatening and colder seas at the southern tip of the Americas. Though the winds were favorable, there was an ominous presence onboard that threatened to hold them back—Thomas Doughty. His behavior had once again flared up in an unfortunate way. He'd propagated discontent, frequently questioning Drake's leadership and decision-making; even suggesting witchcraft was involved. Drake worried that Doughty's underlying ambition was to take over leadership of the fleet. With the weather and sea conditions about to become increasingly harsh, there was no room for other causes of restlessness among the men. He removed Doughty from his captaincy of the *Pelican* and assigned him to the fleet's smallest ship, the *Swan*. For Doughty, it was a glove cast at his feet—a challenge to which he was bound by honor to answer.

Days later, in the throes of a severe storm, Doughty and the *Swan* became separated from the rest of the ships. After the storm subsided, the fleet began searching for the missing vessel. When they finally spotted it, they observed it streaming away from them, at full sail—a clear act of treason. The *Pelican*, a far superior sailing vessel, overtook the fleeing ship. As it drew alongside the *Swan*, its crew threw grappling hooks across the taffrail, locking the ships together. Prouten was first to cross over, accompanied by Lee, Musa and Caber. Drake had chosen not to make an appearance, a not-so-subtle message to Doughty that he was not pleased.

Doughty approached Prouten the moment he stepped on deck. "What is the meaning of this rude behavior, Mr. Prouten?" he shouted, attempting to establish upper ground in the conversation.

"I am afraid, sir, that you appear to be traveling in the wrong direction." Musa and Caber stifled their chuckles at Prouten's dry humor. "Commander Drake has requested your presence aboard the *Pelican*. He feels some navigational instruction is in order." Musa couldn't contain himself. He laughed uproariously, sparking Doughty's indignation.

"This is an outrage, Mr. Prouten. Please inform the Commander that I am well aware of the direction I am headed and have no need of his instruction." Prouten had no desire to engage in debate. He nodded to Musa and Caber. They were more than happy to take hold of the arrogant landsman.

"Unhand me," protested Doughty!

"Take him to his quarters," instructed Prouten, "and ensure he is properly secured until the Commander is prepared to see him."

Doughty recognized it was senseless to struggle with the two strongmen. He went peacefully to his cabin, contemplating Drake's pending visit.

Furious and exasperated, Drake waited a full hour before boarding the *Swan*. Prouten and Lee accompanied him to Doughty's quarters. Musa and Caber, seeing them approach, opened the door. Doughty, seated in the chair behind his desk, rose stiffly as Drake entered. The Commander stood motionless, observing his deserter, saying nothing. Finally, he spoke. "You, sir, are a disgrace to England. You have deceived me, stolen property, lied, and spread discontent among the men. And now you have the audacity to attempt desertion from the fleet. This is most unbecoming of a well-born gentleman. I am therefore relieving you of your command, holding you in contempt of my leadership, and charging you with seditious acts."

"You cannot be serious."

"I assure you, I am." Drake turned to Lee. "Have the men bind this sorry soul to the mast." He knew this would be painful for Doughty, having to watch the men he'd been leading pass by and spit on him. Nothing could be more degrading.

Musa and Caber escorted Doughty to the main deck, smiling as they bound him to the mast before the crew. Many cheered their action. Doughty's brother John was not one of them. Instead, he confronted Drake, "This, sir, is most assuredly an injustice. My brother has done nothing to deserve such demeaning treatment."

Drake responded curtly. "You, sir, may well be an accomplice to your brother's sedition. Another word from you and you shall join him at the mast." He turned to Lee, nodding in John Doughty's direction, "Take this man to the *Pelican* and secure him." Lee nodded to Musa and Caber. They grabbed John by the arms and led him away.

Drake climbed atop a water barrel and called for the *Swan's* crew to assemble. Thomas Doughty, pained by the wrist burn from the rough rope binding him tightly to the mast, watched and listened intently as Drake addressed the sailors. "My good men, you have suffered severely under the captaincy of a fool and a traitor. I apologize for my decision to have him serve as your captain. Mr. Doughty has demonstrated he is unworthy to lead a sailing vessel and has thereby put your lives at risk. You shall shortly have a new captain, appointed from among my officers. In the interim, I shall take command of the ship myself."

Drake ordered the crew back to their stations, took charge of the vessel and asked Prouten to captain the *Pelican*, pending his return. It was now perfectly clear to him—he needed to bring an end to Doughty's continual, troubling interference.

XVII

As the fleet continued south along the Brazilian coast, Drake enjoyed a moment of leisure in his cabin, drawing from memory some of the birds and animals he'd seen in these parts of the world. A knock on the door interrupted him.

"Enter."

Garret walked in, confidently.

"Close the door, if you please."

"Aye, sir." Garret closed it, then turned to face him. "You wanted to see me?"

"Yes. Have a seat." Garret sat across the table from him. "How goes your training under da Silva?"

"It goes well, sir. He is quite skilled. And a fine instructor."

"Good. Good. I expect you to learn all you can. Should anything happen to him, you shall ascend to his role. It is particularly important that you learn everything he knows about Magellan's straits. I understand they are most treacherous."

"Thank you, sir. I will."

"Good. You may go now." Garret hesitated, remaining seated. Drake continued, "Is there something else?"

"If I may, sir." Garret waited for his permission before continuing, "I wish to be entirely clear. I am fine learning the skills of a navigator. However, I hope that will not hinder my participation with the crew in other ways."

"Such as?"

"William and I have discussed our involvement in any assault. We are anxious to prove ourselves in battle."

Drake sucked in a deep breath, blowing it out through clenched teeth. "You continually challenge me, Master Connachan."

"As you have always instructed," she smiled. "I believe strongly that participating in battle shall prove my worthiness before the men."

Drake recognized the truth in her statement. He hesitated for a moment. "As you wish, Connachan. But be mindful of what you wish for—it may well dash your expectations. Or something worse."

"So be it, sir," Garret replied, with an air of confidence. She rose and left. It pained her a little that she hadn't accurately represented William's position. He was less committed to the idea than she. But Garret felt certain he'd be better off for it. Besides, he would never know she'd planted the seed with Drake.

———

The fleet arrived at Port San Julian, seeking fresh water and supplies. The village was inhabited by a small native population. Perceiving no threat, Drake and several others rowed ashore to greet them. They carried little weaponry, signaling peaceful intent. Shortly after landing, the men began unloading tools and supplies to set camp. A group of natives soon approached.

One of the men, Robert Wynter, noticed the natives carried primitive bows, their arrows stored in quivers slung across their backs. Seeking to make a favorable impression, Wynter approached with his own bow and arrow, gesturing with a head nod to indicate he meant no harm. The natives hesitated as he attempted to demonstrate the effectiveness of his English weapon. He drew back on the bowstring, not realizing it was overly weathered by its time at sea. It disintegrated, causing the arrow to drop a few feet in front of him. Perceiving that as a threat, one of the natives deftly drew an arrow from his quiver, loaded it, and hastily pulled back on the bowstring, aiming directly at Wynter. The arrow burst through his rib cage, embedding itself deeply. Blood splattered over the man next to Wynter as he screamed in pain, falling to his knees and grabbing at the arrow as if to withdraw it. A crewmate set and aimed his arquebus at the offending native, but damp gunpowder delivered a misfire, giving the native time to reload. His second arrow pierced the man's skull, sending him backward. He died in silence.

The natives scrambled for cover. Some turned, briefly, to direct arrows at Drake's men, who were charging forward. Garret grabbed hold of the dropped arquebus, expertly re-loading it with dry powder. She picked out the offending native. He was running away at an angle. Taking a deep breath to calm and steady herself, she aimed slightly ahead of him, squeezing the trigger softly to avoid altering the weapon's aim. The bullet ran true, hitting the native on his right side. It pierced through his chest, splattering his blood forward as his body, twisted by the impact, fell to the ground, arms splayed out. His head hit the sand sideways, his eyes open but seeing only darkness. The remaining natives melted into the trees, shocked by the terror of the loud and deadly weapon they'd never before seen.

Observing what was unfolding onshore, men from the anchored ships deployed in longboats. They soon arrived on the beach with a full array of weapons. Drake ordered the crew to secure the perimeter, tend to the dead men, and set camp. The guards occasionally fired warning shots into the forest, alerting the natives to stay back.

———

After breakfast, Drake decided the moment had arrived. He instructed Lee to retrieve Thomas and John Doughty from their detention onboard the ship. Lee soon returned with the two men bound at their wrists. A single rope attached them together at their ankles. Musa cut them loose when they arrived. The crew gathered on the beach. Drake asked several men to provide their testimony regarding Doughty's actions. Some asked Prouten to speak for them. The last testimony was that of the carpenter, Ned Bright. He claimed to have overheard Doughty planning to execute Drake—an act of mutiny.

"You lie, you sea-scum," Doughty shouted at Bright.

"Silence," yelled Drake, unhappy with the interruption.

When the testimonies ended, the Commander stepped forward. "Thomas Doughty, you have heard the charges brought by your fellow crewmen. I myself have found you wanting on several occasions and observed your attempts to undermine my leadership—an act of sedition for which the penalty is death.”

“My good captain. And friend,” Doughty responded, sweat beading on his brow. “I deny each and every one of these allegations.” He dabbed at his forehead with his handkerchief. “I am compelled to request that you postpone this hearing until we return to England, where a proper trial among learnéd men can be undertaken. I shall not be found guilty by a collection of lying, ill-informed and poorly educated sailors.”

“These men, sir, are your colleagues and partners in this endeavor,” Drake replied. “They have no less standing than you. And they have every right to bring you to justice. Postponement is not workable. Nor is it fair to the men. We cannot abort our mission for your singularly selfish request. Nor can I spare men and ships to return you to England.”

“I am a significant investor in this enterprise,” protested Doughty. “And a friend of the Queen. You have no commission from Her Majesty to preside over a makeshift court of law, nor to take any resulting action against me.”

“I could not disagree more, Mr. Doughty. As Commander of the fleet, I have complete authority to conduct any and all affairs that I deem necessary to the success of the voyage.”

“Then let me see your authority. In writing, if you please.”

Drake had no written authority, though he wouldn’t concede the point to Doughty. “I have no need to produce documents. I have Her Majesty’s full blessing for this mission. There is no questioning her authority.” He turned to his master's mate. "Mr. Prouten, if you please, select the most educated of the men to sit in judgement."

Prouten assembled a small jury, being careful not to select any of Doughty's friends. He then read the summary charges aloud. When he was done, Drake addressed the accused man formally, "Mr. Thomas Doughty, you have hereby been charged with seditious acts against a fleet commissioned by Her Majesty, the Queen of England, under my command." He turned to the jury. "Gentlemen, you have heard the charges against Mr. Doughty as provided by your crewmates. I ask that you consider what you have heard and reach a collective decision on Mr. Doughty's guilt, which you shall then share with this assembly."

The jurors conferred, speaking softly to avoid inviting comments from others. Within minutes, they concluded their discussion, having arrived at a unanimous decision. One of the jurors stepped forward. "Commander Drake," he said, "we have considered all that has been said regarding Mr. Doughty. We are all agreed and fully convinced of his guilt in these matters."

"This cannot be!" shouted Doughty.

"Silence!" demanded Drake. He then addressed the entire crew, "Mr. Thomas Doughty has attempted to discredit me and overthrow my command, the likes of which England has never before countenanced. He has been found guilty by a jury of your fellow crewmen. So I ask you now, who here believes this man deserves the penalty applicable to the finding of sedition and mutiny?" The men shouted aye or raised their hands, making it clear they agreed that the proper punishment should be administered for crimes of this nature—execution.

Drake turned to his prisoner, "Mr. Doughty, you have been found guilty by your fellow seamen and sentenced to die for your crimes. Prepare for your sentence to be carried out under my authority. I shall make arrangements for your ultimate punishment on the morrow."

Doughty hung his head in disbelief, unable to accept that his actions had brought him to this sad state. Mr. Lee ordered Musa and Caber to take him to a nearby tent, where he remained under guard.

Garret had been silent the entire time. Though she disliked Doughty, she hadn't shared the experiences of the men who spoke against him. Even if she had, she certainly wouldn't wish to put the life of her friend's father in peril. She determined to speak with Drake privately on Rose's behalf. He might not like her intervening at such a late point but she believed it was the right thing to do. If Drake were to proceed with the execution, how could she ever explain it to Rose, assuming she might see her again? Within minutes, she was at Drake's side. He was alone, appearing to feel the full weight of his decision, and perhaps worried that it might haunt him for the remainder of his life.

"A moment, sir?"

Drake looked up, annoyed. He preferred to be alone. Still, he was fond of Garret and therefore willing to engage. "What is it, Connachan?"

"It concerns Mr. Doughty."

Drake wasn't surprised. If anyone were to challenge him regarding Doughty's execution, it would be this brash young midshipman. "Speak your mind."

"I know his daughter. We attended Ritchfield Academy together. She is a good friend."

Drake paused. He was unaware Doughty even had a child. That was distressing information, under the circumstances. Executing the man would have severe consequences for his daughter. He immediately wished he hadn't learned of the girl's existence. "Why would you choose to trouble me with this?" he replied, rising in frustration.

"You must understand, sir. My friend's life will be placed in jeopardy by this outcome. I feel I must ask you to reconsider."

"This is not simply my decision, Connachan. It was made by the crew."

"Yet surely, you have the right to grant him clemency."

In his heart, Drake knew Garret was right to question the decision. She was merely giving voice to his own misgivings. "I appreciate your concern. But you must understand, my first responsibility is for the well-being of my men. And the men have spoken. I shall not contradict their decision."

Garret sensed it would be imprudent to continue pressing, especially on behalf of a man she disliked so much herself. "Aye, sir." She turned and left.

Drake watched her go. He knew it had taken courage for her to confront him. He admired that. Still, it only heightened the discomfort he already felt, having personally initiated events that would lead to Doughty's demise, and the loss of a young girl's father.

XVIII

On the eve of his execution, Doughty requested that Drake share a final meal with him. Drake obliged, believing it was the honorable thing to do. As the two men dined and drank copious amounts of wine, they reminisced of better times they'd shared back in England. Doughty reminded him of the afternoon at The Blue Anchor, when they first discussed the idea of this grand voyage, with excitement. Now here they were, in a much different place and at a much different point in their relationship.

After the meal, Drake spoke, quietly, "I find this to be a most difficult topic, but I must ask, have you a preference for how you shall receive your punishment?"

Hearing the words suddenly made things real for Doughty. Maybe it was the wine that drew the tears. He wiped at them. "I truly regret my actions, and this most unfortunate outcome. If I am to die, let it be by the axe. I find it cleaner and quicker than a hanging."

Drake nodded, "Let it be so."

Doughty rose, tears now running visibly down both cheeks. "One more thing, if you please."

"By all means." Drake rose as he spoke.

"Assure me that you will see to the well-being of my daughter, Rose."

Drake understood Doughty's pain—final separation from a loved one. He wished it could be otherwise. "You have my word. I shall provide whatever support she requires." He waited for Doughty to compose himself and then called for Caber to return the man to his holding tent. He sent a messenger to fetch Garret.

Garret was curious, and a little worried, about her commander's request to see her. Nevertheless, she came with confidence. Drake stood when she arrived. "Thank you for coming, Master Connachan. Please, have a seat."

Garret nodded and sat. He sat directly across, looking sorrowfully at his midshipman, thinking how her strength of character reminded him of his own, as a young mid under Hawkins. "I have made a commitment to Mr. Doughty that you should be aware of." He paused. "I promised him I would ensure his daughter's well-being."

"Thank you, sir. That is most kind of you."

"I shall need your support in the matter, since you have a relationship with the girl."

"I have not seen her in some time, I am afraid."

"Nonetheless, you know her. It would be of immense help if you could communicate my commitment to her."

"Of course. I shall prepare a message for your review."

"You understand, such a letter must also inform her of her father's passing."

"I do."

"I would prefer that it come from you, not me."

"Why, sir?"

"Because you shall write it from your heart. I do not know this girl. Your words would no doubt bring her more comfort."

Though she'd offered her assistance with confidence, Garret now struggled with how to even begin such a message. There was so much ground to cover with Rose, yet the message needed to be short, given its nature. And it needed to share her own love and warmth for her friend in this time of crisis. She strove to reach out and touch Rose through her words as she wrote that night, and deep into the morning, disposing of several drafts.

Dearest Rose,

Our journeys have taken us to different and perhaps unexpected places. Yet I have always carried your friendship with me. It gives me much warmth. I hope you feel the same.

I am writing to you now from the Southern Seas, blessed to be sailing with Commander Drake. He has taken me under his wing and instructed me well. I am certain you shall instantly recognize that I must therefore be with your father. I have indeed been with him. But I am afraid that I must now share the news of his passing. It is most unfortunate.

You may hear this same news from other sources, including the circumstances of his passing. Please trust that I shall provide you with an accurate account, as well as comfort, when next we meet. There is no question you can ask that I shall be unable to answer.

I can only imagine how you must feel at reading this, since I have never myself experienced such a crushing loss. Please know that your tears will honor your father's memory. He was immensely proud of you. I know he would have wanted you to carry on in the tradition of your family's most honorable endeavors.

Commander Drake has asked me to express his own personal condolences and his assurance of support for you and your family. He deeply mourns the loss of his close friend.

When I return to England, we shall find an opportunity to cheer your father's legend. I so look forward to that.

Your most humble friend,

Garret Connachan

Though still not satisfied with the message, Garret wasn't certain she ever would be—no matter how many times she might rewrite it. Her gravest concern was that Rose might first learn of the circumstances surrounding her father's demise from others. She would be overcome with grief, possibly with no one there to comfort her. Yet there was nothing she could do to avert that, other than offer her own version of what happened in a face-to-face meeting. That was something she could manage. One day. If ever.

———

In the morning, once the men had assembled, Lee and Caber led Doughty to a place at the edge of the beach where a large tree had been cleanly felled. The stump was shaved to a rough finish. Doughty knelt before the stump, bowing his head. Preacher Fletcher uttered a prayer on his behalf. Doughty himself then offered up a prayer. He said it loudly, ensuring all might hear him against the crashing of the surf.

"Dearest Lord, I thank you for your many blessings. And for the friendships I have enjoyed on this voyage. Please keep safe my friends and family, both here and at home. I ask that you protect our dear Queen Elizabeth. I ask that you bless the remainder of this voyage, upon which these many men have embarked. I remain your humble servant and now place my soul in your graceful hands." After his prayer, Doughty looked up at the men. "Please, forgive me of the crimes you say I have committed. I also ask that you forgive my associates and my brother who are here with us—that they might come to no harm as a result of my alleged actions."

Drake responded, "I assure you, Mr. Doughty, no reprisals shall be taken against your associates or your brother." He said it loudly, so the crew would be clear that this was how he wished it to be.

Doughty rose to his feet. He nodded to Drake and then hugged him heartily, as though he were a good friend. "Thank you and farewell, Commander. We have shared better days together."

Drake nodded. He then stepped back as Doughty knelt once again before the stump, slowly resting his chin on it. Fletcher read the Lord's

Prayer, finishing by asking God's blessing of Doughty's soul. Doughty remained silent. He didn't weep, wishing instead to show strength, in order that he might always be remembered for having taken his punishment bravely.

At the conclusion of Fletcher's remarks, the giant, dark-skinned, Musa came forward. The sun glanced brightly off the recently sharpened blade of his dreaded battle axe. Except for the crashing of the waves against the shore, and the squawk of birds flying overhead, there was complete silence on the beach. Musa hovered over the kneeling man. Both men were expressionless. Slowly, the muscled arms of the executioner raised the lethal axe high above his head. In a split second, the axe descended ferociously upon Doughty's neck, decapitating him instantly. Cleanly. The blow sent Doughty's head rolling off the stump, onto the sand, dripping blood.

Deafening silence continued. But for Garret, even the waves seemed to cease their assault on the beach; the birds lost their voices. She hadn't looked away. An execution was something she'd never witnessed. The shocking nature of its conclusion jarred her, much more so than the slaying of a fox at the end of the hunt. Like the fox, Doughty was defenseless. Though he may well have deserved his fate, it hardly seemed fair that he wasn't permitted to fight for his life. Was there justice in this? Was it fair to take a man's life other than in battle? She knew how it felt to bring a man to blood in the course of combat. There was power in that. But there was also a fairness about it. Meting out blooded-revenge, or battle-death, both seemed acceptable for their evenhandedness. One-sided mortal punishment such as this, however, did not. Yet there were other types of killing as well. Like assassination—the killing of another for political purpose. Or the taking of a life for the mere pleasure of it. Both seemed distasteful to her; entirely unacceptable. Her thoughts turned to her friend Rose. She couldn't even imagine the devastation Rose would have felt, had she borne witness to her father's end.

Drake moved toward the headless body with the departed soul. He reached down, grabbing Doughty's pale head by its hair and raising it high in the air. Sand particles clung to the beard while others fell. Blood dripped from the sharply severed neck. "This," he declared, "is the rightful end of traitors!"

Garret watched Drake carefully place Doughty's head back on the sand, next the body. How difficult it must have been, she thought, for Drake to have made the final decision to end the man's life, regardless of the circumstances. She hoped that, if and when she were to become a captain, she might never have to face such a difficult decision.

A handful of natives, observing the Englishmen from distant positions in the jungle, looked on in horror. What gruesome men were these, they wondered.

Later that day, Drake sat on a fallen tree near the beach. His young brother, midshipman Thomas, came to check on him, "Are you alright, brother?"

"I have seen better days, Thomas." He turned and looked out over the blue waters of the ocean, breathing deeply. "But I have learned that leaders must deal directly and quickly with problems that arise. We cannot let them fester and swell into more serious problems." His head dropped as he picked up grains of sand, letting them filter through his fingers. "Still, there is only sadness when my decision results in the loss of even one of my men." Thomas nodded. Drake continued, "Mr. Doughty has paid the ultimate price, yet I am at peace with my decision." He paused and looked at Thomas, "Though it still brings pain and sorrow."

———

He was known for leading from the front. Drake seldom shied away, either from battle or from the rigorous day-to-day tasks associated with running the ship. He worked alongside his men, often performing the same tasks as the lowliest of sailors—with the one exception of cleaning the foredeck slats. He understood how easily a man's morale could be crushed by long days at sea, at times in dark and stormy weather, when heroic efforts were needed to maintain the ship's seaworthiness. There were many reasons sailors might complain—living conditions, demanding work, quality of their food, modest rations, rats, sickness, superstitions and, most importantly, the constant risk of death. By working hard alongside his men, Drake raised their spirits, winning their confidence, favor and support. These were things he would need when faced with future challenges. Unfortunately, the same could not be said of Doughty's friends. They were high-society gentlemen, not sailors. Like Doughty, they viewed the rest of the crew with disdain, believing sailors' work was beneath them. It was just one more thing to undermine his men's morale. Drake felt a need to address it publicly before sailing on to the Strait of Magellan and the enormous challenge of crossing to the Pacific. He gathered the men on the beach as they prepared to leave Port San Julian.

"My fellow adventurers," he began. "We are about to sail where no Englishman has ever journeyed. When we accomplish this mission, we shall be welcomed home as heroes. But, with as many challenges as we shall face, we must work together, as men of one mind, fully committed to doing whatever it takes to succeed. From this point forward, there can be no distinction between the sailors who toil intensely and the gentlemen who accompany us on this mission. Let each man among us, sailors and gentlemen, commit here and now to work together for our collective cause. Let no man put himself above others but rather provide whatever help and support he can to his fellow shipmates."

Drake scanned the men's faces before continuing. His eyes settled on Doughty's brother John, "If any among you cannot accept these terms for the remainder of this voyage, let him speak now. I am prepared to provide such men with a ship, for the purpose of their return to England." He knew full well that John and his gentle-friends were incapable of sailing on their own. He made eye contact with as many of Doughty's friends as he recognized, searching their souls. None expressed dissent.

"Hear, hear," yelled one of the sailors. Then another, and another. The beach virtually shook with the cheers of the men, hailing their leader. There would be no vessel returning to England.

"To the ships, then," Drake ordered.

The men pushed off in their longboats, heading to the four ships anchored in the harbor. The decks were soon heavy with activity as the sailors began weighing anchor and unfurling sails. One ship, however, remained silent—the *Mary*. Drake wasn't confident it could weather the challenges ahead. He had ordered the men to unload her supplies and equipment and then set her aflame. It seemed only fitting that she now join the man who had once captained her.

The weather turned cooler on the edge of an approaching storm as the *Pelican*, the *Elizabeth* and the *Marigold* got underway. Some looked back on the death-shroud of flames and smoke encompassing the *Mary*. Drake saw it as a fitting end to the sorrow they were leaving in their wake.

Garret, William and Thomas stood at the *Pelican's* taffrail, watching the *Mary* succumb to a deadly mix of fire and water.

"'Tis a sad day," offered Garret.

"How so?" Thomas asked.

"Two men slain by natives, Doughty's execution, and now the end of the *Mary*. I, for one, am glad to leave it all behind."

"I have no sadness over Doughty's death," offered Thomas. William nodded in agreement. Neither had liked the man.

"I suppose my sadness over his death is not so much for the man himself as it is for his daughter," Garret replied. "She was my friend at the Academy." Neither Thomas nor William knew how to respond, so neither did. After a moment, Garret continued. "I hope for something better in the days ahead. Something we can all take joy in." As she said it, she realized it was likely to be some time before they were to find any joy. They were on the precipice of a challenging passage to the Pacific.

———

The barren cliffs of the Cape of Virgins evidenced the frequency of harsh weather entering the Strait of Magellan. Even the sun dared not challenge the dark, heavy clouds roiling in the morning sky. Upon glimpsing the ominous sight, Drake had a newfound admiration for the daring Spaniard, Ferdinand Magellan, who had sailed here some sixty years prior. His own fleet would now be the second to attempt the treacherous passage—three hundred miles of swirling, unpredictable currents, spotty islands and hidden sandbars. Biting winds swarming from varied directions would test the bravest of souls, spearing them with unforgiving sea spray and relentless rain. With only primitive navigational logs to assist them, Drake's fleet was at the mercy of his navigator, Nuno da Silva, and his assistant, Garret. The crew were counting on their Captain's seafaring knowledge and skill to master the challenge; that and their own collective strength as time-tested, deep-ocean sailors.

As they sailed past the Cape, Drake sensed both a need and an opportunity to reinvigorate the men, refreshing their commitment to facing the difficulties ahead. He assembled many of them on his flagship, seeing to it that each man was issued a cup of grog. From his place at the bow, the wind roaring hard at his back, he shouted for all to hear.

"My good men. This day marks our entry to the channel that will take us to the Pacific Ocean. Our passage here shall forever be celebrated by our countrymen. In honor of this moment, we drink a toast to Her Majesty, the Queen."

"To the Queen," the men shouted, raising cups and heartily gulping watered-down beer.

"In making this passage," Drake continued, "you shall become heroes of England. Your children and grandchildren, and their grandchildren, shall share the stories of your courage. I drink to you and the legacy you shall leave!"

The men cheered and drank once again.

"In recognition of this moment," Drake continued, "I have chosen to rechristen our flagship. The *Pelican* is no more. From this point forward, as we leave behind the Atlantic, our ship shall be the *Golden Hinde*."

The men laughed, howled and cheered. "The *Golden Hinde*," they shouted, thrusting their cups in the air, showering each other in grog.

"Mr. Fletcher," Drake called out, "lead us in prayer, if you please."

As Fletcher asked for God's blessing of the men and for the safety of the journey before them, Drake bowed his head. He gave personal thanks to God for having brought him to the glory of this exciting, yet worrisome, moment.

Garret stood alongside Thomas and William as the crew began to disperse. She raised her cup. "Good luck to us all." The two mids joined her in the toast. "Let me add that, if for any reason, life is to fail me on this passage, I want you to know that you two have been my most cherished friends. I shall think fondly of you always."

"As shall I," echoed William.

"And me," added Thomas.

They drank, each of them wondering whether they would ever see the Pacific.

Garret pondered her own words. These two mids had become such close friends that her feelings toward them were those one might associate with siblings. It was something she hadn't experienced before, even with her friend Rose. Maybe it was their shared purpose that bound them together. They'd become so close that they thought of themselves as a trio. She was deeply committed to coming through this challenging passage with these friendships alive and intact. No matter what that took.

———

"Cast off the topgallant bowlines," Drake screamed amid the howling of the winds. The crew echoed his call down the lines. The rain pinged hard against the side of his face as he looked upwards to the top of the *Golden Hinde*. "Haul home the topgallant clewlines!" The men following his orders felt the burn and cut of the harsh ropes tugging against and slipping through their already well-tortured hands. It was their thirteenth day battling the ice-breathing dragon that was the Strait of Magellan. Constant, raging winds, blinding rain, churning waters and dangerous outcroppings of rock, tested nerves and weighed mightily on the men's bodies and spirits. For many, it was the most challenging contest between man, sea and weather that they'd ever competed in. The conditions schemed against them, pressing them to their physical and mental breaking points. The weakest among them had days ago begun questioning why they'd ever signed on for this torment. Swears and prayers alternated up, down and below the decks. Even the bravest found private moments alone to shed and hide their tears. Through the misery, they couldn't even envision an end. Clouded darkness daily dissolved into chilling night. Surely, the Gods hated them.

Morning arrived less violently the day the fleet finally emerged from the Strait, on the brink of Pacific water. A tremendous chorus of cheers reverberated throughout the ships. Surprisingly, the rough passage had been completed in half the time it had taken Magellan decades earlier. Yet potential misfortune forever hides around the ocean's corner. The joy of reaching the Pacific was soon crushed by yet another onset of brutal weather. Horrific storming winds and turbulent, thirty-foot swells battered the ships, hammering already deflated sailors.

Thomas Drake was on watch, high among the *Golden Hinde's* web of masts and rigging, as the storm thundered through the day and into the night. The ship tossed and pitched in the winds, swaying severely. Thomas peered below, seeing no ship directly beneath him—only crashing waves flooding the entire ship with racing, menacing water. Death was sure to follow, he thought, gripping the mast tightly in his arms. The ship swayed back. He glimpsed the *Marigold*, melting into the dark, pummeling rain. Squinting hard to pierce the weather veil, he searched for the missing vessel where he'd seen it dissolve. A distant crack spliced through the noise of wind and water, followed by the cries of the men as the sea swallowed the *Marigold* whole, taking their souls with it.

Drake was dismayed by the loss of the *Marigold*. He counted many of its men as friends and mourned their passing. Still, the voyage had to go on, despite the now oppressive fog and weather that exceeded even the fiercest of English winters.

Among the men now doubting the wisdom of this venture was John Wynter, Captain of the *Elizabeth*. With his ship, his men and his own spirits sorely weathered, he made the painful decision to reverse course and head back to the Strait of Magellan, hoping to return to England on favorable winds. Drake and the *Golden Hinde* were suddenly on their own, battling the uncharted, unforgiving southern reaches of the Pacific.

XIX

The Mapuche scout crouched silently among the rocks and trees on Isla Mocha, closely observing several pale- and dark-skinned men setting camp on the beach. His own skin color was a softened brown, contrasted by a loose necklace displaying white shark teeth. He wore a loincloth and animal-fur cloak. His tightly muscled physique and the fresh carcass at his feet suggested he was an agile hunter. A blooded carving knife was comfortably nestled in his grip. Watching Drake's sailors unload long knives, swords, pikes, shields and arquebuses, he studiously took inventory of the men and their weapons. Once the longboats stopped coming ashore, he retreated to his village, to inform his people of the invaders' arrival.

There was no reason to believe these intruders were any different from others they'd previously encountered. They only ever came with hostile intent, seeking to ravage their island. The Mapuches' experience with invaders had finely honed them into fierce, adaptive combatants. Over time, they'd captured Spanish horses and weaponry, and even reverted to cannibalism. They began preparing to engage and defeat this new group of unwelcomed raiders.

It was the need for fresh water and rest that had brought the *Golden Hinde* to Isla Mocha. Nearing sunset, the crew finished setting camp and began readying their meal. Garret watched as a small, unarmed group of Mapuche approached along the beach, bearing gifts. They greeted Drake's men as friends. When one of them spoke, Garret noticed his surprisingly sharpened teeth. Though it disturbed her, she imagined it was a tradition dating back hundreds of years, to help them devour wild prey. The natives smiled, offering up shells, necklaces and fresh fruits. Drake ordered his men to share tools in exchange. The encounter was brief; dinner was ready and night was falling.

The Mapuche walked back casually along the beach, their opening ploy complete. They wanted these intruders to believe they had nothing to fear. And it worked. Drake's men slept at ease that night, with only two guards keeping watch. Familiar with the ways of invaders, the Mapuche fully expected them to leave camp in the morning, in search of fresh water. They sought to deliver something different.

The crew was up before dawn, enjoying a casual breakfast of hardtack and watered beer, around a roaring fire. By the time they'd finished eating, the sun was peering periodically through scattered clouds. Drake ordered an assembly, and spoke, "Gentlemen, Mr. White and Mr. Allan shall keep watch, while the rest of us take the boats upriver to load fresh water. The natives are friendly, so we shall take only swords and shields, allowing more room for casks." Musa stared blankly at Drake, slowly raising his battle axe without uttering a word. Drake noticed. "Yes," he smiled, nodding to Musa, "you may bring your axe." The men laughed as a wide, menacing grin stretched across the black behemoth's face.

A dozen men—and a woman disguised as one—soon loaded into three boats. They rowed against the river's modest current, flanked by overflowing vegetation—tall trees and thick shrubbery. The air pulsated with the songs of countless birds celebrating the morning and scolding the strangers below. The crew rowed deeper into the interior, soaking in the sights and sounds of this much-welcomed calm.

"There," Drake called out, pointing to where the river widened into a sand-framed lagoon, beyond a slight bend. While the river's current flowed toward the sea, there was only a gentle ebb in the lagoon itself. "Secure the boats here and ready the casks."

The Mapuche knew this was a favored spot for intruders to gather water. Crouching in the brush like lions on the hunt, they waited until their prey would secure the boats. The sun broke through as the crew neared the beach. Brewer and Flood, two ordinary seamen, stepped out of the lead boat and began tying it to a nearby tree as the others stowed oars and prepared to disembark. The sun glanced off something that caught Brewer's eye. He watched in horror as a horde of warriors suddenly emerged from the foliage, storming toward him like a crushing wave. Their faces painted in streaks of red and black, the Mapuche voiced blood-curdling battle cries, piercing and shattering the morning's serenity. It unnerved even the most battle-hardened of Drake's men. A shower of arrows and spears abruptly filled the air.

Brewer and Flood scrambled to untie the rope from the tree, their nerves hobbling their efforts. They quickly trudged toward the boats through waist-deep water. Flood screamed as an arrow entered his arm. The remaining sailors readied oars and raised shields to deflect incoming projectiles. As the freed boats drifted back Brewer and Flood found themselves slowed by the water's increasing deepness. Mere moments from being surrounded, Brewer recognized the hopelessness of his situation. He shoved the bow of the boat hard, hoping to save his fellow crewmen. The Mapuche splashed down on him and Flood, brutally slashing at them. The two died harshly, their blood turning the water around them red. Garret watched in horror as the warriors cut into Flood's chest in haste, retrieving and devouring his still-beating heart. This was the most vile of all killing, she thought. Cannibalism. She had to look away.

Despite the men pulling hard on their oars, a Mapuche warrior managed to grab the lead boat's rope. Garret reacted with lightning speed, slashing and splitting the rope with her cutlass. A second warrior emerged from the water, grabbing onto the boat's edge. Garret's cutlass sliced directly across his neck. She felt no remorse. 'For Flood,' she thought.

The men's arms strained under the weight of the boats, unaided by any current. Caber stretched and pulled back hard, finally gliding the boat away as arrows streaked past. Drake turned his head quickly to avoid one. It glanced off his cheek, below his right eye, leaving a thin, blood-red trail.

Several warriors swam after the boats, knives held in their shark-like teeth. One managed to yank an oar away from a sailor. Others slashed at the crew with long knives. Musa wielded his axe with dexterity, detaching arms and ending the lives of two swimmers. Garret's cutlass separated the hand of another.

Several of Drake's men were now wounded, two badly, their blood spewing over others in the boat. Despite the intensity of the attack, those who still held oars continued rowing, their adrenaline pumping every stroke. Finally, they gained advantage of the flowing current crossing the edge of the lagoon. The boats quickly streamed toward the river's mouth. Looking back, the men sadly witnessed painted warriors sharing the hearts of Brewer and Flood, in celebration. The sight hollowed the crew's souls, filling them with a pressing desire for revenge. Harker, a close friend of Brewer and Flood, screamed profanities at the Mapuche.

Nearing their campsite, Drake hailed White and Allan on the beach to load the arquebuses. He signaled Prouten on the *Golden Hinde*, which soon unleashed cannon-shot over their heads, deterring the Mapuche advance.

Longboats from the *Golden Hinde* brought more men ashore. Wounded sailors were taken back to the ship. Though desperately wanting revenge, Drake couldn't risk the lives of any more men. Warning shots kept the warriors at bay while the crew broke down their camp and headed back to the ship. Their welcome to the west coast of the Americas was a bloody one.

———

As the *Golden Hinde* sailed north along the coast, several wounded men were attended to. One failed to see the sun set. In total, three good men had been lost. The following morning, Thomas sat across from Drake, sharing a somber breakfast. The cabin creaked and swayed under rough seas.

"Do you find it odd," asked Thomas, "that some natives are friendly, while others are the most brutal of warriors?"

"It may well depend on their past," replied Drake. "We know from Europe's own history that when differing groups of people are in close proximity, conflict often follows. On Isla Mocha, where there is but one people, their brutal nature must reflect their experience with intruders. Perhaps the Spanish have mistreated them. That might explain their bloody greeting. Hopefully, we shall find places where the Spanish have not yet ventured, offering more peaceful encounters. For our part, we must spread goodwill among the natives at every opportunity. It is in England's best interests. Better we befriend them than create enemies. That can only help us as we compete with the Spanish for the purpose of trading and sharing resources."

Thomas nodded. He thought for a moment, while his brother continued eating. "Tell me, do you have any regrets?"

Drake swallowed and washed down his food with grog. "Fair question, Thomas. Some might say no, they have no regrets, believing that saying yes would show weakness. But I shall share the truth, because doing otherwise would haunt my soul—Yes; I have regrets. I should not have let down our guard, as I did. Had I not, Brewer and Flood might still be with us."

"Perhaps you are right to accept blame. But then, how do you live with that?"

"I *choose* to be at peace, Thomas. I cannot let mistakes weigh on me. Though I may not always make the best decisions, what man does? I simply do my best. What more can anyone ask? When the outcome is unfortunate, I choose to learn from it, to improve future decisions. One must never let his regrets overwhelm him."

"Would you find any blame in others?"

Drake shook his head. "When things go wrong, never look to find blame in others. Rather, look for solutions to the problem that has arisen. And seek to avoid such problems in the future."

"Is it your sense, then, that we should continue to seek fresh water and provisions on inhabited islands like Isla Mocha?"

"Truly, what choice have we? We must be better prepared the next time."

"Indeed." Thomas paused, noting the sadness in his brother's eyes. "Since you accept blame for the lives of the fallen, allow me to forgive you. Not all things are under a man's control."

"Thank you, Thomas. It is not your forgiveness I seek. It is God's."

While Drake and Thomas shared breakfast, Garret was busy assisting Caber with the mainsail lines. She asked his impressions of the Mapuche attack. "I should have liked to get my hands on the neck of one of those bastards."

Garret nodded, understanding. She felt a compliment was in order. "You showed great bravery in rowing without a shield while arrows filled the air."

"It needed to be done," he replied, details of the incident now racing through his mind. "You were smart to cut that rope, so our boat could pull away."

"It needed to be done," Garret echoed, smiling. "A simple reaction to what was happening."

"It saved our lives."

Perhaps, thought Garret, she might finally be earning the crew's respect, something she deeply desired. It was fundamental to the next step—coming clean about her true gender.

XX

He noticed happily that the days were growing longer; warmer. Standing on the foredeck of the *Golden Hinde* as it sailed north, Drake thought about his much-depleted force—now a mere eighty men. And one woman, he noted, grumbling to himself. Yes, she'd proven herself in combat, but he worried constantly that the truth of Garret's gender might slip out, and that he might be deemed complicit in her deceit. At some point, he would need to get in front of that situation—before it could undermine his leadership.

He thought about all the gold, jewelry and artifacts his men had now plundered from Spanish settlements along the Pacific coast. Still, he harbored regret about one village that had been burned to the ground, the unfortunate result of its stubborn resistance. He assured himself that it was all in the name of the English crown. His raids were intended to disrupt Spain's efforts to settle and claim the Americas for itself. But in his heart, he knew he was also driven by revenge for losses he'd personally suffered at Spanish hands, including the killing of his brother, John. His dispute was with King Philip II and his military leaders, not the Spanish people themselves. He felt satisfied that minimizing the killing of ordinary villagers meant he was a good and decent man, as did his graciousness toward prisoners. Still, his soul was haunted by the many lives lost, on both sides. He shook his head to make these thoughts go away, deciding to return to his cabin to draw unusual wildlife he'd seen along the way. That always brought him peace. Though he couldn't sense it in the moment, he was establishing a unique precedent for military leaders—fierce and courageous in war, magnanimous in victory and studious in his quiet time.

Heading back to his cabin, Drake nodded to two crewmen. Neither smiled.

"Damn you," muttered the more vocal of the two, under his breath. Though most of his crew trusted and admired him, these two were his biggest detractors. They blamed Drake for the death of their friends, Brewer and Flood, at the hands of the Mapuche. The mutterer was a Harker, one of the tallest crewmen. His dysfunctional left eye constantly stared straight ahead, with a clouded gray hollowness. It made most men avert their own eyes, so as to avoid having to look into its depths. The other detractor, of comparable size and stature, was Yauggan de Graaf. Half Dutch, half black, he mostly followed Harker's lead. The two had discussed pooling their share of treasure to purchase a ship of their own at some point. In the meantime, Harker was committed to recruiting other like-minded crewmates to his side.

Besides detractors among his own crew, Drake had developed a broad swath of Spanish enemies. They viewed 'El Draque' (the dragon) as the most vile pirata. The Governor of Chile, Rodrigo de Quiroga, was particularly appalled at Drake's exploits at Val Paraiso, where El Draque had stolen wine, food, silver, and twenty-five thousand gold pesos. Recognizing just how poorly defended his coastal villages were, Quiroga ordered a naval warship to find and destroy the *Golden Hinde*. He sent messengers to Chilean villages along the northern coast, alerting them to potential assault. Men and arms were commissioned to help build defensive fortifications. Villagers were instructed to move their valuables to hiding places outside the towns themselves.

The strengthened resistance first became evident at an isolated harbor, where Drake's men had anchored to load fresh water. The small group that headed to shore was spotted by a lookout. Spanish soldiers soon charged, the thundering hooves and spraying sand of their horses catching the attention of the search party. They left their water casks and rushed to take cover. One man, Richard Minivy, was shot in the back. He fell to the sand in writhing pain. The others raced on, leaving him behind.

Seeing the skirmish unfold onshore, Drake ordered the firing of cannons and launching of longboats, causing the Spaniards to retreat. But it was too late for Minivy. They dragged him along the shore before one chose to decapitate him. The man raised Minivy's head high in his extended arms. Spanish soldiers erupted in cheers.

Standing on the deck, Garret, Thomas and William looked on in shock. How could these soldiers descend to such undisciplined, brutal behavior—beheading a wounded, defenseless man, Garret wondered. They were not men, she thought; they lacked a soul. Thoughts of Doughty's execution suddenly returned to her. But that was different, she thought. Justifiable. Or was it? She erased the thought from her mind, turning to William. "We can no longer consider the search for water to be low-risk."

"Indeed. We must always anticipate a 'welcoming' party," William replied, in jest.

"Well I, for one, want to accompany and defend our men in any future search for water. Being here on the ship leaves me feeling helpless."

"Given our experience here, and on Isla Mocha, I doubt the Commander would now even consider us for such a role. We are the youngest, after all."

"Youngest yes, but not the least skilled in battle," Garret insisted. In the back of her mind, she felt confident Drake would provide her such an opportunity—especially since he was complicit in hiding her gender. He knew she needed to prove herself in order to earn the men's respect. That would free him to come clean with them about her gender, on his terms.

"That may be true for you, Garret, but we lack experience," replied William. He placed his arm around Thomas. "*We* still have much to learn."

"I shall make a point of speaking with the Commander about our desires."

"*Your* desires," William corrected her.

The loss of Minivy only emboldened Harker's desire to sow dissent among the crew. And he had a skill for getting inside men's heads. With their spirits low, some were inclined to side with him. For his part, as the days wore on, Drake recognized a need to rally the men.

———

Word of El Draque's exploits had traveled quickly, thwarting any further assaults on Chilean villages. But seaborne targets were still available. It wasn't long before the *Golden Hinde* crossed paths with the *San Cristobal*, a Spanish merchant. Its four gunports on the facing side were closed, the cannons questionably functional for lack of use over the years. Drake had the wind advantage and used it to come quickly alongside the vessel.

The Spaniards had hastily readied themselves for hand-to-hand battle. They watched as grapples flew across the gap, like leashed vultures. Many caught the taffrail. Drake's men drew the two ships together. Musa was first to jump onto the deck, in menacing fashion. Covering fire from the upper masts of the *Golden Hinde* kept the Spanish at bay as Caber, Garret, Lee, Drake and others waterfalled over the side of the ship, weapons in hand. Tovery followed in the second wave, less enthused than Garret about being in the first.

The Spanish fired at the charging horde and wielded cutlasses against the front line. Musa, a large target, was grazed on his right side but still effortlessly dispensed with one man, slashing his axe between his neck and shoulder blade. Drake and Lee attacked with pistols smoking and cutlasses clashing against opposing blades. A large Spaniard challenged Garret clumsily. Her adept parry, followed by a lightning thrust, surprised him. His eyes opened wide as the cutlass speared through his heart. Tovery took a pistol shot to his shoulder, sending him backward. His pike fell from his hand, rattling on the deck.

The Spanish captain, sensing his men were about to be overwhelmed, shouted for the raiders to give quarter. In the din of battle, he wasn't heard.

Two of his men died in front of him. He shouted louder, for quarter, holding his arms high and firing his pistol to the sky. It caught Drake's attention. He called for his men to hold. Within seconds, the deadly clash ended. Spanish weapons were dropped or thrown onto the deck, clattering and skidding on hard, blood-slickened wood.

For a moment, a deafening silence took hold. Drake's boots broke the quiet as he approached the Spanish captain. The man bowed his head, offering up his sword. Drake waited for him to make eye contact before speaking, "Thank you, Captain. Your men have defended your ship bravely. I accept your surrender. You may keep your sword—at your side, if you please," he grinned.

The captain was a fit, muscled and seasoned sailor. He had no understanding of English. Drake motioned for him to sheath his sword. He did.

"Mr. Langton," Drake called out. "Join me, if you please,"

Langton was not a fighting man. He'd stayed behind during the assault, along with Drake's brother Thomas. Having already lost brothers John and Joseph, Drake had no desire to put Thomas in harm's way. Langton jumped over the taffrail and came to his Commander's side. "Please assure the captain that we mean him no harm. His crew shall be imprisoned in the hold while we take control of the ship. The captain shall accompany me to my quarters."

Lee, Musa, Caber and Garret took control of the prisoners, leading them below deck. Tovery, bleeding and in shock, was carried back to the

Golden Hinde, along with two other wounded men. The rest of Drake's crew began searching the ship for supplies and treasure.

Back in his cabin, with Langton present, Drake interrogated the Spanish captain. Cups of grog helped loosen the man's tongue. He spoke proudly of the *Nuestra Señora de la Concepcion,* a Spanish treasure ship. Apparently, it had left a nearby port days before, sailing north—a head start that might require several days to make up.

———

A speck of white blinked on the horizon. Atop the *Golden Hinde's* mainmast, William's eyes lit up. He prayed this might be the storied *Concepcion,* supposedly heavily laden with Spanish gold and silver." He called down excitedly to the main deck.

"Sail Ho!"

Drake was on the bow at the time, conferring with Prouten. "Where away, Tovery?"

"Five points to larboard, sir."

It was a few minutes before Drake himself was able to pick up the bright white speck matching the color, but shinier than, the streaky clouds sweeping high across the deep-blue sky. The ship was moving in the same general direction as the *Golden Hinde.* Drake couldn't be certain whether his prey had spotted him. But even if they had, he suspected they were unlikely to be fearful; only Spanish ships had ever plied Pacific coastal waters. He turned to Prouten. "Let us align our course to overtake this ship. But we shall close the gap in a non-threatening manner."

"Aye sir." Prouten walked off quickly to pass the command.

Garret was at the da Silva's side when Prouten reached the helm to confer with him on the pursuit. "Is it the *Concepcion*?" she asked.

"Do your job and we shall soon have our answer."

For the next several hours, the gap between the two ships narrowed. The crew of the *Golden Hinde* raised the Spanish flag they'd taken from the *San Cristobal,* so as not to alarm their prey. Drake was pleased by Tovery's confirmation that the ship ahead was indeed the *Concepcion*. He maneuvered to take full advantage of the weather gauge. That and the element of surprise would enable him to be aggressive in commandeering the treasure ship.

As they came within hailing distance, Drake ordered the lowering of the Spanish Burgundy and the raising of St. George's Cross. The gun ports popped open. Threatening cannons rolled into firing position, catching the *Concepcion* by complete surprise.

Langton called out on Drake's orders, "Hail *Concepcion*!" He waited for the call to receive proper attention before repeating it. "Hail *Concepcion*! This is Commander Drake of the English ship, *Golden Hinde*. You are now subject to attack. Lower your flag immediately and no harm shall come to you."

Captain Anton, shocked and well aware of just how unprepared he and his crew were to defend an assault on the *Concepcion*, thought immediately about the enormous value of his cargo. How would he be judged were he to surrender? He counted the *Golden Hinde's* guns, now primed and ready; unlike his own. His predator was well-armed. And he'd heard over the years that El Draque was undefeated in battle. Judging his best option was to outrun the pirate, he ordered full sails.

Drake watched the spark of activity on the Spanish deck as they rushed to set more sail and secure the clew lines. He turned to Prouten, "It appears they have not received our invitation with good grace. Let us deliver a little encouragement."

"As you wish, sir," Prouten nodded. He called out to Lee. "Prepare warning fire, if you please." A trumpet blew onboard the *Golden Hinde* announcing their intent. "Shots away," ordered Prouten. In a moment, two cannons roared and recoiled, thrusting out long streaks of orange flame, spearheaded by cannonballs chased only briefly by clouds of black smoke that hung in the air before imploding. Both shots sailed across the bow of the *Concepcion*, sending a showering spray of ocean water high into the air. A loud burst of arquebus bullets peppered the *Concepcion's* sails. The Spaniards took immediate cover, many scrambling below deck.

"Prepare to board, Mr. Prouten," Drake said calmly, observing that the *Concepcion's* crew were unarmed, disorganized, and scurrying on deck. Some of the treasure ship's sails fluttered uselessly as the departing crewmen let go of the lines. There would be no chase. Still, the Spanish flag continued flapping in the wind.

The *Concepcion* rode low in the water, indicating the great weight of its cargo. But its main deck was highly elevated relative to that of the *Golden Hinde*. As their ship came alongside, Drake's raiders hoisted climbing ladders and threw grappling hooks upward, across the *Concepcion's* rails. They scaled the ladders like agile monkeys, scrambling over the side of the ship and onto its deck, swords and pistols drawn. Only a few Spanish hands had remained on deck. Watching armed raiders jump menacingly over the rail, they scattered in search of better cover. Shots rang out in both directions. Ducking and weaving, Prouten, Musa and Garret rushed the captain's quarters. Two guards were posted at the door, swords drawn. Prouten was an experienced swordsman. He paused to see whether a guard might take a swing. He did. Prouten stepped back as the sword swung past and then instantly thrust the point of his own sword directly through the heavy guard's chest and out his back. With his eyes blank and his mouth open, the guard's knees buckled. He dropped to the deck, breathing his last. Prouten withdrew his sword. It offered more resistance than he'd expected.

Garret now had the point of her sword only a few inches from the throat of the second guard. He was frozen, having no desire to suffer his mate's fate. His sword had already hit the deck. He hoisted his hands in the air. The skirmish on deck had already ended abruptly.

"Stand aside," ordered Prouten, nodding his head to one side. The guard stepped away, followed magnetically by Garret's cutlass. Prouten checked the door. It was barred from the inside. He thought for a moment. There was a possibility the captain had more guards inside. Breaking through the door could bring instant death.

"Captain," Prouten shouted, "I am Master's Mate Prouten, of the *Golden Hinde*. We now control your ship. Commander Drake sends his compliments. He asks that we take every measure to ensure your safety. We prefer not to enter by force, putting your life at risk. I ask that you free the door. You have my word—no harm shall come to you."

Captain Anton was fluent in English. He glanced at the two guards in his cabin, considering his options. It seemed unlikely an armed response would favor him. And there was comfort in the apparent sincerity of Prouten's words—he sounded as though he were a man of honor. "Thank you, Mr. Prouten. I am Captain Anton. On your honor, I am prepared to accept your offer. There are two men here with me." He nodded to his guards to lay down their weapons. "They shall surrender their arms. May I have your assurance that no harm shall come to them?"

"You have my word, Captain."

Prouten took Anton prisoner and transferred him to the *Golden Hinde*, where he was piped aboard, befitting a ship's captain. Drake stood on the main deck, waiting. Prouten approached alongside Anton, while Musa and Garret accompanied the Spaniard's principal officer. Anton was a small man, though he had a distinct air of confidence about him. His thick, dark hair matched the color of his prominent eyebrows and penetrating eyes. He sported a neatly trimmed goatee in the fashion of the day. His black coat, embroidered with crossed silver swords, had a narrow white ruff reaching up behind his ears.

Prouten spoke first, "Commander Drake, may I present Captain Anton of the *Concepcion*."

"Welcome aboard, Captain." Drake extended his hand. "Let me begin by apologizing for any damage that has come to your good ship and your men. I shall have my crew work with yours on any necessary repairs."

"Thank you, Commander, that is most kind." Anton's comments struck Drake as surprisingly fluent; almost as though he'd studied at Oxford.

"Of course, you and your men are now officially my prisoners. We shall take ownership of your ship and possession of its contents. I promise you no harm, provided no attempt is made to stand in our way."

"I assure you, none will."

"Excellent. I shall need your patience while we transfer contents of interest to the *Golden Hinde*. In the meantime, you shall be afforded quarters befitting your status."

"As you wish, Commander."

With that, Captain Anton was escorted below deck. Drake ordered his men to sail the two ships further out into the ocean, to prevent their being seen from shore.

Over the next several days, Drake's crew unloaded surprising treasures—numerous chests filled to the brim with coins, twenty-five tons of silver, bars of gold and other valuables and goods. In total, the haul amounted to almost one-half of the Queen's annual tax revenue. It was a remarkable capture, with the death of only one man—Captain Anton's guard.

———

Housed in Prouten's quarters, with Garret as his in-room guard, Captain Anton had become quite fond of this 'young man'. While they were engrossed in conversation, there was a knock at the door.

"Your breakfast, Captain."

"Enter," Anton replied.

"Fresh fish this morning, sir," announced the cook's assistant, setting a tray on the captain's small table. There was also a cup of wine.

"Thank you," said Anton. The assistant turned and left.

"Would you join me, Master Connachan?"

"Thank you, no. I ate earlier, while you slept."

Anton looked Garret in the eye, sampling the fish. "Might I say, Connachan, you have a certain refinement I rarely expect from seafarers. How is it that you came to be part of Commander Drake's crew?"

"My father, sir. He signed me on as a midshipman."

"How old were you at the time?"

"Just turned twelve."

"And did you welcome this life?"

"In truth, I had no idea what to expect. I was rather lonely at first. But my father had spoken highly of the Commander. He felt there was much I could learn."

"Ah, yes. Commander Drake has a reputation as a fine mariner. And he is clearly a gentleman. Still, most in my country think him a pirate. They call him 'El Draque'—the dragon."

"So I have heard."

"Apparently, he trusts you with this important assignment." Anton sipped from his cup.

"He has shown much confidence in me."

"I find you both well-spoken and well-read. Yet, for him to trust you as my personal guard, there must be something more." He sipped again.

"I was well trained as a swordsman."

"Good for you, young man."

His comment pleased Garret. It suggested she was maintaining her secret.

Anton continued, "Might I say, there appears to be something about you that you choose not to share." He grinned and sat back, no longer eating or drinking.

Garret's heart sank. Did he know? Had she given something away during their private conversations over the past couple of days? If so, it could jeopardize her standing with the crew and make things awkward for Drake.

Anton noted Garret's change in mood. Highly observant of human nature, he was now more convinced than ever that Garret was of a certain persuasion—one who enjoyed the company of men over that of women. He leaned in, placing his hand softly on Garret's thigh.

Garret rose abruptly, pushing back on her chair. Her hand instinctively gripped her cutlass. She was speechless.

Anton noticed the shock on her face. He rose, slowly, now regretting his action. "Forgive me. I have made a grave misjudgment."

"Indeed you have, sir. I have no interest whatsoever in your advances. I am a man of honor."

"I promise you, it shall not happen again. I am afraid your manner gave me the wrong impression. I thought perhaps…" he let the comment trail off, not really knowing what to say. An awkward silence left both pondering what came next. Anton spoke first, "We shall not speak of this again. But I trust we might remain friends."

Garret felt her pulse slowing. She nodded, now better understanding the man's actions. Though troubled, she still liked Anton's demeanor and intellect. Their prior conversations had been rich and engaging. She withdrew her hand from her cutlass but remained standing.

Drake also shared time with Anton during his confinement. On one particular day, as the two walked the deck, Garret walked five steps behind, hand-on-cutlass.

"How is it that you find yourself in Pacific waters, Commander?"

"I have longed for things unknown my entire life," Drake replied. "I first saw this ocean while in Panama. It called to me. I could not resist."

"And what have you learned, now that you are here?"

Drake thought for a moment. This ocean was not so different from other waters he'd sailed. But his treacherous crossing of the Strait of Magellan was of some note. "Above all," he replied, "I have learned that no major accomplishment can be achieved on one's own. My success depends entirely on my crew's ability to perform at its best, under the most challenging circumstances."

"You are most wise in this thinking."

"It is merely an observation of fact."

Anton probed a little, "And what do you observe of my guard— young Master Connachan?"

Drake stopped walking and looked at him. It seemed an odd question. He hoped Anton hadn't somehow discovered her secret. "He is among the finest young men of my crew. A future captain, no doubt. He has the required strength of character. And quiet confidence in his abilities. He also shows admirable empathy for his crewmates." As he spoke these words, Garret looked down at the deck, in modesty, allowing herself a brief smile. The sentiment warmed her heart.

"Indeed," agreed Anton. "And wonderful intellect. I commend you for your obvious progress in mentoring him." The two began walking again, Drake winking back at Garret as he turned.

"He is a most pleasant surprise," added Anton.

———

Drake knocked on Anton's door and entered his cabin, carrying a musket and a silver plate. "Good day, Captain."

"And to you, Commander." Anton rose from his chair. Garret also rose.

"I am pleased to report we are returning your ship to your command."

"Thank you, sir."

"As a token of my appreciation for your patience, I should like to present you with this musket. It has been in my family's possession for years. So too this silver plate, with the family name engraved on it." Anton nodded, accepting both, humbled by Drake's thoughtfulness. "I have also set aside a chest of my own silver. I ask that you share it equally among your crew, as thanks for their cooperation."

Drake was well aware of his reputation among the Spanish—as a pirate by those who didn't know him personally, but as a gentleman by those who did. He understood the value the silver plate with his name on it might have for Captain Anton upon his return to Spain. He suspected King Philip might want the plate for himself, and reward Captain Anton handsomely for it; or at least punish him less severely for the loss of the *Concepcion's* treasure.

"I thank you for your kindness toward me," responded Anton, "and for ensuring the safety of my men. We shall part as friends. I hope our two countries might soon come to peace." He extended his hand.

Drake shook the hand heartily. "Farewell then, friend. Perhaps we shall meet again and share memories over a fine meal."

"I welcome such a time, Commander. Under different circumstances, of course. And perhaps you might be so kind as to have young Connachan accompany you," he winked. "He has been a most joyful acquaintance."

Garret and the two men headed to the main deck. Horns announced Anton's upcoming departure. The two captains shook hands once more, demonstrating to their men how leaders, despite their countries' animosities, can still remain gentlemen. They had observed the humanity in each other and cherished the friendship of fellow seafaring officers. But in truth, Anton cherished Garret's friendship more than Drake's. He placed his hand on Garret's shoulder. "Should you become but one-tenth the man your Commander is, you shall be a fine leader."

XXI

As the weeks passed, Drake and his men captured more vessels and raided more villages, amassing still more treasure, ship's supplies, provisions and other cargo. But their activities ended abruptly upon reaching the northern limit of Spanish penetration. Following several days without contact of any kind, Drake stood on the bow of the *Golden Hinde*, contemplating their future direction—north or west. The minor wounds he'd absorbed from the most recent conflicts were healing well, though some remained visible. They added to the legacy of challenges already scribed on his sea-weathered face and body. Perhaps the most notable was the limp he bore from his leg wound at Nombre de Dios. He found it ached in cooler weather.

The stiff, cool breeze blew his long, sandy hair sideways. His thoughts turned to the sailors who had honored themselves in recent clashes. He was particularly impressed by Connachan and Tovery. Both showed promise. From what he'd observed himself, and heard from others, Garret showed surprising passion, fearlessness, and a distinct flair for action. Though Tovery had become increasingly comfortable in combat, he was not as intense. It may have stemmed from his wounded shoulder. Drake was convinced Garret's self-assurance resulted from her extensive military tutoring. She was a truly remarkable swordsman. For most of his crew, that was still a rough skill—one they'd only learned through actual combat. In contrast, Garret's approach was more refined—thoughtful, artful. Some of the men had already approached the young mid for guidance on improving their own swordsmanship. It made Drake smile. If they only knew, he thought.

Still bearing north, beyond the limits of European ventures, there were no maps to guide him or his navigator, da Silva. There had long been discussion and speculation among seafarers about the possibility of a northern passage between the frozen Arctic and the northern coast of the American continent—one that might enable an accelerated return to England. Drake pondered whether to test that theory. As he breathed in the cooler air, many tens of degrees above the equator, Prouten approached, wearing a longer coat than usual.

"What say you, Mr. Prouten? Shall we attempt to find a northern passage?" Prouten knew that finding and traversing the passage, if it even existed, would bring lasting fame. Nonetheless, he had grave concerns. "I worry that potentially freezing weather will challenge us severely. And snow on the land might make it challenging to acquire food and other provisions. There is clearly significant risk, especially as we are now in the latter half of the year. "

"Just so," acknowledged Drake. "Still, let us continue north for a time, hoping to find such a passage before conditions dictate otherwise. If it does exist, and is passable in reasonable weather, then we shall soon dance a jig in Devon." The two stood silently for a few moments, Drake's mind flooded by thoughts of other paths home. One was to reverse course, returning through the Strait of Magellan. That would mean passing through a strengthened line of Spanish defense. Another alternative was to head west across the Pacific, to the East Indies, and on past Africa's southern cape. Though a longer voyage, it would be the first-ever circumnavigation of the globe by an Englishman. For that reason alone, Drake leaned toward challenging the mighty Pacific for immortality. He turned again to Prouten, "I believe a warmer trip across the Pacific is in order. Would you agree?"

Prouten understood the challenges such a lengthy voyage might present. Still, he had high confidence in Drake's ability to tackle and survive whatever the ocean and weather might throw at them. The only unknown segment was from here to the East Indies—one with warmer seas. "I believe the Pacific calls us, sir."

Drake now had two ships, the *Golden Hinde* and a recently captured Spanish frigate. The latter presented an opportunity for his mids to test their recent learning. He gave temporary command of the frigate to his brother, Thomas. Recognizing Garret's promise, he appointed her master's mate. He arranged for da Silva to take William as his new understudy, learning the navigational skills that Garret had already mastered. If inclement weather threatened separation of the two ships, he would detach Prouten to support Thomas.

Later that day, Drake assembled his officers. They arrived in his quarters finding wine on the table. It brought smiles to their faces. They talked and drank until Drake decided it was time to share the news. He banged his fist on the table to gain their attention. "Gentlemen," he opened, winking at Garret as he said the word, "I have made my decision regarding our course home." Everyone but Prouten looked on with great anticipation. "I do not intend to reverse course. There is nothing more to be gained in that direction. Instead, we shall continue briefly north, to find a suitable harbor to provision the ships. We shall then head west to the islands of the East Indies. The

Portuguese have exerted their influence in that part of the world. However, da Silva, here," he nodded to the navigator, " informs me that the native population has enjoyed recent success in pushing back against them."

Prouten responded. "Since our conversation this morning, sir, I have spoken with some of the crew concerning this matter. If I may speak candidly, on their behalf?"

"Of course," Drake nodded.

"Most, though not all, are in fine spirits. Perhaps our success in accumulating treasure has something to do with that," he smiled. The rest of the officers laughed. "To a man, however, they are anxious to return home, to enjoy their newfound wealth. With all respect, sir, they prefer the shortest path."

"A fair point, Mr. Prouten, to be sure. Yet the shortest path by distance may not be the shortest in reality. A return to Magellan's Straits will open us to Spanish challenge. They shall surely be better prepared." The officers nodded to the merit of his statement.

"I cannot disagree," replied Prouten. "When the time comes, I shall counsel the men accordingly."

"Are there any other comments or questions?" Drake asked.

Garret had something to say but chose to hold back. No one else commented either. Drake finished by announcing and toasting the new assignments of Thomas, Garret and William, which the others hailed. When the cheering died down, Drake finished, "Alright then, gentlemen. Drink up. And fair sailing."

As the officers left, Garret stayed behind. "Might I have a word, sir?"

"Certainly. Have a seat." By now, Drake was used to her staying behind to press her case on some matter or other.

"Thank you, Commander. I wish to express a concern."

"I have come to expect that," he smiled, warmly.

"We are in waters that no Englishman has ever sailed. And no real understanding of the risks associated with the Pacific Ocean, or how they may differ from those of the Atlantic."

Drake nodded. "The thought has crossed my mind."

"Señor da Silva assures me it will be a lengthy voyage, with no land to be seen for months. I wonder whether it might be prudent to careen the ships before beginning the cross. It has been some time since we have done that. Doing so would enable us to determine whether these Pacific waters are damaging to the hull in ways we have not seen before."

"Fair point, Master's Mate Connachan." Garret smiled at his formal use of her new title. "We shall do just that."

"Thank you, sir. That is all I wished to say." She began to rise.

"And yet you chose not to say it in the presence of my officers."

"I felt it might be better discussed in private, sir."

"Why so?"

"Frankly, sir, I did not wish to ask a question that might make the other officers feel they were somehow less thoughtful in noting or raising the concern themselves."

Reading something more into her words, Drake suspected her real concern might be that he himself hadn't thought to career the ships before making the cross. And, admittedly, she was ahead of him on the matter. By not raising the point in front of his officers, she had avoided causing him embarrassment. He admired her discretion. He rose from his seat. "You continue to amaze me, Connachan. In so many ways. You should know that a good commander does not always have the answers before his officers do. Indeed, he—or she—relies upon his officers to express their concerns quickly and openly, so that they might be addressed in the moment. No leader can function successfully without open questioning. If you have concerns in the future, you must feel free to share them in front of the others. It is how we increase our collective learning."

"Of course, sir. I apologize for not raising it earlier."

"No, no," he shook his head. "Your apology is unnecessary. My role demands that I make all final decisions. But I am not infallible. I choose to surround myself with the best people—to have the benefit of their thinking. It helps minimize my own mistakes. We are all the better for it. So please, accept my apology for not having prepared you with the confidence to speak openly on such matters."

"As you wish, sir. It is truly an honor to serve under you."

"To serve with me, Connachan. *With* me."

Garret nodded with a smile and left. Drake followed her with his eyes as she exited. She shall make an exceptional leader, he thought. I must do everything I can to accelerate that process.

———

Over the next several days, Drake's two ships skirted the coast in search of a convenient harbor. The weather turned cool, accompanied frequently by thick fog. They spotted an inlet flanked by high hills, promising both good depth in the water and shelter from ocean winds. On his order, the ships sailed through the inlet and turned to larboard at the first opportunity. It wasn't long before the vessels were purposely grounded on a beach near high tide. The cannons and cargo were painstakingly unloaded to lighten their burden on the ships. The crew used ropes to secure the masts to large trees nearby. Using the trees as pullies, they hauled the masts over as far as possible, inspecting the hulls for damage. Days passed as they scraped off barnacles that impeded their ships' speed. They replaced spoiled planks and tarred the exterior, both to prevent leakage and deter organisms from collecting on the wooden frames. Once the process was complete, each ship was reversed, enabling the men to careen the other side. The process took longer than Drake would have preferred but he wished to be thorough. After all, on traversing the Pacific he would be totally reliant upon the seaworthiness of his ships; that and his navigational tools—the astrolabe, cross-staff and compass. And of course, on the spirit of his crew.

With the careening underway, Thomas and Garret led a team that set up camp onshore. They initiated friendly interactions with the indigenous Miwok people. Strangely, the natives believed Commander Drake was a reincarnated ancestral chieftain. They granted him leadership of the tribe and reign over their lands. Drake accepted on behalf of England, informing his officers and noting it in his logbook. This being England's first possession in the Americas, Garret encouraged him to call the territory Nova Albion. Nova was Latin for "new" and "Albion" was the earliest known name for England—something she'd learned from her studies at Ritchfield Academy.

For her part, Garret was much taken with the Miwok children. She loved their curiosity and happy smiles. Before departing, she distributed English coins and gold pesos among them—mementos she hoped they'd cherish. She wondered whether she might ever see them again, just as she wondered about her friend Rose, whom she'd left behind at the Academy. It seemed life had a way of interrupting even the closest of relationships.

When the careening and provisioning were complete, and the weather warm and calm, Drake ordered the men to break camp. They bid farewell to the Miwok and rowed their longboats out to the ships anchored in the harbor, fresh and ready. The natives gathered at the edge of the hills near the shore, watching their visitors depart. They waved in sadness as the two ships left the harbor, heading to open sea, and, they believed, on to the heavens from whence they had come.

XXII

The Pacific Ocean was unexpectedly benevolent. Drake and his men sailed for more than two months without incident, blessed by manageable weather and forgiving winds. Though desperate for any sight of land, nothing had interrupted the ocean's horizon-to-horizon vastness. Then finally, it came—an excited call from atop the mainmast of the *Golden Hinde*. "Land Ho, ahead to Starboard!"

The men on deck rushed to the starboard side, overjoyed and cheering heartily. Prouten ran to Drake's quarters and knocked.

"Enter."

"Thank you, sir. I give you joy of finding land to our nor' nor'west."

Drake smiled. He'd heard the ruckus on deck and knew that nothing else could have generated such jubilant emotion. "Thanks be to God, Mr. Prouten!"

"Aye, sir. Shall you be joining the men on deck?"

"I most certainly will."

The two headed out, finding most of the men at the taffrail. While several were still cheering, a few played musical instruments. Many danced a jig in unfettered delight. Drake smiled broadly. Nearing the landmass of the East Indies, he knew they could now skirt land all the way back to England. Though still thousands of miles away, he could almost smell English soil in the air. For a moment, he let himself dream in earnest for the day when he might once again set foot on his beloved homeland.

The hordes of people and vessels filling the harbor at the bustling port of Ternate surprised Drake. He'd never before seen so many people in such a small area. This was the nominal center of Indonesia's Moluku Islands; home of the deified Sultan Baabullah. He had led these dark-skinned people in freeing themselves from pale-skinned Portuguese oppressors. A sense of joy permeated the very air.

Shortly after anchoring at Ternate, word of Drake's arrival reached the Sultan. He had learned of the famous 'El Draque' through his interactions with the Portuguese and Spanish ambassadors who were still permitted presence at his court. He sent two messengers to invite the legendary commander to an audience at his fortress-turned-palace at São João Baptista, which Drake accepted.

Prouten, Lee, Thomas and Garret accompanied Drake, along with a contingent of lightly armed sailors, including Musa, who had unhappily left his battle-axe onboard ship at Drake's request. As they moved through the hot, humid, dirt streets of Ternate, a growing crowd of onlookers trailed alongside. There was unusual curiosity surrounding this mixed-race entourage bearing a massive, dark chest in a wooden cart. As they reached the outer bounds of the palace, a noisy, babbling crowd waited anxiously, pushing forward to observe the famous pirate and his behemoth black guard. With the

Sultan's overly aggressive soldiers holding the swarm at bay, Baabullah's messenger led Drake's men through the boisterous, clawing crowd, to the palace gate. Once inside, they were ushered into to a museum-like visitation room. The ceilings were twenty feet high, peering down on gold-trimmed entryways and walls covered in fine artwork, draped with a complete rainbow of bright silk fabrics. Massive sculptures were everywhere. The officers looked in amazement at the wide array of jeweled ornaments and accessories. They breathed in the heavy incense that burned from several pots in the room. Musicians played softly on both pipe and string instruments.

Sultan Baabullah was seated in an oversized chair framed in pure gold. He was a tall, able-looking man. His soft, brown skin glistened in the filtered light, his piercing eyes a deep brown. A neatly trimmed black goatee emphasized his sharp jaw. He wore a white silk blouse with gold buttons done up to his neck and a long, black-silk robe with gold-trimmed lapels. His soft black headdress was replete with jewels. Around his neck hung a heavy gold chain. His shoes were a strikingly red leather. Several rings containing turquoise, rubies, emeralds and diamonds adorned his hands. A dozen spear-carrying guards surrounded the throne. To the Sultan's right was a servant with a large palm frond, fanning him in the stifling heat. On his left was a translator, an Italian gentleman who spoke several languages, including Banda, the language of these islands, and passable English.

What a remarkable man Sultan Baabullah was, thought Garret. And so fashionably dressed. Colorful. Tasteful. Either he reflected the rich culture of his people or he was the very architect of it. He was a most handsome man, with a gleaming smile.

The Spanish and Portuguese ambassadors stood at a distance, not pleased in the least by the presence of El Draque and his entourage.

Drake and his men took a knee, in unison. The Sultan uttered a word, in a soft but regal tone. "Arise," said the interpreter.

"Your Great and Honorable Sultan," Drake began, addressing Baabullah and glancing at the translator. "I am Drake, Commander of the good ship *Golden Hinde*. Representative of Her Majesty, Queen Elizabeth of England. I thank you for this audience." The Sultan acknowledged his thanks. "I have brought you gifts from the Americas." Drake waved his hand to the men. They brought forward a chest of gold and silver coins and jewelry, setting it at the feet of the Sultan and opening it. The Sultan looked on, a wide smile emerging on his face.

"The Sultan thanks you for this most generous gift," said the translator. The Spanish ambassador, who was there at the invitation of the Sultan, leaned over and whispered to his Portuguese counterpart. "Dios mio! El Draque steals our treasures and offers them to the Sultan as his own gifts!"

"Our compliments to the Sultan," Drake said. "Please inform him that we are here to trade with his people. We congratulate him on his recent victory over the Portuguese oppressors and their Spanish overlords." Drake looked directly at the two foreign ambassadors with a sly grin. "We are not friendly with the Spanish. Nor the Portuguese. My country is currently in conflict with them. We have come from the Americas, where we challenged their oppressive leadership, just as you have here."

The Sultan smiled, knowing full well the two ambassadors would be fuming at hearing these words. They had no choice but to suffer in silence, in order to maintain their much-valued trading relationship with his islands.

"The Sultan is pleased to hear these words, Commander Drake," said the translator, almost at a whisper, so as not to offend the two ambassadors.

Drake smiled and continued, digging his verbal sword more deeply into the Portuguese ambassador. "We understand the Portuguese have committed heinous acts against your people, and that you have a powerful desire to remove them entirely from your islands." He continued more quietly. "On behalf of England, I am prepared to commit our full support to this cause."

The translator conferred with the Sultan. "Thank you, Commander. The Sultan wishes to know the nature of the support you can provide."

"We have insufficient forces at present to address the Sultan's challenges. But when I return to England, I shall make arrangements with the Queen and her ministers to provide the support you require."

The Spanish and Portuguese ambassadors were unable to hear El Draque's now quieter dialog with the Sultan, but they sensed it was at their expense. They could barely stand still, anxious to expedite word to their own rulers of the presence and brashness of this English dragon, and the potential threat he represented to their trading relationships in the East Indies.

The Sultan responded through his interpreter. "And what is it that you wish in return for such support?"

"With the Sultan's blessing," he said, bowing slightly, "we would ask that England be given exclusive rights to trade with his people for spices and silk."

The translator again conferred with the Sultan, who glanced at the two ambassadors with what seemed like a look of revenge. This was his opportunity to trade for European goods without having to deal with his former oppressors. "This is acceptable," the translator said. "The Sultan wishes you and your officers to dine with him here in the palace, to celebrate this agreement."

It was a stunning banquet that the Sultan had arranged in their honor, featuring a wide variety of meats, fish, rice, vegetables, herbs and spices. Drake's men hadn't eaten well on their long voyage. Nor had they ever tasted food prepared in this way, some of which made them cough from the strength of the spices. Still, they feasted and drank heartily. The interpreter leaned over to Drake. "The Sultan has a favor to ask."

"By all means."

"One of his counselors, a fine young man named Pantas, is desirous of traveling to England with you, as the Sultan's ambassador. Would you be kind enough to honor this request?"

Drake understood the thinly veiled request. This was how the Sultan would hold him accountable for his verbal commitment to provide English support. The Ambassador would serve as a constant reminder of England's obligation and spearhead the negotiations regarding their mutual arrangement.

"But of course," he replied. "It would be my singular pleasure to have Ambassador Pantas accompany us."

"Thank you. At the Sultan's request, I shall deliver a gift of silks and spices in exchange for this favor."

Drake thanked the Sultan through the interpreter, holding his cup in the air to salute him.

The Spanish and Portuguese ambassadors, sitting together at the far end of the table, silently feared whatever it was that the Sultan and the pirata had just agreed to.

"Congratulations on your appointment as Ambassador," Drake said, extending his hand to the caramel-skinned Pantas. A tall, slender young man approaching the age of twenty, he was a beloved nephew of the Sultan. His thick black hair, dark eyes and bright smile gave him a striking, pleasing appearance. He wore a silk robe over a silk blouse, his pants tied at the waist by a silk scarf holding a gleaming dagger with a gold, heavily jeweled handle. Well-schooled, he spoke several languages, including excellent English.

"It is my great honor to accompany you, Commander Drake. I shall be forever grateful."

"The honor is mine, Ambassador. Her Majesty, Queen Elizabeth, shall be pleased to welcome you to her court."

Pantas introduced Drake to his personal aide, Halim, who would accompany him on the voyage and remain with him during his stay in

London. In turn, Drake introduced the two men to Garret. "Master's Mate Connachan shall serve as your personal guide and attendant onboard the ship." Pantas smiled at the fancy title for such a young man, not unlike his own inexplicably lofty designation.

XXIII

Standing at the starboard taffrail on a gusty morning, Pantas sensed it was the coming of a worrisome storm. He gazed out over the distant southern tip of the African continent. Halim was at his side, commenting blandly on the gray dullness of the water, and the seeming convergence of the Indian and Atlantic oceans.

Garret made the turn to starboard on her second circuit of the ship. On her way to Drake's cabin for breakfast with the officers, she'd purposefully left early, needing to flush her lungs. The freshness of the morning breeze liberated the stale air from her quarters below deck. She spotted Pantas and Halim up ahead. It caused her to think about her relationship with the Ambassador. By this point, she and Pantas had spent much time together. His thirst for knowledge of both the ship itself and English culture let flow her passion for her two most treasured topics. Yet despite their many conversations, a critical third topic had never arisen—the secret of her gender. It was becoming increasingly difficult for her to consciously conceal it, given how deeply enamored she'd become of the Ambassador. Her eyes frequently savored his features and mannerisms when he was nearby, though not while he was looking. It was a thrilling new feeling for her—sensual attraction to a man. Perhaps it was his refined nature that drew her interest. It was a trait not displayed by the men of Drake's crew. Not even the Commander himself exhibited such polish and grace. It now occurred to her that through the entire voyage since leaving England, she had never felt anything more than kinship with her fellow crewmates. Even at times when she'd witnessed them relieving themselves, emphasizing the truth of their biological differences, there was nothing that generated in her a sensation of personal or physical attraction…merely a sense of curiosity. She, herself, had always been discreet in handling her necessities.

The difference in her feelings toward Pantas was not entirely self-explanatory. While drawn in by his charm, she understood the folly of making her feelings known to him in any way. She secretly cherished the memory of a moment when he'd brushed by her, touching her accidentally as the ship swayed in the waves. He'd grasped at her arms to steady himself, with a gentleness suggesting a degree of empathy, perhaps even apology. She wished deeply that a time might come when she could judiciously share her feelings with him, so that they might touch in earnest. With purpose.

"Top of the morning Mr. Ambassador; Halim," she said, bowing slightly and nodding to each in turn. "I trust you slept well."

"I find I am becoming more adept at embracing the sleeping arrangements," Pantas smiled. Garret smiled back, knowing he was referring to the use of a hammock. Her mind wandered, imagining herself swaying in one with him, yet realizing that could never happen onboard the ship.

Halim sensed an opening in Garret's pause. On Pantas' behalf, he raised a point they had jointly pondered for some time. "I must say, Master Connachan, I find it most interesting that you hold such a significant role for someone so young."

Garret smiled. "The same might be said of the Ambassador."

"Indeed it might," Pantas smiled. His white teeth gleamed against his caramel skin. "In my case, the Sultan favors me as his nephew. Though I must admit some surprise at his entrusting me with this responsibility. He is a most generous leader."

"As is Commander Drake. He has mentored me for some three years now. I hope to justify his confidence in me."

"Then we have something in common," Pantas replied. As he said it, he sensed a budding closeness between them. Something about this young man appealed to him, though he couldn't label it.

"Indeed. Well, gentlemen, I must leave, to join the Commander for breakfast."

"Then we shall continue our dialogue later," Pantas nodded.

"I look forward to that. Perhaps we can meet on the foredeck in an hour's time." Garret bowed slightly and took her leave.

Pantas watched Garret go, walking with the confident swagger of a seasoned sailor. But there was a degree of refinement in her walk that Pantas hadn't observed in the other crew members. He leaned over to Halim. "What think you of Master Connachan?" he asked in his native tongue.

"There is something more than can be seen. A certain…mysticism."

Pantas nodded without saying anything. Mysticism indeed, he thought.

———

The noise in the Captain's quarters almost hurt the ears, now that the officers had finished consuming their breakfast. Laughing and shouting over each other, they were enjoying a moment they hadn't shared in some time, their being divided between two ships. "Gentlemen," Drake interrupted, pounding the butt of his pistolet on the table. "Order, if you please." The cacophony dissolved into silence. "Thank you. Now, to the business of the day. We are about to make our turn to the northwest. We shall skirt the coast of Africa, careful to avoid being visible from the shoreline and drawing potential confrontation. Our next stop shall be the Cape Verde Islands, for final provisioning. Let us proceed in haste but with caution. In the event we become separated in severe weather, we shall assemble at Praia do Portinho, on the southern tip of the large island."

Thomas, seated next to Garret, leaned closer to her, "It will not be long before we are home. I cannot wait."

Garret nodded agreement. "We must make a point of remaining in touch once we are back. I cherish my friendship with you and William. I have no desire to lose that."

"Indeed. Friends always." He raised his cup in salute. She responded in kind.

"To England," Drake exclaimed, his glass raised.

"Huzzah," cheered the officers.

The voyage to Praia do Portinho seemed excruciatingly long, though it really wasn't—it was the men's anticipation that pulled at their hearts like an anchor in tow. When they finally arrived, they spent a few days hurriedly conducting minor repairs and securing provisions. Pantas and Garret arranged a moment to sit together on the shore in private, near where the ships were anchored. A brilliant sun warmed them. Its heat was lightened by a modest breeze. "I trust we are not long for England," said Pantas.

"We are so close I can almost smell the docks of Plymouth," Garret smiled.

"What is it you shall do once you are home?"

"I shall spend time with my family. It has been far too long since I last saw them. I have much to share."

"Halim and I shall go on to London, of course. Will you be joining us there?"

"I will, yes, at the Commander's request. It is the last thing I must do before seeing my family."

"Then perhaps you might be kind enough to acquaint me with the city while we are there."

Garret looked into Pantas' dark eyes. They made her heart flutter. She hoped she wasn't blushing, yielding evidence of her true self. Perhaps in London, if she could be alone with him, she might finally share her secret. "It would be my pleasure, Mr. Ambassador."

"Please," he said, "after all this time, call me Pantas."

She nodded. "Thank you, Pantas. You may call me Garret."

In the days that followed, the ships sailed on past the Strait of Gibraltar. They gave Portugal a wide berth and sailed by the northwest corner of Spain and the west coast of France. Finally, after three long but adventurous years since departing England, the ships sailed into Plymouth Sound, completing their historic circumnavigation of the globe—the first Englishmen to do so. Unfortunately, disease was spreading throughout the city. Drake ordered his ships to anchor in the harbor. He would wait patiently for word when it would be safe to disembark. In the meantime, he sent Prouten and Garret ahead to London on a smaller vessel, to deliver news to Queen Elizabeth that he had arrived home, accompanied by an ambassador from Indonesia. Pantas and Halim traveled with them, anxious to see the storied city.

———

Arriving in London, Prouten and Garret walked along the Thames. Ambassador Pantas and Halim trailed behind. Clouds filled the sky, casting a light drizzle on the street.

"It is a strange feeling," said Garret. "We have been so long at sea that my mind seems confused by the lack of movement beneath my feet."

Prouten laughed. "Indeed. Yet it is God's blessing that we are back on English soil. In time, you shall appreciate that."

"Oh, I appreciate it even now. Still, my heart longs for all the beauty this world has to offer outside of England. How fortunate are we to have both?"

Prouten nodded. "I have no doubt we shall soon return to the oceans with the Commander. For as long as I have known him, when he is not sailing them, he is planning his next voyage on them. It is his passion."

"I have learned so much these past few years. How lucky I am to have sailed with him. And with you, of course."

"How lucky we both are," Prouten clarified. He paused for a moment. "And yet, how fortunate is he to have had a young student with as much promise as you," he smiled. "You represent the next generation of English seafarers. You shall be their bowsprit, leading them in the principles and traditions of the Commander."

Garret had never thought in those terms. She took pride in Prouten's words. Comfort too. It was pleasing to know he'd gained such confidence in her since that day at Plymouth harbor when he'd placed his hand on her shoulder. It seemed forever ago. The two walked on in silence.

Though he was in awe of the sights and sounds of this bustling city, Pantas found his eyes most frequently drifting to young Garret in front of him, still intrigued by the manner of Garret's walk. He didn't fully understand his own fascination with it.

The four messengers checked into Orion's Tavern. Prouten arranged for a message to be sent to the Queen at Richmond Palace and requested two rooms, one for Pantas and Halim, the other for himself and Garret. Garret was immediately concerned. How difficult would it be, she wondered, to conceal her gender while changing her linens—especially now that her breasts had made their full appearance. Daniel had prepared her for their eventual emergence but hadn't guided her on how best to conceal them. Though she'd always worn her blouse loose, she noticed, particularly in cooler weather, that her nipples would announce their presence against lighter materials. As a result, she'd taken to wearing heavier blouses. Or a doublet. When choosing not to wear a doublet, she folded and strapped a silk scarf around her breasts, to conceal them. It wasn't always comfortable but then, what choice did she have? She longed for a time when such measures would be unnecessary.

Following dinner in the tavern on their first evening, the four headed to their rooms. Prouten chose to retire early. Garret felt it would be best to wait. She sat on a chair, next to a candle, opening a book she'd been reading. Prouten proceeded to change his linen undergarments. She kept her eyes tightly focused on her book while he did so, though intense curiosity ultimately moved her, at just the right moment, to direct her eyes toward him; without moving her head. She stared briefly at his naked, well-crafted body— his shoulders broad, his back muscled, his buttocks firm. He turned slightly, his manhood hanging low from a puff of dark, curly hair. A strange sensation came over her. Though she'd seen many before, they were usually in the process of streaming fluid. This one was not. It hung freely. She forced herself to look away, fighting an urge to take just one more glimpse. Prouten pulled on clean linens. "Do you care which side?" he asked, climbing into the bed.

Her immediate thought was 'the front'. But she caught herself blushing, realizing he was referring to the bed. "No. Either is fine, thank you."

He pulled the covers up over his shoulders and closed his eyes. About fifteen minutes later Garret heard his rough breathing. She closed her book, quietly changed her own linens behind him, and crawled into the bed. There was barely room for her. She turned on her side, away from him, feeling his warm body against hers. She hoped dearly that he wouldn't accidentally discover anything in the middle of the night.

Garret found it hard to sleep. But it wasn't just Prouten's guttural noises; it was the many thoughts swirling in her head. Daniel had never told her what to expect of intimate relations between men and women, though Prouten's features had sprung some ideas in her head. She thought for a long while about the handsome young Indonesian Ambassador, and his own private assemblage. It was quite some time before sleep won out.

XXIV

"How did you sleep last night?" asked Pantas.

Garret hesitated, instantly recalling the naughty thoughts that had kept her up late. "Well, thank you. Very well," she smiled.

"More tea, if you please," Prouten called out to the tavern keeper. The man scurried to the back. Halim noticed some crumbs had spilled onto the table. He brushed them off.

A commotion outside drew everyone's attention. Queen Elizabeth's messenger and a royal honor guard had pulled up. The messenger entered, approaching the keeper. "I have a message for a Charles Prouten."

"That would be me." Prouten stood.

The messenger approached, bearing a sealed note. "Charles Prouten, of the *Golden Hinde*?"

"That I am, sir." Prouten extended his hand.

The messenger extended the note. "From Her Majesty, The Queen, sir."

"I thank you kindly."

The messenger turned and left as Prouten unsealed the message. "An invitation for an audience with the Queen. One week hence."

"Are we all to attend?" queried Garret.

"Drake and his officers," Prouten smiled. "And, of course, the Ambassador and his aide. There shall be a banquet to follow." Everyone joined Prouten's smile. They would be properly celebrated.

The approaching noise of several horse-drawn carriages and wooden carts attracted crowds through the countryside. The carriages were immaculately cleaned and the carts heavily laden with chests of gold, silver, spices, silks and jewels. Word of Drake's exploits and treasures had already spread well beyond Plymouth. So it was no surprise that his procession faced a massive sea of humanity as it neared London. Pushing through the crush of people, Drake ordered a stop at Orion's Tavern, to pick up Ambassador Pantas and Halim, who had stayed there these last several days. They headed on to Richmond Palace, amid the exuberant cheers of commoners bouncing off the cobblestones. The caravan triumphantly approached the palace grounds, seemingly pulling along a horde of onlookers.

Queen Elizabeth waited inside until word came that the procession had reached the courtyard. Drake and his officers, tired from their travel, stepped out of the creaking carriages, dressed in their finest. Broad smiles lightened their faces. Some of the men, led by Musa and Caber, carried a small parade of heavy chests. Once the adventurers were assembled and ready, the painted-faced Queen and her entourage emerged to greet them. Drake knelt on the step. His officers and men also took a knee. Complete silence followed, in anticipation of the Queen's remarks.

"My dearest Commander. I am most joyful of your return. You have brought great distinction to our Empire. I am anxious to have you share the events of your historic voyage. Please rise and join me inside."

"Thank you, Your Majesty." Drake rose to his feet, "I remain your humble servant. I shall be honored to share our remarkable experiences, sailing the world in your name. But first, let me present to you the honorable Ambassador of Sultan Baabullah of Indonesia—Ambassador Pantas."

Though he'd already risen, Pantas once again took a knee. "Your Majesty," he bowed, "It is my utmost honor to meet you. And to be of service to you."

"Arise, Ambassador. You are most welcome to my court. I have heard wonderful things concerning your Sultan. His success in fighting off the scourge of other countries inspires us. I trust he is well."

"He is, Your Majesty. He sends his kindest regards. And these gifts." He motioned to his aide, Halim, who requested the men behind him to bring forward the chests sent by the Sultan. As they were opened, the sun glanced brilliantly off the gold and shimmering silks within. Jewels in the dark wooden chests sparkled and twinkled like colored stars against a night sky.

"These are exquisite, Mr. Ambassador," the Queen smiled.

"The Sultan hoped you would be pleased."

"You may assure him that I am. Exceedingly so."

Drake waited a moment for the Queen to turn to him. When she did, he waved his right arm toward the men standing by the remaining chests. "My men and I would like to present you with a small token of our thanks for your most gracious support." As had become his practice, he winked at Garret, as recognition that she was certainly included in his words: *my men*.

The officers and aides brought forward the remaining, heavy chests. They overflowed with gold and silver coins and bars, and colorful jewels. The Queen again smiled broadly. No words needed to be exchanged. Her delight was obvious. She took Drake's arm. "Come Commander, let us celebrate this wondrous voyage of yours."

Elizabeth escorted Drake and his officers into the palace, where she had arranged an astounding banquet in their honor. They dined with members of the royal court, carefully selected members of Parliament, and ambassadors from other countries, enjoying the finest meats of several kinds, along with fruits, a wide array of desserts, and no shortage of fine wines.

With the banquet nearing its end, Drake and the Queen retired to a private room. It was a small room with a domed ceiling and rich purple carpeting. Grand artworks, beautifully and colorfully painted, hung on all four walls, accented by flowing velvet draperies trimmed in gold. The two sat and enjoyed a cup of port. Drake spoke of his travels, his numerous encounters with the Spanish, his observations of the Pacific Ocean, and his capture of abundant treasures. For two hours, they fully immersed themselves in conversation, the Queen being completely engaged by his stories. Her imagination came alive with the many places he described. They both found the time passed quickly.

"Commander," Elizabeth said, finally rising from her chair. "You have accomplished much on behalf of our Empire. Perhaps more than all but a handful of Englishman before you. I think it reasonable that you set aside a fair portion of the treasures you have brought home—for yourself, your officers and your crew. They are well-earned. I ask that you inventory the balance for the Admiralty Court. They shall arrange for its transportation to the Tower, to be stored and held for the benefit of our beloved country."

Drake had risen with her. "I am profoundly grateful for your kindness and support, Your Majesty. I shall make these arrangements. I hope we might soon visit again. I have many more stories to share. And perhaps we can discuss future endeavors I might embark upon, for the glory of England."

"Most certainly. I look forward to it."

"Excellent. Then I wish you good day and good fortune." He reached out and brought the back of her extended hand to his lips. "Until our next meeting, then."

It was late and dark when Drake's carriages left the palace grounds. Still, small crowds mingled along the streets, hoping to catch another glimpse of the man. Cheers once again filled the path. Drake felt a warm connection to the crowd. They were commoners, just as he had once been. And his father before him. He breathed in their support with pride, thanking them by having his men distribute gold and silver coins among them.

The widespread happiness and good spirits in England were not echoed in Spain. King Philip was outraged by Drake's exploits and success—

at his expense. He sent word to Queen Elizabeth, seeking the return of all treasures El Draque had pirated from the Spanish empire. But Elizabeth had no intent to honor his request. In her mind, the treasure now rightfully belonged to England, as the spoils of the undeclared war between the two countries. She understood their expanding ill-will might well lead to an all-out confrontation between the two nations. But Spain would have to make the first move. She sensed that would bring them disfavor among other European countries who also feared the imposing beast, thereby pushing them toward a deeper alliance with England. In the meantime, she appreciated Drake's efforts in service of the country's interests—without requiring her more formal, written authority. It provided her both distance and options.

————

"If you wouldn't mind, sir, I wish to keep an appointment with a friend." Garret was nervous in asking the favor, but she'd already sent a messenger to alert her friend to the appointed place and time.

Drake wasn't particularly pleased. He and Garret had spent the past two weeks in London, taking advantage of the currency of his accomplishments. They were raising capital and support for his next voyage. Garret had been by his side at his request. He was convinced that her superior intellect, charming youth, and surprising diplomatic skills would prove valuable as he attempted to win over investors. And she'd proven him right. She was cunningly adept at helping him negotiate the terms and conditions of their investments. Her grandfather had obviously schooled her well on the management of her family's finances and business interests. Now here they were, taking a break during an extended negotiation, and the last thing Drake needed was for her to be unavailable for some period of time. "I am afraid that is not possible, Connachan. I need you here with me."

"Certainly you can handle these next two investors without me, Captain. They admire you. It would be an honor for them to have you accept their money," Garret smiled.

"Still…" Drake protested.

"No, sir. I shall have my personal time. I have earned it."

Drake hesitated. Damn this woman, he thought, though he knew she was right. But why couldn't she simply accept his orders, like everyone else did? It pained him. Still, what choice did he have? He certainly didn't want to lose her services. "Alright, then. But be brief about your visit."

"I shall see you in two days, then."

"Two days?"

"Yes, sir. Unless I choose to take a third."

She was toying with him now. And he knew it.

"Get thee gone, seadog. I shall expect you on Friday."

"Agreed. Thank you, sir."

Drake hadn't asked who her friend was, nor did Garret volunteer that information. She was excited to be meeting with the handsome young Indonesian Ambassador. And sharing something rather personal with him.

The two young voyagers met at Orion's Tavern. Halim waited outside. Pantas noticed that Garret was dressed in naval finest, sporting a white ruffed collar and black, broadband hat, accented with a flowing auburn feather. "It is my great pleasure to see you again, Master Connachan."

"Garret," she reminded him. He nodded. She continued. "I thank you for your willingness to see me."

The tavern owner interrupted, "Tea, sir?"

"Yes, and a scone, if you please."

The server nodded and left.

Pantas resumed the conversation, "I was surprised to learn you were still in London. I thought you were anxious to be home with your family."

"I have been deeply engaged with the Commander, arranging financing for his next voyage. But candidly, I had hoped to see you once more before returning home. I value your friendship, Mr. Ambassador."

"Pantas," he reminded her.

"Yes, of course, Pantas," she smiled.

"I, too, value our friendship. I hope it may extend well into the future. I imagine you can be most helpful to my cause here."

Garret looked at him closely. His thoroughly engaging dark eyes seemed so very deep. She sensed her own eyes trying to find their far end. It was distracting, slowing her from saying what she'd planned before the opportunity passed. Would he be receptive to her sharing her secret, she wondered—or simply shocked and appalled. But what choice was there, really? If not now, then when?

Their discussion continued with reminiscences and observations of London. The owner delivered Garret's tea and scone. After he left, Garret finally opened the door, carefully, "I wish to share something personal with you, Pantas. Something you must swear never to disclose to anyone, for it would ruin me."

"My goodness. What could it be?"

"Do I have your word, then?"

"Most assuredly. Upon my death."

She looked directly into his eyes, delivering the words she'd gone over many times in her mind, preparing for this moment, "I am not exactly the person you perceive me to be." She said it softly, allowing the words to float gently in the air, hoping to judge his reaction. She removed her hat, letting her freshly washed hair flow with a small flip of her head. Its long, knotted tail, which she'd maintained since her earliest days at sea, had been carefully undone this very morning. She ran her hand through her hair. A silence hung softly between them as Pantas pondered her statement, observed the fullness of her hair, and noticed something different about her eyes, not entirely certain what it was. They seemed more…inviting? Garret reached for his right hand, touching it softly while she smiled, coyly. It was an unmitigated assault of every subtle clue she could muster.

"Allah be with me!" Pantas whispered, suddenly piecing together her subliminal messaging. "Can this be?"

She knew instantly that he'd picked up on her signals. "Indeed, it can."

"But how?" He shook his head in wonder. "Why?"

"It is a long story. For another time." She glanced around the tavern to check whether anyone was looking on. Then, slowly, she returned her hat to her head, tucking her hair back beneath the ruffed collar. She kept her hand on his. Though tanned, it was still light against his caramel skin.

Her hand sent a wave of warmth up Pantas' arm and into his heart. For the first time, he saw Garret for the appealing young teenager she was. He fought to suppress a sudden urge to place his left hand on hers, realizing that might not be prudent in such a public place. Slowly withdrawing his right hand from her touch, he smiled back, "Perhaps we can meet in a more private venue, where you can share your long story with me."

Garret finished taking a sip of her tea. She placed the cup on the table. "There is a park nearby, next the river. Tomorrow, as the sun is setting, you should visit this park. You shall meet a young woman there." She pushed back her chair and rose from the table. "I wish you good day, Pantas. Until we meet again—for the first time."

He rose from his chair. "Good day indeed, my good sir," he replied, teasingly.

———

Green was the right color, Garret thought. It seemed to go best with her auburn-colored hair. She had hoped to look up her old friend, Rose Doughty, both to catch up and to confer with her on the right outfit to wear to her first meeting with Pantas…as a woman. Never having worn a dress before, she could have used her friend's support. But she hadn't yet connected with Rose following her father's death. It would be impossible to console her and, at the same time, discuss the wearing of a proper dress. Besides, Rose still knew her as a male. That alone would make things awkward. She had left her meeting with Pantas at Orion's Tavern the day before, contemplating all of this. In the end, she'd decided to visit a fine dressmaker's shop, to seek the assistance she needed. The old woman, though surprised beyond measure, had softened when Garret explained how her father's decision had given rise to her dilemma. She had agreed to help and had a dress that, with a modest degree of tailoring, would serve the purpose. And so it was that Garret, umbrella in hand, now walked across the open grass field in the park alongside the Thames.

Pantas could scarcely believe his eyes. Yet he was convinced the woman approaching in a green dress, topped with a white ruff, was Garret. Her body movement, her smile, her hair—they all shouted Garret. He rose awkwardly, taken by her subtle yet obvious beauty. She laughed at his stumble as he rose. "Are you so shocked at my appearance that you have lost control of your legs?"

"I am…" he paused, searching for the right word in English, "…befuddled."

"Befuddled? Is that truly the best you can do?" Garret teased.

"You are as fair as the…"

Garret waited for it. He couldn't find the words. She broke the awkwardness, "As fair as a sailor in a dress."

They laughed together. He drew close. "May I?"

"That depends. What did you have in mind?"

He placed his hands softly on her hips. "Just, to hold you. To look at you."

"I see. And is that all?"

"I wish to orient my mind to the real you. The one before me. This beautiful…young… woman."

"You mean, not the pirata the Spanish would have me be?"

He drew her closer. "Perhaps the most treasured pirata who ever sailed the world's oceans. Treasured by her beauty, not by her prizes."

"Prizes of a different kind, then?"

His head moved close. His right hand touched the bottom of her chin. "Indeed. The most treasured of prizes." He pressed his lips against hers. Softly.

XXV

Gusty winds blew through the port of Deptford, pushing chilly air down the necks of the boisterous, still-growing crowd assembling at the harbor. They anxiously awaited the Queen's arrival. The excitement of this historic moment was palpable. Elizabeth and her entourage, including several ambassadors, approached in glistening coaches accompanied by resplendent cavalry, causing nearby pigeons to scatter into the breeze and take wing. When the procession stopped, the hum of the crowd rose to a crescendo at Her Majesty's appearance, triggering dogs to bark frantically.

Drake had sailed the *Golden Hinde* to Deptford at the Queen's request. She'd chosen this place as the most appropriate venue for the ceremony at which the Commander would be knighted. As she exited her carriage and ascended the long wooden steps to the ship's deck, the crowd's cheers overwhelmed her. She turned to acknowledge them, slipping slightly as she did so. A guard reached out to steady her.

Brass horns announced the monarch's arrival onboard. The crew of the *Golden Hinde*, having spent days readying the ship, stood back in their finest attire, giving Elizabeth and her entourage space. Drake stood in front of his officers as she approached, a broad smile on her face. She stopped in front of him. Drake dropped to one knee and kissed her extended hand.

"Welcome aboard, Your Majesty."

"Please, remain kneeling," she commanded. She looked around, acknowledging the large crowd assembled on the deck. Then she looked back at Drake, raising her voice for all to hear. "It is my immense pleasure, Commander Drake, to bestow upon you England's most precious honor."

Drake bowed his head. A brief, hallowed silence was broken by a gilded sword, unsheathed and handed to the Queen. Under normal circumstances, she would have knighted him by dubbing his shoulders with the sword. But this was an unusual time. Elizabeth was intent on obtaining a display of support from the French for Drake's extraordinary actions. It would send a strong message to King Philip of Spain. She took the sword and handed it to the French ambassador, Monsieur de Marchaumont. As de Marchaumont touched the sword to Drake's right shoulder, and then to his left, the Queen spoke, "My dearest Commander Drake. In recognition of your historic endeavors to bring the highest honor and celebrated fortunes to the English Empire, I hereby pronounce you Knight of the Realm, of England." She paused for a moment and looked at him with a smile. "Arise, *Sir* Drake!"

Drake rose to speak the oath. "My most gracious and generous Queen. I shall obey the laws of England and honor my peerage. I shall defend the realm, its lands, its Queen and its people. I dedicate myself to the noble pursuit of honesty and justice. I pledge myself to the support of my fellow man. I dedicate myself to the persecution and cessation of poverty and hunger. I further pledge myself to the protection of the weak. And I dedicate myself to the cause of Good and the fight against Evil and Injustice."

A rousing cheer on deck ushered in England's newest knight. The assembled crowd smothering the grounds of the harbor couldn't see the actual knighting. But hearing the cheers emanate from the ship, they roared their own approval, with unfettered joy—a prolonged and vociferous recognition for a much-loved hero.

Touched by the moment, Garret felt tears begin to form in her eyes. She was witnessing history for a man she deeply admired and loved platonically. Hearing him speak the oath, she'd felt an affinity for the ideals on which knighthood was based. She knew from her studies that, in its earliest form, knighthood was simply purchased by men of great wealth. Yet here was a man who had earned it through his actions. It meant so much more in this instance. So very much more. She felt blessed to have been part of this epic journey, with the legendary commander as her leader and mentor. As she often did, she harkened back to the moment when she'd stood alone on the cobblestones overlooking Plymouth Harbor, uncertain what future lay before her—on the verge of a different kind of tears. If she'd only known then what she knew now, she wouldn't have been so sad. Her heart would have been bursting with anticipation and excitement. She could barely wait to head home, to share the stories of her adventures with Daniel—the man she knew only as her father.

XXVI

While Drake continued his initial affairs in London, Garret was by his side at every turn. She'd proven exceedingly helpful in wringing every last pence from investors. But when not accompanying Drake, Garret busily pursued her own passions. Her relationship with Pantas had become an obsession. Beyond simple friendship, it had evolved into an exploration of shared intimacy—something they were learning together. For the first time in her life, she was experiencing what it truly meant to be a woman—to feel differently about men; about herself. It was liberating beyond measure. Yet she was still confined in her interactions with others. It only heightened her longing for complete freedom to express who she truly was.

In time, Drake concluded his affairs and headed home to Devon. Garret felt torn; anxious. It was time to return to her own family—Daniel and Gwendolyn, still completely unaware they were not her actual father and older sister but rather her grandfather and mother. Before leaving, she arranged one final meeting with Pantas at Orion's Tavern. She wasn't surprised upon entering to find him already there. The man was always thoughtful of others and the preciousness of their personal time. So much so, that he was committed to never making anyone wait for him. She admired his obvious empathy for others.

As Garret approached, Pantas rose, with sadness in his eyes. He knew she was leaving and was uncertain when he might see her again.

"Good morning, my friend," he said, walking toward her, arms open. He wanted to say 'dearest' rather than 'friend' but here in this place, where she was known by some as one of Drake's men, it wouldn't have been appropriate. She entered his arms and hugged him as any man might hug another. Both knew there was more to their hug than onlookers could ever imagine. Her hair was once again in a knotted seaman's tail, as it always had been but for the time when she had shared her secret with Pantas.

"Good morning, Pantas," Garret said rather formally. "It is always a pleasure to meet with you." She winked and smiled as she said it, signaling her enjoyment of the pleasures they'd shared in his room on prior occasions, including yesterday.

They both sat. Those in the tavern who were watching returned to their own conversations. Pantas looked her in the eyes, loving the way the light filtered through the window to brighten their green color. "You light the room this morning," he whispered.

"God knows why that might be," she replied playfully, knowing full well that her joyful mood following yesterday's encounter was shining through.

"I am beside myself, knowing you will be gone. I wish I were free to accompany you. London shall be a lonely place while you are away."

The owner of the tavern brought her a cup of tea and a scone, her usual order. He placed it on the table. "Will there be anything else, sir?"

"Thank you, no," she said, reaching into her pocket for a coin. "I shall be traveling again, but I do hope to enjoy your fine scones upon my return."

"Thank you, sir," he said, taking the coin. It represented a large overpayment. "It is always a pleasure to serve you." He smiled gratefully, nodded, and left the table.

"Have you decided how long you shall be gone?" Pantas asked.

"However long is simply too long. I shall be thinking of you constantly." As she said it, she glanced around the room, to confirm no one but Pantas was listening. "I shall send word the moment I know when my return shall be."

"It cannot be soon enough. I am most anxious to pick up precisely where we left off."

————

Seeing her daughter approach on horseback, down the long lane leading to the stately residence, a small crack spread through the great wall of sorrow cemented inside her. A manservant opened the door for Gwendolyn as she stepped out into the daylight, to welcome the girl home.

Garret dismounted her steed, looking as confident and in-control as any fine young man might. She strode toward Gwendolyn with a man's athleticism as well, doffing her fine black hat, the knotted tail of her auburn hair bouncing behind. She was radiant in her mother's eyes, which only made the much-troubled woman even more sad. Garret embraced her with a warm, lasting hug befitting the length of time they'd been apart. Gwendolyn was overcome, unable to utter words she couldn't form.

"What a pleasure to be home," said Garret, hoping her cheerfulness might somehow raise the normally depressed spirits of the woman she knew only as her much older sister. She pulled back to look her in the face, searching for some sign of happiness. There was none; simply tears.

"I love you, Gwen," she whispered, pulling her close again. "Tell me, how is grandfather?"

Gwendolyn said nothing, simply pointing toward the door. Garret took her arm. The two women walked inside, one strong and confident, the other a frail, near-empty vessel. The manservant followed.

"Garret!" exclaimed Daniel with all the strength of voice he could muster, which wasn't much above a raspy whisper. "You are a comfort to my soul." He coughed, excessively.

Garret was shocked to find him seated in a chair, wrapped in a blanket, looking gaunt and weak. The man had seemed so healthy and vibrant when she last saw him. She knelt beside his chair, taking his hand in hers and kissing his forehead. It was moist from some unknown illness.

"You poor dear." She turned to the manservant. "Bring me some water, if you please."

"God bless you, Garret. How I have missed you." Daniel's throat hurt so badly he struggled to say the words.

"And I, you, father. Too much time has passed."

He coughed again, this time spitting up bits of blood mixed with saliva. The manservant brought a small bowl of water and a linen cloth. Garret took the cloth, dipped it in the water and wiped his forehead. She wiped the red spittle from his lower jaw.

"Have you heard the news, father?" It was a rhetorical question. She didn't wait for an answer, recognizing that speaking caused him pain. "I have sailed the globe with Commander Drake. There is so much I wish to share with you." He coughed again. The words he'd already spoken made it difficult to say much more. She continued, fearing she might never have a better opportunity than this very moment to express her thanks to the man.

"Father, there is something I must tell you." She squeezed his hand, lovingly. "You have been my life's inspiration. All that I have accomplished has been done on the foundation you laid for me. I cannot thank you enough." His eyes looked deeply into hers and blinked. The emotions he was feeling inside made this the only way in which he could acknowledge her thanks. His head fell backward slightly. He closed his eyes, soaking in the moment he'd so longed for.

Daniel's health was failing badly. Garret suspected this visit with him might well be her last. She committed herself to making the most of what little time was left. She was also concerned about her poor sister's future well-being. Through the years, Gwendolyn had recoiled into a shell, according to the manservant, seldom venturing beyond the house. She was incapable of caring for herself. Garret knew difficult decisions lay ahead.

With the manservant's help, Garret arranged to take Daniel out on his boat, as they'd done frequently when she was younger. They'd shared so much time together on this boat that it had become their place to share stories, reminiscences and innermost thoughts.

Daniel's mood seemed somehow brightened, here on the calming water. Watching Garret skillfully maneuver the boat, he beamed with pride over everything she'd accomplished at such a youthful age. She was still a teenager but had already traveled the globe and seen much more of its civilizations than he could ever have imagined. He was impressed by her maturity, self-confidence and exceptional poise. There was no question but that she would be an excellent successor to the management of his properties and businesses. He felt it was time for her to leave the sea-faring life and attend Magdalen College, to study the law.

Garret loved Daniel dearly. But given her concern over his frailty, she knew the time had come to raise the question that had lurked in the back of her mind the entire time she was at sea, surrounded by men, irritatingly and continuously conscious of her hidden womanhood—what were her his true underlying motivations for raising her as a boy? He'd told her it was to make things easier for her—to give her every advantage he'd once had. Yet her experience was that she'd had to deal with enormous challenges she wouldn't otherwise have had to face. She had to know the root of his decision. Things were becoming extremely complicated. She had no facial hair, nor the deep voice of a male, making it increasingly difficult to continue the façade. What's more, she now had to dig her way out of the hole she'd dug with the rest of Drake's crew. The longer she waited, the deeper that hole would get.

"Father, I must speak frankly with you."

"When have you not?" Daniel coughed with the words, keeping him from smiling the way he might have wished.

Garret waited until he was looking her straight in the eye. Her next remarks weren't something he could be less-than-fully attentive to. "I have reached a time in my life where presenting myself as a man has become enormously awkward."

Daniel dropped his eyes. He'd known this conversation must come at some point. He'd preferred it would be at his initiation, not hers. But he realized he'd waited too long.

"Look at me, father. Please," Daniel looked up. "You know that I have been true to your wishes, despite the challenges I have faced." He nodded. "I cannot continue in this fashion. I realize that changing my story now might damage your own reputation. But I want..." She hesitated. "No. I *need* your support."

Again, Daniel nodded without saying anything, to let her finish.

"I have thought about it constantly, as you can well imagine. Yet I cannot fully understand why you decided I should be raised as a boy." Daniel remained quiet, preserving his strength for the words he would need to utter. Garret sensed she needed to ask him a direct question, to generate a response. "Can you fully explain your reasoning to me?"

It was then that she noticed the sorrow in Daniel's face; the tears brimming low in his eyes. Unable to speak, he held up his hand, as if to ask for time. He slowly reached his frail hand into his pocket, pulling out a wrinkled handkerchief, which he dabbed carefully to his eyes. He composed himself with a deep breath, mustering strength for this important moment.

"I am so sorry." His voice was raspy, hesitant. "But I do not regret my decision." He took another moment to gather strength. "There is so much more to the story. And much sadness in it." He dropped his head.

Garret felt a sudden sorrow for the man she loved so dearly. She put her hand on his shoulder. "I love you, father. I am a big girl now. Surely you can tell me."

"I am not certain where to begin." He coughed, shuffled his position, and struggled to find strength. "First, let me tell you of a young woman I once knew—the daughter of a successful man, though not blessed with his intelligence. Some said her mind was not fully formed." He paused, took a deep breath, and continued quietly. "As she grew into womanhood, her ability to make good decisions about her relationships, and her body, were compromised." He coughed again and wiped his mouth before continuing, "She had the body of a woman but the mind of a child."

"That is so sad; not unlike Gwen."

"Indeed." Daniel steeled himself once again. "There came a young man who charmed her with false affections. He had his way with her." He shook his head as he said it, then paused to wipe his forehead. "Not wanting any complications, the bastard was gone as quickly as he had come. The young woman found herself with child, though hardly knowing what that meant."

"My goodness. How troubling that must have been; both for her and her family."

"It was," Daniel shook his head. Tears beginning to flow, he sniffed and continued, "The young woman's mother was heartbroken; distressed beyond measure." He dabbed at the tears. "Her father feared for his business relationships. Rumors of his daughter having an illegitimate child would surely derail his ambitions."

And there it was. Garret could see the parallels; they flowed in his watery eyes. The young woman her father spoke of had to be Gwen. Was she then Gwen's daughter? But that would mean Daniel was—her *grand*father. She sat, speechless, her eyes wide, her mouth open.

Daniel saw she'd put the pieces together. No further explanation was required. "I am so sorry, Garret." He shook his head.

Garret couldn't speak. Tears brimmed and overflowed onto her cheeks. Daniel continued, "I told others you were my adopted child. How else could I explain it, given that my wife, your grandmother, had not been with child?"

Garret gathered herself, trying to find her voice. She was angry. The truth of the matter was that Daniel had chosen to serve his own best interests, rather than hers. His prior claims of giving her every opportunity he'd had as a boy now rang hollow. "But why a boy?" she pressed. "Why not a girl?"

"The world is simply more kind to boys, Garret. They have advantages you would never have been able to enjoy. I wanted you to have those opportunities." More coughing.

"I know that." Garret's head was down, shaking side-to-side.

"What is more, dearest, I had seen my own daughter taken advantage of. I never wanted that for you."

Garret sensed a deep caring in her grandfather's soft, failing voice. Her anger began to dissipate. She looked up, seeing the traces of pain and sorrow this pale, frail man had been through, and his hopes of a better life for her. As he now averted his eyes and hung his head, she set aside her remaining anger, moving closer and putting her arm around his shoulder. They were both in tears, floating with the drift of the water lapping against the boat.

XXVII

255

The ball at Richmond Palace in Surrey was well attended by nobles and dignitaries from throughout England, Drake among them. The most stunningly beautiful woman in attendance was the young Elizabeth Sydenham, daughter of Sir George Sydenham, the Shire Reeve of Somerset; one of the wealthiest men in the country. Miss Sydenham was constantly courted by the most accomplished men of England and might easily have chosen any one of them. Still, she was uninclined to imagine a life with any of her suitors. Toward the end of the evening, Drake approached her. "Would you care to show me how to dance?" he asked, a broad smile on his face.

"You toy with me, Sir. I have watched you steal several ladies' hearts on the floor."

"Yet none display the level of grace with which you move. I should like to learn from the best."

She took hold of his extended hand. They walked onto the floor.

"They say you are a pirate," she teased.

Drake laughed. "I am a mere adventurer. People define me as they will."

"And how shall I define you?"

"As an admirer. Of you."

"You flatter me."

"For good reason, my dear. All the treasures I have ever obtained pale in your presence."

"Is that all I am to you? Another treasure?"

"Not just any treasure. You are *the* treasure."

In the weeks and months that followed, Drake and Miss Sydenham spent a considerable amount of time together. She was much taken by the dashing young adventurer who mesmerized everyone with his remarkable stories. He had a disarming charm, a sense of humor, and deep knowledge of unseen parts of the world. Yet, at his core, he seemed to her a humble man—one who treated even the lowliest of his countrymen as his equal. She fell deeply in love with him.

When the two finally decided the time was right, Drake paid a visit to the Sydenham residence, to sup with her family. Following dinner, he and Elizabeth's father retired to the study for a glass of port. They spoke of trade and other matters in which they enjoyed mutual interest. When a brief pause offered the opportunity for a change of subject, Drake seized on the moment, "Sir George," he said, placing his port on the table, "I believe you know the great admiration I have for you, and for all you have accomplished. It is no secret that I am also deeply enamored of your precious Elizabeth. She has a poise and intelligence that simply belie her age. And she is clearly the most beautiful of all England's daughters. It would be my great honor to take her hand in marriage, and to become your son, in law. I hope I am worthy in asking your permission and blessing in this."

George rose from his chair. "Sir Drake," he replied, "I am as much an admirer of yours as is the Queen herself. You have proven to be a man of great courage and capability. You have a good heart and you clearly share my concern for our country and our fellow men. I cannot imagine giving the hand of my dear Elizabeth to anyone other than you. You have my full, unencumbered blessing. I welcome you as my son." Drake had already risen. The two men clasped hands and embraced each other over their agreement.

Elizabeth had been sitting nervously on a bench outside the main entrance. She'd wrapped herself in a shawl in the cool of the evening, anxiously awaiting Drake's appearance. When the door finally opened, she rose to her feet. His face beamed with a rich, loving smile. The complete joy in his eyes spurred her to run to him. She hugged him with all her might. "Oh, my precious Knight," she whispered. "This is the very best of all my days. We shall enjoy a wonderful life together."

"Indeed we shall, dearest."

———

The reception following the wedding of Sir Drake and Elizabeth Sydenham was a splendid affair, attended by close family and most of Drake's officers, including Prouten, Lee, Langton, his brother Thomas, William Tovery and Garret Connachan. Ambassador Pantas also attended. Unbeknown to Drake, or the rest of his officers, Garret and Pantas had been seeing each other frequently, and intimately, over the last two years. For appearance purposes, the two had come separately. She remained mostly on the periphery of the gathering, in light of how difficult it had become to continue presenting herself as a man. Still, some of her time had been spent with her closest friends—William and Thomas, so that they might see only minimal changes in her appearance from time to time, blinding them to the fuller picture.

For his part, Pantas spent the better part of this evening engaged in discussion with others, befitting his role as Ambassador. But his eyes frequently wandered in search of Garret. It was well into the night that he finally felt it would be reasonable to approach her without raising suspicions about their relationship. He came holding a goblet of wine, while she was seated at a table with William. "Good evening, Master's Mate Connachan. And to you as well, William." His eyes still on William, he continued, "Might I have a moment alone with Master Connachan? We have some issues to discuss."

"By all means," William said, rising to leave. "I shall see you later, Garret." He walked away, in search of Thomas.

"I have not had a chance to view the grounds," noted Pantas. "Would you care to show them to me?" Garret hadn't yet seen them herself. She rose. The two walked side-by-side through the extensive, beautifully groomed gardens, until they were far removed from others. There was only a slight chill in the evening air, under a bright three-quarter moon, and no breeze. They spoke briefly of the splendor of their surroundings. Pantas felt a need to share something he'd learned in the course of his many conversations that evening. "I hear Sir Drake is not long for England, though you have mentioned nothing of this." He looked into her eyes. "It concerns me. Surely you can understand why."

Garret nodded, not entirely certain how to respond. She felt badly about not having been open with him about her desire to join Drake's next voyage. She was torn by her love for Pantas on the one hand, and her passion for her career as one of Drake's officers, on the other. The two walked on in silence for several moments.

"Perhaps you and I could return to Ternate, to live a proper life in the court of the Sultan," Pantas offered.

Garret stopped. She looked around, wondering whether others were nearby. There were none, though she still felt discretion was required. "You dear, sweet man," she said, holding back the urge to reach out and touch his cheek. "You have my deepest love. I would so enjoy living a proper life, as you say. Yet I am torn by my desire to sail the oceans and see the richness of everything this world has to offer." She immediately saw the sorrow in his eyes. "Perhaps you might join us at sea."

"But how? You cannot be your true self. Surely that is not possible."

"I know. I know." She looked down at the pathway, shaking her head. "I have a difficult decision to make."

"It is an easy decision." He stroked her cheek with his hand. "Choose me."

Garret once again looked into his eyes. Damn those deep, dark eyes, she thought. "Give me time, Pantas." It was all she could think to say. She reached up and squeezed his hand on her cheek, drawing it down and then letting it go. She turned and began walking back toward the reception. He sighed and followed. Tears welled up in her eyes. Though her love for the Ambassador was strong, she had no desire to spend the remainder of her days in Ternate. Perhaps she needed to let him go, to free him for another woman. Holding onto him hardly seemed fair if she were to continue her life on the oceans. She would have to tell him, but it would not be in this moment. Certainly not in public. She reached inside her vest for a linen handkerchief and dabbed gently at her eyes.

———

The weeks raced by, during which Pantas accomplished much in negotiating England's support for his country. Following a meeting that lasted well into the night, he left for his quarters at the inn above Orion's Tavern. The night was dark, the streets empty. Not even the hardened cobblestones offered up a sound. A thin fog had settled in, along with a calm that wafted through his soul, knowing he'd won Garret's heart. He still bore hope that she would at least return with him to Ternate, to be married. Beyond that, he was confident they might find a way to be together. He could hold the position of Ambassador to London for quite some time, if that suited her interests.

Without warning, a dark, imposing figure stepped out from an alley as Pantas approached, blocking his path. The figure bore a long, black coat; a dark hat topped its head. He couldn't make out the face. Pantas stopped, not realizing that a second man had stealthily approached from behind and was now standing near his back.

"May I help…" Pantas' voice stopped. His eyes opened wide as a long blade from behind entered the back of his neck, plunged deeply, and then withdrew. His vision blurred. His eyes closed. He felt the warmth leaving his body as he dropped to his knees, unable to speak. An image of Garret's hand reached into his mind, caressing his face. The dark figure before him drew a cutlass from beneath his coat. The glinting light of its slash brought darkness.

"Morra, seu porco Asiático!" (Die, you Asian pig)

The two assailants looked around, to ensure there were no witnesses. There were none. One of them knelt, being careful to avoid the pool of blood around Pantas' head. There was no indication of any breathing. The killer searched for the jeweled dagger Pantas was known to carry. He found it and placed it in his belt, under his cloak. He rose. The two then turned and walked down the dark alley, blood still dripping from their bladed messengers of death. They'd been paid handsomely to assassinate Pantas, thereby ending further negotiations over England's support for Indonesia.

———

With her ungroomed, black-robed mother beside her, Garret looked down on the grave into which Daniel had been lowered. The words of the preacher went unheard as a myriad of thoughts raced through her mind. She felt a cavernous loss at the man's absence. And she worried deeply over her mother's future well-being. She wanted achingly to be back in London, with Pantas at her side. She couldn't envision spending much more time in this place of stifling sorrow.

"Come, Mother. It is time to go."

Gwendolyn, bitter and troubled, took her daughter's arm. As they turned to leave, she looked back toward Daniel's grave. The man had caused her so much pain throughout her life. She spit hard at his coffin.

———

Within the week, Garret was back in London, anxious to see Pantas. It was late in the afternoon when she sent a messenger, inviting him to meet her at Orion's Tavern on the morrow. In the meantime, she laid her finest naval uniform on the chair, disrobed, and changed her linens, not knowing her note would never make it to Pantas. It was delivered instead to his aide, Halim.

Entering Orion's Tavern the following morning, Garret was surprised that Pantas wasn't already there, as was his custom. She saw Halim seated at a table and walked toward him, smiling. No sooner had she sat than the owner came with her usual tea and scone. She paid the man and reached for her tea. Something wasn't right. Though Halim had acknowledged her presence with a nod, he'd said nothing. She could see he was distraught.

Ever since learning of Pantas' demise, Halim had worried he might ultimately be the one to inform Garret. He knew more about their relationship than she was aware. Pantas had confided in him about her gender, and his plans for her. He'd been sworn to secrecy. But now, that seemed of little consequence. Her moment of pain was a moment away. He'd thought about how best to put it—succinctly, he thought. The words now ran through his mind, suddenly seeming inadequate. Garret interrupted his thinking, "What is it, Halim? Is something bothering you?"

"I am sorry to bring you most unfortunate news, Master Connachan." He hadn't bothered to look her in the eye; that would be too painful. "The Ambassador has been slain. A few days ago." There was nothing more to say, really.

"But that cannot be," uttered Garret. The shock brought no tears. "Who could possibly want him dead?"

Halim simply shook his head, still looking down at the table.

"Was he robbed?"

"Only of his dagger."

"Dear God!"

"He would have wanted you to have these." Halim pushed a bound collection of written pages across the table. Pantas had maintained two journals. One was his official record as Ambassador. The other, the one now before Garret, was filled with only his personal thoughts—ones with no bearing on his Ambassadorial role.

Garret looked down on the papers, her vision now blurred by tears. She recognized the handwriting. Pantas had often sent her messages, all of which she'd kept. She reached out and shuffled through the lifeless sheets. She could see these were his innermost thoughts. Their relationship dominated the latter pages. She felt his presence through the words; his hand on her cheek; his body next to hers. She ran her hand lovingly down one page in particular. Pantas had written about the day she'd met with him here in the tavern, to hint at her true nature.

Today was most surprising. He'd written. *Master Connachan informed me there was something more about him that he needed to share. I had always felt a certain warmth for the young man—a feeling I could not explain. And then <u>she</u> touched my hand.*

Garret's index finger rubbed the underlined word, *she*. Tears now ran freely down her cheeks. She wiped at them, to avoid having them fall onto his writing. She continued reading.

He was in fact not a young gentleman at all, but rather a charming young <u>woman</u>. Her touch was so soft. So alluring. It made my heart race. This is a woman whom I believe could change my life. We made plans to meet on the morrow. I cannot wait to embrace the person she truly is. She has somehow confused my mind yet stolen my heart.

Pantas' words brought back the moment so vividly that she could see him looking at her with those deep, dark eyes. But with a clank of noise in the background, the moment was gone. She sniffed, turning her head and again wiping away free-flowing tears. She breathed in deeply, to gather her composure. It was of little help.

"Thank you, Halim. I must go now." She'd said it abruptly, as she rose. She hurried out of the tavern, hand over her mouth, papers in hand.

Halim sat alone, feeling the loss himself. The tavern door closed loudly, like the falling lid of a coffin.

Her head down, tears streaming along her cheeks, Garret walked hastily across the cobbled lane, wanting to put as much distance as possible between herself and the tavern that had now turned from a locus of love to a cell of sorrow. Memories of Pantas flooded her mind, drowning out any sense of where she was even headed. She remembered the depth of his eyes; the warmth of his smile; the softness of his touch; his self-assured persona. She wept for the many times they'd held each other in moments of deep, shared love and belonging. How could anyone possibly think of taking the life of such a peace-loving, happy, friendly human soul?

She soon found herself alongside the Thames. She noticed the river flowing away from her, thinking how much it mirrored Pantas' departure. She sat, pondering her loneliness—her grandfather gone, her mother fading away, and now Pantas' spirit drifting for seas unknown. There were two things she knew for certain. First, she no longer had any life other than that of sailing the world's oceans. And second, she must somehow find a way to avenge Pantas' murder.

———

The days in London passed drearily as Garret mourned. It was a time of remembrance, of soul-searching. Not anxious to return home, yet having little desire to remain in the city, she viewed returning to the sea as a refuge. Before that could happen, however, she needed to address some pressing issues. Since she was already in the city, it made sense to deal with the vast estate Daniel had left her. Though she was the executor, someone needed to serve as day-to-day manager of all the property, business and financial assets in her absence. That task had taken much longer than she'd expected. When it was done, she headed home to address another important matter— Gwendolyn's health was frail and failing quickly. She needed to find someone, or some way, to attend to the poor woman. That task turned out to be surprisingly easy to accomplish. A nearby institution agreed to take her on, though only at a substantial cost. Once her mother was settled into her new residence, Garret returned to London briefly, feeling a need to make good with Halim. She'd treated him so rudely, leaving him alone in the tavern that day when he'd delivered the devastating news of Pantas' murder. The two met the day following her arrival in the city. Halim informed her that the whisperings at court suggested Pantas had been assassinated. The prime suspects were the Spanish, who sought advantage over England in Indonesia, and the Portuguese, who were now part of the Spanish empire. It hardened her heart against both enemies, just as Drake's own feelings toward Spain had been etched in stone.

Not long after meeting with Halim, Garret left London to visit Drake in Devon, to confirm an assignment on his upcoming voyage. And something more. She no longer had anything to lose. And nothing to hide. It was time to be brutally bold.

XXVIII

Elizabeth Sydenham and Drake joined the ranks of the richest families in England. Yet for her, their wealth came second to their love and friendship. Unfortunately, she would soon learn that her husband's first love was the sea. And her dashing adventurer was about to sail once again, this time at the explicit request of the Queen.

Relations between England and Spain had deteriorated to the point where their undeclared war was an obliterated peace. Spain had already taken control of Portugal and was threatening Holland. King Philip, in retribution for Drake's piracy, had declared an embargo of all English merchant ships at every port around the globe where the Spanish maintained a military presence. His soldiers boarded English ships, unloading arms, munitions and supplies. Queen Elizabeth was infuriated by these egregious actions. She knew she must act quickly, to avoid Spanish domination of the oceans and much of the world's landmass. In her mind, Drake was best positioned to lead her response. Forcing him to set aside a voyage he was planning, she appointed him Admiral, helping him assemble a fleet of twenty-five warships, several smaller vessels and 2,000 men, including twelve companies of soldiers. Drake's mission was to disrupt Spanish supply lines, including their South Seas settlements and, wherever possible, their treasure galleons. If the possibility presented itself, he was expected to retrieve English ships held by Spain.

Drake had assembled much of his crew through word of mouth. Countless others had responded to postings in the taverns of Devon,

Plymouth, Portsmouth, Deptford and Deal, scribbling their marks to sign-up sheets. At home in Devon, eating a breakfast of toasted cheese, he poured over the lists, recognizing several of the names. Virtually all of the men who'd previously sailed with him had signed on for this voyage. He was pleased with the overall interest, though he was challenged by the selection of officers—the prized role being that of Captain of a warship. While many such positions were available, more men had expressed interest than he could possibly accommodate. He knew he must choose wisely. The fleet's success would depend heavily on the intelligence, judgement and leadership abilities of his captains.

Sipping tea as he carried his papers into the study, he heard the approach of a lone rider. Glancing through the window, he saw a white steed canter to the door, Garret astride. She was dressed in what resembled naval attire. She wore a white blouse with a high ruff, covered by a tight navy-blue, V-waisted doublet, its brass buttons gleaming. Her pants were deep-blue silk, above white stockings and black, brass-buckled riding boots. Her auburn hair was just as he remembered it— knotted in a long tail. It fell from beneath a black, auburn-feathered, broadband hat. He continued into his study, placing his papers and tea on the desk and taking his chair. One of his manservants soon entered, announcing Garret's arrival. She waited in the foyer. Drake took one final sip of tea, shuffled his papers together, and proceeded to greet her.

"Good morning, Sir Drake," Garret said, smiling in admiration as he entered the foyer. She could see he looked well, despite the facial scars that distinguished a man who'd fought bravely for Queen and country.

"It is good to see you, Master Connachan." He truly meant it. She'd grown into a handsome young woman, though still presenting as male. He extended his hand, which she accepted and shook. "How have you been, my good man?"

"Your good woman," Garret insisted.

He nodded and smiled. "Just so."

The two headed into his study, choosing to sit by a small table, rather than across from each other at his desk. Drake ordered a cup of tea for her while he retrieved his own. He sat and they talked at length. Garret shared news of her grandfather's passing and the arrangements she'd made for the care of her mother. That led to her bringing up the matter of Pantas' demise. It had been weeks since his death. The loss still darkened her soul but the tears had run out. Drake was already aware of his murder. He'd also heard that Pantas' aide, Halim, was now the temporary Ambassador, in his stead.

"You may have known, sir, that Pantas and I shared feelings for each other."

"I did not, I am afraid."

"It is no matter," she said. "He had hoped I might accompany him back to Ternate, to marry him there; with the Sultan's blessing."

"Good God. You must be heartbroken."

"I am past that, Commander."

"Admiral," Drake interrupted. "The Queen has seen fit to appoint me Admiral for my next mission."

"Of course. Your posters made that clear. My apologies. Congratulations are in order. That is wonderful news. The promotion is well deserved."

"Thank you," Drake nodded. "You were saying…about the death of Pantas?"

"Oh, yes. Well, it was a turning point for me, Admiral. I am now completely committed to taking my revenge on the Spanish. I believe they assassinated him."

"I see. Can you be certain it was the Spanish?"

"He was not robbed, save for his jeweled dagger. It was doubtless taken as proof of his execution. Who but the Spanish would have such motivation?"

"The Portuguese perhaps?"

"Perhaps. But they are now part of the Spanish empire. I make no distinction between the two."

Drake paused before responding, "I must say, he was a most honorable man."

"Indeed he was. I shall miss him, dearly."

"Is this why you have come here today, to inform me of Pantas' death?" He asked it knowing full well that Garret always seemed to have ulterior motives.

Garret smiled. "You know me too well, I am afraid."

"Indeed I do"

"Rather than sign one of your posters, I preferred to meet with you personally." She looked him squarely in the face, understanding the position she was putting him in—facing the difficult choice of *knowingly* permitting a woman to join his crew, at a time when all seamen still believed a woman's presence onboard ship was a bad omen.

Drake leaned back in his chair, returning her gaze. "I admire your pluck, Master Connachan. You seldom hesitate to speak your mind."

"As you have always instructed, Admiral," she smiled.

"Indeed." Drake thought for a moment. Garret had always managed to conceal her true self well. Yet there was a constant risk that her gender would be detected by someone. After all, she lacked facial hair, which one might expect a young man at this age to already have. He glanced fleetingly at her chest. The vest hid any obvious sign of breasts. That was a good thing. Still, should her gender be discovered, he might be accused of contributing to her deceit, putting him in an awkward position, not only with his crew but also with the English navy.

Garret interrupted his thoughts. "I wish to prove myself, Admiral. You know full well that I can wield my cutlass more artfully than most of the men. And I have never shied away from battle. Given further opportunities to demonstrate my abilities, I shall earn the respect of your entire crew."

"You have impressed many already," he acknowledged. "Still, I worry that naval battles are no place for a woman."

"Perhaps not for most women. But I am far from one of those. Being at sea and participating fully in any venture is the only life I desire. I am more than capable of defending myself. And I shall not let you down. You have my word."

After a brief pause, Drake yielded. "Alright, Master Connachan. On your word. You shall be given every opportunity. And no favors."

"Thank you, Admiral. Might I also be so bold as to ask that I be granted the role of an officer?"

Drake had suspected that might follow. He rose and walked to his desk, picking up the sheet containing the roster of men he thought might serve as officers. He turned and leaned against the desk, looking down the list of names. His head swayed back and forth, pensively. After a moment, he looked up at her. He knew how much promise the young woman had. Since her first voyage as a midshipman, he'd been grooming her for an officer role; just as he had the other midshipmen. Yet he'd recognized early on that there was something about her that made her stand out. She and William Tovery had both demonstrated an innate ability to lead. But Garret's intelligence was a singularly striking advantage over every other member of his crew, including his officers at that time. She was officer material; he knew that for a certainty. He also recognized that, were she a young man, he would immediately honor her request.

"You may indeed be so bold as to *ask*, Garret." He waited a moment, toying with her. Then he smiled, "I believe you have earned the right. Captain Patrick Laine has need of a Lieutenant. He is a seasoned officer who, I believe, would mentor you well."

"Would he be ready, sir, to be informed that I am a woman? And to maintain the confidentiality of that, if necessary?" Not waiting for an answer, Garret quickly added, "I am, of course, unafraid to serve openly as a woman. In fact, that would be my preference."

"You ask much, Connachan." Drake shook his head, slowly. "Let me give that further thought…Lieutenant." He smiled.

Garret rose from her chair. "Thank you, Admiral. That is all I ask." She extended her hand. Drake stood and shook it, heartily.

"Make your preparations. We depart in three weeks."

"Aye, Admiral."

As Garret left his study, Drake shook his head. He never could fathom what went on in a woman's mind. But this one was different. It was as though she thought like a man—bold, confident, outspoken. She said what she thought. Straight up. One of the best young officers he'd ever known. Including himself.

———

The grand war-fleet bustled with preparations, readying to depart Plymouth Sound. Drake stood at the bow of his new flagship, the *Bonaventure*. The surrounding sounds served up his most-favored music. He thought briefly about two of his fleet captains. His younger brother, Thomas, would be captaining a warship for the first time. Though not truly ready, Thomas was born of the same father. Surely that bode well for his success. In stark contrast was his most seasoned captain—Patrick Laine. The man seemed more frail than when Drake had last seen him. But there was nothing to suggest his talents were failing him. Garret had been assigned as his master's mate. Drake hadn't yet informed Laine of her true gender. That would have to come later. Soon, he imagined.

General Christopher Carleill stood at Drake's side. He was responsible for all military troops the ships carried. "It is a fine fleet, Admiral."

"Indeed, General. The finest England has ever assembled."

"And it carries her finest troops," Carleill smiled.

Drake smiled back. The thought running through his mind was that two of his own men— Musa and Caber—were stronger, braver and more lethal than any of Carleill's soldiers.

Prouten approached. "Pleased to report we are ready to depart, Admiral."

"Please proceed, Mr. Prouten. Let us put on a show for our countrymen."

It was cold and blustery as the fleet set sail. Hundreds of people lined the shore, huddled together like arctic penguins. They'd come to cheer the fleet and pray for its success. Drake and Prouten walked to the stern of the *Bonaventure*. With one hand on the rigging, the Admiral waved to the cheering crowd. Prouten ordered the cannons fired in salute to Queen and country. The collective noise of the cannon fire was deafening, giving rise to even heartier cheers from the assembled throng.

"Let us pray for success. And God's grace, sir," Prouten shouted over the noise.

"Indeed, Mr. Prouten. The future is ours to write."

———

Since Drake's last expedition, Spain had greatly improved the defense of its South Seas settlements. But King Philip, comfortable with Spain's rulership of the oceans, hadn't anticipated being challenged by a fleet as large as Drake's. It would prove to be a major miscalculation. Not long after leaving Plymouth Sound, the fleet assaulted the Cape Verde Islands, easily capturing the capital, Santiago. They also took control of Praia do Portinho, without resistance. It wasn't long before word reached Philip. He ordered hastened preparations for the defense of all settlements on coastal waters—in Europe, the Caribbean Islands and the Americas.

Captain Laine was charged with securing Santiago. He had invited Garret to his quarters there. She entered, admiring the ease and grace with which Laine treated her and others on this voyage. He bore little resemblance to the traditional image of an overbearing naval captain. Perhaps his age had softened him, she thought. He was a father-like presence for her. She'd already learned much from the man. The old captain sported a robust, white beard and fine naval garb. He was portly. The buttons on his vest strained to contain his garments. His face appeared pale. Beads of sweat dotted his forehead. Sitting awkwardly at his desk, the man was visibly uncomfortable.

"Are you feeling alright sir?" Garret queried.

"I am afraid not. Perhaps something I have eaten pains me." His words were hesitant, slurred.

"How can I help?"

"Perhaps a drink of water."

Garret walked to the credenza on which sat a handled urn containing water, and several cups. She chose a cup and poured the warm water into it. As she walked back toward his desk, Laine slumped over it. She rushed to his side, lifting his upper body and placing his back against the chair. She put the cup of water to his lips. It mostly ran down his chin. Not wishing to leave him alone, she called out for assistance.

Having refreshed their water supplies and provisions in the Cape Verde Islands, Drake's fleet now headed west. Captain Laine rested in his quarters with a dreadful fever, attended by his personal physician. Garret assumed temporary command of the ship. This is my moment, she thought— do as Admiral Drake would; as Captain Laine would. Be decisive. Firm. Fair. Earn the men's respect. It may be temporary but I shall make the most of it.

General Carleill followed behind Drake as they entered his quarters on the *Bonaventure,* to review their plans for military assaults on important settlements in the Southern Seas. Drake turned, placing his arm around Carleill's shoulders. "Stealth shall be the order of the day, General. The Spanish shall not see us coming until it is too late. We must act quickly and decisively, with overwhelming force; both from the sea and on the land." He punched the air with his right hand as he said it. "It is often men's fear of their own annihilation that facilitates their defeat. Overwhelming force and surprise are the sparks to ignite that fear. We shall not fail."

Thinking about the widespread seasickness that had recently incapacitated many of his men, Carleill didn't share Drake's buoyant enthusiasm. "I shall be pleased if the seas alone don't defeat us," he grimaced.

"I assure you, General, they will not. Your men shall soon have their sea legs. Now, about Santo Domingo…"

For the residents of Spain's oldest settlement on Hispaniola, the day's calm was suddenly interrupted. A vast fleet bearing English flags appeared to emerge from beneath the sea, bearing down on their harbor. The long, thin line of warships brought fear to even the bravest hearts in Santo Domingo. While they'd heard rumors of the King's warning, they were shocked by the imposing size of this oncoming force. Dreading a deadly onslaught, they began scrambling for the outskirts of the city, clogging the streets with bodies, carts and animals. It hindered the very movement of their own soldiers.

Drake waited patiently for a sign from General Carleill. He and his soldiers had disembarked the night before, in a nearby uninhabited harbor not visible from the city. Now in position, Carleill signaled their readiness.

"Guns at the ready if you please, Mr. Prouten," ordered Drake.

"Guns at the ready," Prouten echoed loudly. The gun ports crashed open. Fully loaded black-iron monsters rolled forward, nosing through. The sound carried sharply across the otherwise quiet waters just outside the harbor.

"Ready to fire, sir" responded Mr. Lee.

"Fire at will, Mr. Prouten!"

At Prouten's call, the *Bonaventure* and the rest of the fleet lit fire on the city. Massive volleys of cannon-shot streaked through the air, crashing thunderously on the streets, buildings and shore batteries of Santo Domingo. Wooden structures exploded into shards, hurrying and impeding scattering residents. The noise of the cannons was accompanied by the howling of animals, the screech of birds, and the screams of the injured and dying. Smoke, dust and falling debris blanketed people and animals, many stumbling and falling. Some trampled their neighbors in the chaos. Buildings crumbled, disintegrating under iron rain.

The city's shore batteries were soon inexplicably quiet. The element of surprise, chaos in the streets, and the fleet's overwhelming firepower had shrunk the ranks and the response of the shore batteries—to the point where the despair of the firing teams drove them to leave in fear for their lives.

While English cannons raked Santo Domingo, the approach of Carleill's soldiers on land caught the attention of those living outside the city. A rag-tag militia prepared to engage but was quickly turned back by the deafening volley of gunfire from a vast line of arquebuses. The Spaniards let loose a herd of cattle, to charge and disrupt the invaders. But the heavy beasts, frightened by the overwhelming noise of the guns, simply dispersed into the woods in disarray. The English charged forward. Taking their cue from the cattle, the Spanish militia dissolved into the nearby woods, leaving the English free to assault the city gates, uncontested.

Carleill had split his soldiers into two groups. They signaled Drake's ships to hold fire and then stormed Santo Domingo from separate flanks, converging on the city center virtually unscathed. It was all over shortly after it began. The city had toppled in astonishing fashion. Soldiers cheered and celebrated their victory; a handful mounted and raised the English flag on the royal palace and the church of Santa Barbara.

———

Drake was rowed ashore by several of his men, accompanied by his officers. Before his longboat even slid onto the beach, he jumped out into the water, splashing his way toward the soldiers who'd gathered on the shore, including General Carleill himself. The two leaders shook hands heartily as their men cheered. "You have performed admirably, General. My compliments to you and your men. It is a remarkable victory."

"Thank you, Admiral. May we be so lucky as we go forward."

"We shall make our own luck, General. In the meantime, let us establish headquarters in the Cathedral, form a defensive line at the city's edge, and begin our search of the principal buildings and residences—the ones still standing," he smiled.

"My men shall proceed with all due haste." Carleill turned to go but then stopped, remembering the word he'd received earlier of the apparent death of Captain Laine. The man had been a close friend of Drake's. His illness had finally overcome him the day before the assault. "I was sorry to hear of Captain Laine's death, Admiral. I know he was a good friend of yours. And a fine sea captain."

"He was indeed, General. I mourn his loss. Captains of his quality are hard to find."

"Do you have a replacement in mind?"

"There are two who are capable, though one presents certain complications."

"Then I wish you well with your decision."

"Thank you. Now, let us proceed to discover what treasures Santo Domingo wishes to share."

XXIX

The morning after the fall of Santo Domingo, Lieutenant Garret Connachan strode confidently into the cathedral, to meet with Drake. "Good day, Admiral." Her words echoed off the walls and lofty ceilings. "My compliments on the taking of the city."

"Thank you, Lieutenant. All glory to the entire fleet. And to General Carleill and his men." He paused, knowing there was a different matter of importance to young Garret. In fact, he'd half expected her to come, and bring it up. He cleared the area of his attendants and then opened the door to the discussion, "I am deeply saddened to learn that Captain Laine succumbed to his illness."

"It was my pleasure to have served with him, Admiral. He was a fine man, and an excellent mentor—as you had indicated. I shall always value his intense focus on the management of a finely tuned warship and his high level of empathy for his crew, as though they were his extended family."

"Admirable traits of leadership," Drake nodded.

"I must say, following his death, I noticed our flag flapping happily in the wind. It seemed most inappropriate. I ordered the flagman to lower it half the way, in the captain's honor."

"That explains it, then. I had seen the flag flying low and wondered what the meaning of it was."

"With the opening created by his death, sir, I would welcome the opportunity to serve as captain. *And* as a woman. I believe I have earned the men's respect, and that they will accept me for the leader I am, without regard to my gender." She'd practiced delivering these comments in advance and now articulated them with abundant self-confidence.

Her remarks pained Drake. The secret of her gender was fine with him, so long as it wasn't disclosed. Its hiddenness was in fact its beauty—it brought him peace. But she was now forcing the issue…and requesting a captaincy at the same God-damned time. He took a deep breath to calm himself. He recognized she'd already earned the respect of many of his men; even Musa and Caber, perhaps the hardest to impress. Both had witnessed her courage in battle. Da Silva thought her an excellent navigator. Drake, himself, saw her as a natural leader and one of the two he was already considering as Captain Laine's replacement; the other being William Tovery. But she carried risk. Substantial risk. Would learning she was a woman change the men's perceptions in a negative way? Or cause dissension among other members of the crew? Would it cast a poor light on him for having kept this secret from the men?

Garret continued, "I am confident appointing me captain would be well received. I imagine the Queen herself would be pleased to see a woman serve in such capacity." She knew playing the 'Queen' card would resonate well—Elizabeth had established the very precedent for a strong woman to excel in a commanding leadership role.

Not having a child of his own, Drake had taken Garret under his wing long ago; almost as though the brash midshipman were his own child. She'd made an excellent protégé. He could envision her one day following his own path, though he wondered just how difficult that might be given the obstacles she would face—like having to navigate the turbulent waters of being the first woman to ascend to a role always held by men. If he'd learned anything about women through the years, it seemed that few were both courageous and driven. But garret was. And she had the requisite bearing and intellect. He also felt confident, given his standing among the men of England, that he could freely make such a call. Still, it would require his actively selling the decision to his entire fleet, including many men who didn't yet know her.

"Alright then, *Captain* Connachan. Let us proceed on this basis. You shall have your opportunity. And my full support. Let us accomplish great things together."

"We already have, Admiral," she smiled. "May we accomplish many more."

Drake had no doubt they would.

"One more thing, Admiral. I am afraid I have another favor to ask."

"I am almost afraid to hear it," Drake snickered.

"William Tovery, sir. I realize he is currently assigned to your flagship. But, as Captain, I have need of a lieutenant. I believe he would serve me well."

Drake didn't hesitate. "A fine choice. But tell me, would he be comfortable serving *under* you, given you and he were midshipmen together?"

"Not in the least, sir. He and I have a strong bond."

"As you wish, then. Feel free to inform Master Tovery. At your leisure."

"Thank you, Admiral. I shall inform him immediately. But I shall leave the timing of the disclosure of my appointment—and my gender—to you." Drake recognized she was now holding him accountable to deliver on the most important piece—informing the entire crew that she was a woman. She turned and left the cathedral, a broad smile brightening her face.

The following afternoon, Drake's officers assembled in the cathedral. He made the formal announcement regarding Garret's succeeding Captain Laine. It was well received and cheered by all. One of the existing captains felt it appropriate to initiate her into the club. He poured his beer over Garret's head, to a great laugh and a further cheer. She smiled through it, wiping the beer from her face.

Drake, relieved, welcomed the broad support. And since he had it, he knew now was the time to disclose her secret. When the noise settled, he continued, "There is one more matter of foremost importance, gentlemen."

Garret sensed it was coming. Now drying the beer from her hands, her nerves on edge, she contemplated the men's reaction. Hopefully, her past record would be sufficient to gain their acceptance.

Drake continued, "Those of you who have sailed with me in the past know the importance I place on the role of captain. Other than the unfortunate appointment of Mr. Thomas Doughty, I have made those decisions wisely. I make them by drawing on my own experience and that of others who have been successful in the role. It seems only fitting that I pose this question to you all now: What is it that *you* believe determines a captain's success?"

His brother Thomas was quick to respond. "Courage, sir. A captain must be prepared to make difficult decisions affecting the lives of his men. Those decisions must often be made in the face of challenge by others. A captain cannot please everyone. His decisions must be based entirely on doing the right thing—for the benefit of the crew and the mission."

"Well said, Thomas." Drake looked around. "Anyone else?"

"The lives and the success of the crew must come first, sir," said William Hawkins. "No captain can succeed without ensuring the well-being of his men."

"Indeed."

"A captain must lead by example," offered Captain Frobisher. "Asking any man to do that which he would not do himself, will undermine his ability to lead."

"All good points, gentlemen." Drake paused, slowly looking each of them in the eye, taking their measure and ensuring he had their full attention before continuing. "Tell me, does anything you have offered here as traits of a successful captain rule out someone who might be different from ourselves? A man of color, perhaps? Or a Catholic? Perhaps even a Jew?"

The men glanced tentatively at each other, uncertain where the Admiral was headed with this. Drake waited.

"I suppose, sir," replied Edward Poole, "that one might rightfully question whether the crew would be willing to follow such an individual."

"And what if that individual had already proven themselves in battle. And in leadership?" Drake responded.

"Well then," replied Poole, "I imagine the men would be willing to follow."

The others nodded agreement.

"I can see, gentlemen, that we are all aligned on this. And I must now share with you something that requires your complete support. Do I have your word on that?"

"Aye, sir," they said, almost in unison, without hesitation.

"You should know that our distinguished, battle-tested, and proven leader—our new Captain Garret Connachan—is in fact…" he paused briefly to look them each straight in the eyes…"a woman."

Silence. Puzzled faces turned toward Garret. Some searched their minds for any evidence from their prior experiences with Garret. Had they simply overlooked something? Virtually all of them wondered what was beneath her uniform. No one dared comment. What could they possibly say?

"I have complete confidence in Captain Connachan, gentlemen. She shall serve us well. And *openly*. As a woman." Drake paused again. "Are there any among you who would doubt her?"

The men were still playing catch-up. Most shook their heads. A few hesitatingly uttered no.

"Good, then." He pressed on, "Now, let me be clear. My expectation is that every one of you—every one—will support her and treat her with the same degree of respect that you give every other Captain in my fleet."

The men nodded. It was an order, like any other from the Admiral.

"Finally, your responsibility as an officer is to relay this message to your own crews. At once. So that all the men may hear of this at the same time. And I recommend, gentlemen, that when communicating this message, you use the same approach I have here used with you. Before disclosing Captain Connachan's gender, you must first bring your men into agreement on the underlying principles of success for a captain." He scanned the room. "Am I perfectly clear?"

"Aye, sir," the officers replied.

"Thank you, gentlemen. That will be all."

That evening, as Garret disrobed in the cabin that had been Captain Laine's, she took the first moment in what seemed like forever, to observe her naked body in the glass. Her face looked older than she felt, though she believed it was still modestly attractive. She unknotted her hair's tail, allowing it to flow freely. She ran her hand through it, admiring its color. Her young breasts had filled in nicely. They were firm and white, her nipples pink and taught. Her arms and shoulders were more muscled than feminine, but she liked the definition it gave her body. She moved her hands downward from her breasts, along her abdomen. It was tight. Slightly rippled. Her hips curved outward gently, not severely. A puff of soft auburn hair graced the joining of her firm, white thighs. Her longish legs were pleasant enough to look at, though she wasn't fond of her knees. Her feet were wider than she would have liked but, thank God, not like those of a duck. She laughed at that thought and then looked up and down a few times, admiring the strength of the woman in the glass and inhaling the wonderful moment of being a free, fully disclosed and confident female—no longer burdened by the secret she'd borne for so long. For too long. She breathed in deeply, smiling and raising her arms high in the air—in victory.

———

News of Garret's being a woman, disguised all this time as a man, didn't sit well with some of the crew. One man in particular—Harker—now openly challenged her mere presence. He'd been a rebel since childhood. Craftily outspoken, he was adept at intimidating and influencing others. Like all seasoned deckhands, Harker had learned the superstitions of the seas that each generation of sailors passed on to the next, for centuries. He believed that storms and bad omens were brought by the Gods, in retribution for the actions of men that served no good purpose. Actions such as this—bringing a woman on board. Following the announcement, he shared his concern with several crewmates.

In the dark and stillness of a calm night, Harker and his close friend, Yauggan De Graaf, sat by a coiled rope, drinking tankards of beer. "I tell you, it is the Devil's design, having a woman onboard," offered Harker. "And to be made a captain, no less. Trust me, this witch has slept with the Admiral and cast a spell on him. With her leading a ship, we are surely damned."

His large, half-black mate chimed in. "Ever since the loss of Brewer and Flood, the Admiral has made questionable decisions. Perhaps she had already cast her spell on him back then." He paused to think. "We should not have signed on with him again."

"What choice did we have?" replied Harker. "The man is the best hunter of treasure. Would you prefer a fishing vessel?" De Graaf shook his head in resignation. Harker continued, "Best we deal with this witch before the seas rise up against us."

"How might we do that?"

"Perhaps she shall find her way over the side in the middle of the night."

Musa, seated quietly on a stairwell around the corner, overheard the two men talking. Having shared battlefields with Garret, he admired both her courage and capabilities. In his mind, she was as good a seafarer as any of the men. She also had a smartness about her. And a will to succeed that made her something special. He would have none of this talk. He rose and proceeded up the last few stairs to the deck. Harker and de Graaf immediately stopped talking, surprised that anyone had been nearby. Harker was well aware of Musa's reputation as an executioner. The man was the only crewmate he truly feared.

Almost a head taller than Harker, carrying the enormous bulk of his glistening black chest, Musa walked straight up to the disruptor. He reached out with his huge hand, pulling Harker upward by the back of his neck. He angled Harker's head and peered down on his, so that the two were almost nose-to-nose. Without saying a word, he waited until Harker's one functioning eye looked away. He squeezed the neck hard and spoke slowly, with menace in his voice. "You, matey, are a stinking pile of ooze that I would sweep from the deck if Captain Connachan even stepped near you. Slide carefully, you foul-smelling bilge rat." He kept Harker's neck in a tight grip for a few moments, letting the message sink into the man's black heart. De Graaf watched as complete silence fell among the three of them. Finally, Musa released his grasp. He looked at De Graaf and then back at Harker, who stood there with his good eye focused firmly on his feet.

"Do you understand me, fool?" Musa growled.

"Aye," Harker said quietly, suddenly feeling impotent. He resented being handled this way. One day, he thought, he would find a way to deal with both the witch and her henchman.

Musa turned and walked away. He expected there might be more talk of this nature among the men. And indeed there was over the next few days. But he and others who'd seen Garret in action quickly suppressed such talk. They made it perfectly clear to others—Captain Connachan had their support.

———

Following her first breakfast as Captain with the rest of the officers, Garret headed to the main deck. She was comforted by Drake's remarks at the close of the meal. He had confirmed that all the crew members on all the ships had been properly informed of her new rank and 'new' gender. William Tovery was beside her as they walked. "A beautiful morning, is it not?" he remarked.

"A beautiful morning indeed." Wanting to fully affirm who she truly was, Garret took a few moments to unknot her hair. She shook her head, letting the hair blow freely in the light, warm breeze. Though it sent the clear message she wanted, she knew it wasn't the most practical way to wear it. She would soon revert to the knotted tail. But for now, it felt wonderful. She and William stood at the taffrail, looking out over the blue Caribbean water sparkling in the sunlight. She breathed in the freshness of the morning, though a sudden memory of Captain Laine kept her from breathing as long as she would have otherwise. She had awakened the last several mornings sensing the presence of his soul in her cabin—a constant reminder of his loss. She imagined that would pass, in time. "Do you find it odd, William, that the word *morning* brings such a sense of joy, yet the word *mourning*, with a 'u', is pure sadness?"

"I had never thought of the two words in that way."

"Yet here I am—enjoying the morning while still mourning the loss of Captain Laine."

William nodded. "He was a fine man. How lucky for you to have sailed alongside men like Drake and Laine since our days as mids."

Garret turned toward him. "Those early days do not seem that long ago. Yet we have come so far, have we not?"

"And accomplished so much."

"Indeed. The Admiral has given us responsibility well beyond what our youth might suggest we are worthy of."

"You in particular, Garret. He has taken a special liking to you. But that said, it is your merit, not your gender—or your handsome face—that has earned his respect."

Garret sensed a little awkwardness in William's remark about her gender. Perhaps he was still adjusting to the new reality. Or perhaps there was an underlying resentment about her being promoted ahead of him. Or was it the way in which he'd received the news—from Drake, rather than from her? "I must apologize for not having confided in you earlier, William. You are my closest friend."

"I am sure you had your reasons."

"It is a long story. I shall share it with you one day. Over a good cup of wine."

"No matter. Though I do worry about anything inappropriate I might have said to you in the past, regarding women." He said it sheepishly, well aware of how the men frequently spoke of women. Of their conquests. Conversations he'd participated in.

Garret smiled. She couldn't recall anything inappropriate or awkward that he'd said. Though they'd both been part of such discussions, they weren't old enough to have contributed much commentary. Besides, she'd hardened herself to the typical brazen comments of the crew when they spoke of women—almost always either sexual or disrespectful. Or both. But that was to be expected. Most of their experiences were with ladies of the night. Or indigenous women, who commonly gave themselves up for trinkets and mirrors. "You have always been a gentleman, William," she assured him, with a warm smile.

"Thank you, Captain," he nodded, feeling as though he owed her a compliment in return. "And, might I say, it is both a pleasure and an honor to serve under you." It was a comment from his heart. He wished to be clear that there were no ill feelings about her promotion. She was too important a friend to let that get in the way of their relationship. And too deserving of the honor.

Garret touched the back of his shoulder. "Thank you, William. That means a lot to me." Taking a note from Drake's page, she added, "But you serve *with* me, not under me."

XXX

The thriving city of Cartageña was arguably the heart of Spain's Caribbean empire. It was also on the path of Drake's fleet as it sailed from Santo Domingo toward the Spanish Main. Governor Don Pedro Fernandez de Busto had been forewarned about the presence of El Draque's pirate fleet in the Southern Seas. He was well aware of Drake's capabilities and ambitions. In preparation for a likely assault on his city, he ordered the removal of valuables, women and children. Shore defenses were strengthened. His newly organized militia underwent weapons training. Together with his regular army, De Busto now had some two-thousand armed defenders, many black slaves and indigenous people. Basic training began for those who weren't regular soldiers. Weapons were cleaned and sharpened, including those that were traditional among the indigenous population—spiked clubs, spears and poison-tipped arrows. Some six hundred soldiers were assigned to two warships anchored in the harbor. Others, including fifty mounted on horses, were disseminated throughout the city and surrounding areas. But while they covered multiple locations, the land-based forces were widely spread. Coming to each other's aid would be difficult, leaving them vulnerable to a concentrated attack. That attack would come sooner than anticipated.

Alongside his general and other officers, Governor de Busto looked on from the harbor as Drake's two dozen ships and hundreds of white sails closed in from the sea. He felt the hair on the back of his neck stand up. Surprisingly, the fleet altered its course to the west. They sailed past the harbor peaceably, causing confusion among de Busto's military leaders. Some felt their preparations had served to dissuade Drake from launching an attack. Others worried the pirata's maneuver might be a ruse. All had heard of the assault on Santo Domingo. They knew El Draque hadn't deployed his fleet in this manner. They now argued over his crafty intentions.

Experience had taught Drake that fear and uncertainty were weaknesses he could exploit. His sail-by to the west was intended to raise those very emotions among the Cartageñians, making them question their preparations and perhaps make hasty adjustments. It was also a distraction, aimed at drawing their attention away from the east, where General Carleill and one thousand soldiers had quietly unloaded beyond sight of Spanish fortifications and lookouts.

After much argument, de Busto's military leaders decided to quickly withdraw men from their eastern flank, to shore up defenses west of the city, where Drake appeared headed.

Carleill and his forces stealthily hacked through the forest and along the shoreline, in a relentless march to the weakened east side. As they reached a turn where they were forced off the beach and onto an existing pathway, those in the lead were pierced in their lower legs by carefully embedded poisoned stakes. They swore in pain, grabbing their bleeding shins, unaware death would soon call for them. They created a logjam in the path, slowing the raiders' advance. Those behind were forced to hack through the surrounding brush with cutlasses and axes, enabling the rest of Carleill's army to bypass the gridlock. The soldiers continued on, though now with heightened caution.

The path finally ended near a soft marsh. They faced having to wade through it, toward Caleta Point. The Spanish were entrenched on the far side, behind a long, low stone wall. Their now-depleted force, supported by a mere four cannons, was nearly oblivious to what was headed their way. But one of the lookouts spotted unusual movement on the edge of the marsh. The Spanish Captain, Alonso Bravo, sent a small force of cavalry and militiamen to investigate. Nearing Carleill's line, they were shocked by the vastness of the approaching forces. One Spaniard turned his mare, galloping off in the direction of the wall. It caused panic among the others. They, too, fled in retreat.

Watching the small Spanish cadre fall back, Carleill ordered one flank of his men to attack. They poured through the thicket, swarming and buzzing like a horde of angry wasps. Spanish cannons roared, accompanied by arquebus fire. But the cannon shots were too few and ineffective. After the initial volley, the Spanish reloaded clumsily. Carleill's second flank, led by Musa and Caber, took the cue. They charged the wall from the side, delivering a thundering chorus of blood-curdling war cries. A dense cloud of arrows streamed toward the Spaniards, wounding several. In what seemed like mere moments to the Spanish, the raiders from the first flank were scaling the fortress wall, firing pistolets, brandishing swords, and hurling pikes with deadly results. The poorly disciplined and heavily overwhelmed defenders engaged only briefly before scattering, many even abandoning their weapons. Even some of the bravest soldiers questioned whether to follow.

Despite the militia's retreat, Captain Bravo refused to give ground. He and a few of his most skilled soldiers fought admirably, with cutlasses. The clashing of swords was soon the only sound as Carleill's raiders increasingly surrounded the Captain and his men, some engaging, others simply standing near to watch and enjoy the action. Both sides offered up a fine display of swordsmanship, with deft parries, artful thrusts and sweeping slashes. Captain Bravo, gashed and bleeding, fought on bravely. He would only be challenged one at a time, in light of his role. The rest of his men were either slain, severely injured or forced to throw aside their swords, accepting the hopelessness of their situation. At last, fighting alone and having already absorbed six wounds, Bravo was no longer able to lift his sword. He slowly knelt and placed it in the dirt, raising his left arm in surrender. It was the only arm he could raise.

Carleill approached, extending his hand. "Please rise, Captain. You have served your country honorably."

Bravo accepted Carleill's hand. Having taken wounds to his right side, left thigh and both arms, he rose with Carleill's help. He looked at the English soldiers around him and gave them a nod. The raiders collectively cheered, in recognition of Bravo's exceptional display of bravery and swordsmanship—something any warrior could appreciate, no matter his country.

Several of the men who'd fled Carleill's assault began streaming into the city, hotly pursued by hundreds of the General's soldiers. Their startled faces and frenetic pace ignited fear in the soldiers controlling the city's eastern wall. Frightened by the terror they couldn't see but could well imagine, many turned in panic and fled. Carleill's raiders soon descended on the city, greeted by poisoned arrows fired by natives. Several were wounded.

A few died quickly. Seeing the Spanish disengage, the natives saw no point in reloading. They too abandoned their posts.

Within the hour, hostilities ended. General Carleill soon entered the heart of Cartageña. Captain Bravo, still conscious, was carried at his side by Caber and three others. Carleill climbed up on a nearby stone wall. "My fellow soldiers," he yelled, gaining his men's attention. "You have won a momentous victory here today. The mighty Cartageña is now ours." He thrust his sword high in the air. "For England!" he shouted. The warring throng cheered uproariously, thrusting their own swords toward the sky.

The men onboard the two Spanish warships in the harbor had watched in horror as the soldiers defending their city folded and fled. Sensing Cartageña was now a lost cause, and seeing the sudden return of Drake's enormous fleet, they weighed anchor and unfurled sails, attempting to avoid capture of their ships. But in their attempt to escape the harbor, they were stopped by heavy, linked chains. Their own army had strung up the chains days earlier, to prevent Drake's fleet from entering.

Altering course, one of the Spanish ships ran aground on a sand bar. On the other ship, a powder keg inexplicably exploded, shooting flames in the air and quickly burning alive some of the crew. Realizing they were sitting targets, vulnerable to English cannons, the Spanish commander ordered the ships abandoned and set aflame, to keep them from falling into Drake's hands.

Garret and a group of sailors in longboats rowed quickly into the harbor. They breached the defending chains and proceeded to board the burning ships, attempting to douse the flames. Other crewmates took charge of smaller vessels in the harbor.

Many of the Spanish sailors and soldiers rowed toward shore. Others attempted to swim to safety. Some failed to make it, drowning amid flaming pieces of wreckage. Those fortunate enough to reach shore were brutally assaulted by shots from Carleill's army. Aided by the arrival of dusk, many raced to the trees along the shore's edge. All resistance ended.

———

The early morning sun shone on Drake as he stepped ashore at Cartageña. He was guided to a residence that Carleill had taken for his quarters the night before. Arriving as the General was finishing breakfast, he found him in the company of a Spanish officer.

"Good morning, Admiral," Carleill said, rising. "May I present Captain Alonso Bravo. He fought gallantly on behalf of his city. Were he one of our own, we should be honored to have such a fine military leader among us."

Drake shook hands with Bravo—carefully, in light of the man's wounds. "I am sorry to see you have suffered in defense of your city, Captain. Rest assured, you shall have the fine medical attention of my personal physician, Dr. Grant.

"Thank you, Admiral. You are most kind. I have invited the General here to use my residence as his quarters. You are welcome to do the same."

"Thank you. I would be honored to stay, provided it will not inconvenience you and your family."

"I assure you, Admiral, it will not."

Dr. Grant visited Captain Bravo the following morning. After he left, Bravo dressed himself and hobbled outside for some fresh air. He noticed the Admiral, the General and one other captain with a cavalier's hat and auburn feather, with the tail of a white bandana hanging alongside a knotted tail of auburn-colored hair. The three were in deep discussion. Bravo sensed Drake was the one in charge. "Good morning, gentlemen."

"Good morning," replied Drake. "Dr. Grant tells me you are a feisty patient."

"Maldito el Diablo! (*Damn the Devil*) I suppose he means well, Admiral, but he gives me much pain in servicing my wounds."

Drake smiled, knowingly. "He assures me you shall recover in good order."

Aside from his many bandaged wounds, and his use of a makeshift wooden cane, the Spanish captain bore the look of a model soldier. His dark hair, swarthy face, finely trimmed beard and muscled physique gave him a fierce presence. He was perhaps in his late forties. His disciplined military life had extended to his personal life, ensuring a strong physical appearance and good health, aside from his recent wounds.

"Admiral," said Bravo, wincing through a shard of pain in his side, "I must ask a favor. My wife is not well. She was evacuated in advance of your arrival, along with other civilians. I am afraid she is near the end of her days. I must ask your permission to visit her before she dies."

"By all means, Captain. I am sorry to hear this." Drake turned to Garret. "Allow me to introduce you to Captain Connachan. She and her master's mate shall accompany you. You may stay with your wife as long as necessary." He smiled, "On your honor as a soldier, of course, that you shall not take up arms against us. Nor incite your men to do so."

"Thank you, Admiral. I assure you, I am a man of honor. No military action shall be taken." Bravo turned to Garret. "It is my pleasure to meet you, Captain. I had no idea you were a woman. My apologies for having addressed you as one of the gentlemen."

"Apology accepted, Captain. Lieutenant Tovery and I shall be pleased to accompany you to your wife."

During the next several days, Captain Bravo attended to his wife, under the close supervision of Garret and William. They were there to ensure Bravo was true to his promise. Garret had become very fond of the Spaniard. He was not only a valiant soldier but also a caring husband. He spent endless hours at his wife's side. It was a remarkable contrast in human nature— fighting to take a life on one hand while fighting to save one on the other. She wished to learn more from this seasoned military leader. And gentleman. She found an opportunity one afternoon, as he took a break while his wife slept.

"Would you mind if I join you, Captain?" Garret asked.

"Of course. Would you care to share a cup of this drink with me? The Dutch call it *koffei*. They say it has the power to bring energy to the soul."

"I would indeed, Captain."

Bravo poured a cup and handed it to her, watching for her reaction as she drank the hot, dark liquid. Her frown said it all.

"It is quite bitter," she remarked.

He smiled. It was a common reaction for first-timers. "It comes from a rather dark bean that grows here."

"Do you prefer it to tea, then?"

"I drink it daily. I find it gives me strength. It does manage to make its way through my body rather quickly, however," he smiled.

Garret took a second sip. It was less bitter than the first.

"Tell me, Captain," Bravo asked, "how is it that a woman finds herself in the Admiral's navy? Particularly with such high rank? Are you related to him?"

She smiled at the question, expecting she might hear it often in the years ahead. Not sure how best to respond, she decided to be indirect, "And how did you become a Captain in the Viceroy's army?"

Bravo laughed. He saw her implication. How does anyone become a captain—a leader of men? Surely by having earned it. Yet the English were known to sometimes sell this title to those with the means to pay for it. It wasn't always earned. "Did you not pay for it, then?"

Garret was well aware that England's reputation for selling titles extended beyond the country's borders. "I have indeed paid for it," she smiled, "though *not* with money." She regretted the words only moments after uttering them. They'd caused Bravo to raise one thick, black eyebrow, suggesting he may have inferred from her response that she'd used her *body* to curry favor with the Admiral. She blushed. "Paid with *effort*," she clarified. It still seemed awkward.

"Well then, I am pleased to know you have earned it," Bravo comforted, raising his cup to her and nodding.

Garret sipped her koffei. "I am told by others that you continued to fight our soldiers despite your men having already laid down their arms. Can you explain your reasoning to me?"

"It is simply a matter of honor. I have sworn to defend my country. It is my responsibility to do so."

"But surely no man would be asked to give his life under the circumstances you faced in those last moments."

"I choose to lead by example, Captain. What example would I set for the next generation of soldiers were I to throw down my weapon in surrender at the first opportunity?"

Garret nodded. "I believe it is better to die a hero than live a coward."

"Wisely spoken." Bravo thought for a moment, inclined to ask a question about Drake. "Your Admiral's reputation varies among my countrymen. He is widely regarded as an exceptional commander, of course. But many think El Draque simply a pirata. What think you?"

Garret smiled. It was a question she'd often pondered during her travels with the man. Yet how did one define a pirate? Was it someone who stole from others, simply for one's own benefit? If so, then that was not the Drake she knew. "You spoke of honor, Captain," she replied. "This is the Admiral I know. His actions are in service of Queen and country. At every turn. He is not, as your countrymen would call him, a pirata."

"I shall take your word for that. Yet you must be aware that he engages without provocation. He takes what belongs to others. Countless numbers of ordinary citizens have died during his assaults."

"You cannot judge the man solely by his actions, sir," Garret responded, defensively. "It is the context and underlying purpose of those actions that one must understand, to truly comprehend their nature."

"And what might that purpose be?"

"As I have already said, he serves at the pleasure of the Queen. And she, in turn, merely responds to the actions of your King. If there is blame, perhaps it rests at King Philip's feet, not the Admiral's."

Bravo nodded. There was truth in that. Military leaders served at the pleasure of royalty.

Garret continued, "Your King's motives are not always honorable. Would you not agree?"

"That is not for me to say, Captain. I am but his soldier."

"As with you, so with Drake."

Bravo smiled. This young woman had a remarkably quick mind, he thought.

———

Two days later, Garret and William accompanied Captain Bravo back to his residence in Cartageña. Drake was at the door when they arrived. "Welcome back, Captain," he said to Bravo. Pray tell, how is your wife."

"I am afraid her passing is imminent. I find I must ask another favor of you."

"Please," replied Drake, observing the sadness in Bravo's eyes.

"Thank you, Admiral. Once she passes, I should like to bury her on the grounds of the cathedral."

"Let it be so. My men shall make the arrangements. She shall be buried with honor."

On the day of her funeral, Drake attended. He ordered two flags to be flown—one English, one Spanish. Taking a cue from Garret, he decided to fly both at half-mast. He also arranged a booming volley of gunshot to honor the brave soldier's wife.

As Bravo's wife was interred, Garret stood alongside Thomas, Drake's brother. When the service ended, she and Thomas walked together, toward the town square. "Does it occur to you, Thomas, that life is precious, no matter which side you are on? Or which country you serve?"

"I suppose," he replied. "I have never thought of it in those terms. I have no qualms about taking the life of my enemy."

"And yet, that enemy may have a wife. And children. Does that not give you pause?"

"Certainly not in the clash of battle, when it is his life or mine."

"Indeed. I suppose we are obligated to perform the actions our leaders demand of us." She paused. "Are they then to blame for those actions?"

"It may depend upon our leader's motivations. Is he a killer at heart? Or is he honoring or defending his country?"

"Your brother has shown us there can be both honor in battle and generosity following the defeat of a sworn enemy."

"In the case of Captain Bravo, my brother believes he was honorably defending his people, not fighting with hatred in his heart. He has taken the measure of the man and determined this is so."

The two arrived at what had been a small tavern prior to Drake's offensive. The English had commandeered the wine and spirits that were stored on the site and assigned crewmembers to staff the establishment. Garret and Thomas both took a seat and were immediately brought cups of wine.

Garret studied the young man seated across from her. Being the youngest of Drake's brothers who had sailed with him, he was the one the Admiral had felt most fatherly toward. Other brothers remained behind in England. Thomas shared certain features and characteristics with his brother—sandy blond hair, piercing dark eyes, and various mannerisms and speech patterns she associated with Drake. He was near her own age. She felt an attraction to him, though nothing like what she'd felt with Pantas. She enjoyed his company and the countless conversations they'd had regarding their experiences at sea. Since the death of Pantas, she'd drawn closer to both Thomas and William.

"It is a fine day," said Thomas, raising his cup. "And this is a fine drink."

"Cheers to that."

"Speaking of family," he said.

"Is that what we were speaking of?"

"In a way—the families of sailors."

"Oh, I see."

"Do you wish one day to have a family of your own, Garret?" It wasn't a question he wouldn't have asked if he'd still thought her to be a young man. Things had changed.

Garret wondered where Thomas was headed with his question. "I wish to take life as it comes."

"Is that a sea-borne life?"

"It certainly is. For now. And perhaps for as long as I am able. It provides a certain freedom I enjoy. And a need for adventure that pulls me ever deeper into this life."

"It is a passion for me as well," said Thomas, "One I believe I am good at. Therein lies a formula for success in my life—where passion and ability cross paths."

"Well said, Thomas." She raised her cup. "To success in our lives."

"To our success," he concurred, tapping his cup against hers. "With any luck, we shall share numerous successes."

———

Over the next several days, with Captain Bravo's assistance, Drake negotiated with the Governor's representatives for a ransom to be paid, in exchange for returning the city to their control. At one point, sensing the Spanish were not bargaining in good faith, Drake ordered several buildings burned to the ground, to demonstrate what might come. Understanding Drake's intent, and prodded by Bravo, Governor de Busto altered course. He turned over several chests filled with gold and silver coins, and sent numerous bars of gold and silver on horse-drawn carts. It was an enormous payoff. But it had come with a downside. Hundreds of Drake's and Carleill's men had taken ill. By the end of February, nearly one hundred had died from the illness. Drake convened his captains, all deeply concerned about the continuing spread of the sickness and the shortage of men that threatened their ability to continue the campaign. A collective decision was made to return to England.

By mid-April, with the provisioning and repairs complete, Drake stood onshore before departing, alongside Governor de Busto, Captain Bravo, General Carleill, Garret and Thomas. "Gentlemen," he said, directing his comments to the Spaniards, "we leave Cartageña in sadness. You have treated us well. And with honor. A war between countries does not need to mean a war between men of goodwill. We are all honorable gentlemen. But for this war between our countries, I believe we could be the best of friends."

The Governor, displeased with having to turn over his city's treasures to El Draque, nevertheless shook his hand. "God bless you on your journey, Admiral." As he said it, he hoped the pirata might succumb to the same illness many of his men had.

Captain Bravo was more forthcoming. "I am much indebted to you Admiral, for your kindness in the matters of my wife. And for my own health and recovery. I wish you to have this golden necklace my wife once wore, as a symbol of friendship." Drake accepted the gift. "Might I add sir that, were you a Spanish Admiral, it would be my great pleasure to serve with you."

"Thank you, Captain. Perhaps when the war between our countries ends, we shall have occasion to visit each other again."

Bravo turned to Garret. "Farewell to you also, Captain. You have enlightened me on the value in having a woman serve in a leadership role."

"Thank you, Captain. I have enjoyed our friendship. May we meet again one day."

"On peaceful terms!" replied Bravo, smiling and nodding.

XXXI

Hurled by an infuriated King, the silver chalice sailed across the room, forcing the military messenger to duck. It banged off the wall and fell to the floor, dented, dripping what was left of the wine that somehow failed to expel during flight. Philip was infuriated by the news of Drake's crushing defeat and capture of his Caribbean jewels—Santo Domingo and Cartageña. "El Draque has humiliated us," he screamed. "We shall soon be the target of opportunists from every country that chooses to mount a fleet." He pounded his fist on his desk. "This cannot stand." The messenger cowered, his eyes glued to the floor.

Philip shook his head, understanding he must avenge his losses simply to re-establish Spain as the dominant world power. He not only needed to crush England's presence on the world's oceans, but also to plunge his sword into her very heart—invade the country; topple the Queen; lay claim to the English countryside. "Assemble the generals," he demanded.

The grand castle in San Lorenzo de El Escorial was resplendent in the evening light, both on the grounds outside, where a line of carriages and horses waited, and inside the banquet hall, where military leaders and royal advisors were fêted. Following a prodigious feast, during which Philip had refused to consume any alcohol, to ensure he maintained his wits, the King rose to address the assembly.

"My good gentlemen," he said, sans emotion. "We have accomplished wondrous things together. Yet we must never take our success for granted." He scanned the room. "Never," he repeated, this time loudly, gaining the room's full attention. He paused to connect with the eyes of the many faces—the best of the best of his military leaders. He continued with a lowered voice, "Others seek to take from us what is rightfully ours—what we have earned through significant investment and enterprise. They do so at their own peril." Nodding his head several times, to emphasize what he'd just said, he turned to name the specific enemy he had in mind, "England's Queen has betrayed us with empty promises of friendship, while quietly scheming against us. She has used her bloody pirata, El Draque, as her instrument of attack on our interests around the world." He now raised his voice, in full rage, "We simply cannot let this English harlot and her dragon continue to impose their will on us." He paused to sip water from a crystal chalice. "They threaten our very empire," he screamed, flinging the chalice across the room. It crashed loudly against the wall, showering a nearby servant with glass shards. The collected minds instantly froze; unbreathing.

Philip leaned forward, his hands planted firmly on the table, his face flushed with fury. He looked each man in the eye, slowly, sternly. With his voice controlled and strong, he emphasized each word by banging his right palm against the table in rhythmic harmony, "The time has come to take decisive action against England. On every front." He paused and stood up straight. "We shall reaffirm our standing as undisputed rulers of the world. Tomorrow, let us begin building a campaign to crush this outrageous woman and her venomous pirata."

Over the next several weeks, Philip worked closely with his advisors to forge a military campaign strategy. Though several options were considered, the King was most enamored of a plan that included an opening raid on Scotland, to divert English forces. With England's attention deflected, the formidable Don Álvaro de Bazán, the Marquis of Santa Cruz, would lead an enormous fleet to capture the Isle of Wight in the English Channel. That island would then serve as Spain's military base for a subsequent invasion of the mainland. Meanwhile, the Duke of Parma would gather Spain's massive army along the northern coast of France. De Bazán's fleet would transport them to the Isle of Wight, and then later to England, to conquer the English on their own soil.

It wasn't long before Queen Elizabeth's highly compensated informants in Spain sent word that the Spanish were proceeding with a planned conquest of England. Her thoughts immediately turned to Drake, who had only recently returned from his successful campaign. She requested his attendance at Richmond Palace, for consultation. When he arrived, the Admiral was taken to a familiar room, deep within the fortress. The Queen preferred to hold her most private discussions in this thickly walled vault.

"Welcome, Sir Drake. Thank you for coming."

"It is my honor, Your Majesty," he bowed.

The Queen smiled and continued. "England is in precious need of your services. I am certain it comes as no surprise that King Philip is much distressed by your many successes against his ships and colonies. I have been informed that his wrath is now being operationalized. He is actively building and preparing his fleet and armies for the sole purpose of claiming England for himself. This cannot happen."

"Of course, Your Majesty," Drake replied. "Though I share your concern, I know the Spanish well. They are fine sailors but I am confident we can repel any attack the King may be inclined to undertake. His ships are better designed to carry heavy cargo across the oceans than to engage and maneuver in battle at close-quarters."

"Your confidence is comforting Admiral, though I fear the sheer size of Philip's forces could overwhelm us. That is why I am giving you full license to shape our naval forces to combat any threat his forces might present. I shall contribute my own ships to your command, including the *Elizabeth Bonaventure*, which I trust you shall find most suitable as your flagship."

Drake felt this was a good start. "You are most gracious, Your Majesty. I cannot fail with your support. Still, we shall need the support of every ship owner and builder in muscling our naval forces."

"Indeed. I shall speak personally with the Lords and merchants, to ensure the commitment of their resources to the cause. I shall also reach out to our Dutch allies for their support."

"Thank you, Your Majesty. I shall begin preparations immediately." He rose.

"I am not done with you just yet, Admiral." Drake paused, in curiosity. "You have not yet shared with me your stories of the taking of Santo Domingo and Cartageña. I am most interested in hearing them."

Leaving the palace later that evening, Drake was comforted by the thought that he would have at his disposal the largest, most capable fleet his nation had ever assembled. Understanding that this would be the most dangerous test of his life, he nevertheless smiled at the opportunity to demonstrate England's superiority on the world's oceans.

———

Well aware of his brother's close relationship with Garret, Drake asked Thomas to meet with her, to assess her interest in commanding a section of his new fleet. Thomas wasted no time visiting her in London, where she was attending to her family's financial affairs. He hadn't seen her in a few months and was anxious to refresh their friendship. He found her at her much-loved Orion's Tavern.

"What a blessing it is to see you again, Thomas. I must say, you look well; though unusually pale for a seafarer." She smiled as she said it.

"You look well too, Garret." Picking up on her tease, he added, "Save for the odd battle scar, you would be a fetching young woman."

"Those are fighting words, sir," she smiled back. "I choose cutlasses at the break of noon, on the morrow."

Given her unparalleled skill as a swordsman, Thomas countered, "I shall bring my pistolet to your swordfight."

Garret grinned, giving him more than an ordinary gentleman's hug. The warmth of their friendship reheated, she released him. They sat.

"What is it that brings you here? Another brotherly adventure, perhaps?"

The tavern owner brought a cup to the table. He poured the koffei slowly. Garret had brought him a supply of the beans, from her recent travels. The two suspended their conversation until he withdrew.

"Not an adventure in the sense we have come to know," Thomas said quietly, the smile draining from his face.

"You are far too serious, Thomas," Garret chided.

He leaned in, speaking quietly, "You must know that King Philip is displeased with our successes against his empire. He intends to amass a military capability beyond imagination. There is even word he may attempt a full-scale invasion of England, to dethrone the Queen."

"Oh, my. That is most troubling."

"So it is. The Queen has beseeched my brother to build and lead our naval forces in England's defense."

"As I would expect."

"Indeed. That is not a surprise." He paused for a moment, looking her straight in the eye. "My brother would like you to command a small contingent of his fleet. He has informed me that I must not return without your acceptance." He smiled.

Garret didn't hesitate, "It would be my honor, Thomas. Let us drink on that." She lifted her cup, "To Queen and country."

"Queen and country," he responded. They sipped their koffei. Thomas sat back in his chair. "Now, let us share our experiences since we last enjoyed each other's company."

XXXII

Alone in his library, King Philip reviewed his generals' reports on the progress being made in preparation for the assault on England. Though confident of his campaign strategy, he recognized it was possible Queen Elizabeth might learn of his plans in advance and begin readying her defenses. Time would therefore be either his accomplice or his adversary. He had insisted his Generals execute their preparations with utmost haste. Finishing his review, he sat back and sipped wine from a silver goblet. His thoughts turned to the actions he might take, were he in Elizabeth's position. There was little doubt she would tap El Draque to lead the naval resistance. Though he despised the pirata, he begrudgingly respected Drake's formidable skill and success in naval battles. It worried him that his own military forces might be intimidated by the man's reputation alone. For that reason, his plan called for an enormous fleet of ships, the size of which would dwarf anything the world had ever seen—one hundred thirty vessels of war. Their sails would dot the English Channel like snow in a blizzard, giving his own forces confidence and hopefully spreading fear throughout the English fleet. A sly grin and a chuckle emerged—the woman who at one point had turned down his marriage proposal would soon be differently defrocked.

———

It was April when Drake's hastily assembled fleet set sail from Plymouth. Twenty-four ships. Three thousand men. He knew full well it

318

would be dwarfed by Philip's armada, though he was unaware it would be as much as five to one. Shortly after departure, he had called for his captains to assemble onboard his flagship, *Elizabeth Bonaventure*. Wishing to maintain ultimate secrecy, none of them had previously been informed of the fleet's specific mission.

"Gentlemen. And Garret," he opened, standing at the table while his officers sat. "We are about to deliver an English breakfast to a sleepy King Philip—one that comes with a swift kick," he grinned. The officers laughed. "Our naval offensive shall trump any defensive shield we might otherwise have employed. We are about to wreak havoc on a Spanish fleet that is still being readied for battle. We shall press our attack against ships at anchor in their ports, where their ability to maneuver will be limited." Nods of approval circled the table. "Our initial target is Cádiz. I am told a great portion of Spain's armada is assembling there. We shall proceed in haste." He grabbed the handle of his mug, half-full with wine. "God has blessed us with speedy preparation, the element of surprise and, most importantly," he lifted the mug high in the air, "the finest sailors known to man. To our collective success."

A rousing huzzah filled the room, bouncing off the walls as the officers rose, echoing his call for success.

The *Elizabeth Bonaventure* showed astounding speed under the most favorable of winds. It arrived at Cádiz well ahead of most of Drake's fleet. He counted some sixty Spanish ships anchored in the harbor. Several dozen longboats busily dotted the spaces, shuttling back and forth from ships to shore, ferrying supplies and weaponry. Feigning true colors, Drake's ships sported the Spanish Burgundy. As they approached, two Spanish warships weighed anchor to welcome their unexpected visitors. Sensing the opportunity was now, Drake decided not to await the arrival of the balance of his fleet.

"Signal the ships Mr. Prouten, if you please."

Prouten ordered the signalman, who waved his flags, notifying the accompanying ships to immediately turn broadside. Once they were in formation, Drake barked another order. "The colors, if you please, Mr. Prouten."

Prouten ordered the Burgundy withdrawn, replaced by St. George's Cross.

"Cannons at the ready!" Drake shouted.

Prouten echoed the call. A riveting, rhythmic noise reverberated across the water as numerous gunports opened, introducing the harbor to menacing iron.

The approaching Spanish warships, realizing they were about to come under attack, attempted to slow their advance. They began turning broadside themselves, to return fire. Yet the more they turned, the bigger the target they presented to Drake's fleet.

"Fire at will, Mr. Prouten," Drake said casually, his wry smile reflecting his strategically advantageous position.

"Fire all!" echoed Prouten.

"Fire all!" repeated Lee.

From hundreds of yards away, people onshore watched a vast array of orange lights blink and spread across the horizon. Moments later came the blistering, simultaneous roar that instantly drowned out the noise of the busy harbor. Fire and smoke dissipated behind the cannonballs that furiously smashed the two approaching Spanish ships, shattering wood and ripping apart sails like shredded paper. Realizing just how vulnerable their position was, the Spanish captains hastily maneuvered their crippled ships back to the perceived safety of the inner harbor, without returning fire.

"Press the attack, Mr. Prouten."

The signalman waved his flags in the direction of the inner harbor. Drake's fleet angled itself ambitiously forward, where they once again settled into a broadside position. The Spanish fleet was still busy positioning their ships and weighing anchors. The sailors on deck were running more in fear than with purpose, not entirely certain what to do next. Some jumped ship, hoping to distance themselves from the enormous targets they'd been walking on. Longboats scurried toward shore, like sheep chased up a ravine by dogs, at times crashing into each other, creating their own chaos.

Drake's cannons blazed in sequence at several targets, preferring to hit the biggest and broadest ships that represented the largest threat. The residents of Cádiz fled to the castle. They ran in fear, stumbling and trampling others in their haste to reach the castle gates. A few Spanish ships began responding, though they could only muster sporadic cannon fire. One enormous Spanish ship, bearing thirty-two cannons, and well-led by its captain, took on the storming English. It was quickly and mercilessly showered with raining cannon fire, shattering its mainmast and blasting holes below the waterline. It sank quickly to the bottom, taking her crew with it, leaving only the top of its masts standing above water—grave markers in a liquid cemetery. Several other ships were sunk or badly disabled. The bodies and blood of fallen sailors soon began washing up on the shore.

As Drake took control of the outer portion of the harbor, his men disembarked into longboats, seizing several viable vessels. The Spanish gathered their seaworthy ships in the inner harbor and assembled soldiers along the shore, tightening their defensive lines. Prouten and Lee cautioned Drake against proceeding too aggressively against a still-dangerous force.

With dusk beginning to fall, Drake contemplated his options. Always more bold than cautious, this time would be no different. He quickly forged a plan to significantly erode the Spanish defenses with minor risk to his own forces. But he would wait for complete darkness. In the meantime, he ordered his men to unload supplies and valuables from the Spanish ships they'd already captured.

———

Garret had been summoned to the *Elizabeth Bonaventure,* just as Drake himself had once been summoned as a fresh young captain to Commander Hawkins' flagship at Rio de la Hacha. The Admiral informed her she was to take the lead on the next step in the assault at Cádiz. Her orders given, she returned to her own ship, which she'd named *Pantas' Revenge.* She relayed her orders to her Lieutenant, William Tovery.

Cloaked in black in the dark of night, Garret and several of her men scampered along the decks of the Spanish ships they'd seized earlier in the day. They unfurled and tightened every last sail, to capture the breeze wafting toward shore. Kegs of gunpowder were placed strategically on the main deck, with trails of powder leading to each. Anchors weighed, the ships headed toward the inner harbor, their speed increasing. At Garret's signal, the men struck their flints, sparking the long fuses connected to the powder trails. They quickly disembarked into longboats. Garret remained at the helm of the leading ship, long enough to ensure it was on the proper tack. Others helmed the remaining ships, spanning the harbor.

As the fuses burned to their ends, powder trails carried spiking flames forward to the kegs. Garret watched their progress intently. When the flames were within a meter of the barrels, she sprinted barefoot to the taffrail. Hoisting herself onto the rail, she stood momentarily before releasing her grip and diving in, mimicking a hurled spear. A sucking sound accompanied her entry into the water below. Beneath the surface, she heard a muffled series of concussive explosions and saw widespread flashes of fluid light. The flaming vessels continued sailing toward the ships anchored in the harbor. Surfacing from her dive, she treaded water, watching the wall of menacing flames brighten the night sky in a roaring, swirling blaze.

Spanish sailors who'd used the pause in hostilities to catch some sleep awoke suddenly to the crunching of ships. Sweeping flames greeted them as they scurried to the main decks. Terrified, they evacuated in haste. Still treading water, Garret watched them scramble down the sides into longboats or jump into the harbor, just as she had, though without any form. The targeted ships now fed the flames, bringing their own stores of gunpowder to life. Thundering explosions shattered everything, showering remnants high into the night sky.

Comfortable the plan was executing perfectly, Garret turned and swam to an approaching longboat. The men pulled her aboard, congratulating her on the success of the mission.

Drake stood on the *Elizabeth Bonaventure's* deck, watching the chaos unfold. He turned his gaze to the biggest prize—the grand warship owned by the Marquis of Santa Cruz himself. Flagship of the Armada, it was a 1,500-ton giant. Still awaiting the arrival of freshly minted cannons, it was already loaded to the hilt with cannon shot and gunpowder. Drake smiled at his good fortune in finding the flagship only partially covered by other vessels. Garret had guided her flaming ship to split the defense and target the unprepared behemoth. Still, it wasn't enough for his liking. "Mr. Prouten," he shouted, "let us light up the sky as never before. I want that warship drenched in cannon fire."

Prouten shouted, signaling instructions to the fleet. When they were ready, he made the call. "Fire away all. At will!"

The quiet but readied cannons of Drake's fleet roared alive, crushing, and ripping through the hell already smothering the Marquis' flagship. As its stores of gunpowder ignited, red and orange balls of expanding flame hurled upward, their spiraling tongues licking the stars. The suddenly concussed and then powerfully expanded air blew several sailors flailing over the taffrail. Others jumped, dreading the inevitable. Injured sailors, screaming for help, were unable to jump. They met their fate as gunpowder kegs continued exploding in an endless series of fireballs. The great ship began cracking into pieces. It sank within minutes, amid flying debris, thrashing water and a chorus of deathly screams. Throughout the harbor of Cádiz and inside the castle walls, Spanish hearts were demoralized by the devastatingly swift loss of their foremost warship.

Having delivered his message of English strength and superiority, Drake ordered the fleet's withdrawal. There was little more to be gained.

As dawn approached, Spanish reinforcements began arriving from nearby ports. They'd heard the distant roar of battle and seen the underbelly of clouds lit by flames. But they'd come too late. The charred litter of ships' masts rising starkly above lapping water told the story. More than two dozen Spanish ships had been shattered and entombed in the night. Hundreds of bloated bodies swayed with the water and washed against the shore, their souls unaccounted for.

"My good and valiant men," Drake said, addressing the officers in his cabin following breakfast. "We have taken the fight to this would-be armada and set its hopes aflame. The King's very beard has been singed!" A hearty combination of laughter and cheers reverberated through the cabin. When the cheering began subsiding, Drake continued. "You have all participated in a decisive battle that shall forever be remembered as the beginning of the end of Spanish dominance at sea." Another grand cheer arose, echoing across the waves.

The noise settled once again. "I now declare England," Drake said slowly, casually, before raising his voice high, "Master of the Oceans." Cheers followed. He raised his cup of wine, now screaming, "To England!"

"To England!" cried the men, with full measure of voice.

Drake waited once again for the cheers to recede. He looked straight at Garret. "Finally, gentlemen, I wish to salute our *fiery* young Captain Connachan, who lit the sky with a towering wave of flame."

The officers raised their cups, nodding to Garret and cheering her boldly, with three huzzahs, each one louder than the last. The moment took Drake back to the day at Rio de la Hacha when Commander Hawkins had singled him out for his efforts in leading the attack by 'knocking' on Castellanos' door. He'd come full circle.

Following breakfast, the officers dispersed, heading back to their ships. Drake sat in his cabin, Prouten at his side.

"We have won a truly remarkable victory, Admiral," said Prouten.

"Indeed we have. But even a severely wounded animal will lash out with all its might. We must be vigilant. The keys to our success will continue to be thoughtful preparation, the element of surprise, and our ability to adapt as the battle unfolds. Most importantly, we must always grasp the hearts, minds and confidence of our men. No man can lead a battle without their full trust and commitment. We have been much blessed in this way."

"Indeed we have. Without their support, we are but shadows of ourselves. Yet we have not simply been handed the men's confidence. Nor was it purchased. We have earned it."

"Well said, Mr. Prouten. To be sure, we are not leaders if we turn around only to find that no one has chosen to follow." The two men laughed. Drake continued. "They shall only follow us if they know we have their own interests, and those of our country, at heart. This we must always do."

Prouten nodded, sipping from his cup. Drake looked him in the eye. "I am fortunate to have you at my side. Not only here but in countless other endeavors as well. Though I may, in title, be your superior, we are truly partners. As too are we partners with our officers and men. We are but one fire-breathing dragon.

The two men clinked their mugs together, enjoying another sip of the fine wine.

While Drake and Prouten were celebrating, the next generation of leaders had held up on deck. Drake's brother Thomas, William Tovery and Garret wished to have another moment together before returning to their ships.

"Well done, Garret," said Thomas. "Your reputation continues to grow. I am exceedingly happy for you."

"As am I," echoed William.

"Thank you, Thomas. But truly, it is not the glory I seek. It is the adventure. I share your brother's insatiable thirst for the next great challenge."

"May there be many, then," Thomas said, extending his hand. "God be with you."

"And with you, Thomas." She shook his hand and turned to William, "You as well, William." She put her hand on his full, muscled shoulder. "The three of us have much history to write. Together," she smiled.

They disembarked to waiting longboats, each feeling as though they were virtual siblings.

XXXIII

Stark and ominous, the mighty fortress of Sagres emerged from a lifting fog. High on the cliff at the southwest tip of Portugal, it overlooked the eastern end of the Atlantic Ocean. Its gray walls, eight feet thick and forty high, were imposing. Designed to be impregnable, it was constructed at the end of a thin peninsula, surrounded on three sides by sheer cliffs. Observing it from his foredeck, Drake felt a rush of excitement. Capturing it would send yet another frightening message to his enemies. After all, if this fortress were to prove vulnerable, then nothing could be considered beyond his grasp.

Fresh from victory at Cádiz and thirsty for the next challenge, the fleet anchored in the isolated Bay of Belixe, two miles northwest of the fortress. Drake disembarked, along with eight hundred men. They set camp, feasted, and honed their weapons for battle. After the meal, Drake met separately with his officers to lay out the next day's assault plan. There was no alternative but to charge the main gate. The initial runners would carry bales of wood, to set flame to the entry gate. It was a high-risk endeavor—a frontal attack across a narrow, extended plain, exposed to enemy fire from an elevated position.

Later that night, Garret approached Drake's tent. She called from outside, announcing her presence. The Admiral, already retired, was perturbed by the interruption. Nevertheless, he rose to a seated position, recognizing Garret's voice. "Enter," he replied, followed by "if you must," under his breath.

Garret entered. "Thank you, Admiral. I apologize for bothering you at this hour."

"What is it, then?" he responded, abruptly.

"I have been giving thought to our attack on the fortress."

"And?"

"The approach is completely barren, perhaps two hundred yards long and, in places, no more than twenty wide. Runners in the first wave risk a quick entry to Hell. Few can be expected to survive."

"This is not news. We have no choice if we are to succeed."

"Might I suggest, Admiral, that each runner wear dark clothing, and that their exposed skin be smeared with mud. It shall make them less visible."

"That is precisely what I intend," he replied, in irritation.

Garret gathered herself before broaching the reason she'd come, "I wish to accompany that first wave, sir."

Drake didn't hesitate. "That is not possible. I shall be leading the charge. Should anything happen to me, my remaining officers will be needed to lead the fleet. I cannot let any officer face such peril; you included."

"But I have an advantage, sir. I am a slighter target. And a strong runner. I believe I can make it to the gate before any of the men."

Drake saw the determination in her eyes. Her brashness and courage reminded him so much of his own as a youth. Nothing was ever gained without risk, he thought. And she desperately wanted that gain. She would see it through if he let her. And he had to admit, she made a good point—sailors were known for their brute strength, not their running ability. She could easily outrun them all.

"I can take a smaller cache of wood," Garret added, sensing Drake was considering the possibility. "Just the initial kindling. That would enable me to get there even faster."

Drake saw the merit in her argument. If it would improve their chance for success, then it was imperative he act on it. Yet Garret was a highly valued asset. "Perhaps we might find a fast, young midshipman to carry the kindling," he offered.

"I will not stand for that, Admiral!" She said it more vociferously than she'd intended. "Under no circumstances shall a child take my place for such a deadly mission."

Drake flinched. No one had ever challenged him this way—so adamantly; so fiercely. He understood the force of her desire. "You test me greatly, Captain. And not with the honor and respect deserving of a senior officer."

"I am sorry if…" Garret started, her head held high.

Drake raised his hand, interrupting her. "Stop. I am certain this shall be the last time you address me in that fashion."

Garret nodded.

"Your punishment for such rudeness shall be my granting of your wish. You shall lead the first wave. Now leave me before I change my mind."

"Thank you, Admiral."

Garret turned and left, a smile on her face but fear in her heart. Drake returned to his bed, chuckling inside at her insistence that a child not take her place. She wasn't much more than a child herself. Still a teenager, though admittedly one with an adult mind and presence.

The following day, in the late afternoon, Drake peered at the fortress through the foliage at the edge of the approach-way. Hundreds of raiders were assembled behind him. He counted the cannons peering out across the top of the fortress. Between them stood soldiers, alongside mounted arquebuses. Lives were sure to be lost. But there was no turning back, only pressing forward.

"Arquebuses at the ready," he called. The shooters, aligned in a long row just inside the woods, took aim. "Fire at will."

Loud blasts were followed quickly by the sound of lead balls pinging the fortress wall. They merely chipped and bounced off the stone. It was Drake's way of announcing his raiders' presence and readiness to fight. Within moments, Spanish and Portuguese soldiers returned fire. No damage was done. The Admiral waited for their shooting to end. Despite appearances, he knew he was in a favorable position. With his fleet barricading any approach by sea and his imposing force assembled at the opening to the peninsula, he could prevent supplies from entering or leaving the fortress. No one from within the fortress could leave to seek aid. He hoped to encourage those inside to see their self-imposed helplessness. It could avoid casualties, enabling a bloodless seizure of the fort.

Guns now silent, Drake walked out onto the pathway. Garret accompanied him, bearing a large white flag. Langton, his interpreter, walked alongside. They reached a point at which Drake was comfortable they could be heard by enemy forces. Cupping his hands around his mouth, Langton called out the Admiral's remarks, in Portuguese, "Hail, fair soldiers! I am the man you know as El Draque. I mean you no harm. We have come only for your fortress. You are surrounded at sea and on the ground. You shall henceforth be unable to obtain supplies. I urge you to throw down your weapons and open your gates. In doing so, you shall be free to leave this place." He paused to let Drake's words take seed in the minds of the soldiers. After a few moments, he continued.

"Should you oppose us, we shall be forced to impose our will. And I promise you, we *will* take your fortress. You shall either die of hunger and thirst, be slain by our weapons, or become our prisoners. For your own sake, and that of your families, lay down your arms now and walk away as free men."

There was a quiet in the air, interrupted only by the crashing of waves at the base of the cliffs. Five minutes passed; then ten. Still no response. Langton called out once more, "Hail, fair soldiers! My patience runs thin. Decide now—a peaceful return to your families or the end of your days."

Despite the murmurings of his soldiers, the fortress commander was unconvinced by Drake's words. His men were well-supplied and well-prepared. Believing he could wait out the English, he answered Drake's call with a single cannon shot aimed his way. It landed forty yards short, bouncing and rolling harmlessly toward him. The message was clear—Drake would need to proceed with a frontal assault—a virtual death-run.

The soon-to-be battlefield was eerily quiet. Neither side perceived any value in wasting ammunition. The fortress' defenders anticipated a nighttime assault. They smiled inwardly at the thought of it. Targets would be plentiful. A shooter's dream.

Late that afternoon, Drake turned to his officers. "I shall address the men now." They nodded, passing the word for silence. With the breeze at his back and his back to the fortress, he called out to the men with no worries that his words would carry to the enemy. "My brave men. We are about to take this fortress." He smiled confidently. "We cannot scale its walls in the face of fire from above. But their gate is made of wood." He paused. "Wood burns," he smiled. The men laughed. "We shall penetrate that gate. I need thirty brave souls to join me in charging the fortress, under cover of our own fire. We shall place kindling at the foot of the gate, setting it aflame. It shall give us a warm welcome." The men laughed again, this time a little nervously. "Our second wave shall make the charge once the gate is aflame. The soldiers inside will see they are vastly outnumbered. When we pour through the gate, the forces inside shall recognize their imminent demise. Facing a choice between surrender or slaughter, I believe they shall choose wisely." He paused, turning his head from one side to the other. He peered into the eyes of several men, judging their courage. Some looked away. Others nodded. "I shall give you a few moments to think on this. I welcome those who will join me in this charge."

Everyone understood the gravity and riskiness of the mission—a spine-chilling run across an open field, carrying bales of wood. The darkness, their running speed, and covering rifle shots would provide only minimal protection. Many would surely perish on this field. They conferred with those closest to them, making their choices before the horizon completely swallowed the trailing light of a sunken sun.

Drake had sent William Tovery to alert the fleet. They were to open fire on the fortress, on a dual-white-flagged signal, just ahead of the first wave. As complete darkness embraced the peninsula, everyone was at-the-ready. Drake called out once again, "I need thirty brave men. You have each had time to consider your options. So I ask you now: who will run with me?"

Musa, never one to hesitate, stepped forward. Caber offered himself up as well. Matching the courage of these two, a number of other brave souls stepped forward, including Garret, William Tovery and Drake's brother, Thomas. Drake nodded his appreciation. More than fifty had come forward. He selected from among them, denying William and Thomas their chance to participate. Garret was chosen, per their agreement.

"Mr. Prouten." Drake said, "See that these men—and Captain Connachan—are given the bales we have gathered. Have them smear mud on their faces and wear only dark clothing." Musa, his black skin making his broad smile glow in the slivered moonlight, raised his arms questioningly. "No mud for Musa, here," said Drake. The men laughed; haltingly.

———

Thirty raiders were assisted in strapping bales of wood to their backs, preparing for the run of their lives. Adrenaline pumped through their veins, most visibly in their temples. Some chewed on their favored coca leaves, attempting to calm their nerves. Beads of sweat moistened muddied faces. Garret's bale was the primary kindling. Her light load would allow for the swiftest approach to the main gate.

Drake steeled himself to lead the charge. Though the dark had come quickly, the partial moon's light meant the first wave would be exposed. He gathered the runners, advising them of the formation he felt would create sufficient space between them to make the enemy's targeting more difficult. On his signal, the fleet's cannons barked at the fortress. The raiders took off in groups of five, spaced several yards apart and leaving intermittently. They ran as quickly as they could, crisscrossing in swerving paths. Bales on their backs, sweat streaming down their foreheads and stinging their eyes, they charged like slithering snakes. English arquebuses waited patiently for enemy fire before returning it, attempting to suppress it as best they could. Arquebus and cannon shots blazed at the runners, chipping off their wood, kicking up dust, and piercing bone and flesh. A handful of raiders, gravely wounded, breathed dirt, praying for a quick death. Two more were shot dead in their tracks, hitting the ground and sending bales of wood exploding in pieces, with no uniform sense of direction. Several runners absorbed lesser wounds, hindering their movement. They lay tightly glued to the ground, attempting to find cover behind their bales. Bullets pierced the dirt all around them, scattering earth and dust. Men screamed for help, one crying out for his mother as he and others died on blooded soil.

Those who could still run pushed forward. Garret was first to arrive at the gate. Dripping wet, as though emerging from the sea, she pressed herself hard against the heavy wooden barrier, beneath the modest overhang created by the arched stone wall. Breathing heavily and noticing blood on her arm from a wound she hadn't felt, she quickly threw her kindling at the gate's base, pulled threads of it out, and molded them together to catch a flame. She struck pieces of flint near the threads. It took too many tries, in her mind, before they finally caught a spark. She blew softly on the orange glow, brightening it enough to spread. Two other raiders soon joined her at the gate, dripping blood and sweat. They unloaded their bales. Together, they stacked the wood, enabling the fire to grow upward in a spire. The soldiers atop the walls couldn't shoot down at the intruders without bending over the fortress wall and exposing themselves to English fire. Instead, they poured down hot, flaming oil, hoping to set aflame the raiders at the base of the wall. The indentation of the gate provided Garret and the others with much-cherished cover. Drake himself finally arrived, wounded and bemoaning the fact that so many had beaten him to the gate. His raiders used the Spaniards' flaming oil to accelerate the burn of their own bonfire. But they were forced to take cover from the stronger flames now crawling up the gate itself, generating stifling heat. They stood flat against the fortress wall, holding pieces of wood above their heads to avoid the burning oil still raining down from above. Musa and Caber scrambled into the opening, the latter carrying a large chunk of wood to use as a battering ram against the gate, which was now glowing orange at its lowest extremity. Fighting oppressive heat, Musa chipped away at the gate's bottom with his mighty axe, creating narrow channels for the flames to feed on. The gate soon flared on its own.

Seeing the bright glow at the gate, the men of the second wave were emboldened. Prouten ordered the charge, sending a surge of raiders forward at full speed, unencumbered by bales of wood. Fortress defenders were shaken, watching the ominous threat roll toward them—hundreds of blood-thirsty, cutlass-wielding pirates.

Smoke poured into the fortress from flames licking through the base and sides of the gate. The Portuguese commander shuddered as the gate's midsection warped from the crash of Caber's log-ram against the midsection. A vision of swarming raiders pouring through and overwhelming his forces brought him nausea and bile. He screamed at his men to cease firing, pieces of vomit launching with his voice. Several, but not all of his men, lowered their weapons. His vomit gone, the commander shouted orders to his lieutenant at the top of the fortress. They were echoed down to Drake on the other side, above the roar of flames decimating the gate, and the thundering vibration of the approaching, screaming horde.

"Hail, El Draque. We shall surrender. Now—in exchange for our peaceful departure."

His face dirtied by a foul mix of mud, soot, sweat and blood, his hair slightly singed, Drake grinned with pleasure. The power had shifted to his hand. He signaled Prouten, rapidly waving two white flags.

In under three minutes, with the second wave bearing down on the charred, still-flaming gate, the soldiers inside used long, iron rods as levers to remove the gate's iron crossbeam. They pulled back as the battering ram smashed the gate open. Drake's men had their weapons drawn and ready. The Portuguese commander and a few officers stood inside, facing them, swords holstered. One held a pole bearing a huge white sheet. The soldiers atop the fortress looked on, weapons at their feet. The raiders, standing behind Drake and breathing heavily, lowered their weapons, though still grasping them firmly.

Assessing the situation and believing there was no imminent danger, Drake removed his doublet. He held it out front as he jumped through the window of flames. He was followed immediately by Garret and a handful of similarly filthy raiders, most of them wounded, burned and bleeding. Only seven had survived the initial charge. Drake brought himself face-to-face with the Portuguese commander. "My good Captain," he said, observing the man's rank. "I salute you for the valiant defense of your fortress, and for preserving the lives of your men." He extended his hand in greeting.

"Commander Draque," the captain replied, bowing his head and taking Drake's hand. "I thank you for your consideration of our surrender. You may take possession of the fortress and its contents. We count on your promise of safe passage to our homes and families, asking only that we be permitted to take our personal belongings." Drawing his sword slowly, with his left hand, he offered it up sideways, in both hands.

Drake accepted the sword. The two leaders again shook hands on the terms of surrender. At their captain's signal, the Portuguese soldiers left their weapons on the ground and proceeded to collect their belongings. Within the hour, they began leaving the fortress, unarmed and unharmed.

Daring and deadly, Drake's assault had accomplished his objective. In the morning he and his men buried their fallen aside the small fortress cathedral. He said a prayer, asking God's blessing for the courageous lost souls. He then looked up at those assembled, "All of these men we have lost, are heroes. They willingly sacrificed all, for England. I honor them as among the bravest I have ever known. Though their lives were short, their stars shall shine in the night sky forever. God bless their souls."

———

After a few days of celebration and rest at Sagres, Drake's men began leaving, taking all surplus weapons, gunpowder and supplies. Some would stay behind to control the fortress. Thomas, Garret and William planned to leave later, with the Admiral. They stood on the gunners' walkway, looking out over the assault plain at the disorganized parade of their departing mates.

"Those who made the first run shall forever be hailed as the bravest of us all," William lamented. "It was a singular chance to make our mark. I envy you, Garret. You thoughtfully engineered your participation. And reputation."

"Your time shall come, William. Of that, I am sure."

Thomas felt a need to defend his brother's decision to hold him and William back. "As disappointed as I am, I understand my brother's decision. It was no whim of the moment. He knew how deadly the charge would be.

Were all three of us to join him, and perish in the assault, it would leave a gaping hole in the leadership structure—big enough to…sink the fleet."

William and Garret laughed. For that moment at least, the mood was lightened. Garret's thoughts ran to a different victory at Sagres—one she'd fought long and hard for. No longer would she have to face any of the men questioning her courage or capabilities. She was now one of them; unquestionably among the very best.

XXXIV

Drake's fleet sailed north from Sagres, along the southern coast of Portugal, avoiding being visible from shore. They launched surprise assaults on small ports along the way, destroying or damaging most of the Spanish and Portuguese ships they encountered. It was all part of the Admiral's plan to cripple King Philip's supply lines and military capabilities. In time, the fleet reached the bustling city of Lisbon, where a large component of Philip's Armada was being readied. Drake had learned the Marquis of Santa Cruz, commander of the King's fleet, was there, overseeing naval preparations. He composed a message for his Spanish counterpart and asked Garret to deliver it personally, assuring it would be read by the Marquis. Langton, the fleet's interpreter, would accompany her. The two were rowed ashore under a white flag.

Stepping onto shore, Garret and Langton were met by a Spanish captain and several armed soldiers. The captain was in full naval dress—a long red overcoat with braids of gold and large black cuffs. He wore a gold-colored belt at his waist and a white silk bow at his neck, topped by a black captain's hat and finished with gray stockings above black, buckled boots. He was dark-haired, bearded and physically imposing.

"Buenos dios, Capitán," said Langton, extending his hand. "Mi nombre es Langton—interpreter for Sir Drake, Admiral of Her Majesty, Queen Elizabeth's, fleet. He gestured to his left, "Mi asociado—Capitán Connachan."

The Spaniard smirked at this 'Captain' Connachan. She was but a young woman, masquerading, he thought, as a captain. Garret responded to his disrespectful glare with a look of her own—supreme confidence. Her chest thrust forward, shoulders back, she made her womanhood fully apparent. The Spaniard was distracted for a moment, perusing her breasts. Langton cleared his throat to regain the man's attention.

The captain returned his gaze to Langton. "May I ask your intentions, señor?"

"We have a message for the Marquis. From the Admiral."

"Let me see this message," replied the Captain with an air of firmness, extending his hand.

"I am afraid the letter is private. For the eyes of the Marquis only."

The Spaniard looked at him, angrily. "I shall take it to him."

"Apologies, Captain, but the Admiral has instructed us to deliver his letter to the Marquis in person."

The captain paused, looking straight at Langton. He didn't like a man of lesser rank telling him what to do. It was not the way of military order; you simply did not go around an officer of superior rank. Still, he recognized the letter was being delivered on the Admiral's orders. Though he preferred to open and read it, he understood that interfering with its delivery to the Marquis could lead to awkward circumstances—ones he might come to regret.

"As you wish, señor," the captain conceded, determined to still exercise some authority. "But I must insist that my men search you and your…associate…for the presence of any weapons."

Langton was unarmed. Garret had a visibly holstered cutlass. One of the soldiers stepped forward quickly to search them. He smiled as he brushed Garret's breasts with his hand while drawing it down to remove her cutlass from its sheath. Instinctively, her right hand reached for the handle, while her left grabbed the man's offending arm.

Langton intervened. "Please, Captain," he pleaded, "surely you understand that Captain Connachan must always carry her sword."

The Spaniard begrudgingly agreed, motioning to his soldier to leave the cutlass. The soldier did so but continued on, kneeling down and feeling along Garret's legs slowly, with a smirk on his face. He looked inside the rim of her boots, finding a thin-handled knife sheathed there. He withdrew it and rose up, tossing it to his Captain. He then proceeded to walk behind Garret. He stroked her buttocks leisurely and asked that she raise her arms, pushing them up gently. She accommodated him. He felt under her armpits and once again stroked the sides of her breasts, sliding his hands down to her waist and back to her buttocks.

"Are you quite finished pleasuring yourself?" Garret asked, in English. Langton smirked. None of the Spaniards understood what she'd said. The captain ordered his soldier to move on and search Langton. He did so quickly, and nowhere near as thoroughly. The man then stepped back. He looked straight at Garret with a smile, waving his hands as though he were once again fondling her. He pushed his tongue through and beyond his lips, a couple of times. Garret looked away.

"Follow me," said the Spanish captain, motioning them toward the city.

The Marquis was a distinguished-looking gentleman. Almost completely bald, he had traces of silver hair above and behind his ears. His beard was mostly white, highlighted by the up-turned ends of a stylish mustache. He wore a white ruff at his neck and dark, gold-trimmed armor, which he'd often sported on official occasions. A lifelong military officer, following in the giant footsteps of his father and grandfather, he was remarkably fit for being in his sixties. His standing as General Admiral of the Spanish Navy was befitting of his unblemished naval career—he simply did not lose. He made Drake's messengers wait for no good reason other than to display his own importance. Finally, Garret and Langton were led into his spacious quarters and introduced. She was immediately taken by the Marquis' fatherly appearance and pale blue eyes. Standing up from his chair, he looked over the two of them, smiling and nodding at Garret in particular.

"Thank you, Capitán," he said to the Spaniard who'd brought them. "You are excused."

"As you wish, Admiral," said the Captain. He bowed briefly from the waist, then turned sharply, making a dramatic, formal exit.

The Marquis motioned for Langton and Garret to have a seat on the far side of his ornate, polished desk. He waited for Garret to sit before taking his own seat. "I am told you bring word from your Admiral." His English was reasonably fluent.

"Indeed," said Garret. She withdrew the letter from her doublet, extending it to the Marquis. "With Admiral Drake's compliments."

"Thank you, Señorita."

"Captain," she corrected him.

"Indeed," he nodded. The Marquis took the letter, placing it directly in front of him, unopened. He turned first to Langton. "Tell me, how long have you served with the Admiral?" Garret was appalled that he'd spoken first to the person of lesser rank, thinking it must be because he was a man, not a woman.

"Since he was first appointed Captain."

"And you?" asked the Marquis, turning to Garret.

"I joined him as a midshipman. At my father's request."

"It was not your own ambition?"

"Not at the time. Though it has certainly become so."

The Marquis leaned back. "Do you not think it extraordinary that a woman serves with an officer's rank?"

"With all respect, Admiral, would you ask the same of my Queen?"

The Marquis laughed aloud, pounding his desk with his hand. This was one feisty young woman, he thought. A quick mind. And bold. When he'd gathered himself, he responded, "You are very much younger than Her Majesty. Her granddaughter, perhaps?"

"My youth is my advantage, sir," she said confidently. "I am unrelated."

"And does your Admiral favor you for your naval skills?" He paused, with a teasing grin, "Or is there something he values even more?"

Garret waited a moment before answering. His fatherly appearance suggested he may have children of his own, though she couldn't be certain. She chose to deflect his implication. "Were I *your* daughter, Admiral, would you think I had obtained my rank through disreputable means?"

The Marquis laughed again. He absolutely loved this woman's wit; her quickness; her strength of character; and her surprising diplomatic skills— particularly given her youth.

"El Draque has chosen wisely, Capitán," he nodded.

Langton became impatient with this idle chat. "The letter, Admiral," he interjected. "Admiral Drake would appreciate a timely response."

"Yes, yes, of course. All in good time. Please, be our guests for this evening. I shall provide you a letter of my own, on the morrow."

Langton and Garret exited the Marquis' quarters, accompanied by the Spanish captain who'd been instructed to find them separate rooms and arrange for their dinner. Over a fine meal that evening the two recounted their meeting with the Spanish captain on the shore, and their audience with the Marquis.

"I surely do not know how you put up with all that, Captain," Langton stated.

"There is a certain feeling of power," she replied, "that comes from toying with men whose minds are so easily distracted. It makes them vulnerable."

Langton laughed, raising his glass of wine and nodding in admiration of her emotional maturity.

Later that evening, the Marquis unsealed Drake's letter, reading it more than once.

"*My dearest Marquis,*" Drake had written. "*I am well aware of your reputation for victory in battle. It is not unlike my own. We are now at the same place, at the same moment in time. I ask that you surrender your forces and spare the shedding of blood on both sides. In exchange, I shall guarantee your men safe return to their families. But understand that you and your senior officers will need to accompany me to England. You shall all be well-accommodated.*

Should you choose not to accept my terms, you must prepare to engage immediately in a battle to determine which of us is the superior commander of forces.

I graciously await your reply."

In the moment, the Marquis' men and ships were unprepared to take the fight to Drake. The old commander knew it. He suspected Drake also knew it, since he'd so brashly challenged him to do battle. He crafted a message of his own. Though he'd been kind and engaging in his meeting with Drake's emissaries, he was uninclined to be so gracious in a matter of such military consequence. His letter was intended to teach the younger English Admiral a lesson in naval manners and diplomacy. He sealed his note and handed it to Garret the following morning, not sharing with her the nature of its contents.

"I wish you good day, Señor Langton and Capitán Connachan. It was my distinct pleasure to have met you. I wish you well—though not in the event we meet in battle," he nodded and smiled.

———

In his quarters, Drake unsealed the letter Garret handed him—the Marquis' reply. He read it aloud, in the presence of Prouten, Langton, Garret and his brother Thomas.

"El Draque. You, sir, are a pirata. A man of questionable honor. You challenge me with my ships at anchor, not yet ready to fight on fair seas. This is no way to determine which of us is the superior commander. I shall not surrender. Nor shall I engage at such a sharp disadvantage. If you are indeed an Admiral, not a mere pirata, you shall honor me with your retreat. I welcome an opportunity to engage at a future date, on open water."

Drake placed the letter on his desk while looking at his officers. "He is one crafty gentleman; I give you that." He thought for a moment. He knew he could destroy the Marquis' fleet, just as he'd done at Cádiz. His passion pushed him toward unleashing his anger on the old commander by decimating his fleet. But the crusty warrior had implied that that would show no honor—as an Admiral or a gentleman. And Drake knew the Marquis was right—it wouldn't prove his superior skill, given such a substantial advantage. Though his gut thirsted for battle, his sense of honor won out. Best to pull back, to await a time when he could meet the Marquis on equal footing. And then beat him ruthlessly. In that way, there could be no disputing either his honor or the superiority of the English navy. He sent Garret and Langton back with one more message.

"My Dear Marquis. I have served my country with honor and distinction. My actions and reputation show this to be true. I take your words harshly and long for the day when we shall meet on open seas. I shall then feast on your forces. Please proceed with all haste to join me."

The Marquis' ships remained safely anchored in the harbor, unthreatened by Drake. Though he had avoided conflict and demise, not challenging El Draque caused the Spanish Admiral to suffer unexpected humiliation from his own countrymen. The Italian ambassador, who was in Lisbon at the time, was overheard telling his associates, *"Truly, the English are Masters of the Sea, and hold it at their discretion. El Draque is the finest commander of the oceans.*" At least the *verbal* battle had gone in Drake's favor.

XXXV

The light afternoon breeze brought a pleasing call from the crow's nest—"Sail ho!" Drake quickly exited his cabin, hoping the just-sighted vessel was King Philip's treasure ship, the *San Felipe*, rumored to be in the area. His fleet had sailed almost due west from Lisbon for days, searching for it. Looking out across deep blue water, he waited patiently for the gap to close. More than a few hours passed before he could truly study his prey. With twenty-plus cannons, the galleon was significantly larger and arguably more deadly than his leading warships. Nonetheless, a smile broke slowly across his face. The ship was alone. No match for his fast, seasoned fleet.

The *San Felipe* was well aware it was being stalked—a proud, heavily antlered buck with wolves circling. Fully sheeted, its cannons at the ready, it maintained course, letting the predators face its buttocks. Its sheer size and powerful weaponry exuded confidence. It would not be taken without a severe price being paid by these English dogs.

Drake closely trailed the galleon through the day. He sought to take full advantage of the weather's calm. Garret had lobbied Drake for the role of lead assault vessel, disclosing that she had long ago prepared a full set of blackened sails for an assault such as this. Well before dusk, the *Pantas' Revenge* took a wide flanking position beyond view of the *San Felipe*. The sails were hurriedly exchanged for their blackened brethren. As darkness crept in, and before the wind began to falter, her darkly shadowed ship cruised well ahead from the flank. She stood on the foredeck, waiting for the full darkness of night to trigger her assault. Except for the *Pantas' Revenge*, Drake's fleet stalked the galleon from behind, beyond range of its deadly cannons. His ships were well-lit, to hold the attention of the *San Felipe*, providing Garret with a distraction. The galleon fired occasional warning shots at Drake's fleet from its stern chasers. They echoed distantly in the quiet stillness.

Garret and William stealthily disembarked from the *Pantas' Revenge*, leading a group of darkly cloaked longboats on a clandestine approach from the flank. Together, they had carefully selected the men to accompany them. Musa and Caber were first on the list. The assault plan called for them to board the ship and overwhelm its crew. That would avoid damaging the ship itself, risking the loss of its cargo.

Several minutes passed before the sizeable stern chasers of the *San Felipe* once again cracked the air. Two flaring lights from their discharge lit the darkness. The cannon shots fell harmlessly into the water ahead of Drake's slow pursuit. Garret's longboats, drawn by the strongest of rowers, skimmed rapidly over the flat water from the flank until they were directly alongside the galleon's hull. They'd gone undetected as a result of the Spaniards' intense focus on Drake's stalking fleet. When another round of shots fired, the raiders stealthily scaled the sides of the floating palace, nearest the bow. Ascending perilously, they dropped light incendiary devices with medium-length fuses into open gunports, to disorient and disable the cannons. Some raiders remained in the longboats, ready to fire at the taffrail if necessary, to keep the Spanish at bay during the ascent.

Small explosions began ripping inside the gun deck. Garret and Black Jack scrambled over the taffrail. An avalanche of others followed, including

William. The *San Felipe's* captain, finally comprehending what was happening at the far end of his ship, realized he'd been outsmarted. At the frightening view of black-faced raiders pouring onto the deck, he feared for the safety of several hundred passengers, some of them dignitaries, who'd retired below deck for the evening. He instantly raised his hands wide, ordering a halt to the stern chasers and a lowering of the Spanish Burgundy. His second-in-command, standing to the side, waved a white kerchief frantically.

Garret saw the surrender. "Hold," she yelled, throwing her hands wide to her sides but keeping her cutlass pointed forward. Within moments, the raiders came to a halt. She and William strode slowly toward the captain as the others waited behind, weapons at the ready.

The Spaniard drew his sword with his left hand, laying it flat and then offering it up with both hands.

"Please," he said, "I beseech you. Spare my passengers and crew."

"No one dies here," Garret shouted to her compatriots, making her intentions perfectly clear. She accepted the captain's sword."

An hour later, Drake and Prouten boarded the *San Felipe*. "My good Captain," Drake nodded to the Spanish commander, "I commend you for avoiding the loss of life. Let you and I mark this good fortune for our men by sharing a fine wine aboard my flagship this night. Our officers shall join us."

"I thank you, Admiral." The Spanish captain extended his hand. "It is an honor to surrender the ship to a man of such grand reputation."

"You have surrendered your ship to a *woman*, Captain," Drake replied, turning and smiling at Garret. "And *her* reputation is likely to approach mine in time." He turned his eyes back to the captain. "Now, please, show me to the hold of your vessel. I wish to inspect your cargo."

Drake, Garret and William walked to the hold, led by the Spaniard. As they opened the door and peered inside, Drake was surprised to see how small it was for such a large vessel. It contained a normal array of ships' materials and provisions.

"I am sure you jest, Captain. This is clearly not the hold I had in mind."

"No, of course." His modest attempt to shield his precious cargo hadn't fooled anyone. "My apologies. I presumed you meant to inspect our supplies and provisions. We are carrying some exceptionally fine wines."

"I have finer things in mind, Captain."

The group continued on to the main cargo hold. As one of the captain's men opened its locked doors, Drake's eyes widened in amazement. The room disclosed enormous treasures, primarily from the East Indies— precious spices, silks, and tons of ivory, gold and jewels. It was easily the second most valuable capture Drake had ever made. He turned to Prouten. "I believe a course to England is in order. Immediately, if you please."

XXXVI

With his ships securely anchored in Plymouth Harbor and final preparations made, Drake traveled once again to London, to report to Queen Elizabeth. As she'd done before, she welcomed him and his officers with triumphant ceremony and a feast in their honor, attended by the most important political and business leaders of the day. Drake regaled the attendees with stories of his fleet's actions at Cádiz and Sagres, and of the capture of the treasure-laden *San Felipe*. Attendees were enraptured by his storytelling and cheered his victories, frequently toasting Drake, his officers, the Queen, and the honor of England.

When the dining ended, Drake and the Queen exited for a quiet personal meeting, as was their tradition. Sitting alone, wine in hand, Elizabeth raised her chalice. "I commend you, Admiral. Your exploits on behalf of England continue to amaze me. You have done more for this country than any military leader in our history. For that, I am deeply grateful. You shall retain a generous portion of the *San Felipe's* treasures. What remains shall be reinvested in our fleet and military capabilities."

"Thank you, Your Majesty. My men are most deserving of your gratitude. They shall share equally in my portion of the treasure."

Elizabeth smiled, "You say *men*, yet I have come to understand that there is, shall we say, something more among your officers."

Drake returned her smile. "You refer to Captain Connachan, I presume."

"The very same."

"She is as deserving as any of my officers. Perhaps even more so."

"And how is it that the participation of this fine young officer has not previously come to my attention?"

"Entirely by accident, I assure you. She first joined me as a midshipman. Disguised as a male, I might add. She was smartly able to maintain that secret for much of her time with me. Her intelligence and courage eventually earned her the unquestioned respect of my men. She has been well-accepted by them, even in her role as an officer."

"I welcome an opportunity to meet this amazing young woman."

"Indeed, Your Majesty. I shall make it so."

Elizabeth continued on matters of a more serious note. "You must know that your success will further motivate King Philip to exact revenge on our empire. We cannot let that happen. I am entrusting you with the continued defense of the realm."

"It is my high honor to serve England, Your Majesty."

———

The sound of crystal smashing against the stone walls of El Escorial was no longer uncommon. Philip felt a personal humiliation exceeding that of the Marquis at Lisbon. Drake's successes at Cádiz and Sagres, and his capture of the *San Felipe*, had deeply impacted the King's preparations for his

Armada. His rage gave rise to the hurling of crystal almost as often as he thought of El Draque. Spain's reputation as a military power was faltering. With his military leaders assembled before him, he fully vented his anger. "This is beyond unacceptable," he screamed. "I order you to make all necessary preparations to avenge the extensive damage Queen Elizabeth and her pirata have brought us. We shall spare no expense. Fail, and I shall have you all executed for treason."

XXXVII

Seated at the desk in his study, his nerves already on edge, King Philip shook his head at the decision he'd made just a few days ago. It was not optimal; not in the least. He'd spent two years with his military leaders preparing for the conquest of England. And then suddenly, his most experienced naval commander, the Marquis of Santa Cruz, died unexpectedly. The man had never lost a battle at sea and was expected to deliver the success Philip so deeply desired. His untimely death meant having to appoint a lesser commander in his stead. Unhappy with his naval officers in general, Philip chose Alonso Pérez de Guzmán, the Duke of Medina Sidonia, as the Marquis' replacement. De Guzman would have full command of sea-going operations. A seasoned military leader in his late thirties, the Duke had no naval experience. He would, however, be supported by officers well-seasoned in naval warfare. The King's land-based forces would be led by Alessandro Farnese, the dashing Italian Duke of Parma—de Guzman's senior by just a few years.

The two Dukes arrived at El Escorial together. Hearing the noise below, Philip rose from his desk and strolled to a window overlooking the palace entry. Watching the Dukes enter, his thoughts turned to the coming conflict with England. They were soon interrupted by the announcement of the Dukes' arrival at his study.

"Good day, gentlemen. I trust you are ready."

"We are, Your Majesty."

"Excellent. Please, have a seat."

Philip strolled back to his desk, picking up the papers he'd been reviewing. "We have invested heavily, gentlemen. The cost of building a military force to bring England to its knees is high—more than one hundred warships, twenty-four hundred cannons and thirty thousand men. These are the assets I am placing at your disposal. I trust they are everything you need to be successful."

"They are indeed."

He replaced the papers and took his seat. "I am happy to report that our mission has the full blessing of the Pope. You shall carry our Lord's blessings with you. And with your capable leadership, we shall defeat this heretic nation, bring home our treasures, and deliver ultimate glory to our beloved Spain."

"Just so," the Dukes acknowledged, understanding the criticality of their mission.

"We must give Queen Elizabeth and El Draque no quarter. I wish you to bring them to me alive, if possible. We shall imprison her for the balance of her life, so that she might daily regret her actions and deceits against me. As for El Draque, he deserves the fitting end for a pirata. We shall behead him for all our citizenry to witness and celebrate." The Dukes nodded and smiled. Philip rose again, "May God bless you both, and reward you with a grand victory."

De Guzman's fleet launched in July, with the objective of seizing control of the English Channel. The Duke of Parma's army marched toward France's northern coast. From there, the fleet would transport the soldiers to England, to secure the countryside and capture the Queen. Elizabeth, however, had made her own preparations. Twenty thousand English soldiers were strewn across the southern coast. Fire beacons mounted on scattered hilltops along the coastline would warn of any approaching enemy ships. A reserve guard of elite soldiers had been formed, specifically to protect the Queen herself. England's naval forces would be nominally led by the Queen's aging cousin, Charles, known commonly as Howard of Effingham. His role as Lord High Admiral was one of nobility only. Drake would serve as 'Vice Admiral' by title, but ultimate leader of naval operations. The aging John Hawkins, his former commander, would share planning and other aspects of the naval initiatives. Drake had chosen the forty-gun *Revenge* as his flagship. It carried two-hundred-fifty men.

Philip suspected Elizabeth had no desire for all-out war with Spain. She would have little to gain and much to spend. He devised a plan to have his ambassadors distract her with a peace overture while his forces proceeded to the opening positions of their assault.

Upon receiving Philip's emissaries and welcoming their peace proposal, Elizabeth ordered her forces to pause preparations. Upon hearing this news, Drake, Hawkins and Admiral Howard were shocked and concerned. All agreed Drake should visit the Queen, to dissuade her from delaying their arrangements.

It wasn't until after the Spanish fleet had gathered at Lisbon, that Drake received word of the Queen's willingness to meet with him. Recalling Elizabeth's expressed desire to meet Garret, he asked that she accompany him. He sensed her presence would help sway Elizabeth's thinking. Upon their arrival at Richmond Palace, they learned Elizabeth had precious little time for them. They were hustled to her meeting room and introduced. Drake got straight to the point, "Thank you for agreeing to see us, Your Majesty. I understand I must be brief." She nodded agreement. "It comes as no surprise that King Philip has extended an offer of peace. I imagine that is comforting to you. But, as your military commander, I must always ask myself two questions. First, 'What is the worst that could happen?' And second, 'Can I live with that?' In this instance, the worst situation would be that the King extended his peace offering solely to delay our military preparations. That would expose us to rapid, overwhelming defeat. His forces have already assembled in Lisbon. So the clear answer to the second question is—no. Neither you nor our empire can live with that outcome. I am afraid we have no choice. We must proceed with all haste to finish building our offensive and defensive capabilities."

The Queen considered Drake's position. As always, he was both succinct and convincing. But with Garret present, she felt it appropriate to seek confirmation. She turned to the young woman, about whom she'd heard good things. "What say you, Captain Connachan?"

"Your Majesty, I fully concur with the Admiral. I would add my belief that our best *de*fense is an aggressive *off*ense. We must attack the Spanish on our terms, not wait for them to press their attack on our homeland."

The Queen smiled and sat back. "Well said." She paused briefly. "I find your combined counsel informative. And wise. I shall continue to engage in negotiations with the Spanish, on the chance that it might avoid conflict. But I concur with your thoughts. Let us prepare to press the attack." She rose from her chair. They rose as well and bowed. Elizabeth turned to leave the room. She paused to look back at Garret. "I look forward to an opportunity when we shall have more time to share thoughts, Captain." Garret nodded. Elizabeth left with a smile on her face, thankful for having met this intelligent young woman with such strength of character.

————

It materialized from the thick English mist in a myriad of slivers, seven leagues off the coast. Garret used her hand to clear her eyes before taking another look. She sought to be absolutely certain what she was witnessing. King Philip's imperial fleet—125 vessels strong—emerged in an alarming, two-mile-long front, spread across the gray horizon. A rush of adrenaline coursed through her entire body. She breathed quickly. Heavily. As the wall of intruding warships grew, she knew the Spanish greatly outnumbered their English counterparts, creating an aura of invincibility. Onboard Spain's armada were thousands of armed soldiers and eight thousand sailors, determined to obliterate the English navy and take control of her country.

"Set the longboats aflame," Garret ordered. It was the signal Drake had requested.

Though England's fleet was anchored at Plymouth Sound, Drake and Admiral Howard were high in the hills above, playing a game of bowls with their officers when William Tovery arrived.

"Pardon the interruption, Admiral. The signal has been lit. The King's fleet is at hand."

"Thank you, Captain."

With calm confidence, Drake turned to his officers. "Let us finish our game, gentlemen." He was comforted by his forces' readiness. And the Spanish had done exactly what he'd expected. Besides, his fleet needed to wait for the late-afternoon tide, in order to exit the harbor. When the game ended, he ordered an assembly of captains onboard the *Revenge*.

The buzz of anticipation filled Admiral Howard's quarters, where the captains had assembled. Drake called the men to order. Admiral Howard addressed them, "Gentlemen. You represent the absolute best of England's navy. Your hour is now at hand. The Spanish threaten to violate our Channel with their fleet of bloated warships. Spain's intent is anything but honorable. Though we are outnumbered, our ships are faster, more maneuverable and sufficiently lethal. I believe the ultimate edge in battle is ours. I have full confidence in you and am honored to serve alongside you, on behalf of Her Majesty. But let us hear from your *true* Admiral." He nodded to Drake, smiling.

"Gentlemen," Drake began, "you are the finest collection of officers I have ever had the pleasure to serve with. Acting together, without division, we cannot fail. In addition to what the Lord High Admiral has said regarding the abilities of our ships, we have the unflinching courage of our men. Their hearts and minds are fully committed. Further, our opening strategy shall give us the weather gauge, increasing our speed of attack. Finally, we shall have the advantage of surprise because this night, under cover of darkness and rain, we shall proceed to our opening positions. You are to be both bold in your actions and cautious in your defense." He paused to look at the talented assemblage before him. "I have never been more proud, nor more confident, to lead you. We shall soon prove we are the most dominant naval force the world has known. Go with God's grace—for our wives, our children, our Queen, and our blessed England. God speed, gentlemen."

The men cheered heartily, "For England!"

Garret looked at Drake with a frown on her face. He saw it immediately.

"I say again—God speed gentlemen. *And* gentlewoman," he smiled, nodding toward her. She smiled back as the men laughed.

Under cover of night, Drake's fleet had stealthily passed behind the Spanish, moving into position with the wind at their backs. They were now ready to surprise and challenge the dreaded Imperial Fleet.

The sun didn't break at dawn. Instead, heavy clouds brought darkness and thundering rain. Blustering winds howled the coming of chaos. As Drake had planned, the Spanish awoke in disbelief. They'd failed to spot El Draque's encroaching fleet until it was closing fast from behind, advantaged by heavy winds. Cannons announced their arrival, launching the battle for supremacy of the English Channel over several storm-filled days. Smoke from innumerable over-heated cannons filled the air day and night. The Spanish armada held its lines tightly. The English sailed aggressively to attack and then avoid opposing fire, in thrust-and-parry form. Low-hanging clouds were lit by the flames of battered ships, headed for disaster. In close range, rifle shots peppered the decks of ships from both fleets. Shattering wood and tumbling masts spread death and fear on both sides, as ships were beaten and decimated. In the din of battle, thundering storms went unheard.

As the bloody engagement wore on, Drake's *Revenge* took advantage of the already storm-damaged *Rosario*, an enormous Spanish warship captained by Admiral Pedro de Valdés. Following an overwhelming barrage of cannon-fire, Drake had Langton call out to the now-limping vessel on his behalf.

"Commander of the *Rosario*! I am Vice-Admiral Drake, of Her Majesty's Navy. Hold fast your weapons and strike your colors. If you do not, no quarter shall be given. Many will perish. Let us not expose our men to such needless suffering. I await your reply."

Admiral de Valdés contemplated his options. His failing ship was in no position to take on El Draque. He faced not only losing the engagement but also forfeiting the lives of many Spaniards. "Commander Drake," he replied, through an English-speaking interpreter, "I am Admiral de Valdés of King Philip's navy. I agree—engaging now seems pointless. But unless we are granted safe treatment and sole possession of our goods and materials, we are prepared to engage in the King's honor."

"This is not the time for negotiation, Admiral," Langton called out at Drake's direction. "Strike your colors now. You have my word—you and your men shall not be harmed."

Admiral de Valdés recognized his inability to negotiate terms, given his circumstances. He ordered the Burgundy lowered, relying on rumors that El Draque was magnanimous in victory.

Drake's officers and their guards, led by Master-at-Arms Lee, boarded the *Rosario*. As de Valdes' men stood by, weapons lowered, he raised his cutlass horizontally. "I offer this sword as a sign of surrender, asking only that my men be spared in return."

"You have my word, Admiral." Lee bowed, accepting the sword. He motioned de Valdes to disembark, to meet with Drake onboard the *Revenge*, before taking charge of the *Rosario*.

Drake had invited the Spanish Admiral and his officers to dine with him. Admiral Howard and his own officers would attend. As the men stood before the table, awaiting the meal's arrival, Howard opened the discussion, directing his remarks to de Valdés, "I toast you and your officers for your honor in battle and for your thoughtful decision to avoid further endangering the lives of many men. On both sides."

"Hear, hear," said Drake. "To your great honor." He raised his silver cup of wine and drank the toast. The officers on both sides followed suit, raising their cups and drinking. "To the Admiral," they saluted.

Admiral de Valdés returned the honor, "Thank you, Admiral Howard." He turned to Drake.

"Vice-Admiral," he said, "you have shown uncommon seamanship and battle intelligence. I admire your boldness and strength. I toast your honor and your humanity."

Again, the officers echoed his toast. "To the Vice-Admiral!"

The officers took their seats. The meal was placed at the table with proper ceremony, the three Admirals being served first. They ate finely presented fish and fowl. Together, the men from both sides enjoyed not only the meal, but also a discussion of the things they shared in common—the challenges and adventures they had all experienced in sailing the high seas. They'd found a common bond, forming at least a temporary friendship—in the image of their admirals.

At the time of capturing the *Rosario*, Drake was unaware it carried enormous treasure. It was the reason Admiral de Valdés, before his surrender, had requested that he be allowed to maintain possession of all goods and materials onboard the ship. The following morning, Master's Mate Prouten received a message from Mr. Lee, informing him of the discovered treasure. He went straight to Drake's quarters.

"With Mr. Lee's compliments sir, there is news from the *Rosario*. Apparently, the ship bears substantial treasure—primarily gold and silver coins. It appears this may have been the pay ship for the entire Spanish fleet."

"I'll be damned! Thank you, Mr. Prouten. My compliments to Mr. Lee. Please arrange with haste for the transfer of all valuables to the *Revenge*."

News of Drake's capture of a Spanish Admiral and his treasure ship soon reached London. Bonfires were lit in celebration. Though it was an encouraging sign, the war was far from ended. English and Spanish ships continued pursuing and battling each other throughout the Channel, exchanging untold thousands of cannon shots. Countless sailors met their end as numerous ships on both sides were either destroyed or incapacitated. Near the Isle of Wight, off the southern coast of England, the Spanish gathered their remaining forces and pressed the attack. The island was key to their long-term strategy. They needed it as a base to gather the Duke of Parma's land forces, in preparation for an assault on the English mainland. The island's residents gathered in the hills, watching in fear as the two fleets engaged. The English here were led by Garret's flagship. Her success inspired the island's residents. They cheered in full voice as the Spanish ultimately retreated.

Humbled but still dangerous, the remains of the Spanish fleet headed toward a port on the northern coast of France, where Parma's army was gathering. It stopped first at Calais, anchoring in the harbor. The naval commander, de Guzman, waited onboard his flagship for news of Parma's army. Unfortunately, word arrived that the army was still days away. What's more, a number of Dutch ships had surrounded the port where the army was headed, creating a challenging barrier. De Guzman ordered his fleet to remain in and near the harbor at Calais, setting dual anchors to maintain a steady position against the heavy current that flowed directly to the port. They would await their army's readiness while plotting strategy for an assault on the Dutch blockade.

Having vanquished the Spanish, Drake's fleet began gathering near England's southern coast, to rest the men, conduct repairs, and plan their next steps. Drake was anxious for news from the remainder of the fleet. He called for a briefing from Prouten, who'd been busy gathering as much information as he could over the last two days.

"What news of our forces, Mr. Prouten?"

"We cannot be certain, sir, but it appears we have lost upwards of twenty ships. Far fewer than the Spanish"

"What of my brother, Thomas?"

"Pleased to report he is well, sir."

"And Captains Connachan and Tovery?"

"Some remarkable victories, sir. Connachan has defended the Isle of Wight, sending two Spanish warships to watery graves. Three others were severely hobbled. Her own ship has suffered, but nothing that cannot soon be repaired. Tovery has also enjoyed some success. Perhaps most remarkable is Captain James Wenman. He apparently has five kills—the most of any of our ships."

"Excellent news. Thank you, Mr. Prouten. I shall rest well this night."

———

It was near midnight. A lookout onboard de Guzman's flagship alerted the Duke to the approach of English ships—eight or nine by his count. The Duke didn't see this as much of a threat since the English would be greatly outnumbered. Drake's plan, however, was drawn from an older page in his playbook. Garret and her crew had organized this array of the fleet's weakest and damaged ships, recently outfitted with black sails. They were splayed out in a line parallel to the port of Calais and sailed directly toward the Spanish fleet. The dark sails had enabled a relatively blind approach, so that the ships were already extremely close when first spotted.

"Set the powder," Garret ordered. Onboard the lead vessel, flint rocks were struck to light the long fuses appended to gunpowder trails leading to loaded powder kegs. The men then quickly evacuated. On signal, the other ships ignited their fuses. With the fuses burning, the deadly ships neared the outer edge of the Spanish fleet. Pulsating roars erupted as barrels of explosives burst into soaring pillars of flame, creating a stunning sensation of near-daylight in the darkness of the night. The harbor was instantly filled with a glowing wall of orange flame, sucking the light from the stars filling the black sky. The concussed air of the explosions sent Spanish sailors on nearby ships sprawling. Several panicked. Sailors ran along the decks, hacking, cutting and hauling the ropes and chains to their anchors, in an attempt to set sail and flee the hellfire. The Spanish fleet, in complete disarray, suffered gravely.

Dawn soon emerged. Drake's fleet pressed its attack. The tattered, disorderly Spanish ships that managed to flee the firestorm attempted to form up near the port of Gravelines, straddling the border of France and the Netherlands. The English warships, maintaining the weather gauge, peppered the broken armada with crushing broadsides. The Spanish lost five warships and more than two thousand men, who either died in action, suffered severe wounds, or were taken prisoner. Several other Spanish warships absorbed crippling damage. De Guzman understood the perilousness of his position. He ordered an immediate retreat from the Channel, imagining the humility the Marquis of Santa Cruz must have felt when he cowered from Drake's challenge at Lisbon. Unable to reverse course, de Guzman's remaining ships sailed north along the eastern coast of England. Once north of the island, they proceeded west, along the Scottish and Irish coasts, with Drake and his fleet in relentless pursuit. Unfortunately for the Duke, the northern waters turned against him. His ships became separated, many succumbing to severe damage in stormy weather off the rocky Irish coast. Few survivors made it safely to shore.

By the time de Guzman straggled home to Spain, he'd lost one hundred-eighty men on his flagship. And his own health was failing. He was rowed ashore in a longboat, consumed by misery. Spain's dominance of the world's oceans had finally come to an embarrassing end at the hands of Philip's mortal enemy—El Draque.

———

The English nation celebrated Drake's decisive victory with bonfires and feasts, hailing him as their most revered hero. In due course, he and his officers traveled to London, to once again be fêted by the Queen. At her lavish banquet, she addressed the conquering heroes, "My most honorable captains—never before could we claim mastery of the oceans. But thanks to your courageous efforts, against enormous odds, the Spanish have been completely vanquished. We now rule the oceans!"

She raised her crystal glass in toast. "To England. Ruler of the Waves!"

The captains cheered heartily "To England! Hurrah! Hurrah! Hurrah!"

Later, alone with Drake, the Queen confided in him. "You and I have enjoyed much success—on numerous occasions and on several fronts around the world. But I must admit that I worried constantly about the possibility of our demise, given the overwhelming forces King Philip assembled. What you and your officers have accomplished, with much smaller numbers, is a testament to your own preeminence as a military planner and leader. It is unclear what the fate of our country would be, were you not leading our campaign." She raised her glass. "On behalf of a grateful nation, God bless you and give you benefit of the rewards that come with victory."

"Thank you, Your Majesty. I live but to serve Queen and country, and will do so until my days and capabilities are at an end."

"Let that be far in the distance."

They drank to each other. "Now, my good man, I should like a private audience with this young female captain of yours. Connachan," she smiled.

"Indeed." He motioned to one of the guards stationed near the door. "Find Mr. Prouten, if you please. Have him escort Captain Connachan to these quarters." The guard turned and left. While waiting, Drake shared his story of the *Rosario's* capture. Elizabeth smiled frequently, enthralled by the man's expert storytelling. Before he finished, they were interrupted.

"Master's Mate Prouten and Captain Garret Connachan," the Queen's guard announced.

"Come, please," Elizabeth responded.

Prouten bowed. Garret quickly followed with a bow of her own, grandly sweeping her captain's hat, low and wide. A traditional woman's curtsy seemed to her ill-placed, given she was wearing a naval uniform, not a dress. The Queen laughed at her rather audacious maneuver. Drake smiled—it was typical of Garret to deliver the unexpected.

"Thank you for accompanying Captain Connachan, Mr. Prouten," the Queen said. "I believe she is capable of handling herself. You may take your leave."

"Thank you, Your Majesty." He bowed and, in the proper manner, took three steps backward before exiting the room.

"Please, Captain, join us," Elizabeth said, motioning to a chair.

"Thank you. It would be my honor, Your Majesty." Garret sat.

The Queen smiled broadly at this surprising young woman, savoring her whole presence. She turned to Drake, not seeking a response, "She is so much younger than one might expect." She turned back to Garret. "It is good to see you again, Captain. I am sorry our last meeting was so brief and impersonal. We have more time together this night." She paused to sip her tea. "Admiral Drake tells me you come from good stock."

"My grandfather was a successful lawyer and landowner. He has since passed. My mother is in poor health and remains in the care of others."

"They have clearly prepared you well for such a challenging life."

"Indeed, Your Majesty. The Admiral has played a role as well, providing me with every opportunity to prove myself." Drake nodded his thanks.

"I am certain the Admiral is an excellent mentor." The Queen changed course. "Tell me, what are your future plans?"

"The oceans are now my home. I shall be at sea whenever I can." She paused before posing a question of her own. "Have you yourself sailed the oceans, Your Majesty?"

"Only in the hearts of my Ambassadors, I am afraid," she hesitated, "though I have set foot on the Admiral's ship." She smiled at Drake, remembering the day at Deptford when he'd been knighted.

"And was that a successful journey?" Garret smiled.

"It was indeed. A most memorable one, however short." She continued looking at Drake and then turned again to Garret. "I have little doubt that your stories of adventure are much more interesting than mine. Perhaps you would be kind enough to share one with me?"

Drake smiled, recognizing he'd just been given a signal. "Shall I leave the two of you?"

"You shall never leave me," Elizabeth smiled. "But you may take this opportunity to share your wondrous success with the rest of the fawning nobles."

"Thank you, Your Majesty. You are most kind."

When Drake had exited, Elizabeth turned to Garret, "Would that I had *your* life."

Garret laughed. "Well, I *am* constantly surrounded by real men." Elizabeth joined her laughter.

"Tell me Captain, are you truly married to the sea?"

"I am. It is my deepest passion."

"You are a woman whom I would very much love to have here at court—perhaps as a military advisor."

Garret was floored. She'd only met the Queen once before. And briefly at that. How could Elizabeth so quickly conclude that she might be a worthy advisor? She found the suggestion flattering. "You are most gracious, Your Majesty. Perhaps in time I shall be worthy. But I have much to learn and so much more to accomplish. I must first glean everything I can from Admiral Drake."

Though disappointed, Elizabeth understood—Garret was young and naïve. "One day, I shall again ask you this question. And I want you to remember this—when someone offers you a gracious opportunity, accept it. Even if you feel unworthy. You shall find out later how to succeed; especially with the support of the person who has made the offer." She smiled.

"Duly noted, Your Majesty."

XXXVIII

Word of her arrival interrupted what had so far been a stress-filled morning. Drake put down his quill and left his study to greet her at the door. He watched as Garret dismounted her well-groomed, white steed, handing the reins to his manservant. The familiar combination of grace and swagger with which she approached delivered an unexpected wave of nostalgia.

"Top of the morn, Admiral." Her broad smile lightened both her face and his day.

"A pleasure to see you again, Captain. Would you care for a sip of tea in my study or perhaps a walk through the gardens?"

"Tea, if you please. The ride has been lengthy."

Back in his study, Drake stood, waiting for her to sit. But Garret was unwilling to accept the traditional grace offered to a woman. She was here as a naval captain, after all. "Please, Admiral," she smiled, pointing to his chair.

Drake smiled back. "Am I that old—that I must be seated first?"

"You are my senior in both rank *and* age. Choose your own reason."

He took his chair; she hers. The manservant brought a silver tea service and poured their cups. The hot, dark liquid steamed above the rim. Drake thanked the man. He left.

"So, Garret, what brings you?"

"Is it not enough that I merely wish to visit an old friend?"

"For as long as I have known you, your visits have always carried an agenda," he winked, "so why would I expect this one to differ?"

Garret smiled. "You know me well." She sipped her tea. He waited. "I am adrift," she continued. "I find the seas have been writing my story, as my grandfather liked to say. Saltwater has come to define me. Without it, I am almost uncertain who I am."

"I, too, miss the sea. It seems my days have been overtaken by parliamentary duties on behalf of Devon."

"And as the Shire's Reeve, no doubt."

"That as well. And prize commissioner." He shook his head at the number of administrative tasks he'd agreed to take on at the request of others. They competed with, and interrupted, his own interests and business pursuits.

"And what of the fortress?" Garret asked. She referenced the building now underway in Plymouth; construction he was overseeing.

Drake sat back and breathed deeply. He looked at her, a new thought running through his head. "Would you have any interest in assisting me with these many responsibilities?"

"Not on your life," she laughed. He joined her.

As she sipped more tea, it struck Garret that the man had aged more than she'd anticipated. His skin was pale, his laughter a little pained. She needed to know more. "Speaking of life—how is your health, Admiral?"

Drake had no desire to address the subject. The many wounds he'd accumulated through the years, combined with the too-cold weather, exacted a daily price for his life of adventure. "I have seen better days," he admitted.

"Perhaps another voyage would do you well. I know it would me."

"You may be right." He paused. "If I may confide in you…"

"You may."

"Her Majesty has asked that I prepare a fleet for another campaign in the Southern Seas." Garret smiled, saying nothing. He looked at her, oddly. "You know this already?"

Garret nodded. The Queen had previously shared the mission with her, asking that she accompany the Admiral. Though Elizabeth hadn't said it explicitly, she was concerned for the Admiral's health. If it were to fail him, she wanted Garret to be there—to take charge. Elizabeth chose not to share those thoughts with the Admiral but rather to have Garret herself request a role.

"Her Majesty wishes that I further my training under you."

"Surely you jest. She knows you are already among the finest of England's naval captains."

"No matter. I am here to ask that I be permitted to join you."

"So, there was indeed an agenda," Drake smiled.

"That too," she smiled back.

———

Within months, the fleet of twenty-seven ships and twenty-five hundred men was assembled and ready. Drake was mere days away from launching when word came that the Queen had a change of heart. Based on intelligence from her sources in Spain, she was increasingly worried that Philip might once again amass forces to attack England. Her message informed the Admiral that he was to patrol the coast, rather than head for the Southern Seas.

Drake had no desire to play the role of border guard, certainly not this late in his career. Deeply enmeshed in finalizing administrative matters before his departure, and feeling a little under the weather, he asked Garret to visit the Queen on his behalf, well aware Her Majesty had grown fond of her.

"Your Majesty," said Garret, "It is my honor and pleasure to see you once more."

"Mine as well," replied Elizabeth. "Might I add that you look even younger and more radiant than I remember."

"Thank you. You are most kind."

"And you are most deserving. You have accomplished more at such an early age than any woman I know. An English Joan of Arc, no less."

Garret smiled. "I imagine Joan would roll her eyes at your remark."

Elizabeth laughed. "So, what news do you bring from our favorite Admiral?"

"I am pleased to report that a Spanish treasure galleon, the *Begoña*, has been severely damaged by a heavy storm. She is repairing at the island Cristobal Colon called Boriken. Many now refer to it as Puerto Rico. The ship reputedly carries two-and-a-half million ducats. Without such resources, King Philip would surely be unable to assemble another fleet large enough to challenge England. It is unclear how long the *Begoña* may be detained to finish her repairs. Our fleet and military forces are ready now, to capture her for England."

"This is most interesting news."

"If we are to take full advantage of this opportunity, Your Majesty, we must leave as soon as possible; before the *Begoña* is seaworthy. The Admiral and I seek your blessing in carrying out this mission. We believe it is both an offensive and defensive imperative."

Elizabeth observed Garret wistfully, wishing she might wear the young captain's shoes, rather than her own. She weighed her concerns about Philip's possible intentions to attack England, against the chance to strike his source of funding. Timing was a critical consideration. "How soon might you and the Admiral execute the mission and return to England, to lead the defense of our shores?"

The unpredictability of ocean voyages gave Garret pause. She sought to avoid offering such a conservative response that the Queen might say no. "Perhaps a few months, with God's blessing. But, should we be successful, there shall be no need to fear a Spanish attack on England, no matter the timing of our return."

"Well said, Captain." Elizabeth sipped her tea and returned her cup to the saucer. "The Admiral and I have come a long way together. I can see you and he share a deep passion for this mission. With all my heart, I want the two of you to strengthen England's security in the manner you believe is best. But I must insist that you conclude the mission with all haste. The fleet must be back in position to defend us, even if, as you say, the risk of King Philip's assault would be diminished. He has other means to raise funding."

Garret had learned long ago from Drake that, the moment you receive approval, you should draw the conversation to a close; extending it ran the risk of an alternative outcome. "Thank you, Your Majesty. Admiral Drake is the ultimate mission commander. We shall accomplish our objectives and return home expeditiously." She rose.

"Excellent. And when you return, I may well have an interesting opportunity for you. Perhaps you shall take me up on it."

"I am always at your service, Your Majesty." Garret smiled, knowing she had no choice but to accept the Queen's next request.

"Except when you choose otherwise," the Queen teased. "God speed, then, Captain. Be sure to give my best to my beloved pirate."

———

With summer beginning to recede, Drake stood on the docks at Plymouth Harbor, holding his lovely wife, Elizabeth, in his arms. He placed his hand softly under her chin and raised her head, gently wiping the tears from each of her eyes. "I promise you, my dear, this shall be my last adventure abroad for England. When I return, we shall live our remaining years as Lord and Lady of Devon. And when I sail again, it shall be with you, in a pleasure craft."

She smiled back at him, through tears, deeply concerned for his failing health. He was no longer the vibrant young adventurer she'd first come to know. He'd aged rapidly. "I would love that," she replied.

"Then hold fast and be strong. I have the finest fleet and the best sailors at my command. I shall return with wonderful stories and much honor." He hugged her one last time and kissed her with all his heart. He loved the woman dearly, causing him to question his decision to leave her one more time, especially given his pain and discomfort. But this was his calling in life. He was a man of the seas and a champion for his country. How could he possibly walk away from that in times of conflict between England and Spain, and still maintain his self-respect?

Drake was soon rowed aboard his flagship, *Defiance*, and set sail once again for the Southern Seas. Standing on the deck at the ship's stern, he waved goodbye to Elizabeth and other friends on shore, and then turned toward the bow, torn between love for his wife and duty to his country.

It was Garret's ship, the *Discovery*, that first spotted the Cape Verde Islands. She and the Admiral had made frequent stops there. Following their arrival, the fleet's crews were busy conducting minor repairs and provisioning the ships for the much longer second leg of their voyage.

Their stay at Cape Verde was short, Drake being anxious to leave. Shortly after departure, he'd been informed that two of the men had fallen deathly ill, raising concern that the disease might spread. That was just one of many curses faced by mariners, but the one they most feared—a silent killer. Despite the two men being quarantined, others managed to catch the contagion as they proceeded to the Caribbean Islands. Frustrated by not finding the Begonia, Drake made hasty decisions that failed to take account of the illness now sweeping his entire fleet, taking several lives. He suffered military setbacks in the face of strong Spanish resistance. Stress and uncertainty weighed heavily on him as he, too, fell ill, unable to leave his cabin for days. Prouten visited late one morning, holding a handkerchief over his mouth and nose. "Good morning, sir. I am most sorry to trouble you."

"No. No problem, Mr. Prouten." Drake's voice was rough, halting. "What is it?"

"I am afraid our water supplies have diminished to a point of concern. I believe we must dispatch a search party to replenish our holdings."

"Very well. Make it so."

"Thank you, sir." Prouten left, deeply worried about his commander's rapidly failing health. He sent word to Garret, asking that she lead a small party to gather fresh water supplies at an uninhabited section of the Panamanian coast, where a river entered the sea directly.

———

Garret and her twelve-man search party rowed ashore, about one league east of Nombre de Dios. They were unaware that lookouts posted in the hills above the rebel village of Santiago del Príncipe had spotted them. The lookouts, like most of the villagers, were former black slaves who deeply distrusted the Spanish. They were there specifically to provide warning of any approach by their former overlords. Spotting these particular Europeans, they signaled the village. A makeshift militia quickly gathered. Well-armed, they rowed along the mainland in a mass of swift piraguas, converging unnoticed near the site where Garret and her crew had since landed.

While she and her men busily filled casks in the river and loaded their longboats, one of them spotted the rapidly approaching piraguas. There was no possibility of evacuating. A shower of poisoned arrows quickly dusted the sand, embedded in the trees, and impaled Garret's crew, wounding several and killing a few. Ill-prepared to defend against such overwhelming odds, Garret ordered a retreat. The few who were still able to run headed for the jungle. Garret, with the help of another crewman, dragged a wounded man off the beach, hiding him in surrounding shrubs. Laying low and looking back, she noticed one of her men crawling toward her through the sand, an arrow piercing his back. He looked up, making eye contact. She rose slightly, contemplating a run to save him. He shook his head—no. Another arrow dusted him with sand. One grazed his leg. Garret cringed—angry; frustrated; helpless to assist. The wounded man continued dragging forward as the first of the villagers' periaguas hit the shore. They leaped onto the beach, spearing both the wounded and the already dead.

Exhausted from the heavy labor of loading water casks, Garret's few remaining men had little energy to run through thick jungle in stifling heat and humidity. They chose instead to take cover closer to the edge of the foliage than they would have preferred. They peered through the shrubs at the horror unfolding on the beach. Armed with only short daggers or a cutlass to defend themselves, they were highly vulnerable, if found. As the horde of villagers surged forward, some decided to run after all, drawing attention. They were showered with arrows and spears. Garret took advantage of the villagers' distraction to make her own stealthy charge into the jungle, crouching low. The villagers proceeded to slaughter every last man.

Her heart pounding, Garret ran deep into the jungle, alone but for the screams of dying crewmates that wouldn't leave her. Aided by pulsing adrenaline, she continued running, though occasionally tripping and falling. Her anger grew with every step, every fall. Finally drained of energy, she stopped—bent at the waist, hands on knees. For a moment, the world seemed oddly at peace. The jungle smelled fresh.

After a moment, she rose and began treading slowly through thick foliage. She listened beyond the soft crunch of the plants beneath her feet, for any sound of men following her. There was none. The sound of babbling water streaming through a nearby ravine raised her spirits. She headed toward it, knowing it would be difficult for anyone to track her progress along the water. She slid carefully down the side of the gully and then walked cautiously along the slippery, rocky ground bordering the creek. It was several minutes before she found what she sought. At the base of two trees surrounded by high, leafy shrubs, was an opening through which she could wriggle inside. She withdrew her cutlass, entered the cover and sat, placing the sword on the ground. Her heart beating hard, her lungs laboring for air, she breathed in deeply to slow everything down and regain her composure. A slick layer of sweat covered her entire body.

Garret's thoughts went immediately to her men. Had any survived? She felt the heavy weight of guilt. Men had just died under her leadership. She now sensed how Drake must have felt under similar circumstances, recalling the deadly charge at Sagres. For the first time, she felt sorry for the Admiral, having to carry such a burden for so long, dating back to his attacks on Nombre de Dios. It was now icily clear that his hatred for the Spanish was in some way an expression of his accumulated guilt. She felt the same. If she were to survive this massacre, these villagers would one day taste the fury of her hatred.

Several minutes passed before Garret's attention was sparked by the sound of approaching footsteps. Her heart sank. It appeared the villagers hadn't simply completed their slaughter and moved on. Peering out from her hiding place, she spotted movement at the top of the ridge. A small man was carrying a pistolet, scanning the jungle. She looked to see whether he had any other weapons. There was a dagger stuffed in his belt, on his left. Two weapons. She could deal with that if she had to, though she'd need the element of surprise.

The man continued on by. She breathed more easily. A few moments later, she heard the snap of a fallen stem not far from her. It was a second villager, this one approaching along the creek. He came into view—a huge man, barrel-chested and heavily bearded, with cutlass in hand and a dagger in his belt. Given his bearing, he would pass directly by her current position. But this was no time to move. Gently, cautiously, she slid her hand back along the ground. Her fingers curled around the grip of her cutlass. The babbling water now offered little calm as her predator steadily approached. She breathed slowly but deeply, remaining perfectly still.

The heavy-set man was now only a few yards away. If he spotted her in this seated position, she was exceedingly vulnerable. She couldn't risk that. Thrusting herself up and out from the shrubs, she raised her cutlass to a ready position. Though surprised, her predator reacted instinctively, with a slashing blow of his sword. The slash was so fierce that Garret chose not to block it, sensing it might well knock the cutlass from her grip. But as she leaned back to avoid the blow, she slipped on the damp, uneven undergrowth, her cutlass jarring free as her hand hit the ground hard. It clattered along the rocks, into the creek. There was no time to pursue it. The predator lunged toward her, cutlass first. She dodged the thrust, rolling awkwardly into the creek. A large rock battered her side, sending a shard of pain through her body.

The villager dislodged his cutlass from the tree it had hit. He hesitated for a moment, shocked to see that the pirate he was about to slay appeared to be a woman. A vicious, half-toothless, grimace widened slowly from deep within his black beard. He would have his way with her first. He stepped toward Garret, throwing aside his cutlass, unafraid of this now bleeding, unarmed female lying prone in the slowly streaming water.

Her cutlass well beyond reach, Garret's mind raced for a defense. The small, thin-handled knife sheathed inside her boot was an option, but not a favorable one, given the sheer size of the man. She maneuvered her position, securing her hands against rocks in the creek and coiling her knees up against her chest, leaving the boot-knife as an option.

The man, now laughing huskily at her dilemma, came within a foot of her feet. He removed his boots and untied the rope holding up his pants. They fell to the ground. He stepped out of them, one leg at a time, his growing arousal on full display.

Garret smiled. He'd just given her a more precise view of the target she needed to hit. From her seated position, supported by her arms behind her, she opened her legs to the man in inviting fashion. He was now fully erect, glancing between her open legs and disarming smile. She knew then that she had him—men were so predictably vulnerable, she thought, no matter their race. His next step toward her was the one she'd waited for. It fully exposed the target. Pushing hard against the rocks at her back, Garret thrust her boot firmly into his testicles, putting the full weight of her body behind it. Excruciating pain instantly transformed the expression on her assailant's face. He doubled over, falling on his knees just to the side of her. One knee cracked hard against a rock, sending searing pain up and down his leg. He screamed in agony, drawing the attention of the searcher on the ridge above.

Garret grabbed a rock, slamming it hard into the large man's left temple. He splashed face-first into the water, his arms unable to soften his fall. She drew the knife from her boot and plunged the full length of the short blade into the back of his neck, several times. Blood spurted and bubbled, spraying her hand and flowing into the water. She staggered to her feet, dripping wet, still holding the blood-soaked knife. The predator, now fallen prey, lay still, his head underwater. His protruding buttocks forced the water to flow around it. She rose quickly and stomped down hard with her boot on the man's head, feeling the crunch of bone.

A pistolet shot from the ridge above whizzed past Garret's arm, glancing off a rock and embedding itself in the ground on the other side of the ravine. Turning quickly, she saw the shooter fumbling to reload. In his haste, he dropped the ball. Grabbing her cutlass, she scrambled up the side of the ravine. The man dropped to his knees, nervously searching to retrieve the ball from the ground. He found it but his shaking hand caused him to struggle in an attempt to load it into the chamber. Garret threw herself toward him, slashing his left shin with her cutlass. He screamed and fell forward. She brought the cutlass down on the back of his head. He made no further noise. Power and victory coursed through her veins as she used a two-handed thrust to bury the cutlass deep in the man's back.

———

Lying on his bed, his sheets wet and soiled by night sweats, Drake sent word for his brother, Thomas, to join him. He arrived holding a handkerchief against his nose and mouth.

"Thomas," said Drake, struggling to breathe, let alone get the words out, "my days have almost certainly come to an end." He stopped. "Water. Please."

Thomas poured the precious little fresh water into a cup and raised his brother's head to drink. After a moment, gathering strength, Drake continued. "I must add a codicil to my will. The papers are in my desk."

"Surely you shall recover," Thomas lied, sensing death was imminent. Tears welled up in his eyes.

"No, Thomas. My time is done." Drake coughed. "The oceans have defined me. They shall now claim my body." He gasped for breath.

"More water?"

Drake shook his head, no. "My papers." His eyes closed, as if to bring comfort.

Thomas walked to the desk. He retrieved the handwritten will and brought it to Drake's side, along with a quill and small bottle of ink. He looked sadly at his emaciated brother.

Drake coughed, opening his eyes once again. He glanced at the papers. "Add a sentence, naming yourself as executor." Thomas did so. He added the date as well and then handed the quill to Drake, who scribbled an indecipherable name.

"Take command, Thomas." He paused. Thomas stroked his brother's damp forehead and hair with a cloth. "My love to 'Beth." He coughed. "I am afraid I have failed her."

"I shall comfort and care for her, brother."

"Thank you." Drake inched his arm toward Thomas. His eyes closed.

Thomas kissed his cheek. "God be with you." He rose and left, resigned to what lay ahead.

As he emerged on the deck, Prouten approached him, "What news, Thomas?"

"Nothing good, I am afraid. My brother breathes his last." Prouten hung his head in silence. Thomas put his arm on the man's shoulder. "He has been fortunate to have you at his side these many years."

His head still down, Prouten nodded, unable to speak. Thomas felt the tremble roll through his brother's long-time partner. He held back his own tears, with difficulty.

"I must go," said Thomas, taking a deep breath. Prouten nodded.

William Tovery, standing nearby, gave Thomas and Prouten time alone. As Thomas walked away, William called out, "A word, Thomas?"

"By all means."

"Did Prouten brief you on the search party he sent to find Garret and the others?"

"No. We were discussing another matter."

"I am afraid they have returned with sad news. The bodies of the men are strewn along the beach near the river." He shook his head. "It was a massacre."

"My God. Are all of them accounted for?"

"There was no count. The search party dared not approach the site. They merely viewed it from a distance."

Thomas' thoughts turned to his virtual sibling, "And Garret?"

William shook his head, shrugging his shoulders. He had nothing to offer.

"I see. Let us send a larger recovery party, in the dead of night. God willing, they shall find her alive. And others, of course."

In the dark of the early morning, Admiral Drake, hero of the English empire, and the greatest naval officer who had ever lived, asked his attendant to dress him in his uniform. When he'd finished, the aide placed Drake's sword beside him. It was Drake's last request, to die in naval attire. The preacher, Mr. Bride, came. He placed Drake's hand on his sword. They prayed, asking forgiveness and for the saving of his soul. In the midst of his prayer, his spirit sailed quietly to the land of souls.

The officers gathered onboard the *Defiance* later that afternoon. Drake's body had been placed in a lead coffin, draped by an English flag. Preacher Bride spoke of the kindness of God toward all men. He asked the Lord to welcome home this revered traveler who'd brought fame, fortune and much joy to his men, his family and his country. He ended with the Lord's Prayer and closed his Bible. Two sailors blew their horns. Musa, Caber and several others lifted the heavy casket onto a broad wooden plank resting on the taffrail. They raised the near end of the plank, enabling Drake's body to slide into a welcoming blue sea. Gunners fired thundering cannons, announcing his passage.

———

The oars lap rhythmically in the relatively calm water. I can see the longboat across from us, its oars pulling in time, though not coordinated with ours. The sun feels warm on my face. It brings me peace. The moment is somber, the men quiet. Their emotions tug at them, occupying their minds. The massacre of our crewmates who joined me in the search for water weighs heavily on all of us. No one has a desire to speak.

I notice a large gray fish swim by, just beneath the surface, as though nothing has happened. Yet so much has happened. I think back to the day when I stood on the cobblestones at Plymouth Harbor. I can almost feel Prouten's large hand grasp my shoulder, even now. He had promised me great adventure. At the time, I had no idea adventures could be full of both joy and sorrow—sometimes simultaneously.

The blood on my arm is dry. I have no desire to clean it off. It is all I have left that seems to connect me to the men I have just lost. Visions of their own blood haunt me now—and probably will for the rest of my days. At least until I can avenge their deaths.

Boom! Boom! Boom! The distant sound of cannon fire splits the air. Numerous shots in rapid sequence. They appear to be coming from our ship. "I hope that is not bad news."

William looks at me—sadly. Even more sadness than his somber face displayed mere moments ago. "The Admiral," he says. I can tell he sees the confusion on my face. "He has left us."

"Left?"

"Gone. To be at peace with the ocean."

"Surely not?"

"I am sorry. His illness had pressed on. Thomas did not expect him to make it to morning."

Thoughts of Drake fill my mind. Tears fill my eyes. The loss is unimaginable. With all he has given me, I have returned so little. But his loss is not mine alone. Poor England. Poor dear England. Her life continues without her favored son. And she is oblivious to it.

Drake's legend shall surely go on. But so must his legacy, of which I am a part. Perhaps but a small part; yet certainly one that must carry his legacy forward. It is my obligation—the very least I can do to honor the man. I must become the leader he wished me to be—one who would lead for the benefit of others, as did he. *For Queen and country*, he would have said. His words compel me to rise and be counted.

I look to the sky. It is blue as ever. White puffy clouds pass, shifting shape; as will I. I shall rise and make my own mark. For Drake.

END

I hope you enjoyed Pyrate Rising. If so, please take a few minutes to leave a review on my Amazon (USA) book page:
https://www.amazon.com/dp/B09M5L3XLC/

Be sure to catch the preview of 'Pyrate Assassin' at the end of this book.

Facts & Clarifications

Historical facts are funny things—particularly when presented by others several years, decades, or even centuries after the actual events themselves. And often, they're based on questionable memories and stories told or interpreted by others along the way. That said, let me do my best to provide you with what I suspect are 'real' historical facts around the events covered in this novel…

Chapter 2: Rio de la Hacha was Drake's first conflict with the Spanish as a captain.

Chapter 4: Commander Hawkins and the Minion did eventually return to England.

Chapter 6: The raid on Nombre de Dios actually happened, in the rain. Drake was severely wounded and later became unconscious. His raiders were unable to penetrate the storehouse.

Chapter 7: Diego was a real person. Drake did leave for Cartageña. His brother John was killed in the manner described.

Chapter 8: Drake's brother, Joseph, did die of the disease.

Chapter 9: Drake did climb a tree overlooking both the Caribbean Sea and the Pacific Ocean.

Chapter 10: The raid on the mule train was indeed sabotaged.

Chapter 11: This raid on the caravan along the Panama Trail was successful. Le Testu was killed. Drake did leave on a makeshift raft, hoping to find his ship. He did return to save his men.

Chapter 12: Yes, they called it Slaughter Island.

Chapter 14: Yates was a real person and was killed.

Chapter 16: Thomas Doughty and his ship were caught deserting.

Chapter 17: Wynter was a real person and was slain by the natives. Thomas Doughty was tried and found guilty.

Chapter 18: Doughty was beheaded. Drake did rename the Pelican: the Golden Hinde. Captain Winter (not to be confused with Wynter, above) and most of his men returned to England. They were viewed as deserters.

Chapter 19: Drake and his men were attacked by the Mapuche while attempting to obtain fresh water. Brewer and Flood were real men who lost their lives in the attack, supposedly in the manner described.

Chapter 20: Drake did capture the Concepcion.

Chapter 21: Drake did careen his ships in San Francisco Bay and was thought by the Miwok people to be the reincarnation of a former King. They apparently granted him rights to New Albion.

Chapter 22: Drake did meet with Sultan Baabullah at Ternate and offer England's support.

Chapter 25: Drake was knighted at Deptford by the Queen, although the French Ambassador did indeed wield the sword.

Chapter 27: Drake did marry Elizabeth Sydenham.

Chapter 28: Drake and Carleill took Santo Domingo roughly as described.

Chapter 30: Drake and Carleill took Cartageña roughly as described. Captain Bravo was a real person and the events surrounding him and the death of his wife are apparently true.

Chapter 32: Drake did attack Cadíz, pretty much as described.

Chapter 33: Drake did assault the fortress at Sagres with a frontal attack and supposedly ran with the first wave.

Chapter 34: Drake did arrive at Lisbon, exchanged messages with the Marquis, and withdrew.

Chapter 35: Drake did capture the San Felipe.

Chapter 37: The events surrounding the Spanish Armada are roughly as described, though certainly it's unfair to give such an historical event such light treatment.

Chapter 38: Drake's belief that the Begona was crippled is supposedly true. The party searching for water was indeed ambushed by the residents of Santiago del Príncipe. There was only one survivor—name unknown. But hey…it had to be Garret, right?

Okay, Garret Connachan is a fictitious character.

About Drake – 'Pyrate Knight'

Pirates. The word conjures up visions of hard-living, rum-drinking, sword-bearing, swash-buckling villains of the seas, sporting bandanas, eye patches, wooden legs, and painted faces designed to instill fear in their enemies. Ruthless in battle, they were feared both by merchant seamen and Spanish galleons. Their treasure maps are the stuff of lore and fascination.

But who were these men? Where did they come from? How and why did they choose to join forces in these collective efforts?

Most pirates had once served as ordinary seamen, often sailing under tyrannical captains of merchant ships or naval vessels. Some were mutineers who rose up against their captain, taking over the ship and dispensing him. Some had sailed on sea-going vessels that were captured by pirates. If they had special skills, like carpenters or navigators, they were encouraged, or coerced, to join the pirates. Others were given a choice to join the pirates' ranks and seek greater riches from captured treasure than from paltry seafarer wages.

Some pirates had never intended to be sailors. Rather, they were poor landsmen who'd been abducted on the streets by armed squads, under the orders of seafaring captains, and pressed into service, handling menial tasks onboard ship.

Virtually all pirates had rebelled against oppressive leadership, poor conditions and/or brutal punishments for even minor misbehavior. In all, they were a collection of free and generally 'equal' men with a grudge to bear, with lethal weapons at their disposal, and with allegiance to no country and no one but their fellow pirates.

These dangerous men that we commonly think of were primarily white Europeans. But there were also blacks from Africa and Madagascar, Asians, Polynesians, and men of other races and color, many of whom had once been slaves. Some had been imprisoned and chained below decks, aboard ships captured by the pirates. They were set free by the pirates and offered the chance to join their ranks.

Some pirates entered the trade as boys. They grew up on South Sea islands and were easily enamored by the lavish and free lifestyle enjoyed by pirates, who anchored their ships in the harbor and threw around gold doubloons and pieces of eight in the shops and cafes of seaside villages.

Frequently overlooked is the fact that pirates functioned collectively as a primitive form of democracy. They were all considered to be of the same social standing. They shared equally in their acquired treasures, with the small exception of the captain and a few other key men in leadership roles or those with specialized skills. And captains were seldom self-appointed; they were more generally elected by majority vote of the pirates. If pirates lost confidence in their captain, they would vote for a new one from among the crew. In some instances, competing sailors would fight to the death for the right to captain the ship.

On occasion, these free men lived by a 'pirate code'. Pirate Captain Bartholomew Roberts' written code, for example, covered the sharing of captured prizes, conduct on the ship, and a ban on women onboard his vessels.

Some argue Drake was a hero; some say villain. None would argue whether he was a titan of his era. His fearlessness and thirst for adventure took him to places unknown and challenges unforeseen. At a point in history when most leaders were, and had been, dictators and tyrants, he cared deeply for his men, brought out their best, inspired them to follow him, and earned greatness through their trust and confidence in him.

Though Drake shared similarities with the pirates we think of today, there were clearly differences that separated him from our traditional notion of pirates.

Where he was similar with pirates was in his raiding of ships and villages. He was also alike in considering his men to be generally of the same standing onboard ship, regardless of their role, race, color or native origin. They shared equally in the work and the distribution of spoils.

In his early years, Drake was not a captain of the English navy, formally commissioned in the service of Queen and country. He was of humble origins. In many ways, he was similar to the South Seas pirates we're so familiar with. But those pirates were primarily a creation of the late seventeenth and early eighteenth centuries…more than one hundred years after Drake sailed the oceans. If anything, he was a forerunner of the 'Golden Age' Caribbean pirates.

Where Drake differed from traditional pirates is significant. He proudly bore allegiance to England, virtually always sailing with his Queen's verbal blessing. In that regard, he was an early version of a 'privateer'…captains who were not officially part of the navy but were nonetheless commissioned by nobles (usually with a written 'letter of marque') to wreak havoc on ships and villages of foreign enemies.

In Drake's case, his close relationship with Queen Elizabeth, and their unwritten agreements on his many missions, provided the Queen an ability to deny any official authorization of his ventures, much to the chagrin of Spain's King Philip II, the constant target of Drake's initiatives. Queen Elizabeth, while calling him her beloved pirate, saw fit to honor him with a Knighthood.

Freedom, equality and democracy were things we've come to grudgingly admire about pirate culture. But Drake also parted ways when it came to ruthless behavior. He was a gentleman who believed in minimizing casualties on both sides. Whenever possible, he went to great lengths to avoid armed conflict. Rather than slay the captains of captured ships, he often treated them as guests, inviting them to dine with him and sharing the comradery of men in the same profession. Nor did he set his enemies afloat on small boats in open seas. Instead, he frequently returned their captured vessel to their possession.

Whether or not Drake was an actual pirate in the usual sense, remains open to debate. But he was clearly different in ways and actions, driven by principles and allegiance to his country that few pirates seldom, if ever, had.

Acknowledgements

No one writes a book of any kind without the inspiration and support of others. The kindling was laid decades ago, by Robert Louis Stevenson's <u>Treasure Island</u>, which transported me to the world of pirates. Fanning the flames more recently was John Sugden's exceptional book: <u>Sir Francis Drake</u>, Pimlico 2006. But the spark that ignited the kindling and led to this novel came from my son Blake and his wife Jen, who named their son, my first grandchild, Drake.

Before writing my first book, I noticed that writers commonly acknowledged the support of their spouse. I wondered whether that was simply a must-do for the Acknowledgements section. I can now assure you—it's not. In my case, it wasn't merely the extreme level of patience Wendy showed, nor her words of support. An English scholar and prolific reader of novels, she read and re-read my drafts, challenging me constantly to make the writing better. She also added critical insight into the mind of a woman. After all, what man can truly write a female protagonist without the support of an intelligent, thoughtful and caring woman at his side?

Don Drucker, a former colleague, long-time friend, and voracious reader, has been my consigliere on countless projects—including this novel. Like Garret Connachan, he never hesitated to call out things that required change, evolution, or even a toss in the round bucket.

The amazing Natalia de Oliveira Dal' Evedove, from Brazil, was a beta reader from one of my target audiences—young women interested in pirates and novels. An entrepreneur in her own right, she offered constructive feedback and interesting ideas, of which I took full advantage.

Inspiration comes in many forms. A shout-out to my pirate-loving friends on Facebook, particularly: Adam Morrow (Shipwrecked with Captain Marrow), Mark Forget (Festival Des Pirates) and Dave Carroll, co-author of <u>Thatcher: The Unauthorized Biography of Blackbeard the Pirate</u>. Beyond inspiration, their posts have provided research information and context that have proven helpful. Other deserving Facebook Groups include: Pirates; Pirate Nation; Hoist the Colors, Pirate Enthusiasts; Queen Anne's Revenge – Blackbeard; The Republic of Pirates; World Pirate Party; World Wide Pirate Community; The Crew of the Scavenger and the blog: A Pirate's Life for Me. The managers and members of these groups are much appreciated for sharing their insight, humor and inspiration.

A special shout-out to Edgar Barragan, aka Commodore Crimson, and his Crimson Tide Pirates and Privateers.

This not-for-profit organization's quest is "to rebalance the lines of plunder by drawing on those who have so much, to assist those who've suffered without—one charitable endeavor at a time."

A portion of the proceeds from my Pyrate Series is going toward Edgar's foundation.

I also have to thank Page Turner Awards, whose support and guidance led to this novel's selection as a Finalist for their 2021 Writing Award.

Finally, a special thanks to JerichoWriters.com. Their website, and the aspiring writers who participate in their forums, have helped immensely, schooling me on writing and pointing me to needed resources.

My thanks to all.

Irish Proverb

There are good ships and wood ships

Ships that sail the sea

But the best ships are friendships

May they always

Pyrate Assassin

I

The white fullness of its taut sails belied the hollow blackness of the ship's future. It emerged as a distant speck, interrupting the clear horizon separating two distinct blues—Caribbean Sea and cloudless sky. And for a brief time, Espíritu de Los Santos sailed calmly, unnoticed.

The young spotter at the crow's nest of the pirate ship Red Knight turned to scan yet another section of the white-capped waters. The warm, stiff breeze tossed his unruly hair. His eyes passed, and then quickly returned, to the far-off image. "Sail ho," he shouted to the main deck, over thirty yards below.

"Where away?" Harker yelled back.

"Five points to starboard, Captain."

Given his lower angle and inferior vision, it was a few minutes before the vessel came into Harker's view. He turned to his quartermaster, Yauggan De Graaf. "Merchant or warship—what think you?"

De Graaf squinted at the white fleck, unable to differentiate its masts. "Let it be merchant," he grinned.

As the minutes wore on, Harker noticed his prey's white sails began reflecting the descending sun differently. The unaccompanied ship was turning—seeking to avoid contact, he surmised. Likely a merchant, then. English? French? Dutch? Spanish? Its flag yet wasn't large enough to tell. No matter, whatever sailed these waters was fair prey.

"Full sails," Harker shouted. "Lively now." He turned to De Graaf, smiling, "Let the chase begin."

Several crew members scrambled up the rigging to unfurl the remainder of the sails. The soiled and tattered canvas sheets billowed in the wind before being pulled taut and secured. The tiller spun, maneuvering the Red Knight into an intercepting direction.

With the sun virtually tasting water, the gap between the two ships had finally narrowed to firing distance. Harker noticed the Spanish-flagged merchant sailed low in the water, heavy with cargo. It explained why he'd been able to close on it so quickly.

"Bring her alongside. Ports open," he shouted. "Hoist the red." His drapeau-de-guerre was blood-red, the color of death. It delivered a message to the captain of his quarry—choose to resist and you shall pay the ultimate price: your blood. A rough-sewn, crimson flag jerkily ascended the mizzenmast as the Red Knight slid alongside its target's stern. The men below, hunching in the four-foot-high gun deck, had already primed and loaded their cannons. The gunports flipped open, hammering against the ship's starboard side. Long, black-iron cylinders rolled loudly into forward position, noses out. Gunners secured the wheels.

Espíritu de los Santos hailed from Cádiz. It was returning home from Panama with a variety of South American goods. It also bore several chests containing gold and silver, received in exchange for supplies and merchandise it had brought from the motherland and sold. Captain Jose Rodriguez, the nephew of King Philip II of Spain, stood on the foredeck watching the Red Knight maneuver into position. Given his royal connection, Rodriguez was a much-favored trader, sailing frequently to Caribbean ports and the Spanish Main. A distinguished-looking gentleman, he wore an elaborately embroidered black-velvet, V-waisted doublet, embellished with brass buttons. His well-groomed, black beard came to a sharp point below his chin. He had attempted to outrun the unflagged vessel the moment he spotted it, his experience suggesting it was likely unfriendly. Unfortunately, the weight of his cargo had constrained his retreat like tight reins on a horse. The two ships had closed like attracting magnets. The hoisting of a red flag and opening of gunports signaled imminent peril. Though ill-prepared to resist attack by a seasoned band of brigands in a faster, well-armed vessel, there was no other choice. His cannons, too, were in position, peering through open ports.

Harker's cannons roared first, delivering four-pound iron balls pursued by streaking orange flames and light-smothering smoke. A few were aimed high, targeting Espiritu's masts and sails; others targeted the gun deck. None were aimed below the waterline; he needed the cargo afloat, not sinking. Espíritu's mainmast took a glancing hit, spraying the main deck with knife-edged, wooden shards. The ship's sides were peppered, leaving jagged-edged holes near the gun deck, sending unlucky gunners screaming and flailing backward to the far side.

Men on both ships' main decks traded shots from pistols and crossbows. Grappling hooks flew across the gap, gripping the sides of the Spanish merchant like the claws of a hungry hawk. Harker's men furiously hauled the two vessels together, ducking projectiles. A defiled Espíritu de Los Santos would soon yield her treasures.

———

Head down, William Tovery strode hastily along the cobblestones, holding his wet cavalier hat tightly against the brisk wind. His long navy overcoat was drenched, flapping at his knees. As he opened the door to Orion's Tavern, the bell mounted above rang out. He stepped inside, cursing, shaking off the water, and hanging his hat and coat on a wall hook.

Captain Garret Connachan laughed. She'd done the very same herself, only minutes earlier. Seated at a table near the back, she warmed her hands on a fresh cup of hot black koffei—a beverage Spanish Captain Bravo had introduced her to during her time in the Southern Seas. She'd brought supplies of the dark, hardened beans back to London, convincing the tavern owner to purchase some. But aside from Garret and a few of her associates, he'd had little success selling the hot, bitter liquid.

William spotted her. He waved to the owner and pointed to Garret's koffei. He, too, had grown fond of it. As he approached her table, Garret rose to greet him. She was fashionably dressed. Naval style. Though her vest, pants and boots were masculine, she sported a playfully bright green blouse with a white ruff at the collar. The green complemented her eyes. Her auburn hair flowed longer than she'd ever worn it—evidence she had openly and fully embraced her womanhood. Years of presenting as male had finally given way. She had Admiral Drake to thank for it. That and her own efforts to prove herself. Bordering twenty, she had already accomplished more than most men would in their lifetimes.

Her skin bore a soft, reddish tint, the result of spending considerable time outdoors—practicing daily with sword and pistol, hunting foxes, and overseeing the construction of her new flagship. The relaxed expression on her face was reflective of someone happy with their life. Her uncommon appearance drew continual attention from the men in the tavern. She sensed their interest but chose to ignore them.

William was the closest thing to a brother that Garret had. The two first met while serving as midshipmen under Drake. Through numerous voyages and naval engagements with the Admiral, each had earned their captaincy. Garret's had been more difficult to come by, though she'd been given it sooner.

She noticed his curly, dark-brown hair was neatly knotted in a seaman's tail, much like she herself wore at sea. He now sported a well-trimmed beard, accenting his similarly reddish-tanned face. His eyes were dark brown, his smile broad as ever. He strode toward her with the gait and swagger of a seasoned sailor. "Give me ocean spray over this damned constant rain," he said.

"Good day to you as well, William." She greeted him in the manner of a gentleman—with a firm handshake. Though she'd long since come clean with her crewmates about her gender, she selectively maintained mannerisms that were male in nature. It helped avoid awkwardness with the men. She was committed to simply being 'one of them', particularly onboard ship.

"Apologies." William pulled back the well-worn wooden chair across from her. "I am quite ready for my next voyage. I find the firm ground underfoot most discomforting." He sat.

"Agreed." Garret sipped her koffei. "It has been far too long, William."

"Indeed. I thank you for the invitation. Knowing you as I do," he smiled, "I presume you have something specific to discuss."

"You know me better than anyone."

"Except Pantas," William winked, referring to her former lover, the Indonesian Ambassador to England. "God rest his soul."

"God rest his soul," Garret echoed. "He knew me differently, not necessarily better." She smiled. Though the pain of loss still lurked deep within, it was okay for William to bring up Pantas. The three had been friends.

"I am in the early stages of forming a small fleet, bound for the Southern Seas. I have a score to settle, as you well know." William nodded in response. "And I intend to return with a portion of King Philip's purse." The pursuit of treasure was something she and William were both passionate about. It was a disease they'd caught from Drake. "I would welcome your joining me."

William understood there were actually two scores Garret hoped to settle. The first was to avenge the massacre of a dozen men under her leadership by the villagers of Santiago del Príncipe. She alone had escaped that slaughter. The second, and harder score to avenge, was the assassination of Pantas. While they both suspected the Spanish, there seemed little likelihood of ever discovering the actual perpetrator.

"Sounds ambitious," William replied. Though anxious to sail again, he planned on it being for England's navy, rather than as a privateer. The difference was significant. Sailing for the navy would enable him to continue charting a path up the chain of command, in the hope of becoming an Admiral. Privateers, like Garret, were separate from the navy. Though formally commissioned by the Queen or other nobles to pursue specific interests, privateers were not part of Her Majesty's naval forces. Consequently, they had no direct path to the admiralty. Nor to the societal standing, fame, and pensions that accompanied that rank. Even more bothersome to him, privateers would forever be perceived by naval officers as second-class sailors.

"It would be an honor to sail with you again, Garret. Besides you and Thomas, there is no one else with whom I would prefer to sail." The 'Thomas' he referred to was Drake's younger brother, their former fellow midshipman. William warmed his hands on the cup of koffei the server had just placed in front of him. "But I intend to serve with Her Majesty's navy." Garret masked her disappointment. William sipped his koffei and changed course, "May I ask how you are funding your venture?"

"I have not shared much of my personal matters with anyone; other than Pantas, of course. My grandfather was a counselor to high-profile merchants. He added greatly to the significant wealth and property he had already inherited from his mother. When he died, I became sole heir and executor. The yearly revenue earned through farming alone is substantial. I am drawing on a portion of that to fund this voyage. But I have also gained the support of several investors." She leaned in and grinned, "Their eyes gleam at the promise of Spanish treasure delivering outsized returns on their investments." She sat back. "Having previously assisted the Admiral in securing funding has helped immensely."

"No doubt your relationship with the Queen has helped as well."

Garret nodded. William continued, "I envy your economic position. It must be rather freeing to pursue your own agenda."

"It is. Although, wealth must be carefully managed. I have employed advisors for that purpose. I must say, however, they are not entirely onboard with my decision to invest in a private fleet."

"And what of Thomas? Have you approached him about joining you?"

"Dear Thomas. The man is so dedicated to preserving the memory and estate of his legendary brother that he is committed to staying in Devon. At least for the foreseeable future. He also serves as an advisor to the Queen, on military and diplomatic matters."

"So I understand. He and I see each other on occasion, when he journeys to London. We often reminisce about our days together at sea. I always imagined he would continue in his brother's footsteps."

"I am afraid not. He made that quite clear to me. It is no longer his future path."

"Hmmm. So, without Thomas or me, you shall be needing new leadership."

Garret smiled, wryly, "I have not given up on you, William."

xx

Books by Reidr Daniels

Pyrate Rising

Pyrate Assassin

Pyrate Crossover

Pyrate: Black Flag

Check out Pyrate Publishing at:

- PyratePubs.com
- Facebook: Pyrate Publishing